T0304838

MADE FOR MURDERS

A collection of twelve murder mysteries
featuring Master Hardy Drew,
Constable of the Bankside Watch

MADE FOR MURDERS

A collection of twelve murder mysteries
featuring Master Hardy Drew,
Constable of the Bankside Watch

Peter Tremayne

HEADLINE

This collection of short stories first published in this edition in 2024
by HEADLINE PUBLISHING GROUP

1

Cataloguing in Publication Data is available from the British Library

ISBN 978 1 4722 9613 9 (Hardback)

Typeset in 13.05/17.4pt Adobe Garamond Pro by Jouve (UK), Milton Keynes

Printed and bound in Great Britain by Clays Ltd, Elcograf S.p.A.

HEADLINE PUBLISHING GROUP
An Hachette UK Company
Carmelite House
50 Victoria Embankment
London EC4Y 0DZ

www.headline.co.uk
www.hachette.co.uk

For Vick Van Leeuwen,
the first of my family to read a
Hardy Drew tale and approve it

Contents

Methought You Saw a Serpent

Methought you saw a serpent

All's Well That Ends Well, Act I, Scene iii
William Shakespeare

Master Hardy Drew, the newly appointed deputy to the Constable of the Bankside Watch, gazed from the first-floor latticed window onto the street, watching in unconcealed distaste as a group of drunken carousers lurched across the cobbles below. The sounds of their song came plainly to his ears.

> *Sweet England's pride is gone!*
> *Welladay! Welladay!*
> *Brave honour graced him still*
> *Gallantly! Gallantly!*

The young man turned abruptly from the window back into the room with an expression of annoyance.

On the far side, seated at a table, the elderly Constable of the Bankside Watch, Master Edwin Topcliff, had glanced up from his papers and was regarding the young man with a cynical smile.

'You have no liking for the popular sympathy then, Master Drew?' the old man observed dryly.

Hardy Drew flushed and thrust out his chin. 'Sir, I am a loyal servant of Her Majesty, may she live a long life.'

'Bravely said,' replied the constable gravely. 'But, God's will be done, it may be that your wish will be a futile one. 'Tis said that the Queen's Majesty is ailing and that she has not stirred from her room since my lord Essex met his nemesis at the executioner's hands.'

It had been scarcely two weeks since the flamboyant young Robert Devereux, Earl of Essex, had met his fate in the courtyard of the Tower of London, having been charged and found guilty of high treason. Rumour and disturbances still pervaded the capital, and many of the citizens of London persisted in singing ditties in his praise, for Essex had been a hero to most Londoners, and they might even have followed him in overturning the sour, aging Queen, who now sat in solitary paranoia on the throne in Greenwich Palace.

It was rumoured that the auspices were evident for Elizabeth's overthrow, and even the usually conservative Master William Shakespeare and his theatrical company had been persuaded to stage a play on the deposing and killing of King Richard II but a couple of weeks before Essex's treason was uncovered. It was claimed that many of Essex's supporters had, after dining together, crossed the Thames to the Globe to witness this portentous performance.

In the middle of such alarums and excursions, young Master Hardy Drew had arrived to take up his apprenticeship in maintaining the Queen's Peace with the aging constable. Drew was an ambitious young man who wanted to create a good impression with his superior. The son of a clerk, he had entered the Inns of

Court under the patronage of a kindly barrister, but the man had died, and Hardy Drew had been dismissed because of his lowly birth and lack of social and financial support. So it was, he found himself turning from one aspect of law to another.

Old Master Topcliff rubbed his nose speculatively as he examined his new assistant. The young man's features were flushed with passionate indignation. 'I would not take offence at the songs you hear nor the people's sympathies, young man. Times are in a flux. It is a time of ebb and flow in affairs. I know this from reading the Almanacs. What is regarded as seditious today may not be so tomorrow.'

Master Drew sniffed disparagingly. He was about to make a rejoinder when there came a banging at the door, and before he or Master Topcliff could respond, it burst open and a young man, with flushed features, his chest heaving from the exertion of running, burst into the room.

'How now? What rude disturbance is this?' demanded Master Topcliff, sitting back in his chair and examining the newcomer with annoyance.

The youth was an angular young man of foppish appearance, his clothes bright but without taste. Topcliff had the impression of one of modest origins trying to imitate the dignity of a gentleman without success.

'I am from the Globe Theatre, masters,' gasped the young man, straining to recover his breath. 'I am sent to fetch you thither.'

'By whose authority and for what purpose?'

The young man paused a moment or two for further breaths before continuing. He was genuinely agitated. 'I am sent by

Richard Burbage, the master of our group of players. The count has been found murdered, sirs. Master Burbage implores you, through me, to come thither to the crime.'

Topcliff rose to his feet at once. 'A count, you say?'

'The Count of Rousillon, master.'

Topcliff exchanged an anxious glance with his deputy. 'A foreign nobleman murdered at a London theatre,' he sighed. 'This does not augur well in the present travails. There is anxiety enough in this city without involving the enmity of the embassy of France.'

He reached for his hat and cloak and signalled Master Drew to follow, saying to the youth: 'Lead on, boy. Show us where this Count of Rousillon's body lies.'

The Globe Theatre was half a mile from the rooms of the Constable of the Bankside Watch, and they made the journey in quick time. There were several people in small groups around the door of the theatre. People attracted by the news of disaster like flies to a honey pot.

A middle-aged man stood at the door, awaiting them. His face bore a distracted, anxious gaze, and he was wringing his hands in a helpless, almost theatrical gesture. Hardy Drew tried to hide a smile, for the action was so preposterous that the humour caught him. It was as if the man were playing at the expression of agitated despair.

'Give you good day, sir,' Master Topcliff greeted breezily.

'Lackaday, sir,' replied the other. 'For I do fear that any good in the day has long vanished. My name is Burbage, and I am the director of this company of players.'

'I hear from your boy that a foreign nobleman lies dead in your theatre. This is serious.'

Burbage's eyes widened in surprise. 'A foreign nobleman?' He sounded bewildered.

'Indeed, sir, what name was it? The Count of Rousillon. Have I been informed incorrectly?'

A grimace crossed Master Burbage's woebegone face. 'He was no foreign nobleman, sir.'

'How now?' demanded Master Topcliff in annoyance. 'Is the constable to be made the butt of some mischievous prank? Is there no murder then?'

'Oh, yes. Murder, there is, good Constable. But the body is that of our finest player, Bertrando Emillio. He plays the role of the Count of Rousillon in our current production.'

Master Topcliff snorted with indignation.

'An actor?' Master Topcliff made it sound as though it was beneath his dignity to be called out to the murder of an actor. He gave a sniff. 'Well, since we are here, let us view the body.'

Burbage led them to the back of the stage, where several people stood or sat in groups quietly talking amongst themselves. One woman was sitting sobbing, comforted by another. Their whispers ceased as they saw the constable and his deputy. From their appearance, so Drew thought, they were all members of the company of actors. He glanced across their expressions, for they ranged from curiosity to distress to bewilderment, while others seemed to have a tinge of anxiety on their faces.

They followed Burbage to what was apparently a small dressing room, in a darkened corridor behind the stage, that was full of hanging clothes and baskets and all manner of clutter. On one basket was a pile of neat clothes, well folded, with a leather belt and purse on top.

In the middle of this room lay the body of a young man, who in life had been of saturnine appearance. He was stretched on his back, one arm flung out above his head. The eyes were open, and the face was masked in a curious expression as if of surprise. He wore nothing more than a long linen shirt that probably had once been white. Now it was stained crimson with his blood. It needed no physician to tell them that the young man had died from several stab wounds to his chest and stomach. Indeed, by the body, a long bone-handled knife, of the sort used for carving meat, lay discarded and bloody.

Master Topcliff glanced down dispassionately. Death was no stranger to the environs of London, either north or south of the river. In particular, violent death was a constant companion among the lanes and streets around the river.

'His name is Bertrando Emillio, you say? That sounds foreign to me. Was he Italian?'

Master Burbage shook his head. 'He was as English as you or I, sir. No, Bertrando Emillio was but the name he used for our company of players.'

Master Topcliff was clearly irritated. 'God's wounds! I like not confusion. First I am told that he is the Count of Rousillon. Then I am told he is an actor, one Bertrando Emillio. Who now do you claim him to be?'

'Faith, sir, he is Herbert Eldred of Cheapside,' replied Burbage unhappily. 'But while he treads the boards, he is known to the public by his stage name – Bertrando Emillio. It is a common practice among us players to assume such names.'

Master Topcliff grunted, unappeased by the explanation. 'Who found him thus?' he asked curtly.

As he was asking the question, Master Drew had fallen to his knees to inspect the body more closely. There were five stab wounds to the chest and stomach. They had been inflicted as if in a frenzy, for he saw the ripping of the flesh caused by the hurried tearing of the knife, and he realised that any one of the wounds could have been mortal. He was about to rise when he saw some paper protruding under the body. Master Drew rolled the body forward towards its side to extract the papers. In doing so, he noticed that there was a single stab wound in Bertrando's back, between the shoulder blades. He picked up the papers, let the body roll into its former position on its back, and stood up.

'Who found him thus?' Master Topcliff repeated.

'I did,' confessed Master Burbage. 'We were rehearsing for our new play, in which he plays the Count de Rousillon. It was to be our first performance this very Saturday afternoon, and this was to be our last rehearsal in the costumes we shall wear. Truly, the stars were in bad aspect when Master Shakespeare chose this day to put forward his new work.'

'You are presenting a new play by Master Shakespeare?' queried Hardy Drew, speaking for the first time. He had ascertained that the papers under the body were a script of sorts, and presumably the part was meant for Bertrando.

'Indeed, a most joyous comedy called *All's Well That Ends Well*,' affirmed Burbage, albeit a mite unhappily.

'Let us hope that it pleases the loyal subjects of the Queen's Majesty better than your previous production,' muttered Master Drew.

Master Topcliff shot his deputy a glance of annoyance before turning back to Burbage. 'This is a comedy that has turned to tragedy for your player, Master Director. All has not ended well here.'

Burbage groaned theatrically. 'You do not have to tell me, sir. We must cancel our performance.' His eyes widened suddenly in realisation. 'Z'life! Master Shakespeare is already on his way from Stratford to attend. How can I tell him the play is cancelled?'

'Isn't it the custom to have an understudy for the part?' asked Hardy Drew.

'Usually,' agreed Burbage, 'but in this case, Bertrando was so jealous of his role that he refused to allow his understudy to attend rehearsals for him to perfect the part. Now the understudy has no time to learn his part before our first performance is due.'

'What is known about this killing?' interrupted Master Topcliff, bored with the problems of the play-master.

Burbage frowned. 'I do not follow.'

'Is it known who did this deed or who might have done it?'

'Why, no. I came on the body a half an hour since. Most of us were on stage reading our parts. When Bertrando did not come to join us, I came here in search of him and found him as you see.'

'So you suspect no one?'

'No one would wish to harm Bertrando, for he is one of . . . *was* one of our most popular players with our audiences.'

Hardy Drew raised an eyebrow. 'Surely that would not endear him to his fellow actors? What of this understudy that he has excluded from rehearsals? Where is he?'

Burbage looked shocked. 'You suspect one of our players of such a deed?' he asked incredulously.

'Whom should we suspect, then?' demanded Master Topcliff.

'Why, some cut-throat from the street who must have entered the playhouse in pursuit of a theft. Bertrando surprised the man and was stabbed for his pains. It seems very clear to me, sir.'

Hardy Drew smiled thinly. 'But not to Master Topcliff nor myself,' he replied quietly.

Master Topcliff looked at his young deputy in surprise and then swiftly gathered his wits. 'My deputy is correct,' he added, addressing Burbage.

'Why so, sir?'

Master Topcliff gave a shrug. 'You tell him, Master Drew.'

'Easy enough. Your Bertrando, master-player, did not enter this room to surprise a thief. Bertrando was already in this room. Someone then entered while he was presumably dressing to join you on stage. The purpose of that person was to kill him.'

Burbage looked at him incredulously. 'Do you have the second sight? By what sorcery would you know this?'

'No sorcery at all, sir, but by using my common sense and the evidence of my eyes.'

Master Topcliff was regarding his deputy anxiously. He did not like the word *sorcery* being levelled at his office. Such a charge could lead to unpleasant consequences. 'Explain yourself further to the good Master Burbage,' he suggested uneasily.

'I will and gladly. There was a single stab mark in Bertrando's back. I would say that the culprit entered the dressing room while Bertrando was donning his clothes with his back to the door. He had only his shirt on. The murderer raised the knife and stabbed Bertrando between the shoulder blades. It was a serious wound, but Bertrando was able to turn – with shock and surprise he recognised his assailant. The assailant in a surge of emotion, raised

9

the knife and struck not once, not twice, but in a frenzy of blows, born out of that emotion, delivering five more stabs to Bertrando's chest, each a mortal wound. That is an indication of the rage that the murderer felt towards him. Bertrando sank to the floor. Either he was already dead or dying within seconds.'

Master Topcliff looked on approvingly. 'So you think this was done by someone who knew Bertrando or whatever his name is?'

'Sir, I am sure of it. No cut-throat would commit a murder in such a fashion. Nor is there sign of any theft.'

'How can you be so sure?' demanded Burbage.

Master Drew turned to the neat pile of clothes on top of the basket. 'I presume that these are Bertrando's clothes of which he divested himself, stacking them neatly there as he changed for the stage?'

Burbage glanced at the pile as if seeing the clothes for the first time. 'Yes,' he admitted. 'Yes, I recognise his jacket. He was a vain man and given to gaudy colours in jacket and hose.'

Master Drew pointed. 'Then I suppose that the leather belt and purse is Bertrando's also?'

Burbage's eyes widened. 'That they are,' he agreed, seeing where the logic was leading.

Master Drew leaned forward, picked up the purse, and emptied the contents into his hand. There fell into his palm a collection of coins. 'Would a thief, one who had been prepared to murder so violently to secure his theft, retreat leaving this rich prize behind? No, sir, I think we must seek other reasons as to this slaughter.'

Burbage bowed his head. His nose wrinkled at the smell of blood, and he sought permission to cover the body with a sheet.

'Now,' Drew said, turning to Burbage, 'you say that most of you were on stage when you noticed that Bertrando was missing from your company?'

'That is so.'

'Can you recall anyone who was not on stage?'

Burbage thought carefully. 'There were only a few that were late-comers, for I needed everyone on stage to rehearse the final scene; that is the scene set in the Count of Rousillon's palace, where the King and all the lords, attendants and main characters gather.'

Master Hardy Drew hid his impatience. 'Who was not with you then?'

'Why, Parolles, Helena, Violenta . . . oh and young Will Painter.'

'You will explain who these people are.'

'Well, they are all characters in our play. Well, all except Will Painter. He was the understudy for Bertrando, who was excluded from the task. The only thing I could give him to do was to be a voiceless attendant upon our King.'

Master Drew scratched his chin. 'And he was one with a motive, for, with Bertrando dead, he could step into this main role and win his reputation among the luminaries of your theatre. Fetch this Will Painter to us.'

Will Painter was scarcely as old as Hardy Drew. A fresh-faced youth, well dressed and with manners and mode of speech that displayed an education that many theatrical players did not possess.

'Will Painter? That is a familiar name to me,' Master Drew greeted him, having once more sought the permission of his superior to conduct the inquiry.

11

'It is my father's name also, and he was admired as a writer of plays,' replied the youth, nonchalant in manner.

'Ah, indeed. And one who provided well for his family. It is strange that his son would seek such lowly footings in the theatre.'

'Not so.' The youth flushed. 'To rise to be a master-player, one must know and experience all manner of theatrical work.'

'Yet, methinks that you would have preferred to play the role of the Count de Rousillon in this new comedy?'

'Who would not cast an envious eye at the leading role?'

'Just so. Did you cast such an envious gaze in Bertrando's direction?'

The youth flushed in annoyance. 'I do not deny it.'

'And were you irritated beyond endurance by the fact that Bertrando was so jealous of his part that he refused that you understudy him in rehearsal?'

'Irritated by his popinjay manners, yes, but not beyond endurance. One must bear the ills with the joys of our profession. I admit that I liked him not. But dislike was not enough to slit his throat.'

'Slit his throat? Why do you use that expression?'

Will Painter frowned. 'I do not understand.'

'What makes you think that his throat was slit?'

'Why, Master Burbage waxing lyrical about a cut-throat having entered the theatre in search of plunder and killing Bertrando. What other method would such an assassin use?'

Master Drew uncovered Bertrando's body.

Will Painter saw the stab wounds and turned his face away in disgust. 'I liked him not, but 'tis oppressive to see a man so reduced as this.'

12

'And you cannot hazard a guess as to the identity of anyone who would wish him so reduced?'

The young actor shrugged. 'In truth, if I were to name one, I would name many.'

'How so? Master Burbage says he was well disposed to the entire company?'

The youth was cynical. 'Well disposed, but more to the feminine gender of our company than aught else.'

'Women?' asked Master Topcliff, aghast. 'Do you mean that you have women as players?'

'Aye. Master Burbage experiments in using women to play the female roles, as is common in Europe. Bertrando cast his net like a fisherman and trawled in as many as he could. However, he lives . . . *lived* with Hester at the Mermaid Tavern in Mermaid Court.'

'Hester? And who is she?'

'The maid that plays Helena in our comedy. I saw Bertrando and Hester arrive at the theatre together. She was already dressed for her part, and so Bertrando went towards the dressing room, presumably to change. I saw Bertrando no more.'

'Did you go near the dressing room?'

'Not I. I went off to seek a flagon of ale in the Globe Tavern opposite, and there I remained until I heard the sound of disturbance. Master Fulke will tell you that I departed as he arrived, for he brushed past me as I quit the tavern, although he didn't greet me.'

'Master Fulke? And who is Master Fulke?'

'You have not heard of Raif Fulke, who plays the part of Parolles in our play?'

'Parolles?' mused Master Drew. 'Let me stick with Master

13

Fulke and not be confused by such a choice of names. You say that Master Fulke brushed past you?'

'I did.'

'Did he go to speak with Bertrando or Hester?'

'I did not stay to see, but I think not. He is at enmity with them, for Hester once lived with Master Fulke and he bears no fondness for Bertrando. It is well known that Fulke is jealous of Bertrando and his success both on stage and with women.'

'Well, Master Painter, do you go to call this Hester here, but do not go beyond the confines of the theatre until we tell you.'

The girl Hester came almost immediately.

Old Master Topcliff and his assistant, aware of the niceties and refinements, had stopped her from entering the dressing room with the dead body and proceeded to question her outside. She was an attractive woman whose silk gown may have seen better days but which still enhanced the contours of her figure, leaving little to the imagination. That she had taken the news of the death of her lover badly was written on her tearstained features. Her skin was pale and her eyes red with sobbing.

'I hear you were Bertrando's lover?' began Master Drew without preamble.

The girl sobbed and raised a square of muslin to the corner of her eye and dabbed it. 'Lover? I am Mistress Herbert Eldred,' she announced, raising her chin slightly. 'So have I been these past two years. I have a paper to prove it.'

Master Drew blinked, but it was the only expression that he gave of surprise.

Master Topcliff sighed as if totally puzzled. 'Faith! Who is Herbert Eldred?' he demanded in bewilderment.

Master Drew glanced swiftly at him. 'The actor, sir, Bertrando Emillio. Herbert Eldred is his real name.'

'Ah, I had forgotten. Why these people cannot stick to one name, I have no understanding.' He looked hard at the girl. 'I am of the impression that no one in this company of players knows that you were married?'

'Herbert – Bertrando as was – felt it better that we keep our marriage a secret lest it impede his career. If you want proof of our marriage, then I have –'

Master Topcliff made a dismissive gesture with his hand. 'No need for proof at this stage. So, if you are the dead man's wife, you, therefore, had no cause to kill him?'

The girl stared at him in indignation. 'Of course I had no cause to kill him! But there be others . . .' She hesitated as if regretting what she had said.

Hardy Drew was swift to follow her words. 'Others?'

Her eyes were now narrowed in suspicion. 'But why speak of that when I understood that a thief had attacked him and killed him?'

'Who told you that?'

'It is common talk among the players.'

'Were you in this part of the theatre while the others were gathering on stage for the rehearsal?' pressed Drew without answering her previous question.

'For a moment, no more.'

'When did you last see Bertrando?'

'I came with him from our lodgings to the theatre. I left him to change for the rehearsal while I did the same, and then I went to the stage, but Bertrando was not there. When he did not come, Master Burbage went to fetch him.'

'You left him well?'

The girl pursed her lips in a grimace. 'Bertrando was always well. I left him entering that room behind you. Is that – ?'

Master Drew nodded in answer to the unfinished question. 'Please wait for us in the theatre and send us the player who plays the part of Violenta.'

A tall fair-haired young girl appeared shortly after Hester Eldred had left them. From a distance, she looked the picture of maidenly virtue and innocence. Only when she grew near did Hardy Drew see the hard lines around the mouth, the coldness of the blue eyes, and the smoldering resentment in her features. Her body was too fleshy and would grow to fat in middle age, and the pouting mouth would turn to an ugly form.

'I am Nelly Porter,' she announced, her voice betraying signs of the West Country. 'What is your need of me?'

'I understand that you play the part of Violenta in this new drama?'

'A joyous "comedy",' she sneered. 'And what of it? I have played many parts in the French theatre.'

'How well did you know Bertrando?'

She gave a raucous laugh. 'As well as any maid who trod the boards of this theatre, aye, and who came within the grasp of the pig!'

'There is hatred in your voice, mistress,' intervened Master Topcliff mildly.

'Hatred enough,' affirmed the girl, indifferent to his censure.

'Hatred enough to kill him?' demanded Hardy Drew.

'Aye, I'll not deny it. I could have killed the pig who ravished girls and left them to bear his children and fend for themselves.'

16

'He did that to you?'

'So he did. Two years ago. But my child died.'

'And did you kill him for vengeance' sake?'

'No, that's God's truth. But I do not grieve nor do I condemn his killer. If that is a crime, I am ready to be punished.'

'You are honest enough with your dislikes. Where were you just before the rehearsal?'

'I was late getting to the theatre from my lodgings, that's all.'

'Did anyone see you arrive at the theatre?'

'None that I know of. I went straight to the stage on my arrival, so only the people there saw me.'

'I see. Wait for us now on stage and send us the actor who plays Parolles. I believe his name is Master Fulke.'

She walked away without another word, and they watched her go before exchanging glances.

'She is not exactly grieving over her former lover's death,' Master Topcliff observed, stating the obvious.

Master Fulke was poised, could pass as a gentleman, but was not exactly handsome. He was too round of the face, and too smooth of skin and too ready with an ingratiating smile.

'Well, Master Fulke . . .'

'You want to know where I was before I joined the gathering on the stage?' Fulke greeted them a little breathlessly.

'You seem to know my mind,' replied Drew gravely.

The genial actor shrugged. 'It is hard to keep a secret among so small a company. I was delayed, if you wish to know. I arrived late at the theatre –'

'Late from where?'

'From my lodgings in Potters Fields. I have a room in the Bell Tavern overlooking the river.'

'That is but ten minutes' walk from here.'

'Indeed so.'

'Why were you delayed?'

The man rolled his eyes expressively. 'A rendezvous.' He smiled complacently.

'And this, this *rendezvous*, it made you late for rehearsal? Did anyone see you arrive?'

'I brushed by that young upstart, Will Painter.'

'But you did not see Bertrando?'

Master Fulke sneered. 'Bertrando! Yes, I saw *Master Herbert Eldred*. He, too, had a rendezvous . . . I saw him go to his dressing room. Then I saw someone enter after him. It was not my concern. So I went on my way to join those on stage for the rehearsal.' He sniffed. 'We were fifteen minutes into the rehearsal when Master Burbage began to worry that Eldred had not appeared. I told Burbage where he might be found.'

Master Topcliff tried to suppress his excitement. 'God's wounds, man! Do you tell me that you actually saw his murderer?'

'No, I do not, sir. I said I saw someone enter his dressing room after Eldred had gone in. I have no way of saying this was the murderer. I did not stay longer, as I said, but passed on to the rehearsal.'

'Describe the person,' Topcliff ordered sharply. 'Who else would it be but the murderer?'

'A man, short of stature, of wiry appearance, I would say. He wore his hair long and dark, underneath a feathered hat. There was a short cloak. He wore boots. The colours were dark and tailored in the latest fashion. I could see no more in the gloom of the passage. In truth, though, there was something familiar about him, though I cannot quite place it. It may come to me later.'

Master Topcliff was pleased. He dismissed Master Fulke and turned to Hardy Drew with grim satisfaction on his face. 'Well, at least we know our killer was a man, and that he was no common cut-throat but someone who could afford to dress well.'

Drew looked at his mentor blankly. 'Yet this does not lead us any closer to apprehending the man.'

'There are too many of this description on the streets of this city for us to single one out and charge him,' agreed the old constable.

'Do you plan to leave it so?'

'For the time being. Come, Master Drew. I will have a word with this Burbage and his players before they are dismissed.'

The company was standing or sitting on stage in gloomy groups. A tall balding man, well dressed, was engaged in earnest conversation with Burbage.

'Ah.' Burbage turned. 'This is the constable, Will. Master Topcliff, this is Master Shakespeare.'

The balding man inclined his head to the constable. 'What news? Can you say who engineered the death of our player, sir?'

'Master Fulke saw the murderer enter your actor's dressing room and has given a full description –'

There was a gasp from several members of the group, and all eyes turned to Master Fulke, who momentarily stood with flushed surprise. He had not expected the constable to reveal his attestation.

'So you mean to arrest the culprit?' queried the playwright.

'Not immediately, Master Shakespeare. We will consider our

move for a while. Master Fulke here has given a good description, but he has not, so far, recalled where he has seen the person before, though he is sure he recognised him. We will wait to see if his memory improves.'

Fulke made a move forward as if to deny the constable's interpretation, but Master Topcliff turned and glared at the man, so that Fulke lowered his head and hurried off.

The old constable turned to the assembly and bowed low, flourishing his hat.

As he left the theatre, Master Drew came trotting in his wake. 'I do not understand,' he ventured as he hurried to keep up with the long strides of the constable.

Master Topcliff paused in the street and turned to him. 'Are you city bred or country bred, young man?'

'City bred, Master Constable.'

'I thought so. I am country bred and raised in the fields of Kent. When the quarry goes to ground, what does the huntsman do? You know not? Of course, you know not. What is done is that you prepare a lure.'

Hardy Drew frowned. 'Then you have prepared Fulke as a bait in a trap?'

'If our murderer is one of the gentlemen of Master Burbage's company, he will come this night to make sure that Master Fulke's memory does not return.'

'A harsh judgment on Fulke if we are not there when the murderer visits him.'

'Indeed, but be there we will. We will go to the lodgings of Master Fulke and prepare our snare with Fulke as the unknowing decoy.'

Master Drew looked at the old constable with a new respect. 'And I thought . . .'

Master Topcliff smiled. 'You must learn the ways of the game-keeper, young man, and learn that it is always best to tell the poacher where you have set your traps for him.'

They took themselves to the Bell Tavern in Potters Field. A few coins pressed in willing hands were able to secure a booth with curtains from which they could view the front entrance of the tavern. This station fell to Master Topcliff, while Hardy Drew, being the younger and hardier, took up his position at the rear entrance of the tavern, so that either entrance to Fulke's rooms might be observed.

A little the worse for drink, Raif Fulke entered the tavern towards ten o'clock and made his way immediately up to his room.

It was well after midnight that there was a scream, and the innkeeper's wife came running to Master Topcliff, her eyes wide and frightened. ' 'E's dead. Master Fulke is killed!'

Master Topcliff called to a young man hefting barrels to run around the back of the inn and inform Master Drew. Master Topcliff tried to make for the stairs but found the innkeeper's wife clinging to his sleeve and expanding in detail on her fright.

No one had entered from the back door; of that Hardy Drew was certain. He hurried into the inn and up the back stairs to the bedchambers. He saw one of the doors open at the end of a cor-ridor and ran in.

Master Raif Fulke lay on the floor. A candle burned nearby, but it scarcely needed the light to see that there was dark blood oozing from several wounds on the man's chest. Miraculously, Fulke's chest still rose and fell. He was not yet dead.

Drew knelt by him and raised his head. 'Who did it, Fulke, who did it?'

The actor opened his eyes. Even in his condition, he smiled, though grimly. 'I would not have known him . . .' he wheezed painfully. 'Like Rousillon, I knew him not . . . Why? Why, young sir? Jealousy is a fierce foe. That was the reason.'

He coughed suddenly, and blood spurted from his mouth.

'Take it easy, Fulke. Name the man.'

'Name? Ah . . . for, indeed, he was mad for her, and talked of Satan, and of Limbo, and of Furies, and I know not what . . .'

He coughed again and then smiled, as if apologetically.

'The web of our life is of a mingled yarn, good and ill together; our virtues would be proud if our faults whispered this not; and our crimes would despair, if they were not cherished by our virtues.'

'The name, man, quick, give me the name.'

Fulke's breathing was hard and fast. 'I am a'feared the life of Helena . . . was foully snatched . . .'

'Helena?' demanded Drew. 'Do you say that Helena, Hester Eldred, that is, is now in danger from this man?'

Fulke forced a smile.

'Helena? Methought you saw a serpent . . .' he began.

Drew compressed his lips in irritation.

'Concentrate, Fulke, name your assailant.'

Fulke coughed again. He was growing weaker and had not long.

'The play . . . the play's the thing . . .'

Then his eyes dilated and for the first time he realised that he was going to die. The moment of truth came for Master Fulke in one horrible mute second before he fell back and was dead. Master Topcliff hurried in, having shaken off the terrified inn-keeper's wife.

'Did he say aught?' he asked breathlessly.

Drew shook his head.

'He was rambling. His last words were something about the play being the thing . . . what thing?'

Master Topcliff smiled grimly.

'I fear it was only a line from Master Shakespeare's tragedy of the Prince of Denmark. I recognise it well, for it is a play of murder and intrigue that held much meaning for me. "The play's the thing wherein I'll capture the conscience of the king." No use to us. This is my fault. I was too confident. I let this murderer out of my grasp.'

'How did he get in? I can swear that he did not pass me at the back door.'

'Nor from the front,' vowed Master Topcliff.

He peered round. The window was still open, the curtain flapping. There was a small balcony outside, built out above the waters of the Thames. The river, smelly and dirty, was lapping just below. The window and balcony were on the side of the building, for it was built sideways on to the river, and was blind to the scrutiny of anyone watching the front and back.

They stared out onto the darkened waters. The assailant must have come by rowing boat and pulled up against the wall of the inn, under the balcony. It was high water, and easy to pull oneself up towards this balcony and then climb through Fulke's window.

'Our man will be long gone by now. Now, truly, all we can do is return to our lodgings and secure a good night's repose.

Tomorrow morning, I think we will have another word with Master Will Painter. Logic shows him as our likely suspect.'

Hardy Drew sighed with exasperation as he stared down at the actor's body. 'Faith, he rambled on so much. Had he known he was dying, I doubt whether he would have quoted so much from his part in this play.'

He suddenly spied a sheaf of papers on the bed. Bending, he picked them up and perused them.

'*All's Well That End's Well*,' he quoted the title. 'A bad ending for some.'

He was about to replace it on the bed when he spotted a line on the pages to which the play script had fallen open. 'Methought you saw a serpent,' he whispered. He turned to the old constable. 'Are you sure those words "the play's the thing" come from this other tragedy you mentioned? Are they not used in this new play?'

'I have seen the tragedy of the Prince of Denmark, but I have not seen this new comedy, nor has anyone else, remember? They were just rehearsing it for its first performance.'

'True enough,' Drew replied thoughtfully. After a moment or so, with a frown gathered on his forehead, he tucked the play script under his arm and followed the old constable down the stairs, where Master Topcliff gave instructions about the body. There was nothing further to do but to return to their lodgings.

It was morning when Master Topcliff, sitting over his breakfast, observed a pale and bleary-eyed young Hardy Drew coming into the room.

'You have not slept well,' he observed dryly. 'Does death affect you so?'

'Not death. I have been up all night reading Master Shake-speare's new play.'

Master Topcliff chuckled. 'I hope that you have found good education there?'

Drew sat down and reached for a mug of ale, taking a mouthful. He gave an almost urchinlike grin. 'That I did. I found the answer to many mysteries there.'

Master Topcliff gave him a hard look. 'Indeed?'

'Indeed. I learnt the identity of our murderer. As poor Raif Fulke was trying to tell me – the play's the thing, the thing which reveals the secret. He was quoting from the play so that I might find the identity of his assailant there. But you are right – that line does not occur in this play, but the other lines he quoted do.'

An hour later they stood on the stage of the Globe with the players gathered in sombre attitude about them. Burbage had recovered from his shock of the previous day and was now more annoyed at the loss of revenue to his theatre by the delays. 'How now, Master Constable, what now? Two of our good actors are done to death and you have named no culprit.'

Master Topcliff smiled and gestured to his deputy. 'Master Drew will name the assailant.'

Drew stepped forward. 'Your comedy says it all,' he began with a smile, holding up the play script. 'Herein, the Count of Rousillon rejects a woman. She is passionate to have him. She pursues him, first disguised as a man.'

There was a muttering.

'The story of the play is no secret,' pointed out Burbage.

'None at all. However, we have Bertrando, who actually plays Rousillon, in the same situation. He is a man of several affairs, our Bertrando. Worse, he has rejected a most passionate woman, like Helena in the story. Bertrando is married and likes to keep his marriage a secret, is that not so, Mistress Eldred?'

Hester Eldred conceded it among the expressions of surprise from the company.

'So one of his lovers,' continued Hardy Drew, 'that passionate woman, likes him not for his philandering life. Having been rejected, like Helena in the play, she pursues him. However, unlike the play, she does not seek merely to win him back, but her intention is to punish him. She stabs him and ends his life.'

'Are you telling us that a woman killed Bertrando?' gasped Burbage. 'But Fulke saw a man enter the dressing room.'

'Fulke described a man of short stature. He was positive it was a man. Unfortunately, we' – he glanced at his superior – 'decided to allow Fulke to act as bait by pretending he knew more than he did. Thus lured out, the assailant murdered Fulke before we had time to protect him. Luckily Fulke was not dead. He survived long enough to identify his assailant . . .'

He turned to Hester Eldred. She read her fate in his eyes, leapt up with a curse, and ran from the stage.

Master Topcliff raised a hand in signal, and a burly member of the guard appeared at the door and seized her.

A babble broke out from the company.

Burbage raised his voice, crying for quiet.

Nelly Porter moved forward. 'I thought you were going to accuse me. I was Bertrando's lover, and thanks to him, my child died. I had more reason to hate and kill him than she did.'

Hardy Drew smiled softly. 'I did give you a passing thought,' he admitted.

'Then why – ?'

'Did I discount you? When we arrived, Hester was on stage in a dress. Now her part, as I read the play, calls for her, as Helena, to appear in men's clothes. Yet she clearly told us that she had arrived at the theatre with her lover, left him to change while she went to change herself. Presumably from her own clothes she would change into that of her part as a man. But Will Painter said that he saw her arrive with Bertrand, already dressed for her part in the scene. She told me that she had left Bertrando and went to change into the clothes for her scene. When we came to the theatre, she was in a dress and had been so from the time of the rehearsal. She had, therefore, killed her husband while in the male clothing, changed into a dress, and joined you all on stage.'

'But her motive? If she was passionately in love with Bertrando, why would she kill him?'

'The motive is as old as the Earth. Love to hatred turned. For Bertrando was just as much a ladies' man during his marriage as ever he had been. Hester as his wife could not abide his philandering. Few women could. She did not want to share him with others. I could feel sympathy for her had she killed in hot blood. But she planned the scene and brought her victim to the theatre to stage it. She also killed Fulke when she thought that he had recognised her –'

'Who knows,' intervened Master Topcliff, 'maybe he had recognised her. Didn't Will Painter say they had lived together before she took up with Bertrando? Painter implied that Fulke still loved her. Even when dying, perhaps for love, he could not name her outright but, for conscience' sake, gave you the coded clue instead?'

'One thing this deed has also killed,' interrupted Master Burbage. 'We shall no more experiment with women as players. They bring too many dangers with them.'

Master Hardy Drew turned and smiled wanly at Master Topcliff. 'By your leave, good Master, I'll get me to my bed. It has been a tiring exercise in drama.' He paused, smiled, and added with mocking tone, 'The king's a beggar now, the play is done.'

Fear No More the Heat O' the Sun

Fear no more the heat o' the sun,
  Nor the furious winter's rages;
Thou the worldly task has done,
  Home art gone, and ta'en thy wages . . .

Cymbeline, Act IV, Scene ii
William Shakespeare

A wailing March wind was blowing from the north-west along Bankside, causing the Thames to move in choppy wavelets and froth an angry white around its quays and the massive piles of the great London Bridge. Wisps of thatch were being blown hither and thither among the debris of the streets, plucked from the houses and even from the roof of the stately Globe Theatre. The wind howled down Pepper Street, causing the painted wooden sign of the Pilgrim's Wink tavern to rattle and shake in spite of its iron fastening.

Screwing up his eyes against the icy smack of the wind, Master Hardy Drew, Constable of the Bankside Watch, opened the lattice window on the first floor of the tavern. He held it ajar a fraction in order to lean out, pull closed a loose, banging shutter and fastened it, before, thankfully, securing the window latch again.

29

It had been a cold winter and the elderly Queen, insisting on going for her walk in the February chills, had caught cold and had been ailing since. In fact, the talk was that the poor lady would not recover. She lay in her Palace at Richmond surrounded by members of her Privy Council and attended by her physicians and even the elderly Archbishop John Whitgift of Canterbury. All that day, Sunday, the nation had offered prayers for her recovery. Master Drew himself had gone to the church of St Saviours to offer his supplication but it seemed a forlorn hope. Yet, after forty-five years, it was impossible to imagine England without Elizabeth upon its throne.

He turned back into the room that he rented on the first floor of the tavern and rubbed his forehead to massage warmth back into his cold flesh. The distant cry of a night watchman proclaiming the hour turned his thoughts to bed. He had finished the piece of cold mutton pie and the pint of ale that comprised his supper and glanced undecided at the dying embers of the fire. He paused wondering whether to place another log on it and continue reading for a while longer.

Above the threatening cry of the wind, the occasional bang and crash of some object being pushed along the cobbled street before it, he suddenly became aware of a new sound. The rattle of a coach on the stones outside and the nervous whinny of horses caught his ear. Then he realised the coach had halted outside. He stood, head to one side, listening. Sure enough, there came a thunderous knocking on the door below. He made no stir for he heard Master Cuttle, the landlord, already grumbling at the door. Only a moment passed before he heard rapid footsteps on the stair and there came a knock on his own door.

In answer to his invitation, it swung open and Master Cuttle stood nervously on the threshold for a moment.

'Gen'leman to see you, Master Drew,' he mumbled before scurrying off.

A tall man of some fifty years entered and pushed the door closed behind him. Master Drew caught the sweet smell of a tincture of roses, noted the finery of the cloak and hat, which the man proceeded to cast off without waiting for an invitation, throwing them carelessly over the nearest upright chair. His clothing not only proclaimed him a gentleman, but a man of some status and substance.

'Do you recognise me, Master Drew?' he demanded without preamble.

Master Drew's features had formed a frown of recognition. He had seen the Attorney General of England several times when his duties took him north of the river to the law courts of the realm. He made a hurried bow.

'Sir Edward. Please take a seat before the fire and tell me how I may serve you at this hour?'

At the same time, Master Drew moved quickly to the fireplace to put an extra log on the embers.

Sir Edward Coke moved unsmilingly to the indicated chair.

'I have heard good things of you, Master Drew,' he said, as he seated himself. 'You have a reputation as a solver of puzzles. A man with the ability to supply solutions to the most difficult conundrums, and withal you are a man of discretion. Is this not so?'

Master Drew grimaced.

'I am not responsible for what others say, Sir Edward. I can

31

only say that I have had a little success since my appointment as Constable of the Bankside.'

Sir Edward smiled quickly, as if satisfied with the answer.

'Modesty may be a virtue, Master Drew, but it does not put a pension in your pocket or put a prefix before your name.'

'My ambition is to keep my name and save a little to buy a small farm out beyond Moorfields where I might, in simple comfort, spend the twilight of my years.'

'Modest enough. But with your talent, ambition should look further.'

'I am well content. But I fear it was not talk of my ambition that is your reason for coming to call here on such a night.'

Sir Edward sighed.

'Indeed, good Master Drew. I have a puzzle to set before you. I will pay you well for your consideration of the matter.'

Master Drew raised an inquisitorial eyebrow.

'Perhaps you would be so good as to elucidate the matter?'

'I will tell you in the coach. We have to go to Holborn, north of the river.'

'But the gates on the bridge will be closed. And I have no jurisdiction on the north bank of the river.'

Sir Edward laughed.

'The gates of London Bridge will open to me. I am the Attorney General and will tell you where your jurisdiction is.'

Master Drew sighed deeply, casting a wistful look at the fire where the log he had recently placed on the embers was blazing merrily.

It was scarcely fifteen minutes later when, having given instructions to Master Cuttle to have a care of the fire and seizing his worn but woollen cloak and hat, Master Drew found himself north of the river, seated in the Attorney General's coach. They had crossed London Bridge with amazing rapidity. The sentinels at the southern Stone Gate and then at the northern gate marked by Nonsuch House had given one glance at Sir Edward's coat-of-arms emblazoned on the carriage doors and had waved it through with all speed. Sir Edward was relaxed in his seat opposite Master Drew.

'In plain truth, Master Drew, the young cousin of an acquaintance of mine has been killed. Two men set upon him as he came to the town house of my acquaintance in Holborn. He had not long been in London, I'm afraid, and took a fancy to a stroll around the Chancery courts and gardens, returning on foot at dusk. We need to be satisfied that this was either an attack by thieves to rob the unfortunate young man or whether there was some more sinister design.'

Master Drew was surprised.

'Sadly, as you well know, sir, such attacks are not unknown. The footpads will have vanished into the slums around the Fleet. If you are asking me to track them, I fear I shall not be successful. That is, unless they took some singular object by which they can be identified if and when they attempt to sell it.'

Sir Edward was shaking his head.

'The young man was not robbed, sir. At least, his purse was still on his body.'

'Then were the thieves disturbed?'

'They were seen bending over the body but they had plenty of time to carry off the purse, if that was their wish.'

'You imply that it was not?'

'I do not wish to imply anything, Master Drew. I am here at the request of my acquaintance who wishes some investigation and assurance about how his young cousin met his death.'

'Surely, this is a matter for the City of London Coroner?' Master Drew knew that scarcely a day went by when some poor soul was not attacked and robbed and even killed on the streets of London. Only if a person was of some status and wealth was an investigation held and that usually by the coroner.

'This must be an inquiry of a strictly confidential nature, Master Drew. Five guineas will be yours for the use of your discretion.'

Master Drew stared in surprise.

'I would need some enlightenment on this matter. Who was the victim?'

'The young man was cousin to Sir Christopher Hatton who owns the house in Holborn to which we are going. We are going to Hatton Gardens.'

Master Drew frowned as he searched his memory.

'Hatton?'

'You are acquainted with the name?'

'It has a passing familiarity. Ah, I have it but . . . but Sir Christopher Hatton died eleven years ago.'

Sir Edward shook his head.

'This is Sir Christopher's heir; a great-nephew of the Sir Christopher of whom you speak.'

'I see. The Sir Christopher that I recall had been Captain of the Queen's Guard, a Privy Councillor and, I recall, Lord Chancellor. He was given the Palace of the Bishops of Ely by the Queen

and was buried in St Paul's Cathedral. There was a rumour . . .'
Master Drew paused and his lips compressed.

Sir Edward smiled in amusement.

'We are alone, Master Drew. Anyway, I know the rumour.'

'The Queen was frequently a visitor at Ely Palace and was very solicitous when Sir Christopher was dying. It was said that when he died he was indebted to her by some forty thousand pounds.'

'You speak of the facts, not the rumour. They are true. Since you are reticent about the rumour, I will tell it. Sir Christopher was the Queen's favourite.'

'Such was the rumour,' affirmed Master Drew, gravely.

'Let us discard the rumour then. It is of no consequence. It is known that Ely Palace is now called Hatton Gardens after Sir Christopher. When he died, which, as you rightly say, was about eleven years ago, his heir was a nephew, William Newport, who then adopted the name Hatton. He died six years ago and his cousin, the current Sir Christopher, inherited. Sir Christopher is of my acquaintance. In fact,' he grew slightly embarrassed, 'when Sir William died, I married his widow.'

Master Drew made no comment. The behaviour of the wife of Sir Edward, the former Lady Elizabeth Hatton, was one of the scandals of London. When they married, she had refused to take his name, preferring to keep the title Lady Hatton. They had often been witnessed arguing in public places and it was rumoured that the elderly Queen had forbidden her entry to any palace in which she resided. It was known that the vivacious Lady Hatton was twenty-six years junior to Sir Edward and an unrepentant flirt, if not worse. They had, apparently, gone their separate ways over a year ago in spite of having a child in common.

Master Drew cleared his throat and brought his mind back to the present matter.

'So who was this cousin who has been killed?'

'His name was Henry Hatton.'

'His age?'

'Nine and twenty.'

'You say he had only just come to London?'

'He had been living on an estate owned by the Hattons in Waterford in Ireland. Ah, we are here.'

The coach had halted and one of the footmen alighted and hurriedly opened the door. As Master Drew followed Sir Edward to the steps of the considerable town house outside which they had drawn up, the door opened and a distinguished-looking gentleman came hurrying forward. Anxiety marked his features. His glance encompassed Master Drew, and the constable was aware of a deep intensity of observation in that brief look.

'Sir Christopher, this is Master Drew, of whom I have spoken,' said Sir Edward.

Master Drew started to bow but Sir Christopher quickly waved a hand that seemed an invitation to dispense with such etiquette.

'You will want to see the body?' he asked immediately.

'I will also want to speak with anyone who witnessed the attack or was at the scene soon after.'

'My man, Joseph, will show you to the body,' muttered Sir Christopher. 'You will join Sir Edward and myself in the drawing room,' he indicated a door in the hall of the house, 'when you have finished.'

A stony-faced footman dressed in Hatton livery moved forward.

'If you will follow me, sir?'

He led the way up the wide winding stairway to an upper floor and into a bedroom.

'Was this the guestroom where Master Hatton was staying?' Master Drew asked, as the room clearly showed marks of occupancy.

'It was, Master Constable,' replied the footman. 'When Master Hatton arrived, Sir Christopher assigned him this room, being one of our guestrooms.'

'When did he arrive?'

'Two days ago.'

The body was laid out on the oak four-poster bed. It was a man of around thirty years. There were bloodstains on his satin doublet and white linen shirt, both of which had been loosened, obviously in some attempt to staunch the wound as the man lay dying. Apart from the doublet and shirt no other items of his clothing had been touched. Even his stockings and fashionable shoes were still on his muscular legs.

He was a handsome man. His skin was fair, almost white, and his hair, drawn back from a broad forehead, could be called red but standing more towards a pale ginger. The features seemed disconcertingly familiar to Master Drew. Certainly, the man was richly attired. His hands were well manicured and there appeared no indication that he had ever lifted anything heavier than a rapier in his life.

Master Drew frowned suddenly and turned to the liveried servant who stood impassively at the door.

'Joseph, was this gentleman wearing a sword?'

'Not when he was brought in from the street, Master Constable.'

'You mean he was wearing one when he went out that afternoon?'

'I recollect that he was, sir. It don't do for a young gen'leman to be abroad in London without a good rapier to ward off the footpads and the like. Though much good it did the poor gen'leman. Maybe the thieves stole it.'

Master Drew continued his examination. His eyes, returning to the well-manicured hands, noticed a white circle of skin on the man's signet finger, which indicated the habitual wearing of a ring.

'Where is the signet ring he used to wear?'

The footman looked bewildered. He leaned forward as if he had only just noticed that it was not there.

'I do recall that he wore a ring, a large one, if it please you. But in the turmoil of the events . . .' He shrugged. 'It seems that the thieves made off with that also.'

'Yet they stopped and removed his signet ring when it would have been easier to cut the man's purse . . .' Master Drew muttered reflectively as he glanced to where the dead man's purse still hung at his waist. He reached forward and felt it. It was heavy and clinked with its metal contents. Master Drew removed it, untying its fastening and emptied its contents into his hand. 'A silly young man to carry so much. A good three years' wages to a wherryman on the river. Throats have been cut for less.'

'Yet the purse remains, sir,' pointed out the servant, stoically.

'Aye, indeed, good Joseph. The purse and its contents remain.'

Replacing it, he bent over the body again, peering at it carefully and then finally he examined the wounds.

'Someone has attempted to clean the wounds since death.'

'On Sir Christopher's orders, sir. Mary and Poll from the kitchen did their best to clean away the blood.'

Master Drew was thoughtful. There was, in fact, only one clean wound. One small incision which would lead the blade directly into the heart. Master Drew had seen such wounds before and they were usually made by a swift thrust of a rapier – a gentleman's weapon – and not the weapon favoured by cut-throats, footpads and brigands of the London backstreets.

'Did this young man have his own servant?'

'He did, sir,' replied Joseph with a tone of disapproval. 'He brought with him an outlandish sort of fellow who came with him from Ireland, who speaks a gentleman's English, though accented and interspersed with his gibberish Irish tongue. In fact, he was the one who spotted the footpads that attacked Master Hatton, causing them to run off, before he brought his body into the house.'

Master Drew was surprised at this new intelligence.

'What is the man's name?'

'He tells us that he is called Broder Power from a town called Waterford.'

'Ask him to join me here.'

The footman looked as though he would raise an objection and then, meeting Master Drew's steely gaze, inclined his head for a moment and went off to fulfil his task.

Master Drew took the opportunity of the servant's absence to make a quick search of the bedroom. There was a small walnut writing bureau. Obviously Master Hatton had neither inclination nor time for letter-writing for the interior showed no sign of recent usage.

There were clothes in the closet that spoke of good taste and quality. Henry Hatton certainly did not want for money to buy the best that master tailors could offer. He riffled through the silks and satins. One cloak caused him to pause; it was a dark blue satin cloak that had a collar edged with pure white fur and black flecks and even the edging was of the same. Master Drew frowned. He recognised the fur as taken from one of the weasel family, prized for its tail of pure white fur and black tips. He grimaced and then shut the closet door.

An intricately worked walnut dresser contained articles of a toilet nature, with bottles of scents and fragrances that again spoke of good taste. Some drawers were filled with stockings, undergarments, all of good quality. He was about to turn away when he saw something bright under some of the silk clothing. It was a small silver locket on a chain of similar metal. He took it out – inscribed on the silver was a shield and a motto. The shield displayed two bull's heads divided by a chevron from a third bull's head. Master Drew knew the motto as French as he had a little knowledge of the language. *Le plus heureuse* – The most happy. He opened the locket. There was room for two small miniature portraits in the locket. The one on the left-hand side had been removed, but clumsily so, leaving tiny splinters of the wood base on which it had been painted. The second portrait, on the right-hand side, was still there. It revealed the

40

features of the young man who currently lay dead on the bed before him.

Taking the locket in one hand, Master Drew went to the bedside and peered down. There was no doubt of it. This was a miniature of the young man who had met his end by a single thrust of a blade. The constable shook his head, closed the locket, pausing briefly to look at the arms again, and then, hearing a step outside the door, he placed it down on the side table.

There was a tap on the door and he bade the person who knocked enter.

Joseph, the footman, came in followed by a tall, broad-shouldered man in his early twenties, dark hair, fair skin and with the build and manner of a soldier rather than a servant.

'This is Broder Power, Master Drew,' said the liveried footman, indicating his distaste with a grimace.

'You may wait outside, Joseph,' Master Drew replied.

The footman hesitated and then shrugged and removed himself.

The young man who entered glanced at the body on the bed and his hand moved to touch his forehead. Then he realised Master Drew was watching and he caught himself.

'I am not interested in your religion, Master Power,' the constable said immediately, realising that the man was about to make a sign of the cross. 'Though, out of curiosity, was your late master a Papist?'

'He was not, *a dhuine usal* . . . I mean, your honour. But no finer heretical gentleman have I served.'

Master Drew smiled.

'Then I would choose your words more carefully while you are in England at this time.'

Broder Power nodded quickly.

'It is hard to be indifferent in the presence of the dead, your honour.'

'I have a few questions for you. How long have you served Master Hatton?'

'Just over one year.'

'And you are from Ireland?'

'Master Hatton had an estate outside the city of Waterford, from where I come. I served in my lord, the Earl of Clancarthy's troops and after Lord Mountjoy defeated us at Kinsale . . .' he shrugged. 'Well, I was taken prisoner but Master Hatton gave me my freedom if I served him faithfully.'

'Then you are a soldier, not a house servant?'

'*A Dhia na bhfeart, a dhuine usail*, it is so. Master Hatton hired me to guard his person but I have failed in that duty.'

'Why did he need a bodyguard?'

'He said he had enemies in high places and wanted to be sure that he had protection against an assassin's knife.'

'Why were you not with him when he was killed?'

'He ordered it so.'

'Why did he come to London?'

'He told me that he had to fulfil that to which he was born.'

'When did he tell you this?'

'Two weeks ago. A messenger came to him in Waterford. I know not what news he brought. But Master Hatton said we must sail to England forthwith and it took us time to get a ship and sail to London. We arrived scarcely two days ago.'

'He used to wear a signet ring, I am told.' Master Drew changed the subject abruptly.

'He did, *a dhuine usail*. I saw it many times.'

'Yet he is not wearing it now.'

Power took a step towards the bed and stared.

'By the powers, he is not.'

'Do you know what happened to it?'

'He was wearing it when he left here this afternoon.'

'And his sword?'

'I think the footpads fled with that, also he used to wear a Venetian stiletto on his left side. As I recall, he was not wearing that when I found the body.'

'Before we come to that, cast your memory back. What was on the signet ring? Can you recall its emblem?'

'Oh, that I can, *a dhuine usail*. I used to laugh at it for Master Hatton was a young man of action and I would have thought he would have had some emblem depicting that. A fighting animal or bird – an eagle, a raven, a lion or even a bull. No, the emblem he wore was that of a pelican.'

Master Drew let out a soft breath.

'A pelican, say you?'

'A white pearl pelican set against a ruby stone.'

'And his sword? Was there anything that distinguished it?'

'It was of fine workmanship. There were roses worked around the handle guard and some Latin inscription on the blade. I can't recall exactly what it was.'

'Tell me of the events of today. How it was that Master Hatton, being so afeared of assassination, told you to remain here and went abroad alone?'

Broder Power rubbed his jaw with his hand.

'Just as I say, *a dhuine usail*. He told me to remain. I think a messenger came to the house with a note. On the intelligence he received from this note, he told me that he was going to the Chancery buildings not far away and there was no reason for me to accompany him. I protested but a little. But he girth on his sword and dagger, laughed and departed. I was unhappy. Master Hatton was a good man, albeit an Englishman, and I vowed to serve him well. I followed at a distance. Indeed, he went directly to the Chancery buildings, I believe them to be your courts of law?'

Master Drew nodded.

'In a small garden, among those buildings, I saw him encounter a young lady.'

'Can you describe her?'

'That I can and well, *a dhuine usail* . . . I mean, your honour, for she had called at this very house the day we had arrived. I heard Sir Christopher greet her distantly and call her Lady Hatton.'

Master Drew stared for a moment at the man.

'Lady Hatton?' he echoed thoughtfully. 'And you felt there was some animosity in the greeting from Sir Christopher?'

''Twas like watching two skilled fencing artists exchange an opening clash of their blades. I heard her say she wished to be introduced to her new cousin, by which I think she meant my master. But Sir Christopher told her he was not within the house. God save him, but that was a lie for he was within his room.'

'And this was the same lady that met with your master in the Chancery gardens?'

'It was, er . . . your honour. And that is the truth of it. I observed them for a while. They appeared in long discussion. But I misdoubt that it was a comfortable exchange of kinsfolk. There seemed some anger in the air. My master stood up and took his leave. Thinking that I could quickly catch him, I lingered to watch the lady who walked to a shaded arch. I noticed there was a coach there, a coach and two horses. A man leaned out and she spoke awhile to him and once pointed in the direction my master had taken.'

'Did you observe this man? What was he like and were there any distinguishing marks on the coach?'

'There was a shield on the coach, I think it had blue and white horizontal bars on it and some animals but, in truth, I would not be able to tell one of your English heraldic signs from another. I know the man in the coach had a tawny beard, reddish hair and as he leaned from the coach window it seemed to be the gentleman was crooked of back, though it might have been the angle from which I was observing the encounter. The coach moved off and I quickly followed my master. *Dia linn!* I lost sight of him until he reached the very street wherein we were dwelling with Sir Christopher. Dusk was falling but I saw several things at once that demanded my attention.

'I saw the same coach disappearing down the street. I saw my master on the ground and two men were bending over him. One held my master's sword, which he had obviously wrenched from him for it was still in its scabbard. The other was . . .' Master Power paused and exclaimed, '*A Dhia!* One was tearing at his hand. He must have been taking the signet ring. I yelled, stupidly, for I was some distance away and unable to close in on the thieves. They looked up, saw me and took to their heels. I thought it more important to get my master to the house and call for help rather than chase them.'

Master Drew spoke sharply.

'Can you describe them?'

'They had dark cloaks about them and hats that shaded their faces. One thing I observed – that they wore good boots.'

Master Drew raised an eyebrow.

'Good boots? Why would you observe that?'

'It occurred to me only later. I have seen some of the poor in the city. Many, like in my own sad country, go barefoot or cannot afford good quality leather to wear and resort to wooden shoes or the like. These men had good boots.'

'So you brought Master Hatton inside. And then?'

'He was pronounced dead. It needed no physician to confirm it. Sir Christopher was in a great state of anguish, naturally so, it being his cousin. We placed him here. The other gentleman, Sir Edward, was with Sir Christopher at the time and there was some discussion. Then Sir Edward left and on his return he brought you here, *a dhuine usail*. These are the facts as I know them.'

Master Drew sighed and was troubled.

'Tell me, Master Power, do you have your means of support?'

Broder Power looked at him curiously.

'I have my health, a good blade and a fair sword arm, a purse with scarce a guinea in it. I relied on the patronage and employment of my master.'

'Accept my advice, Master Broder Power, and return to your own country and do so immediately. Better still, join your countrymen in France and Spain, for now Mountjoy has defeated

O'Neill, I do fear that things will not go well for your people in Ireland. Slip away from this house this minute while it is still dark and vanish as quickly as you can. It is better that you do not know the reasons why, but I urge you to do so if you value your life and liberty.'

Broder Power stared at Master Drew curiously and then he glanced to the corpse on the bed.

'Then my master was an important person? This was the assassination he feared?'

'You are an intelligent man, Master Power,' replied the constable. 'At this time, in this place, an intelligent man knows when not to seek answers to such questions.'

'I will do as you say, *a dhuine usail* . . . your honour.'

Master Drew left Broder Power and was conducted by the stony-faced Joseph down the stairs to the drawing room where Sir Edward and Sir Christopher were waiting impatiently.

'You have been a while, Constable,' greeted Sir Christopher in a surly manner. 'The hour grows late.'

'The constable has a reputation for thoroughness,' intervened Sir Edward in a conciliatory tone. 'Is it not so? Have you come to some conclusions, Master Drew?'

Master Drew smiled thinly.

'Will you assuage my curiosity, Sir Edward?'

'Of course, of course. Sir Christopher, a glass of malmsey for the good Constable.'

Master Drew declined the wine and said: 'I do not seek to cause offence, but I was wondering about Lady Hatton, Sir Edward. I mean Lady Elizabeth Hatton, your wife.'

Sir Edward's brow creased in a frown of annoyance.

'My wife and I have led separate lives this past year or so.'

'I was merely curious, forgive me, but what was her family?'

'She was a Cecil, Master Drew. The daughter of Thomas Cecil, Lord Burghley. Why do you enquire?'

Master Drew sighed deeply as if he had suspected the answer.

'Forgive me, as I say, it was but a passing curiosity on my part.'

'And so to your observations,' snapped Sir Christopher. 'My cousin's death must be officially pronounced before we can begin the burial procedures . . .'

Master Drew turned to him.

'I believe . . .' he began.

There was a thunderous knocking at the door that startled them all. They could hear servants scurrying to the door, voices raised and then Joseph opened the doors but, before he could speak, a small man came pushing into the room. Behind him were two men wearing the livery of the Queen's guards, their weapons were not drawn but they were well armed.

Sir Edward was the first to recover from his surprise.

'Sir Robert! What brings you abroad at this late hour?'

Sir Robert was a slight man, dwarfish in stature with a humpback, reddish hair, a tawny beard and large green eyes that had a hard quality to them. They swept the gathering with a coldness that did not match the grim smile on the man's thin lips. Master Drew bowed stiffly for it did not achieve anything to antagonise Sir Robert Cecil, Lord Chancellor and Secretary of State to Her Majesty.

'Business of state brings me abroad at this hour, as you should know well, Sir Edward.' He made no reference or apology for the armed guards at the door.

'How can I serve you, Sir Robert?' Sir Christopher came forward, nervously.

'I have lately come from Richmond Palace. Her Majesty is dying and will not, according to her physicians, last out the week. She has, as Sir Edward will know, consistently refused to name or approve a successor. These are perilous times, gentlemen. Claims and counterclaims to the throne will plunge this kingdom into the bloodiest civil war since the Queen's grandfather overthrew Richard of York at Bosworth. Pretenders and claimants gather like conspirators. It is my task to protect the kingdom and, on intelligence from the physicians, I have now sent a draft constitutional agreement to the Queen's cousin, the King of Scots, in that if His Majesty so desires he may proceed here to London on Her Majesty's demise and be accorded the Crown of England as well as Scotland.'

The announcement did not seem to surprise Sir Edward. He merely inclined his head almost as if in surrender.

'It was good of you to seek me out and tell me so, Sir Robert. I will repair to Richmond forthwith as my duty lies with being at my sovereign's bedside at the hour of her death.'

Sir Robert made a curious motion of his hand.

'Yet I hear, Sir Christopher, you have also had a death here at your house?' He glanced to Master Drew. 'I understand that you have sent for an official to make enquiries into the manner and perpetrators of this death.'

Master Drew swallowed slightly. He knew that Sir Robert ran a web of spies and informers and, indeed, assassins, which protected the realm from any perceived threat by the Queen's enemies.

'Master Drew has not yet had time . . .' began Sir Christopher.

'On the contrary,' Master Drew said decisively, 'I was just about to deliver my summation.'

Sir Christopher seemed to exchange a frightened glance with Sir Edward and both men were tight-lipped and anxious.

'It is a sad matter, but not an uncommon one,' went on Master Drew. 'I understand that Sir Christopher's young cousin, Master Henry Hatton, was but lately arrived from Ireland. New to London and London ways, he went abroad this afternoon and, on his return, was attacked by two footpads who stabbed him through the heart. While they were proceeding to rob him, taking his ring and sword, they were disturbed by his servant who rushed upon the scene. They fled and the servant carried his master's body here, whereupon he was found to be dead. I am afraid the matter was a simple one. We may never find the perpetrators.'

Sir Robert raised his eyebrows and, for the first time, there was amusement on his features.

'Simple? Very well. Perhaps we should seek confirmation from the mouth of this unfortunate young man's servant? He being the only witness.'

Joseph, who had been standing silently at the door, coughed and spoke apologetically to Sir Christopher.

'I beg your pardon, sir, but at the time of the arrival of Sir Robert I was coming to inform you that Master Hatton's servant has fled. I suppose, seeing no means of further employment, the rogue did take the purse that was still on his master's body and, indeed, searched a few drawers. For their contents were spilt. I do not know what other valuables he has made off with. But the window was left open and it is an easy passage to the ground from there. I fear he has vanished into the streets of London.'

Sir Robert was smiling grimly.

'Then it seems we will have to leave his apprehension in the hands of the thief takers. I suppose he will be as hard to find as the footpads that killed your young cousin. So, Master Drew, you have no hesitation with your findings? May I send a magistrate tomorrow to take down your statement for the record? We would not want any false rumours to spread abroad as to the circumstances.'

'I will expect the magistrate to call on me tomorrow, Sir Robert. I am content in my resolve,' agreed the constable.

'And you, Sir Christopher? Art content? It is but poor hospitality your cousin received here in London. And you, Sir Edward? Are you both content?'

Sir Edward nodded while Sir Christopher said shortly: 'I wish nothing more than to accord Henry a speedy burial. He was almost a stranger to us and there will be none in our family who will long mourn him. Alas, he came to London at the wrong time.'

Sir Robert grimaced.

'A sad time, a sad time for all of us. A shadow hangs over the realm, gentlemen. Our good lady has served us well and deserves rest from her worldly chores. Soon she will fear no more the burden of government of this realm. She may go peacefully to her rest. Before the week is out, we, who remain, shall see if a brave new era of prosperity will begin or whether we shall sink back into the dark days of civil war and blood feuds. I hope for the sake of all of us, gentlemen, that we may come through this time of mourning.'

Later that night, Master Hardy Drew sat gazing thoughtfully into his own fire. He had been extravagant enough to build up the fire and heat some mulled wine, even cutting himself a slice of cold mutton pie. Such luxury was compensated by the thought of the ten golden crowns that Sir Christopher had given him which now lay locked away in the small wooden box he kept under his bed. It had been an exhausting evening and one which still sent chills through his body. He hoped that Broder Power would make it safely to France or Spain. He would be glad when Sir Robert's magistrate had officially taken down his version of the story.

He was not sure how Sir Christopher had planned to present the young man called 'Henry Hatton' as heir and claimant to Elizabeth's throne on her death? Well, that plot was ended and he was lucky to have extricated himself from involvement in it.

Who exactly was 'Henry Hatton'? His features proclaimed him to be a Tudor. His resemblance to the portraits of Elizabeth were obvious. The locket bore the coat of arms and motto of Anne Boleyn, Elizabeth's mother. Elizabeth was known to have still revered her executed mother and despised her father for the state murder. Who would Elizabeth love so much to present that locket to? And the signet ring, so described by Master Power. The pelican on a ruby background. The pelican was one of Elizabeth's favourite symbols, used to portray her motherly love for England. The legend had it that in times of food shortages, pelicans plucked flesh from their own bodies to feed their dying young. And then there was the ermine-edged cloak – a status symbol which only high nobility and royalty were allowed to wear. The missing sword, with roses on the hilt – Tudor roses?

'Henry Hatton' had been no ordinary person. It was obvious to Master Drew that Hatton had been a Tudor, sent into exile by Elizabeth for safety. Was he Elizabeth's own son? Sir Christopher Hatton, dead these eleven years, had been known to be her favourite. Was Henry a child by him? Or was Henry a child by someone else, given to Sir Christopher to take care of until such time as he could come forward and be recognised? Did Lady Elizabeth Cecil, during the time that she had been married into the Hatton family, come to learn this dark secret? Certainly, she was instrumental in Henry Hatton's death. Hearing of his return to London as the Queen lay dying, Lady Hatton had arranged a meeting with the young man to identify him. Having done so, she had reported to her uncle, Sir Robert Cecil, the spymaster and chief assassin, who favoured the King of Scots as heir to the English throne. Master Drew had no doubt that Sir Robert had given the orders for his men to kill the young man and remove any evidence that would link him to the Tudors.

Master Drew shivered at how close he had come to being arrested by the Lord Chancellor – or worse.

He was still unsure whether Sir Edward and Sir Christopher had brought him into their conspiracy to investigate as a witness against the Cecils or to give an official pronouncement in support of the footpad theory that would allow them their freedom, proclaiming them innocent of the knowledge of the identity of the young man and therefore the reason for his assassination. Had they expected Master Drew not to realise the truth or to disguise it?

At times, Master Drew reflected, as he stretched before the fire, it was far better to pretend ignorance than boast his talent for gathering and interpreting the facts.

It was in the early hours of Thursday morning, four days later, that it was announced that Elizabeth of England had passed peacefully to death in her chambers at Richmond Palace. She would, as Sir Robert said, fear no more the heat of the sun, for she had fulfilled her worldly task and gone to receive her heavenly wages. The nation was in mourning. Already, a cortège had left Holyrood Palace in Edinburgh and was heading south into England bearing the thirty-seven-year-old James Charles Stuart, King of Scotland, Duke of Rothesay, Duke of Albany, Earl of Ross and Baron Ardmannoch, who had now been proclaimed Elizabeth's successor.

A Walking Shadow

Life's but a walking shadow; a poor player,
That struts and frets his hour upon the stage,
And then is heard no more . . .

Macbeth, Act V, Scene v
William Shakespeare

The message that the boy who was dressed in the livery of the
Worshipful Company of Mercers had handed to Master Hardy
Drew was brevity itself.

'Sir Thomas Bennett requires and requests Master Drew, Constable of the Bankside Watch, to wait upon him forthwith at
Bridge House.'

It was not the fact that Sir Thomas was reputed to be one of
the richest men in London that sent Master Drew scurrying in
search of his best doublet, pear-shaped breeches, trunk hose and
new cloak. Nor did it concern him that Sir Thomas was a leading
member of the oldest and premier Livery Company of the city
whose Royal Charter had been bestowed in 1394. It was the fact
that Sir Thomas Bennett was Lord Mayor of the City of London
and a man who was powerful enough to have the ear of Lord

Burghley, Lord Chancellor to the newly crowned King James, the first Scottish King to ascend the throne of England.

Thus, within five minutes the Constable of the Bankside Watch was hurrying along, still adjusting his dress, following the nimble-footed youth along the crowded cobbled Thameside streets, past the cylindrical theatre of Cuthbert and Richard Burbage, heading for the south end of London Bridge. It was there that Bridge House stood as a portal to the great structure.

London Bridge was the only entrance into the city across the Thames from the south. No one really knew when the first bridge had spanned the broad, dark, sluggish river. In its present form, it had stood since the time of King William Rufus. The bridge spanned nineteen piers, across which numerous buildings balanced precariously, leaving room only for a narrow road between them. The buildings along both sides of the bridge rose many storeys. They were timber-framed with wattle and daub walls and *haute-pas* galleries running from the third storeys, linking houses on either side of the narrow bridge road. These structures overhung the bridge supported on great wooden beams. Most of the first storeys were given over to shops with gaudily painted signs in which all manner of merchants and artisans plied their trade. Over the years, the shop counters had gradually inched out into the narrow road across the bridge until they so impeded the passage of coaches that many accidents began to occur. It had only been twenty years ago that a new law had been passed restricting the protrusion of shop counters to a width of only four inches from the faces of the buildings.

The buildings on the bridge, as crowded and precarious as they were, were much sought after, as the Bridge district was one of the healthiest areas of the city. Being right on the river, there was no problem about sewerage and the water works at the northern end of the bridge, built twenty years before by Peter Morris, ensured a good water supply. Thousands now dwelt in the tenement blocks that rose on the old construction. Tolls were no longer charged for crossing the bridge, but all manner of rents were collected by the Bridge House Estate, a proprietary company whose trustees were the Corporation of the City of London.

These thoughts were on Master Drew's mind as he halted on the steps of Bridge House, for he knew that it was from this building that all activities upon the bridge were administered. He also knew that Sir Thomas Bennett, as Lord Mayor of the City, was chief trustee of the company governing those affairs.

The boy guided the constable through the offices, clerks regarding him suspiciously under lowered brows. The boy paused before a dark oak door and tapped lightly. A stern voice bade him enter but he merely opened the door and sung out, in a voice somewhere between boyhood and pubescence, 'The Constable of the Bankside Watch!' Then he stood aside for Master Drew to enter.

The constable entered a dimly lit room, hesitated a second, then doffed his hat and executed what he imagined to be a courtly bow to the only occupant of the room. That occupant was a man of middle age with a commanding appearance, broad shoulders, and a muscular frame.

'Do I address Sir Thomas Bennett?'

'You do, sir, you do,' replied the Lord Mayor. 'I have heard from His Grace of Winchester that you have a gift, sir – a gift for solving puzzles. Is this so?'

Master Drew reflected for a moment. Thomas Bilson, the Bishop of Winchester, whose estates included the Bankside and a great deal of property on the south bank of the Thames, was the constable's employer.

'I have had some small success in resolving matters that some considered conundrums,' he conceded.

The Lord Mayor sighed deeply and sank into a seat beside the fire. Then, as if in afterthought, he waved Master Drew to a facing chair.

'Seat yourself, sir. Seat yourself. Will you take a glass of good Canary Sack, sir?'

Master Drew declined, for it was too early in the day to be indulging in fortified wine. However, he accepted the invitation to sit and waited politely. It was clear that the Lord Mayor was having some difficulty in gathering his thoughts. Eventually he cleared his throat.

'Are you aware of the large number of Scots who have inhabited the city since His Majesty arrived here six months ago?'

Master Drew was indifferent. 'Surely that is not to be remarked upon? When His Majesty of Scotland was invited to ascend the throne of England it was to be expected that he would bring with him many retainers, nobles, and others of quality from his native land. Now that His Majesty of Scotland has been duly crowned His Majesty of England, we may expect many more Scots to be appointed to the royal court and to enjoy the patronage of the King.'

Sir Thomas glanced at him sharply. 'There is no censure in your voice, Master Constable.'

Master Drew shook his head. 'I am concerned with facts and not with censure, Sir Thomas. I leave it to others to be concerned with politics.'

Sir Thomas regarded him with deep-set dark eyes, unblinking and almost snake-like. 'Thus you would have no prejudice against the Scots?'

'No one has questioned my loyalty to legally held authority,' he responded, deflecting the question.

Sir Thomas smiled cynically. 'By the Holy Rood, Master Constable, I do fear that you sound like a lawyer, and many a lawyer's tongue has led him to Tyburn Tree.'

'I gather that you wish to consult me with a problem, Sir Thomas,' the constable said after a moment or two. 'What has this problem to do with the new influx of Scots into London?'

Sir Thomas paused a moment and then continued. 'As you rightly say, when His Majesty came to London, he had an abundance of his countrymen in his retinue, nobles among them. I speak with frankness, Master Constable. They be a ravenous brood, come to seek fortune and fame here. You may know that their antics have begun turning public opinion among our good English citizens against them. Yet, it is one Scot in particular with whom I am now concerned.'

'Indeed?'

'Sir Alan Kerr of Fernieshurst Castle. He is one of those who accompanied His Majesty hither.'

'A nobleman, sir?'

'A *Scottish* nobleman,' returned Sir Thomas without enthusiasm. Then he sighed again. 'And, by the Fate, he be cousin to the King's favourite, a handsome young wretch named Robert Carr. Rumour has it that His Majesty plans to make this self-same Robert Earl of Somerset ere many days have passed.'

'I warrant that this is interesting, sir, but, pray you, how is this business connected with me? What has this Sir Alan Kerr done that would make you call upon me as Constable?'

'It has fallen to those connected with the royal court to provide for His Majesty's retinue. Houses and estates were found for those who could afford them and apartments for the poorer among them. I was asked by His Majesty's newly appointed High Chamberlain, Lord Suffolk, to find a suitable property for Sir Alan to rent. One suitable property was available on London Bridge, as the previous tenant had absconded without payment of his rent in March.'

Master Drew's eyebrows raised a little. 'Upon the bridge, sir?'

'You may know that as Lord Mayor I am chief trustee of the bridge and may use my role to bestow favours, especially when requested by the High Chamberlain of the realm. Sir Alan now resides in Nonsuch House.'

That made sense to the constable. Nonsuch House was one of the most expensive properties on the bridge; indeed it was one of the most valuable properties in the City of London itself. Reserved for the use of nobles, it stood at the southern end of the bridge and was called locally 'The House of Many Windows', for its richly decorated exterior attracted many visitors who came simply to stand and marvel at it.

Master Drew recalled when the building had been erected some five and twenty years before. It was unique in that it had been built in Holland, then shipped to England in pieces and reconstructed on the bridge, secured to it by large wooden pegs. It was a fine house. If any property on the bridge would suit a visiting noble, it would be Nonsuch House.

Sir Thomas saw that the constable was impressed and smiled

with a certain amount of pride. 'Nonsuch House should be rented for a hundred times the rent that the Bridge Estate is allowed to ask. We have many gentlemen applying for its rental and some even offering bribes to our clerks to ensure their applications are met with favour. Why, we had the devil to pay from would-be tenants when Sir Alan moved in. There were protests from those who felt they should have had preference. Even my master clerk had to be overruled. I could not ignore the wishes of the Royal Chamberlain.'

'How long has Sir Alan been the tenant?'

'Since His Majesty arrived in London in April.'

'So, nearly six months? What problem now assails Sir Alan Kerr?'

Sir Thomas pursed his lips hesitantly. 'Did I say a problem assailed him?'

'There exists a problem, otherwise the Lord Mayor of London would not be spending his time gossiping about His Majesty's retinue with a lowly Constable of the Bankside Watch . . . and certainly not with one who does not have jurisdiction over the bridge. You may have forgotten that my authority ends at the very steps of this house. The Bankside and its territory is my watch. The bridge has its own watch, sir.'

Sir Thomas smiled quickly. 'Under my warrant, Constable, you are given that authority. But you are right. A problem has arisen. Sir Alan's manservant has been murdered. Sir Alan swears that he, himself, saw the murderer. This is a delicate matter and I cannot afford to take chances with a routine investigation by the solid but unimaginative officials of the Bridge Watch.'

The constable was puzzled. 'But it appears, from your words, that the case is simple. If Sir Alan saw the culprit and raised the alarm, it should be a straightforward matter to apprehend the miscreant.'

Sir Thomas gave a troubled sigh. 'Sir Alan says that he saw the figure of the murderer. He bethought it was a man . . . but the figure had no head. It subsequently vanished before his eyes.'

Master Drew's eyes widened a fraction and he sat silent for several moments. Then his lips twitched a little in scepticism. 'Shall I presume that the body of the servant vanished as well?'

Sir Thomas shook his head quickly. 'No. The young man had been stabbed in the chest. After the Bridge Watch examined the body, a mortician removed it.'

'I would venture, Sir Thomas, that phantoms are not in the habit of committing murder by physical means. I hold no belief in phantasms and spirits. Wheresoever there be a physical body slain, there be usually a corporeal culprit. I have been privy to no evidence nor observation that would contradict that reasoning.'

Sir Thomas was unhappy. 'Yet there do exist possessors of malevolent supernatural powers – witches and demons who concoct mischief.'

'You have observed such?'

The Lord Mayor shook his head. 'God be thanked, I have not. But I have had discourse with Sir Edmund Anderson who judged the case of that witch, Elizabeth Jackson, last year.'

Master Drew compressed his lips in disapproval. He was familiar with the case. Elizabeth Jackson was only one of twenty-five poor miscreants Anderson had sent to the gallows in recent years on the grounds that they were witches.

'Sir Alan believes he has been bewitched?'

'He believes he has been assailed by a phantom. I have sought your expertise in this affair, Master Drew, to discover the truth. But it must be done discreetly. As I have told you, Sir Alan is cousin to the King's favourite. You may not be aware that His Majesty is the author of a book, which I understand was printed six years ago, called *Daemonologie*. He is much interested in this subject and I am reliably informed that he plans to pass an Act shortly against what he sees as the practice of witchery in England. Imagine, good Constable, the damage to the reputation of our bridge company should this story be voiced abroad, especially if whispered into the ear of His Majesty – witchcraft and phantoms on London Bridge! Knowing His Majesty's humours he might order the entire bridge to be burnt down to extirpate the evil.' He shuddered as if in emphasis.

Master Drew noted the tone of desperation in the Lord Mayor's voice. 'And I have the authority to question whom I may upon the bridge?'

'I have had my master clerk draw up your warrant,' confirmed Sir Thomas.

Master Drew rose from his chair. 'Then, by your leave, I shall haste me to Nonsuch House to see Sir Alan and hear his account of this so-called haunting.'

Sir Thomas also rose, nodding rapidly. 'I have forewarned Sir Alan that you might be expected.'

'I presume this Sir Alan speaks English?' Master Drew said as an afterthought.

'After a fashion,' Sir Thomas said with a grimace. 'He speaks it in the Scottish form that I find hard to comprehend, but repetition and patience withal may see you through.'

Master Drew stood for a moment in thought, fingers touching

the door handle. 'Have you a clerk who might be acquainted with the houses on the bridge? I may want to seek information about Nonsuch House.'

The Lord Mayor frowned. 'Master Gregory, my master clerk and surveyor of the bridge, who has drawn up your warrant, has full knowledge of the bridge and is in charge of all revenues from those that rent upon it. I will instruct him to co-operate with you.'

Master Gregory was a man with thin, earnest features and dark hair.

The constable took the seal-embossed warrant from him. 'Sir Thomas tells me that you will be able to advise me of any matters affecting the houses on the bridge.'

'Aye, sir, I will do my best.'

The constable frowned at the other's manner of speech. 'Are you a Scot, Master Gregory?'

'If it please you, Master Constable.'

'One who has recently followed His Majesty from Scotland?'

'Indeed, no, sir. I came here nearly twenty years ago to seek my fortune.'

'Were there no fortunes to be made in Scotland?'

'Alas, I took service with the wrong master. My Lord of Gowrie fell out of favour and suffered execution by command of the Privy Council of the Scots. I was scarce twenty at the time and knew nothing of politics. I came to London, found work on the bridge and have been master clerk to the Bridge Estate for the past five and ten years.'

'Then you are the man that I may need upon my return.'

* * *

64

The door of Nonsuch House was opened by a barrel-chested man clad in a leather jerkin and a type of skirt which the constable believed was called a kilt. His bare, muscular arms and long hair and beard gave him a wild appearance. He wore a dagger and broadsword at his waist and another dagger strapped to his right leg below the knee. The man exchanged some incomprehensible dialogue with an unseen party before allowing Master Drew to enter.

He found himself in a small, red, oak-panelled entrance hall from which a staircase ascended to the living rooms of the building. A man stood on the bottom stair.

Sir Alan Kerr was a thin, hook-nosed man with fiery red hair and the temperament to go with it. He was no more than thirty years old and dressed in a manner that proclaimed him well acquainted with London fashions.

When Sir Alan initially spoke, Master Drew found his dialect difficult to follow and confessed himself at a loss. At this, Sir Alan sniffed in displeasure and said, '*Excusez-moi, Monsieur. J'en suis désolé. Parlez-vous français?*'

His host regarded him with apparent surprise when Master Drew confessed that he could not understand French either, and once more tried his native dialect, speaking slowly and repeating himself at intervals until his manner of discourse became more understandable to Master Drew. After the preliminary introductions, Master Drew fell straight to his task. 'May I ask you to recount the events of the night of the murder to me?'

''Twas nearing midnight when I heard a moaning sound within the house.'

'Who was within the house at the time?'

'My manservant, Rob. Davy here,' he nodded towards the man-at-arms who had taken up a position by the door, 'has been acting as my guard since Rob's death. Apart from Davy and poor Rob, I have existed with no other servants this last week and more, for I have been awaiting the arrival of my retainers from Scotland.'

'Prior to this moaning sound, nothing else had disturbed you?'

'Nothing. I was so distracted by the moaning – it was like a man in pain – that I lit a candle and made my way below stairs to seek out the cause of such a piteous sound. I called to Rob several times but he answered me not.'

'And then?'

'I came to the bottom of the stairs and raised my candle high. It was then that I saw the apparition. In truth, sir, I was unable to move at the spectacle.'

'This was in the very hall where we now stand?' pressed Master Drew, glancing around the dark oak-panelled room. It was a curiously shaped hall, reflecting the fact that it had been fashioned around the overhang of the bridge – a fairly plain room with a staircase leading up to the larger reception chambers and bedrooms. There was an area off to the side partially hidden by a wooden screen. There were no other doors apart from the door that gave onto the bridge road and there were only two windows. Both gave a view of the river. When Sir Alan nodded the constable added, 'Explain exactly what you saw.'

'The light of the candle was not strong, of course. It gave a shadowy flickering light. But I saw the phantom clearly. A tall person of masculine appearance with a long dark cloak . . . but no head was upon those broad shoulders!'

'Then why do you say it was of masculine appearance? Explain the dress in detail.'

'Would it not be more efficacious to send for a minister of religion to investigate this phenomenon?' demanded Sir Alan irritably.

'My warrant from Sir Thomas Bennett is to secure the facts, so please try to remember what it was wearing,' replied Master Drew.

'The thing was clad all in black except for a white ruff collar which was small in the new fashion. It beset the neck or where the neck should have been, for above this collar there was nothing at all. No neck, no head.' Sir Alan shuddered at the memory.

'And from this ruff, did the cloak fall away, covering the whole body?'

'No. It came down to mid-calf. But it was open in the front and I could see a doublet of the peascod belly type.'

Master Drew frowned. 'You appear well acquainted with our new fashions, Sir Alan,' he observed, inflecting it as a query.

Sir Alan spoke again with irritation. 'We are not behind the fashion north of the border, Master Drew.'

'I would not suggest otherwise, Sir Alan,' Master Drew replied smoothly. 'Yet you have a sharp eye for fashion and, by the Holy Rood, it seems your spectre was a veritable fashionable phantom.'

Sir Alan glanced at him as if he was unsure whether or not the constable was making fun of him.

'The doublet and hose were masculine in fashion?' Master Drew pressed when he did not respond.

'Yes. Hence I refer to this phantom in masculine terms.'

'Very well. Now, I presume that you came down the stairs here . . .?' The constable indicated the red oak staircase. On receiving a nod he went on, 'And, standing at the bottom of the stairs, you held out the candle to examine the phantom. How tall or short would you estimate this spectre to have been?'

'Oh, tall. Of that I have no doubt. I am not short but I had to look up to observe the line of the ruff, and if a head were where it should have been, I would venture that the spectre would have exceeded two yards in height.'

'What then? Was anything said? Did the spectre threaten you?'

'Words were uttered,' Sir Alan admitted, to Master Drew's surprise.

'And these words were . . .?'

'*Thoir am baile muigh ort!*'

The constable looked blankly at Sir Alan.

It was Davy, the man-at-arms, who replied. 'It is the old language of our country, which is now spoken mainly in the north and to the west. It is the fashion to call this tongue Yrisch to distinguish it from our Scots Inglis.'

'And do you and Sir Alan understand this tongue?'

'All too well, sir,' snapped Sir Alan. ' "*Thoir am baile muigh ort*" means "get out of the house".'

'For what purpose would the phantom seek to expel you from this house? Does any explanation come to your mind?'

'None.'

'And why would the phantom speak to you in this – what did you call the language? This tongue? Why not address you in your own language?'

''Twas once the language of all Scotia,' muttered Davy.

'Who knows the ways and meanings of phantoms?' replied Sir Alan, ignoring him. 'All I know is that this house must be bewitched by some evil spirit.'

'You heard this voice clearly?'

'As clear as now I hear you.'

'The voice came from the phantom?'

'A deep voice, a hollow voice, as if coming from its bowels.'

'And then?'

'Then my eyes fell upon the floor and I saw poor Rob. He was lying there with a dark stain on his clothing. I saw the handle of a dagger. In truth, sir, I was so distracted I forgot about the phantom for an instant. When I raised my eyes again the phantom had vanished. I sounded the alarm for the night watch at once, but when they heard my account, they were much afeared. I then sent for Davy here, my trusty man-at-arms, who has lodgings nearby. He agreed to stay on at Nonsuch House as my protector until this matter is resolved. This morning the good Sir Thomas informed me that he would send a man to investigate the manner of this slaughter. There is nought else to tell.'

Master Drew nodded thoughtfully. 'Let Davy here take up the position of the phantom, and you, Sir Alan, stand in the position where you were when you espied it.'

At Sir Alan's direction, the places were assumed.

'And the body of the manservant Rob? Where was that?'

Sir Alan pointed in front of him and slightly to the right of the stairs.

'Take the position on the floor, Davy,' instructed the constable, 'while I assume the position of our phantom in your stead.'

When this was done, Master Drew searched the part of the

room that he was in and then dropped to one knee to examine the floor.

The wooden screen stood near Master Drew, partially obstructing Sir Alan's view of the room. Behind its slight cover, Master Drew's eyes fell on that which he expected to find and he smiled. He moved across, grasped a metal rung sunk in the floor and pulled, revealing an aperture eighteen inches square – cut into the floor to allow tenants to throw effluence into the river. Directly below were the frothy waters of the Thames, crashing up against the piers on which the bridge was supported.

Master Drew knew how dangerous the passages under the bridge were. In addition to the hazards posed by the massive piers supporting the bridge, there were those posed by the water wheels under the arches at the north end of the bridge and the water-powered grain mills under the southern arches. The Thames could rise six or seven feet and its level varied greatly hour by hour. 'The London Bridge is for wise men to pass over and for fools to pass under' went the saying along Bankside. Boatmen who tried to prove their masculinity by attempting to 'shoot the bridge' often capsized and were drowned.

'What is that?' demanded Sir Alan, coming around the screen and peering down.

'That,' smiled the constable dryly, 'is where your servant empties your chamber pot.'

Master Drew paused, then lay at full length on the floor. Removing his hat, he put his head through the aperture. Just below was a precarious roped walkway along which, so he imagined, those artisans who maintained the structure of the bridge could make their way while inspecting the timbers on which the houses were supported. After a moment, he drew himself up.

'How long did you say that your attention was given to concern for your dead servant?' he asked Sir Alan.

'A moment or two. I was in a state of perturbation seeing the figure, hearing the voice, and then seeing my servant dead. When I glanced up the phantom had vanished.'

'A moment or two was all that was needed. Your phantom vanished, but not as an ethereal being but a corporeal one who exited through this aperture and onto the rope walkway below.'

'In faith, are you claiming that this headless spectre was a man of flesh and blood?' Sir Alan looked aghast. 'By the just fate of the odious Riven crew, I'll disembowel the knave with my own sword.'

'It is my belief that it were so,' replied Master Drew gravely, wondering what curious Scottish curse the man had just pronounced.

'I have no understanding of this matter,' Sir Alan said with a shake of his head, 'but find me the miscreant and he shall be dealt with, never fear.'

'Bear with me and I will endeavour to solve this conundrum.' The constable paused, then said, 'Have there been any strange warnings or threats given to you or your manservant which might indicate someone was seeking to frighten you into leaving this house?'

Sir Alan rubbed his jaw reflectively. 'Rob had been speaking freely with some of the natives hereabouts and one of them, a clerk who takes care of the bridge properties, told him that the ghosts of many Scotsmen haunt the dwellings on the bridge.

Many of my countrymen who perished in the wars between our two nations, including our great hero William Wallace, had their heads displayed on long poles on this bridge, and Rob was told that a number of those heads were displayed exactly where this house now stands.'

'So you were told of this before the apparition came?' Master Drew asked with interest.

'I was and, for shame, I paid them no mind, as I could see with my own eyes that the heads of miscreants are not displayed here but at the other end of the bridge at the place called the Great Stone Gate. Such idle gossip I dismissed. But . . .'

'But?' pressed the constable.

'Poor Rob had been told only yesterday that there was much truth in the story. He was most disquieted.'

'What did he learn?'

'That this house was built on a place called Drawbridge Gate which was taken down less than thirty years before and it was, indeed, at that time the very spot where the heads of traitors were displayed. Davy there believes in the phantom and claims to know the purpose of the spectre's visit.'

The constable turned to the stoic man-at-arms with an unspoken query.

'We live with vengeance in our country and often die with it,' said the man.

'All this means is that some person intends to scare your master from this house,' returned Master Drew sharply. 'The question is why. Certainly, it is a desirable property and many seek it. Yet why go to such lengths to frighten you, Sir Alan, out of the tenancy?'

That question was uppermost in his mind as Master Drew made his way back to Bridge House. Vengeance. Curses. He tried to remember the Scotsman's quaint curse. 'By the fate of the odious Riven crew . . .' Riven? That surely meant 'to tear asunder'? It made no sense. He reached Bridge House but was told that Sir Thomas was lunching with His Grace the Bishop of Winchester and would return later. The master clerk, Master Gregory, was about some business on the bridge but one of the assistant clerks informed him that Sir Thomas had left instructions that everyone at Bridge House should accord the constable whatever help he might demand.

Master Drew, on impulse, demanded to see the rental accounts for Nonsuch House.

He went quickly down the names of previous tenants before Sir Alan Kerr. He was looking for Scottish names but could not seem to find any. The tenant immediately before Sir Alan had been a person called Ruthven. Master Drew frowned. Ruthven did not even appear to be Scottish.

He called to the young clerk who was still hovering nearby. 'Have you any details on this Master Ruth-ven?' The constable pronounced it with two clear syllables. 'He was the tenant before Sir Alan.'

The young lad immediately laid a bundle of papers before him. 'We keep reports on all foreigners who rent our properties, sir. It is a requirement. It should be . . . ah, yes . . . here.' He solemnly handed a paper to Master Drew.

The constable read quickly. 'Archibald Ruthven, refugee from Scotland, hired Nonsuch House at the Calends of February, 1601, on recommendation of Robert, Lord Burghley, as being a fit person. He is recommended for his service to Her Majesty, the Sovereign lady Elizabeth, against the interests of his former liege of Scotland. He departed the tenancy on Ash Wednesday, 1603, leaving without due notification and owing four florins.'

The constable smiled. How political times had changed. Before Her Majesty's death there had been talk of war with the Scots and their French allies. King James of Scotland had been seen as an enemy. Scottish refugees were used as spies and informers. So this Archibald Ruthven was one such. He had quite probably fled in haste when it was announced that James VI of Scotland would ascend to the throne of England.

The young clerk pushed another paper into his hand. Again Master Drew glanced at it. It was the report of another such informer.

'November, 1600. Archibald Ruthven has fled to London following the Scottish King's declaration that the name of Ruthven be proscribed in Scotland, and all titles, honours and lands of the family be forfeit. He is of a mind to give what assistance he can to the English cause. In August of this year, Ruthven's father John and his uncle Alexander enticed the Scottish King to John's town house in Perth and made him prisoner. The King's loyal courtiers quickly ascertained his whereabouts and effected a rescue during which both men were killed.'

The constable sat back with a frown. There was much intrigue here. 'Do you know what happened to this Archibald Ruth-ven?' he asked the lad.

The clerk shrugged. 'I did hear that he fled to France the moment His Majesty of Scotland was named as heir to the throne of England. I believe there was some assassination attempt by agents of His Majesty in March of this year and that this was the cause of his flight.'

'It says here that the titles, honours and lands were forfeit and even the name of Ruth-ven was proscribed in Scotland. Is there any knowledge of such titles?'

'I have no knowledge, sir.'

Intrigued, the constable retraced his steps back to Nonsuch House. After he was ushered into Sir Alan's presence, he came directly to the point. 'Your pardon, Sir Alan, know you anything of a family called Ruth-ven?'

He was disappointed to see Sir Alan Kerr immediately shake his head. 'What makes you ask, Constable?'

'I had thought the name was well-known in your country until a few years ago when it was proscribed.'

'Ruth-ven?' Sir Alan repeated and was shaking his head again when he paused and a smile spread slowly over his face. 'Fetch pen and paper, Davy,' he called to his man-at-arms. 'Let the constable write this name.'

After the constable had written the name, Sir Alan peered at it. He nodded in satisfaction, but was clearly troubled. 'Yon's proscribed name, indeed, and proscribed in the name of His Majesty In Scotland, should it ever be pronounced again, we say Riven.'

'Riven? So that was the curse you mentioned!' Master Drew exclaimed in satisfaction. 'Tell me of his background and estates.'

'The family held the title of Earl of Gowrie.'

'Gowrie?'

'Aye, 'tis a title that my family bears no liking for. Nigh on thirty years ago they nearly wiped out the Kerrs in a feud. Their patriarch, William Ruthven, the first to hold the title, was executed some ten years later. His eldest son inherited the title, but disappeared shortly thereafter, never to be heard from again. A few years thereafter he was presumed dead and the title passed to William's second son, John, who became the third Earl of Gowrie. He, too, met with an unsavory end, not three years past – killed in a plot against the King. Best not mention that name again, sir. No man may say aught of them for they are traitors all.'

'Do you know the name of the previous tenant of this house, sir?' asked the constable softly.

Sir Alan shook his head.

'Very well,' the constable spoke decidedly. 'I will take my leave for I have much to do.'

By the time he returned to Bridge House, Sir Thomas was back from his lunch and awaiting him.

'Have you tracked down our phantom, Master Constable?' The Lord Mayor exuded bonhomie and it was clear that several glasses of Sack had followed the first as well as a good lunch.

'I believe I have, sir.' Master Drew was grim. 'I believe there is a conspiracy here, sir, and would fain ask you to send for your clerk, Master Gregory.'

Sir Thomas at once sent for his clerk, regarding the constable with a frown of curiosity.

Master Gregory entered, glancing quickly at Master Drew, then standing nervously before the Lord Mayor.

'You came to London twenty years ago, you say?' demanded the constable with an abruptness that made the clerk start.

'I did so, sir.'

'You told me that you had been under the patronage of a lord named Gowrie?'

'I was in his service, sir.'

'You were a loyal servant?'

'I always give my loyalty to my masters, sir.'

'You said that you came to London after this lord was executed?'

'Indeed I did, sir.'

'And was the Lord Gowrie you served the father of one John Ruthven, third Earl of Gowrie – a man killed three years ago while trying to enact a coup against His Majesty of Scotland, having unlawfully imprisoned him?'

Master Gregory compressed his lips for a moment. 'I believe he was, sir.'

'And Archibald Ruthven,' Master Drew said, pronouncing the name correctly, 'is the son of that third Earl of Gowrie?'

Sir Thomas let out a hiss of breath. Master Gregory paled and then nodded.

'And are you uncle to this Archibald Ruthven?'

Master Gregory's eyes were desperate. 'Sir?' He raised his shoulders helplessly.

'What is your name? Gregory Ruthven? I believe that you were not, as you claim, merely a servant to Lord Gowrie, but that, in fact, you are his eldest son, a son who inherited the title but subsequently fled Scotland and was presumed dead.'

There was silence. Sir Thomas was trying to follow the conversation.

The constable continued remorselessly. 'I believe that you are involved with Archibald Ruthven and, for some reason I can as yet only guess at, you are both trying to frighten Sir Alan from Nonsuch House. Further, I believe that you are the play-actor who pretended to be the phantom. Did you not provide intelligence to Sir Alan's servant that Nonsuch House once stood on the site of Drawbridge Gate where executed traitors' heads were displayed, emphasising that among these were Scottish rebels?'

Master Gregory's face was filled with dismay.

Sir Thomas cleared his throat and spoke sharply to his master clerk. 'Confess if you are guilty, man, for it will be the worse for you if you don't. A short meeting with the rack will not only stretch your limbs, but your tongue as well so that it will wag freely.'

Master Gregory spread his hands. 'It is true that I acted the spectre, sir. It was merely to scare Sir Alan into vacating the house for a while. The servant, Rob, however, was not taken in by my disguise. He came at me with his dagger and we struggled. It was not my intention to inflict a wound upon him. He lay moaning for a while before I heard Sir Alan coming down the stairs. I decided to brazen it out according to the plan. It seemed to work, for Sir Alan was of little backbone, being true to the tribe of Kerrs whom my father defeated.'

'You spoke to him in . . . what is the language called? Yrisch?'

'The true language of my country, sir – what we call the Gaelic. Aye, I warned him to leave and when he turned his attention to his servant's body, I left the way I had come, along the rope walkway beneath the bridge.'

'And are you, as the constable claims, the son of this Lord Gowrie?' demanded Sir Thomas.

'I am and I am proud of my name, though for the sake of politics I have long hidden it.'

'And you are even now in league with Archibald Ruthven? But why? To what purpose can you want to chase Sir Alan from his house? So that your nephew will be able to take possession of it once more? That would be impossible. He absconded from the tenancy and the name of Ruthven would convict him as so many supporters of the Scottish King – of His Majesty, for he is King in England as well as Scotland now – know of the name and the proscription on it.'

'I can tell you no more, sir. I would only ask one favour of you, Sir Thomas – that you mention my situation straightaway to my Lord Burghley.'

'To the Lord Chancellor?' Sir Thomas's eyebrows shot up in surprise. 'Why so?'

'You know him well, Sir Thomas. I can say no more.'

As the constable left with Master Gregory in his charge, he turned to the worried Lord Mayor. 'If you will take advice from me, Sir Thomas, I would suggest that you send such a message to Lord Burghley by a trusted source. I would not advise you to mention this affair as yet to Lord Suffolk.'

Master Gregory was removed to a nearby jail in the thoroughfare from which it took its name, Clink Street.

The next day Sir Thomas sent for Master Drew. The constable had been expecting the early summons.

Sir Thomas was waiting to greet him and told him to go straight to his chamber, but surprisingly Sir Thomas waited outside. The man awaiting Master Drew in Sir Thomas's chamber was of middle age, handsome, and richly dressed with a heavy gold chain of office. The constable had seen a row of liveried guards standing beside a coach outside Bridge House when he had arrived. The coat of arms emblazoned on the coach clearly announced the identity of the man before he spoke.

Robert Cecil, Baron Burghley, Lord Chancellor and Keeper of the Privy Seal of England, examined Master Drew with an interested scrutiny. 'Do you know the Latin expression *a fronte praecipitium a tergo lupi*, Master Constable?' he asked without preamble.

'My lord,' the constable replied, 'I regret that I did not have the opportunity to construe Latin in my youth.'

'It means "a precipice in front, wolves behind". In other words, the choices facing me are equally dangerous. I hear you are an honest man and so I shall be honest with you. You are too good at your profession. Had Sir Thomas come to me with this problem, I would have told him to leave matters in the hands of the Bridge Watch. They have enough imagination to believe in phantoms but not enough to piece together the puzzle in the manner you have done.'

'My lord, I have pieced nothing together,' replied the constable. 'I have merely uncoiled a few strands on a ball of twine.'

'You are too modest,' said Lord Burghley, then without preamble, stated, 'The Ruthvens were working together in my service.'

Constable Drew did not blink for he had spent much of the night considering the possibilities of the matter.

Lord Burghley tapped his fingers on the arm of the chair, watching the constable's impassive face closely. 'You are not surprised?'

'It is known that for many years you ran Her Late Majesty's intelligence service, as your father did before you.'

Burghley sighed and hesitated a moment before he looked again into the constable's eyes. 'You will not be surprised then, that early this morning Master Gregory effected an escape from the jail on Clink Street. And, as Lord Chancellor of this realm, I will tell you what you must now do to save it from bloodshed.'

'There is something at Nonsuch House that must be retrieved?'

Lord Burghley smiled and nodded. 'I am not mistaken in you, sir. You have a sharp mind. As Constable, with Sir Thomas's warrant, you will present yourself at Nonsuch House and request that Sir Alan, and any servant or servants he may have, vacate the house for the rest of the day. You may make the excuse that Master Gregory, the culprit that you so ably apprehended, has escaped and is believed to be plotting an assassination attempt on Sir Alan. You must tell Sir Alan that you plan to lay a trap in his house and that he must remove himself for his own safety.'

Master Drew was silent.

'You will proceed immediately to Nonsuch House with six liveried men,' continued Lord Burghley. 'They already wait outside for you. Once you have despatched Sir Alan and his servants from the house, one of these men shall go to the main bedchamber. His task is to remove some documents that he neglected to take with him when he left residence there.'

'This man being Archibald Ruthven?' the constable said, smiling.

'You will then allow the men to return here,' Burghley said, not responding to the question. 'You will later inform Sir Alan that you have discovered that Master Gregory has fled to France. Indeed, both Ruthvens will have done so by this evening. That will be an end to your work in this matter.'

Master Drew inclined his head briefly. 'I am at your command, my lord.'

He made to move for the door but Lord Burghley called him to stay a moment. 'You are a good man, Master Drew. An official without political ambition who offers loyalty without question. His Grace of Winchester keeps me well informed. Do you not want me to smooth away any concerns that you have?'

The constable turned back with a shake of his head. 'My lord, I know that in politics loyalties may change quickly. What is patriotism one day may be treason another. I know that there were many who were unhappy with the King of the Scots being made King of England. Sir Walter Raleigh, now languishing under sentence of death in the Tower, has been found guilty of plotting to put the Lady Arabella Stewart on the English Throne. I suspect that there were many more involved in that enterprise. Now that James has been placed firmly on the throne, many serve him who would have preferred to serve the Lady Arabella. They would have cause to regret having stated their allegiances if their names were now discovered. Indeed,' he added, 'just as Sir Walter probably now regrets having acted on his.'

Lord Burghley's eyes met the constable's and there was amusement in them. 'You are truly a man of wit and discernment, Master Drew. You already know what is hidden in Nonsuch House. Names were unfortunately put down on paper and hidden there. When Archibald Ruthven had to flee, he did not have time to secure them from their hiding place and was unable to contact his uncle until recently. And when he did, there was a new resident at Nonsuch House. A blood enemy of the Ruthvens, no less. Archibald Ruthven had been working for me with other Scots who wished to see the Lady Arabella replace James on the throne of Scotland and ascend to the throne of England in his stead. My name is the first one on that list. I did not learn until last night that the Ruthvens had been working on a plan to secure entrance to the main bedchamber in order to retrieve the documents which would have sent myself and hundreds of others, including His Grace of Winchester, your patron, to the execution block. It was a bizarre plan, a silly plan, and one doomed to disaster.'

He sat back and sighed. 'The political world has changed, Master Constable. England has welcomed the Scottish King. We must tread a cautious path. Thomas Howard has been made Lord Suffolk by King James and appointed Lord Chamberlain. I probably will not be long in my office. And if the names of those who would have preferred Lady Arabella in place of James were known, not only would many be at the execution block but there might be civil war tearing its bloody way through the country, not to mention a new war with the Scots. What I do now, I do in the name of justice for the people of this realm. Now, can you forget all that, Master Constable?'

Master Drew smiled grimly. 'I have already forgotten it, my lord. I am a simple man and not a politician. You are still Lord Chancellor of England. So long as you serve justice for the people, I shall serve that justice. I am not so naive as to believe that justice is a synonym for the law.'

This Thing of Darkness

This thing of darkness.
I acknowledge mine

The Tempest, Act V, Scene i
William Shakespeare

Master Hardy Drew, Constable of the Bankside Watch, stood regarding the blackened and still smoking ruins of the once imposing edifice of the house on the corner of Stony Street near the parish church of St Saviour's. There was little left of it as it had been a wood-built house and wood and dry plaster were a combustible mix.

'It was a fine old house,' Master Drew's companion said reflectively. 'It once belonged to the old Papist Bishop Gardiner.'

'The one who took pleasure in burning those he deemed heretics in Queen Mary's time?' asked Master Drew with a slight shudder. He had not been born when Mary had been on the throne but he knew it to be a strange, unsettled period when, during those five short years, she had earned the epithet of 'Bloody Mary'.

Master Pettigrew, the fire warden, nodded.

'Aye, Master Drew. The same who condemned some good men to the flames because they would not accept Roman ways.'

'Well, it is not infrequent that buildings catch alight and burn. You and your sturdy lads have put out the flames and no other properties seem threatened. Why, therefore, do you bring me here?'

Master Pettigrew inclined his head towards the smouldering ruins.

'There is a body here. I think you should see it.'

The constable frowned.

'A poor soul caught in the fire? Surely that is a task for the coroner?'

'That's as maybe, good Master. Come and examine it for yourself. It is not badly burned,' he added, seeing the distaste on Master Drew's features. 'I believe it was not fire that killed him.'

He led the way through the charred wood and the odd standing wall towards what must have been the back of the house and into an area that had been partially built of bricks and thus not much had been destroyed by the conflagration.

Master Drew saw the problem straightaway. The body of a man was hanging from a thick beam by means of iron manacles that secured his wrists and linked them via a chain over the beam. He breathed out sharply.

'This is a thing of darkness. A deed of evil,' he muttered.

The constable tried not to look at the legs of the corpse for they had received the force of the fire. The upper body was blackened but not burnt for, by that curious vagary which fire is often prey to, the flames had not engulfed the entire body. The fire seemed to have died after it had reached the corpse.

The body was that of a man of thirty or perhaps a little more. Through the soot and grime it was impossible to say much more about the features.

85

Master Drew saw that the mouth was tied as in the manner of a gag. The eyes were bulging still and blood-rimmed, marking the struggle to obtain air that must have been filled with smoke and fumes from the fire.

'You will observe, Master Drew, that the upper garments of this man speak of some wealth and status and the manner of his death was clearly planned.'

The constable sniffed in irritation.

'I am experienced in the matter of observation,' he rebuked sharply.

Indeed, he had already observed that, in spite of the blackened and scorched garments, they were clearly garments affected by a person of wealth. His sharp eyes had detected something under the shirt and he drew the long dagger he wore at his belt and used it to push aside the doublet and undershirt. It was a gold chain on which was hung a medallion of sorts.

Master Pettigrew let out a breath. He was probably thinking of the wealth that he had missed, for being warden of the fire watch around Bankside did not provide him with means to live as he would want without a little aid from such items collected in the debris of fires such as this.

Using the tip of his dagger, Master Drew was able to lift the chain over the head of the corpse and then examine it. Master Pettigrew bent over his shoulders.

'A dead sheep moulded in gold,' he breathed, peering at the symbol.

Master Drew shook his head.

'Not a dead sheep but the fleece of a sheep. I have seen the like once before. It was just after the defeat of the Spanish invasion force. They brought some prisoners to the Tower and I was one of the appointed guards. One of the prisoners was wearing such a symbol. When one of the sergeants wanted to divest him of it, our captain rebuked him saying it was the symbol of a noble order and that the prisoner should be treated, therefore, with all courtesy and respect.'

The warden looked worried.

'Some nobleman murdered here on the Bankside? We will not hear the last of it, good Constable. Nobles have powerful influence.'

Master Drew nodded thoughtfully.

'A nobleman, aye. But of what country and what allegiance? This order was set up to defend the Papist faith.'

Master Pettigrew looked at him slightly horrified.

'The Papist faith, you say?'

'This is a Spanish order for I see the insignia of Philip of Spain on the reverse.'

'Spanish?' gasped Master Pettigrew. 'There are several noble Spaniards in London at this time.'

Master Drew's features hardened.

'And many who would as lief cut a Spaniard's throat in revenge for acts of previous years. Were there no witnesses to this incendiary act?'

To his surprise, Master Pettigrew nodded an affirmative.

'Tom Shadwell, a passing fruit merchant, saw the flames and called the alarm,' returned Master Pettigrew. 'That was at dawn this morning. My men managed to isolate the building and extinguish the flames within the hour. Then we entered and that was when I found the body and sent for you.'

'Well, one thing is for certain, this poor soul did not hang himself nor set fire to this place. To whom does this building now belong?'

'I think it must still belong to the Bishop of Winchester for he has many estates around here. Such was the office of Bishop Gardiner but he has been dead these fifty years during which it has remained empty.'

'That's true,' Master Drew reflected. 'I have never seen it occupied since I came here as assistant constable. No one has ever claimed it nor sought to occupy it.'

'Aye, and for reasons that local folk claim it to be haunted by the spirits of the unfortunates that Bishop Gardiner tortured and condemned to the flames as heretics.'

Master Drew pocketed the chain thoughtfully and glanced once more at the body.

'Release the corpse to the charge of the coroner, Master Pettigrew, and say that I will speak with him anon but to do nothing precipitous until I have done so.'

He was about to turn when he caught sight of something in the corner of the room that puzzled him. In spite of the fire having damaged this area, he saw that the floorboards were smashed and that, where they had been torn away, a rectangular hole had been dug into the earth. He moved towards it.

'Is this the work of your men, Master Pettigrew?' he asked.

The warden of the fire watch shook his head.

'Not of my men.'

Master Drew sniffed sharply.

'Then someone has excavated this hole. But for what purpose?'

He bent down, peered into the hole and poked at it with the tip of his long dagger.

'The hole was already here and something buried, which was but recently dug up and removed and . . .' he frowned, moved his dagger again and then bent down into the hole carefully, trying to avoid the soot. With a grunt of satisfaction, he came up holding something between thumb and forefinger.

'A coin?' hazarded Master Pettigrew, leaning over his shoulder.

'Aye, a coin,' the constable confirmed, scraping away some of the soot with the point of the dagger.

'A groat?'

'No, this is a shilling, and an Irish shilling of Philip and Mary at that. See the harp under the crown on the face and either side, under smaller crowns, the initials P and M? Now what would that be doing here?'

'Well, Bishop Gardiner was a Papist during the time of Mary and approved her marriage to the Spanish king Philip. It is logic that he might have lost the coin then.'

Master Drew looked down at the hole again. He knew better than to comment further. Instead, he slipped the coin into his pocket and moved towards the exit of the blackened building. Outside, groups of people were already gathering. He suspected that some of them had come to forage and pillage if there was anything worth salvaging.

'Where are you away to?' called Master Pettigrew.

'To proceed with my investigation,' he replied. 'I'll speak to the fruit merchant who first saw the conflagration.'

'He has the barrow at the corner of Clink Street selling fruit and nosegays to those visiting the folk within the prison.'

The constable made no reply but he knew Tom Shadwell, the fruit seller, well enough and often passed the time of day with him as he made his way by the grim walls of the old prison.

'A body found, you say, good Constable?' Tom Shadwell's features were pale when Master Drew told him of the gruesome find. 'I saw only the flames and had no idea that anyone dwelt within the building. Had I known, I would have made an effort to save the poor soul. So far as I knew, it had been empty these many years.'

'You would have been too late anyway,' replied Master Drew. 'It is murder that we are dealing with. Therefore, be cautious in your thoughts before you recite to me as much as you may remember.'

Tom Shadwell rubbed the bridge of his nose with a crooked forefinger.

'The first light was spreading when I came by the corner of Stony Street to make my way to my pitch. I was pushing my barrow as usual. It is not long after dawn that the prison door is opened and visitors are allowed to go in. I usually start my trade early. I was passing the old house when I saw the flames . . .'

He suddenly paused and frowned.

'You have thought of something, Master Shadwell?' prompted the constable.

'It is unrelated to the fire.'

'Let me decide that.'

'There was a coach standing in Stony Street, not far from the house. Two men were lifting a small wooden chest into the coach.

90

It seemed heavy. Even as I passed the end of the street they had placed it inside, then one climbed in and the other scrambled to the box and took the reins. Away it went in a thrice. I then crossed the end of the street towards the old house and that was when I heard the crackle of the fire and saw its flames through the window. I pushed my barrow to the end of the street, for I knew Master Pettigrew, warden of the fire watch, dwelt there. I was reluctant to leave my barrow – prey to thieves and wastrels – but there was no one about, so I ran along to his house and raised the alarm. That is all I know.'

'This coach, could you identify it?'

Shadwell shook his head.

'It was dark and the two men were clad in dark cloaks.'

'Well-dressed fellows, would you say?'

'Hard to say, Master Constable.'

'And which way did this coach proceed? Towards the bridge?'

Shadwell shook his head.

'In this direction, towards Clink Street or maybe along to Bankside, not towards the bridge.'

Having ascertained there was nothing more to be gathered from the fruit seller, Master Drew turned past the Clink Prison to the adjacent imposing ancient structure of Winchester Palace that dominated the area just west of the Bridgehead. Southwark was the largest town of the diocese of Winchester. In the days when Winchester was capital of the Saxon kingdom, before London reclaimed its Roman prominence, the Bishops of Winchester were all-powerful. Even after Winchester fell into decline as a capital, the bishops remained within the royal court circles and therefore had to be frequently in London for royal and administrative purposes. So the grand Winchester Palace was built on the south bank of the Thames.

Master Drew explained his business to the gatekeeper of the palace and was shown directly to the office of Sir Gilbert Scrivener, secretary to His Grace, Thomas Bilson, the Bishop of Winchester.

'The house on the corner of Stony Street? We have large estates in Southwark, Master Drew, as you know. But I do vaguely recall it. Unused since Bishop Gardiner's decease.'

'You have no personal acquaintance with the house, then?'

'My dear constable,' replied Sir Gilbert, 'I have more things to do with my time than to personally acquaint myself with all the properties controlled by the diocese. As for the burning of this building, and the murder of foreigners, it is not to be wondered that they and empty houses are treated in such a manner – since it is, it may be a blessing for it has long been His Grace's wish to rebuild that crumbling edifice and set upon the site something more useful to the church and the community.'

'So you are acquainted with the house?' frowned Master Drew sharply.

Sir Gilbert spread his hands with a thin smile.

'As I said, not personally. But I am His Grace's secretary. I fear you do but waste your time for do we not live in Southwark and is it not said that these mean streets are better termed a foul den than a fair garden? Its reputation is best described as notorious. Bankside itself is a nest of prostitutes and thieves, of cut-throats and vagabonds.'

'And playhouses,' smiled Master Drew grimly. 'Do not forget the playhouses, Sir Gilbert.'

Sir Gilbert sighed impatiently.

'I cannot spare you more time, Master Constable. I wish you a good morning and success with your endeavours.'

Outside the gates of Winchester Palace, Master Drew paused, frowning, his hand fingering the golden chain that reposed in his breeches pocket.

He sighed deeply. It was going to be a long walk to where he felt his next enquiry was going to take him. His allowance as Constable of the Bankside Watch would not stretch to what the justices of Southwark might deem unnecessary expenses, a wherry-man to ferry him across the river. So, with a shrug, he set off towards the entrance to London Bridge. He was walking towards it when a voice hailed him.

'Give you a good day, Master Constable.'

He glanced up to see old Jepheson, the tanner, guiding his wagonload of hides towards the bridge. He knew him well for he had prevented the old man and his wife from being attacked and robbed one summer evening in their tannery in Bear Lane.

'Good day, Master Jepheson. Wither away?'

'To deliver these hides to The Strand.'

Master Drew smiled broadly. Here was luck, indeed.

'Then I will seek the favour of a ride with you there for it will save an exhausting walk and the wearing of my shoe leather.'

'Climb up and welcome. I am already in your debt.'

Master Drew obeyed with alacrity. While old Jepheson prat-tled on, Master Drew could not help but dwell on the meaning of the golden chain in his pocket. The symbol of a Spanish noble order found on the corpse of a murdered man. All England knew that the long war between England and Spain was coming to a negotiated end. Envoys from the two kingdoms were even now meeting in the palace built by the Duke of Somerset. Since 1585 the war had continued with no side gaining any advantage. With the death of Elizabeth and the accession last year of James VI of Scotland as James I of England it was felt time to end the long and wasteful war. The old enemy, Philip II of Spain, was also dead and Philip III now ruled there. Six leading Spanish noblemen had arrived with their entourages to conduct the negotiations that would, hopefully, lead to a treaty.

Somerset House was on the north bank of the River Thames. Southwark was south of London Bridge and a separate jurisdiction from London. It owed its importance to its position at the southern end of the only bridge spanning the Thames and thus the main thoroughfare to the south. And its population had grown by making itself a pleasure ground for the more law-abiding north bank of the Thames. It had only been in 1550 that the City of London had decided to attempt to control the lawlessness of Southwark by setting up justices and constables, such as Master Drew's own office.

Southwark still felt separate and would not be forced to obedience of the justices of London. It became the headquarters of the rebel Sir Thomas Wyatt in 1554 when he raised an insurgent force to move on London to prevent Queen Mary's intended marriage to Philip II of Spain. Only the fortification on the northern end of London Bridge and the training of the cannons of the Tower of London across the river on the homes and churches of the people of Southwark, forced the withdrawal of the insurgents.

It was because of this independence, this freedom and laxity in the laws, that the Bankside area became a place where playhouses had sprung up outside of the restrictions put on them by their neighbours on the northern banks of the Thames. The Bankside had become a haunt of prostitutes, pimps and thieves. And it was with this separation in jurisdiction that Master Drew realised he would be unable to exercise authority on the northern bank.

Master Drew left Jepheson and his wagon of hides in The Strand and walked to the gates of Somerset House. In the court-yard an officer of the guard stopped him and shook his head when he said he wanted to see one of the Spanish delegation or their secretaries.

'You have no jurisdiction here, Constable,' replied the officer. 'I can let no one through here without legal authority.'

'Master Drew?' a sharp voice suddenly called behind him.

The constable swung round. A man of small stature, crook back, with a tawny-coloured beard and hair and sharp green eyes was examining him. He had apparently emerged from a nearby doorway. The officer of the guard stiffened and saluted while Master Drew performed a clumsy bow as he recognised the Lord Chancellor of England, Sir Robert Cecil.

'I thought it was you,' Sir Robert said, with a soft, malicious smile. 'I never forget a face. What business brings you hither?'

Master Drew tried to repress thoughts of how Sir Robert came perilously close to having him arrested for conspiracy to High Treason while Elizabeth lay dying the previous year.

'A matter that may be one of national importance, Sir Robert.'

The Lord Chancellor raised his eyes and then waved away the officer of the guard.

'Then, come walk with me, and tell me what you mean.'

Master Drew, with little wasted words, explained what had happened as they paced the courtyard and ended by presenting Sir Robert with the gold chain.

The Lord Chancellor frowned as he examined it.

'I have seen the like before and recently. You have in mind that it belongs to one of the Spanish delegation?'

'And even worse,' agreed Master Drew. 'That the owner of the chain and the body in the house on Stony Street might be one of your Spanish nobles. If it is so and one of the ambassadors has been murdered at such a fraught time . . .' He shrugged.

The diplomatic implications were not lost on Sir Robert.

'If so, then, indeed, we face perilous times,' he said softly. He turned back to the officer of the guard and called to him.

'Go to the apartment of His Grace, the Duke of Frias, and ask him if it would not be troubling him too much if he could attend me in my chamber. I pray you, put as much courtesy and politeness in the request as you can.'

The officer went off on his new errand.

Sir Robert guided Master Drew into the building and through to a chamber where a fire crackled in the hearth.

'I have seen the Duke of Frias returning from his morning ride, so I know he is safe,' confided Sir Robert. 'He is the chief ambassador of the Spanish and should be able to assist in this matter.'

It seemed only a short time passed before there was a knock on the door and the officer of the guard entered and stood to one side.

'His Grace Juan de Velasco Frias, Duke of Frias, Constable of Castile,' the guard announced solemnly.

A tall, dark and elegantly dressed man entered and made a sweeping courtly bow to them.

Sir Robert went forward to greet him.

'Your Grace, forgive me for disturbing your morning's pre-occupations, but we must ask for your advice and information on a pressing matter of concern to both our nations.'

The duke smiled but with a movement of his facial muscles only. His dark eyes looking enquiringly at Master Drew, taking in his slightly shabby clothing and appearance which clearly did not place him as a courtier or officer of state.

'It is what I and my compatriots are here for, Sir Robert. But I have not had the pleasure of your companion's acquaintance.'

'This is Master Drew, Constable of the Bankside—'

'*Master* Drew? And a constable? I am Constable of Castile. Do you not have to be of the knightly rank to be a constable in this kingdom?'

'There is a difference in office, Your Grace,' Sir Robert explained hurriedly. 'Suffice to say, Master Drew is much in our confidence. Tell me, have you seen all your compatriots this morning?'

The duke frowned.

'All? Indeed, we breakfasted together to discuss some points to raise at our sessions later today. Why do you ask?'

'Master Drew has something to explain.'

Master Drew cleared his throat and repeated his story and then held out the chain for the Spanish duke to inspect.

'The Order of the Golden Fleece,' the duke whispered softly. 'It bears the insignia of His Majesty, Felipe the Third.' The expression on his face told them he recognised it. He turned his dark eyes to Sir Robert. 'Can someone ask the Count of Villa Medina to join us?'

Sir Robert glanced towards the guard who had remained by the door and issued instructions.

When he had gone Master Drew asked, 'Does Your Grace think that this belongs to the Count of Villa Medina?'

The Duke of Frias shook his head.

'I know that the Count of Villa Medina is not a member of this noble order. However, he will, I am sure, be able to cast light on the person who held this honour.'

Again, it was not long before the door was opened to a nervous man whose movements reminded Master Drew of a bird, quick and unpredictable. He possessed the habit of running his hand quickly over his small, pointed beard each time he spoke.

This time, the Duke of Frias spoke rapidly in Spanish and then turned to Master Drew and asked him to hold forth the golden chain.

The count's face paled as he examined it.

'I can identify the owner of this,' he said slowly. He spoke a fair English but without the fluency of the duke.

'And the owner is . . .?' queried Master Drew.

'My secretary, the chevalier Stefano Jardineiro y Barbastro.'

Master Drew frowned.

'Stefano Jardineiro?' he echoed.

The count made a quick motion with his hand, stroking his beard rapidly.

'He is of an English family who fled to Spain on the death of Mary, the former Queen Consort of Spain.'

Sir Robert sniffed in embarrassment. 'Stefano Jardineiro was a nephew of Bishop Stephen Gardiner. That is why the name is familiar. I recall the family.'

Master Drew tried not to hide his surprise.

'Bishop Gardiner of Winchester?'

'The family was granted asylum by the late King Felipe who gave them an estate in Barbastro,' added the count. 'The chevalier proved his nobility and loyalty in service and so was ennobled by the court and made a member of this order.'

Sir Robert glanced keenly at Master Drew.

'I am aware that Bishop Gardiner sent several worthy men to the flames as martyrs for the Protestant cause, therefore there might be some who would see the death of one of his family as just retribution. But before we seek conclusions, let us establish facts. I presume the chevalier is currently unaccounted for?'

The count looked embarrassed and nodded.

'I sent for him this morning to discuss notes appertaining to the Treaty but was told he was not in his chambers and that his bed had not been slept in. He has not been seen since last evening.'

'And why has an alarm not been raised?'

The Count of Villa Medina shrugged.

'The chevalier is a young man and there are many distractions in this city to preoccupy him.'

Master Drew looked sharply at him. The manner of his speech was careful to the point where it seemed obvious that he was withholding something.

'If I am to expedite this matter, I need to know all the facts.'

The count hesitated but the Duke of Frias spoke to him sharply in Spanish.

'It is true,' the count said, answering the duke in English. He turned to Master Drew. 'Very well, the facts it shall be. The chevalier said he had to go out last evening, as he wanted to collect an old . . . how do you call it? *Una reliquia de familia.*'

The duke translated for him.

'A family heirloom. He spoke to the count of this within my hearing. He mentioned no further details.'

Master Drew sighed deeply.

'I would be grateful if the count would accompany me to Bankside in order that he may formally identify the body. After all, it may not be the chevalier. But if it is, let us confirm it. Perhaps, Sir Robert, you might provide a coach to take us south of the river? I cannot ask the count to walk with me.'

'Even better,' replied the Lord Chancellor, 'there is a boat by the quayside at my constant disposal that will make your journey shorter.' He turned to the officer of the guard. 'Captain, take you two good stalwarts of your guard and accompany Master Drew and the Count of Villa Medina. You are the constable's to command, and his commands may be given in my name. Is that clear?'

The officer saluted and turned to fulfil his task.

A moment later the count and guards were seated with Master Drew in the boat, whose four oars were manned by men in the livery of the Lord Chancellor. It pushed off from the north bank, making its way swiftly over the dark waters of the Thames, south towards the less than salubrious quays and wooden piers that lined the Bankside.

An elderly man limped forward to help tie up the boat in the hope of receiving a coin for his trouble. Master Drew recognised the man as one of those unfortunates who regularly frequented the quays to scavenge or pick up the odd job here and there. A thought suddenly came to him.

'Were you about the quays last evening?' he demanded sharply.

The man touched his cap awkwardly.

'That I was, Master Constable. I do be here most times unless the ague confines me to the pot room at The Bell, wherein I do be given a place by the fire by the good office of the innkeeper.'

'Did you notice a boat similar to this one?' He jerked his head towards the boat they had arrived in. 'Did a young man land here last night?'

'There be many young men come to the Bankside, good master. You know as well as I. Young rakes in search of a good time at the taverns or theatres and the company of low women.'

Master Drew took out a penny and fingered it before the man's eyes.

'This man would have been well dressed and foreign withal.'

'Foreign, you say? Spoke he like a Dago?'

Drew's eyes narrowed.

'You spoke with him?'

'By my soul, I did. It was late and I was about to go back to The Bell. There were few folk around. He came from the quay and asked if I could direct him to Stony Street, which I did. He then asked if I knew whether the Gardiner house still stood. That I could not say for I had never heard of it. But when he confided that Gardiner was once the bishop here, I said he had best call at Winchester Palace and enquire there. I told him where that was and he gave me a coin and went on his way. That's all I do know.'

Master Drew dropped the penny into the man's hand and

instructed the boatmen to stand ready to transport the count back to Somerset House. The mortuary was not far away and, as soon as the count had confirmed that the body of the young man was, indeed, his missing secretary, the chevalier Stefano Jardini-ero, he was despatched with one of the guards back to the boat with assurances that his murderer would soon be found.

With the officer and the other guard in attendance, Master Drew made his way directly to Winchester Palace and went straightway to the gatekeeper who was the same man who had been on duty earlier.

'Who was on watch here last night between dusk and mid-night?' he demanded without preamble.

The man looked nervously from the constable, whom he knew, to the liveried soldiers behind him.

'Why, old Martin, Master Drew.'

'And where shall I find old Martin now?' snapped the constable.

'About this time o' day, he'll be in the Bear Pit Tavern.'

It was a short walk to the tavern, which was on the quayside, and old Martin was soon pointed out.

Master Drew seated himself opposite the elderly man.

'Last evening you were the watch at the entrance to Winches-ter Palace.' It was a statement and not a question.

Martin looked at him with rheumy eyes.

'I cannot deny it.'

'A young foreign gentleman called there?'

'He did, good master. That he did. He asked me if the Gar-diner house still stood.'

'And you told him?'

'I told him that all the houses belonged to the diocese of Winchester and which one did he mean? He was trying to explain when Master Burton came by and took him aside. They were in deep conversation for a while and then the foreign gentleman . . . well, he went off looking quite content.'

'You saw no more of him?'

'None.'

'And who is this Master Burton?'

'Why, he be manservant to Sir Gilbert Scrivener.'

Master Drew sat back with a curious smile on his face.

Within fifteen minutes he was standing before the desk of the secretary to His Grace, the Bishop of Winchester, with the officer of the Lord Chancellor's guard at the door. Sir Gilbert was frowning in annoyance.

'I have much business to do, Master Constable. I trust this will not take too long and I only condescend to spare the time as you now say you come on the Lord Chancellor's business.'

Master Drew returned the man's gaze steadily, refusing to be intimidated by the man or his office.

'I would tell you a brief story first, about one of the Bishops of Winchester. He fortunately died in the time of Queen Mary and so did not have to account for the Protestant souls he cast into the flames to cure them of what he deemed as heresy. He was a wealthy and influential man who owned many houses here when he occupied this very palace. One building, in particular, he used to interrogate and torture heretics. You know the one; the one that was burnt down last night.

'It seems he gathered some wealth, a chest of coins, that, if Mary lost her throne and the Protestant faction came in, would help him escape to Spain and ease his exile. In the end, Mary outlived him so it was members of his family who had to flee to Spain. Before his death, he seems to have written instructions to his family in Spain as to where they could find that chest of coins. But war between Spain and England prevented any member of the family coming to England to seek it out . . . until now, nearly twenty years later when, it so happened, one of his family was appointed as secretary to the Spanish ambassadors who are now in this country to make a treaty of peace, ending the war.'

Sir Gilbert looked stony faced.

'Are you coming to a point, Master Constable?'

'Last night this scion of the Gardiner family, now known as chevalier Jardiniero y Barbastro, came in search of the Gardiner house wherein the box was buried. He made the mistake of being too free in his enquiries.'

'Are you saying that someone decided to kill him out of vengeance when they knew he was a relative of Bishop Gardiner?'

Master Drew shook his head.

'Not for such a lofty motive as vengeance was he killed, but merely for theft. He was followed and watched and, when he had dug up the chest of coins, he was attacked, bound so that he could hardly breathe and left to the tender mercy of the fire that had been set. The thieves hoped the conflagration would destroy the evidence of their evil. They had a coach waiting and set off with the chest. That much was seen.'

Sir Gilbert raised an eye, quickly searching the constable's features.

'And were they thus identified?'

'When the chevalier came here asking directions, he was told the way by Master Burton,' Master Drew went on, avoiding the question.

'Master Burton? My manservant?'

'Where is Master Burton?'

Sir Gilbert frowned.

'He set out this morning in my coach with some papers for Winchester itself.'

'With the chest of money?'

'If he is involved in such a business, have no fear, I will question the rogue and he shall be punished. You may leave it in my hands.'

Master Drew smiled and shook his head.

'Not in your hands, I am afraid, Sir Gilbert. Master Burton had an accomplice.'

'And do you name him?' Sir Gilbert's jaw tightened.

'You were that accomplice.'

'You cannot prove it.'

'Perhaps not. But you revealed yourself earlier when I asked you about the ownership of the house. I had not mentioned anything about the body or the possibility of its Spanish identification – yet you said to me that the burning of a house and murder of a foreigner was not to be wondered at in this city. How would you know that the body found was that of a foreigner unless you shared Master Burton's secret?'

Sir Gilbert's eyes narrowed.

'You are clever, Master Drew, and with the tongue of a serpent. But when all is said and done, I am an Englishman with good connections, and the young man was a foreigner and a Spaniard at that.'

'The war is over, Sir Gilbert, or will be when this treaty is signed.'

'My answer will be that I was retrieving what is rightfully the property of the Bishops of Winchester from theft by a foreigner. I shall say that he tried to make away with this treasure and Master Burton and I prevented him and reclaimed it for its true owner.'

Master Drew paused and nodded thoughtfully.

'It is, perhaps, a good defence. But there is one aspect that may not sit well on such a plea; that is, the chevalier Stefano Jardiniero y Barbastro was a member of the delegation currently negotiating the treaty. True, he was but a secretary within the delegation, and there are arguments to be made on both sides as to whether the treasure to which he had been directed was his family property or whether the subsequent Bishops of Winchester had a right to it. And, of course, we will have to ascertain whether Master Burton has gone directly with the chest to the Bishop of Winchester or whether he may have had cause to rest with it awhile in your own manor at Winchester town. And, even when these arguments are all set in place, it will come down to a simple fact of politics. How badly does the Lord Chancellor and His Majesty desire this treaty ending the twenty years of war with Spain? The Spanish ambassadors may seek to be compensated for the murder of one of their number before agreement can be reached.'

It was at the end of August of that year of 1604 that the treaty of peace and perpetual alliance between England and Spain was finally signed in Somerset House. Two weeks before the agreement, a certain Master Burton was taken from Newgate in a

106

tumbrel to Tyburn Tree and hanged. A year later, a prisoner in the Clink caught typhoid, in spite of the payments he had been able to give the jailer to secure good quarters during his incarceration. He was dead within three days. It was rumoured in the prison that he had once been a man of some status and influence and had even dwelt in the grand palace of the Bishop of Winchester, adjacent to the prison.

Made for Murders

By nature made for murders

Titus Andronicus, Act IV, Scene i
William Shakespeare

Master Hardy Drew, Constable of the Bankside Watch, halted briefly before turning down Bear Alley and exhaled in an exaggerated sigh of relief. His daily circuit along Maiden Lane with its rowdy taverns, and oft-times rowdier playhouses, had been completed without incident. It had been a quiet day. Now, and not without some relief, all he had to do was turn down Bear Alley to the Bankside and return along the Thames to his lodgings in Pepper Alley, where he rented rooms in the Pilgrim's Wink tavern and where Mistress Cuttle, the landlord's wife, would even now be preparing his supper.

He smiled at the thought, for she had promised a mutton and veal pottage. He could almost visualise her preparing it; a rack of mutton, a knuckle of veal, boiled with oatmeal and all manner of herbs, such as thyme, sweet marjoram, succory and marigolds, sage and sorrel. He inhaled deeply and imagined he could smell those odours of the scented mixture already.

His mind was thus distracted when a voice, raised in greeting, penetrated his thoughts. He stopped and realised that Master Redweard, the mortician and apothecary, was lounging outside his mortuary at the end of Bear Alley, a clay pipe in his mouth. He was leaning against the wall as if enjoying a break.

'Give thee a good day, Master Drew,' the man repeated now that he had the constable's full attention.

'How fares your day, Master Redweard?' Master Drew responded almost indifferently.

'Middling well, Master Drew,' the mortician replied, inhaling from his pipe before letting the black, pungent fumes drift from his mouth. 'Middling well. At least I do not want for customers.'

Master Drew tried not to show his distaste of the tobacco odours that assailed his nostrils. He knew that, as a mortician, Master Redweard had picked up the habit as defence against the noxious odours that assailed him. It was a habit many people had adopted since returning traders from the colonies of the New World had started to bring tobacco into England.

In this regard, Master Drew was a supporter of King James who, two years before, had imposed a stringent import tax on tobacco, having written that it was a 'custom loathsome to the eye, hateful to the nose, harmful to the brain, dangerous to the lung and in the black and sticky fume thereof, the horrible stygian smoke of the pit that is bottomless'. Nevertheless, the custom had been growing for forty or more years. Master Drew had tried to read John Frampton's translation of the Spaniard Nicólas Manardes, who praised the virtues of tobacco, claiming it was good for toothache, bad breath or halitosis, worms and other maladies. Master Drew was not convinced and preferred to carry a rose-scented cambric to stop the stench of the Bankside assaulting his senses.

'I believe you are at work on a corpse by the manner in which you have come out into the street to dull your senses with the foul aroma of that weed?' he remarked with a disapproving smile.

Master Redweard did not take offence.

'In truth, it be so. There be little that passes your eye undetected, Master Drew. That is well, for it proves you are well endowed for your profession.'

Master Drew could not suppress an immodest smile.

'So whose cadaver keeps you occupied this day?'

'That I know not nor am I likely to. Just a poor unknown waif found on the street. A young girl collapsed beyond recovery on the doorstep of a generous citizen.'

Master Drew's eyes widened. 'A generous citizen? By what means generous?'

'When the corpse was found, and she not long perished, the man sent her body to me to take charge of with the instruction to prepare it to be interred in the pauper's plot at Saint Saviour's.'

'Then the citizen was generous indeed. I presume you took some coin and did not undertake the task for nothing?'

'I have not lost control of all my senses, Master Drew. I am not a charity, but honest in my labours.'

'So the corpse has no name to be entered on the parish list?'

The mortician chuckled sourly. 'Of all people along the Bankside, you have the best guess at how many unknown bodies are taken from the river or the streets surrounding it and buried without identity. Aye, the poor girl had nothing on her to identify who she was or whence she came.'

'And did you discover how she met her death? Lack of food or some pestilence or street malady, I suppose?'

'Of a broken neck, constable,' the mortician replied acridly. 'I would hazard that she had been suffocated by a powerful pair of hands that broke her collar bone as well as stifling the air from her lungs.'

'Then it be murder?' Master Drew inhaled sharply. 'You should have spoken of this before. You say that you have no clue to who she is?'

'No clue as to who she is or whence she came,' Master Redweard reaffirmed. 'Had it not been that she was found on the doorstep belonging to Master Armin, and he volunteered a groat for me to prepare her for burial, then she would likely have remained where she fell until she rotted.'

Master Drew frowned as he caught the name. 'Master Armin? You don't mean Master Robert Armin, the playwright and actor of the Chamberlain's men?'

'I have knowledge of his name only since the corpse arrived here on a wheelbarrow pushed by two street urchins. But, since you ask, I think I must have heard mention of the name since you connect it with play acting.'

Master Drew shook his head as if in disapproval. 'There is only one Master Armin and he is both distinguished as a playwright and a balladeer. I have often seen him acting not only in his own plays but in those of Will Shakespeare. He is a famous comedian, often playing the part of the fool in Master Shakespeare's dramas.'

Master Redweard smiled patronisingly. 'I knew you were a frequenter of the playhouses here. Such entertainment is not for me. Give me a less cerebral entertainment – bear baiting or wrestling or some more bloody sport.'

'Methinks that you would have had enough of blood in your business,' Master Drew sniffed judgmentally.

'My business, as you say, is a bloody one. Frequenting the houses of such sports has its advantages. Where else do you think I could pick up good anatomical specimens that would help me advance my art? Many are the injuries of those who welcome my attentions. Often, I have access to the injured who are beyond saving so that I can practise my theoretical studies. By dissection, one learns much of the anatomy.'

In spite of his years of dealing with the dead and dying of the Bankside, Master Drew could not suppress a sudden shiver.

'So, Master Armin sent you this corpse by means of two young lads in a barrow. Who were these lads?'

'Oh, you must have seen them about these streets plying their trade by carrying goods on their hand barrow. They are often up and down Maiden Lane and the streets down to the Bankside. The senior is called Frankie the Filch and his companion is Bert.'

'I know them well. Young gallows bait, both. Some kind hearts feel sorry for the boy Frankie. I gather he is so named because his father was a Frenchie. Hanged at Wapping as a pirate, if I recall. That was not long after the boy's birth. He had to fight his way through childhood on these streets, surviving by cunning and guile. That has played upon some kind magistrates that have kept him out of Marshalsea. And, say you, they brought the corpse to you and handed over the groat? Very well. Before I depart I will have a look at this corpse that you say is unknown. I cannot neglect the fact that the girl was the victim of an unlawful death.'

'I see little profit in that,' replied the mortician. 'I do not doubt that there is many a corpse within a yard or two of here that has met their end by unlawful means.'

'Nevertheless, I will view this cadaver.'

Inside the mortuary Master Drew had to resort to his rose-scented cambric as he encountered the curious musky odours. The corpse was laid out on a table, naked but covered by a thin, soiled sheet for propriety's sake. The sad thing was, in life, the girl had been attractive and was young, scarcely out of her teens. Even a little brown mole on her left cheek had a curious appeal. Master Drew had seen ladies of fashion with such moles and they enhanced them by means of some cosmetic decoration. However, the main thing that the constable noticed was the flaxen hair that was clean and well cut; neither ragged nor dirty, as if it were cared for.

The bruising around her neck was obvious.

Master Redweard came forward with a lamp that he turned up, the better for the constable to make his observations.

'As you see, the bruising around the neck and the fact that bones were broken there implied someone of strength. You will notice the abrasions and bruising on her face. She was badly treated before her death.'

'I see the girl was well nourished.' Master Drew frowned thoughtfully. 'Does that not imply something to you?'

Master Redweard shrugged. 'That she was no street beggar, I suppose. Maybe she worked in one of the brothels or was kept by a single patron until her death.'

Master Drew was examining the hands of the corpse.

'And have you noticed the hands?' he asked.

'The hands?' frowned the mortician. 'I admit that I have not made a thorough examination as of yet.'

'These indicate that she was definitely no skivvy. They are finely textured and the nails are well tended without any dirt under them. I guarantee she has never done a day's rough work in her short life.'

Master Redweard gave an inward drawing of his breath, forcing a whistling sound through his teeth.

'And, if I mistake it not,' went on the constable, 'there is a mark on the fourth finger of her left hand. That would indicate she once wore either a wedding band or a ring announcing an intention. The marks indicate she wore it for at least a year or two.'

'You find the marks on many abandoned women,' the mortician dismissed with cynicism. 'Married women are often abandoned. The ring is removed by them to get money for a meal.'

'Yet this is a young girl. Well fed. Was the ring removed before or after death?' Master Drew mused. He turned and began examining the feet.

'So what do you deduce from your examination,' the mortician replied, almost in an attempt to sound bored at the constable's deductions, but he was clearly irritated at missing the items.

'Like the hands, the feet are well cared for. The feet have never been crammed into ill-fitting shoes.' He stood back, frowning. 'Tell me, in what state was the girl found?'

'Found? You would have to ask Master Armin, as it was he who found her.'

'How was she brought here? Naked?'

The mortician shook his head. 'She was clad in a piece of sackcloth and nothing else when the two lads brought her here from Master Armin's house in a wheelbarrow.'

That made the constable frown. He turned to the corpse and placed an exploratory hand on the flesh.

'I know little of your art, Master Redweard, but the body has signs of advancing rigor. Was this rigor mortis apparent when the body was carried in the wheelbarrow?'

'It had to be strapped on to secure it. Indeed, it was stiffening.'

'Which led you to believe that the slaying of the girl had happened sometime during the night or the evening before?'

'I can tell you little more. All I know is that it was this morning that the two lads turned up here saying they had been stopped by a Master Armin and handed a groat to bring the body to me and a further groat to give to me to prepare it and conduct it to a pauper's grave at Saint Saviour's.'

Master Drew was thoughtful for a few moments.

'Why send the body to you? For charity's sake, the body and a coin could have been sent to one of the surrounding clergy who would have been happy to say a quick prayer and bury it in a pauper's plot in the local church. It seems an unlikely thing to do.'

Master Redweard shrugged indifferently.

'A groat is a groat, so I thought not to ask. Better a groat to me than to a fat parson. Probably Master Armin sent the body to me because of the manner of death, which might not have sat well with a parson.'

It was as he was turning to leave that something else caught Master Drew's eye. An incision had been made to the right side of the corpse. It was fairly fresh for the skin had not knitted together but there was no blood.

Master Drew turned a stern face to the mortician.

'Have you begun to work upon the cadaver already?' he demanded.

'I don't know what you mean,' protested the mortician.

'You notice this incision? You know there is a good market for body parts among certain medical men?'

'God's wounds, Master Drew,' protested the mortician, 'it was not I that made that cut. Look closely and perceive that it was made before the body was brought here. I would only sell bodies to the hospitals as being complete and unclaimed, and even then not without permission of the magistrate.'

'This is unusual, by my troth. Why is this incision not even sewn and made after death, for I accept the poor creature was strangled. Why cut there? What lies there?'

The mortician shrugged.

'The liver, the kidneys. Nothing a general physician would be unaware of.'

Thoughts of the supper being prepared by Mistress Cuttle had completely vanished and Master Drew's jaw was set in grim determination.

'Master Redweard, I command you to keep this corpse awhile for 'tis clear that the remains are that of no poverty-struck harlot. There has been foul play here and I must seek an explanation from Master Armin. I will make a report to the magistrate.'

The mortician shrugged. 'Well, at your insistence, I shall keep the corpse but cannot guarantee to do so more than two days thither. I have my business and health to think of.'

'It should not take me long because I know where to find

Master Armin within a short step from here. He's at the Rose theatre rehearsing a tableau with Master Alleyn and that is where I shall hasten now.'

It was, indeed, but a fleeting period before Master Drew ascended the steps into the Rose playhouse in Maiden Lane and sought out the man he knew. The actors were huddled on the stage discussing the order of appearance and by their raised voices and scolding of one another, it seemed that all conspired to play the narcissist by claiming major attention to their part. Master Armin was approaching his fortieth year and his booming tones had not lost the faint Norfolk burr of his home county. His manner and gestures were now and then exaggerated. Master Drew recalled the times he had watched the actor play the fool in some adventure in the theatres of Bankside.

As the constable ascended the stage, Master Alleyn, apparently in charge of the players, recognised him and immediately declared a pause to their proceedings. Master Drew inclined his head in acknowledgement but went to the comedian directly.

'What business have you that disturbs the work of good honest thespians?' demanded Master Armin.

'I must broach the subject of a woman's corpse that you found,' the constable declared. 'I have just come from Master Redweard's mortuary.'

He was disconcerted when he found Master Armin staring in bewilderment at him.

'What game's afoot? The subject of a woman's corpse?' the actor demanded in perplexity.

'I talk of the corpse that you handed to two street urchins.'

Master Armin paused uncertainly. 'Alas, good Constable, my

wit is either out or I have imbibed a strong liquor that has chased away memory. I know nought of what you say.'

He seemed sincere enough even though an actor.

'I am told that earlier today you gave two groats to two young urchins to use their barrow to transport a corpse that you had found discarded outside your house. You asked them to take it to the mortician in Bear Alley with instructions for him to oversee the body's burial.'

There was no mistaking the genuine look of incomprehension on the actor's face.

'I share not your wit, Constable. How, tell me, am I supposed to have found a corpse outside my house and then engaged someone with a barrow to transport it all the way to this side of the river from my house to some mortician?'

'That is the understanding of the mortician who took delivery of the body.' The constable frowned, picking up the interpretation of the answer. 'What mean you by "transporting it all the way across the river"? I am told that you hired the boys close by St George the Martyr?'

'Then it is not I. It is a fact that I reside by St Botolph's in Aldgate, north of the river. If I discovered a corpse there, why would I engage someone to bring it here for burial? If I had discovered a corpse, then all I had to do was call the local constable, or slip a coin to the parson, who resides next to me anyway.'

'You do not know a street urchin by the name of Frankie the Filch?'

'My dear Constable, am I of such a disreputable character that I would associate with young sneak thieves? For I presume this Frankie the Filch is one by your choice of his nickname?'

'This is not good, Master Armin, for why would street urchins make so free of your name and in such a matter, about the disposition of a young woman's corpse?'

The actor drew himself up with a snort of indignation.

'I am obliged to say, Constable, that is your concern and not mine. I am not responsible for any child of these parts who makes free of my name for the name is posted a many time along the streets hereabouts from the Rose to the Globe and other playhouses.'

'True enough,' Master Drew conceded with reluctance.

'Then I shall bid thee a good day for I have better things to do than dwell on street urchins and corpses. I am a comedian well known to many of influence, I have more serious matters to fill my time.'

As he sat in the snug of the Pilgrim's Wink tavern, before the supper that Mistress Cuttle had prepared for him, Master Drew felt irritated that he had lost his appetite and could not force his mind into an appreciation of the fayre that had been served for him. His mind kept turning over the problem. That he felt almost sure that Master Armin was not lying to him, for what gain would be made unless he was sure that the boys would be unable to identify him and not name him as the man who had handed over the corpse or even to the point where the boys could obviously identify the house near Marshalsea where they had picked up the body.

The next morning found him in a querulous mood.

He had swallowed a tankard of ale and devoured a slice of bread and cold beef sausage and was making his way out of the inn when he paused at the door and asked Master Cuttle, the landlord, if he knew of the whereabouts of Frankie the Filch. A broad smile spread across the man's heavy features.

'Bless thee, good Constable, I do be seeing him this five minutes gone. He be down at the Steps unloading a lighter just come up from Gravesend. If you be quick, you'll catch him there.'

Along from the Pilgrim's Wink, by Pepper Alley Steps, where river boats loaded and unloaded goods along the Thames, a crowd was fighting over the few pennies that the lightermen were offering to young men, scarcely children, to help with their wares. Master Drew spotted young Frankie, the sneak thief. He strode quickly up, coming up behind the boy unobserved. He clamped a hand immediately on the body's shoulder.

'Remain still, otherwise your next steps will be a dance on the gibbet along Marshalsea.'

The boy glanced up and recognised the threatening constable and began to whine piteously.

'T'weren't me, mister,' he protested. Anyone else but the Constable of the Bankside Watch and the boy would have shown a clean pair of heels, but Frankie had survived thus far by knowing that Master Drew's reach was long and his memory was boundless.

'You and your friend Bert took a body to Master Redweard, the mortician, yesterday.' It was a flat statement of fact.

'The gennelman do give us a groat to do so, and another groat to give to the corpseman.'

'You mean the mortician, Master Redweard?'

'If that be his name; him what trades in corpses in Bear Alley. I swear, we didn't keep back a penny o' it, if that be his 'plaint.'

'You told him a Master Armin commissioned you in this task?'

The boy frowned, not understanding.

120

'What was the name of the man who gave you the money and showed you where to pick up the body?' pressed Master Drew.

'He said his name were Master Armin.'

'Had you seen him before?'

'Stranger to me, master.'

'Where did you meet with him?'

'Me and Bert were coming down Talbot. We'd been up at the 'ospital, taking a barrer load of spuds to the kitchens. Sometimes we pick up a bit of work there but as there were none we were coming back along where this cove stopped us and says 'e had work. The work being, as you say, to transport a stiff that he had found near his house to the corpseman in Bear Alley. For this we got coin.'

It was quite a long speech for the lad. Master Drew could not help but reflect on the lack of feeling when the boy mentioned the corpse. Drew had been battle-hardened by years fighting the Queen's enemies in the Low Countries, which had qualified him for the task of constable in one of the most crime-ridden areas south of the capital. He was used to death in all its hideous forms. But this was a lad of thirteen who could look with indifference on the murdered and naked body of a girl, who had been attractive and animated in life, and think of her as no more than an object. The constable sighed. He might feel hardened but these children, growing up in warrens of crime, often seeing their own parents murdered, were taught violence was normal and there was no other way of life for them. They had no other means of measuring mortality.

'And the man's house was in Talbot Street?' Master Drew interrupted his own thoughts harshly. 'Near the hospital?'

'Near there, but it were in an alley called Angel Court. Near the prison – Marshalsea. That's where the cove said that the body were found.'

'And was it?' Master Drew caught the nuance of what the boy said. 'He told you that you would find the body there. But he did not show you where it was?'

'He said that he had business at the hospital so could not show us. Nevertheless, we found the stiff there as he told us.'

'Didn't he say the corpse lay on his doorstep?'

'We picked it up along the alley by the side entrance of a big house in Angel Court.'

The constable frowned for a moment.

'So, now you will show me,' he decided.

'An it please you, sir, but I must pick up a penny for food this day,' he gestured to the lighter being unloaded at the steps.

Master Drew smiled grimly.

'I fear the best pickings have already been taken by your companions. I'll see that you do not lack sustenance this day, boy. Think of this as a job I give you.'

The walk from Pepper Alley south towards the more salubrious streets which opened out to the main highway to Canterbury, through the gentle countryside of Kent, was an easy one. As they walked, he questioned the boy about the man who called himself Master Armin. It soon became clear that the boy was confirming what the actor had asserted. The description was nothing like him. The boy described an aged man with a salt-and-pepper-coloured beard of unruly style. Ice blue were the eyes and he had a scar diagonally across his left cheek, with the rolling gait that indicated a life on shipboard.

All in all, Master Drew was impressed at the boy's descriptive ability.

'So, now you must take me to the house where you say you were hired.'

The boy was reluctant but, with a reminder of his precarious position, by the constable, the young lad reluctantly led the way along the Canterbury Road. Finally, a little beyond Marshalsea Prison, the boy pointed.

'That's the alley. There's the house where the body were.'

The house was, indeed, large, but bleak looking, seeming as if it was decaying. There was no sign of any inhabitant. In spite of the once grand elegance of this corner house, beyond stretched a dark abyss of tenant dwellings.

Master Drew's attention was immediately distracted by the appearance of the very man the boy had just described as commissioning him and his companion to take the corpse to Master Redweard. But the man had not come out of the indicated house but the house next to it; one on the corner of the alley. He was engaged in sweeping the porch of the building. Master Drew was able to correct the boy's description by noticing that, rather than elderly, he was certainly not much beyond middle age. A broad and muscular man but who had certainly led an outdoor life and the manner of a sailor was clear.

Master Drew approached him and the man, seeming to recognise him, in spite of the barefoot urchin trailing behind, laid aside his broom and touched a finger to his forehead in a sailor's salute.

'You be the constable, b'ain't you? I see'd you bringing convicts down to Marshalsea, from time to time.'

'That is so. Who are you?'

'Will Cherry. They call me Cheerful Will, former steward on the old *Nonpareil*, thirty-two guns. Leastways until they put us ashore in ought-three and relaunched the old ship as the *Nonsuch*, damn their eyes.'

'And whose house is this?'

'Why, Cap'n Sir Anthony Borrer, sir. He were cap'n of the *Nonpareil*.'

'So you served him at sea and now you do so on shore?'

'I do so, Master Constable. I served on the *Nonpareil* five and twenty years. Now I serve the cap'n as steward just as I did when he was fighting the Dagos.'

'Another question. How come you felt able to make free with the name of Robert Armin?'

The former sailor hesitated. He cast a furtive look towards the house.

'Meant no harm, master. I didn't want the cap'n bothered if folk associated me with being in his service. It were a name I just came up with.'

'And how were you so free with your coins to be able to pay the boys and a mortician to get rid of the body?'

'Not his money, constable,' rasped a new voice. Master Drew noted the steward's gaze, which was fixed on the door of the house, had widened perceptively.

Master Drew turned to find himself being scowled upon by an elderly bandy-legged man dressed in fine broadcloth and silk that proclaimed him certainly as a seafarer. He had emerged out of the house unnoticed by Master Drew, but now stood regarding him with the belligerent eyes of someone still in command of a fighting ship.

'Not his money,' repeated the seafaring apparition which was obviously none other than Captain Borrer. The captain was hostile. 'I paid for the corpse to be removed from that alley as I did not want my servants and visitors distressed by the sight of what this Sodom and Gomorrah leaves on the streets and further, that very night, I was host to Admiral Sir John Buxton, and his flag lieutenant, who has the fortune to be engaged to my niece from Norfolk. Indeed, my niece is expected here tomorrow or the day after to join her fiancé. Do you think that I would wish them offended by such a sight as the rotting dross of the street?'

Master Drew had heard of Admiral Buxton of the Channel Squadron.

'Well, I trust there were no other corpses to offend your guests.' Master Drew could not help the cynical utterance.

'Thanks be, my guests did not arrive before my steward had seen to the removal of the corpse at my instruction.'

'So you are saying that, when you learnt there was a body abandoned outside the next house in the street, you instructed your steward here to give coin to someone to dispose of it . . . to take it to the mortician?'

'I believe my English was plain enough?'

'Did you take a close look at the body?'

Captain Borrer was indignant. 'I did not, sir. Why should I wish to look at the remains of a strumpet who had abandoned her God? I have better things to do with my time. So I will give you a good day.' He turned on his heel back into his house.

Will Cherry looked after his captain with a curious expression which seemed to be almost a mixture of relief or self-satisfaction.

He broke in quickly as if in corroboration of his master's statement.

'That is the right of it, Constable. Can't say I gave more than a glance at the corpse either. Leastways, no more than to check whether she be dead or drunk. Bodies don't bother me none. Seen too many blown to pieces in my time. You'd be surprised what even a culverin or a saker could do to a body.'

Master Drew knew what cannons could do no matter their size.

'I am told you found the two boys on Talbot Street near the hospital.'

'That's the truth. I had a job there. So I spies the two lads and gave them the task.'

'You found the body yesterday morning?'

'Up before dawn, that's me.'

'That empty house there, it looks derelict.' Master Drew changed the subject, indicating the building. 'That is where you found the body? To whom does it belong?'

'That I can't rightly say, sir. Heard tell it belonged to the old Abbot before the religious changes. You know, 'twas when St Mary Overie were an Augustinian priory before they disbanded it. Dissolution, they called it. So the hospital was run by the priory when it came back into being. The young king set up the hospital, cos there were many poorly lying about the streets and disturbing the gennelmen of the parish. But many a tavern or building owned by the old prior were sold off. Aye, master; like the Tabard Inn. Now that used to belong to the abbot until fifty years gone. Now 'tis all private. Maybe it's part of the new hospital estate.'

'So no one lives there?'

'It be still used, that's for sure,' the former sailor said with a knowing smirk. 'Not what you call a regular household. But now and again I do see young buckos go there, taking their doxies. God damn their souls.'

Master Drew frowned. 'I thought I knew all the bawdy houses and brothels in this area. I don't recall this one?'

'That's because the young gennelmen keep their doings a secret. Glad you know now that 'tis they who reap benefits while us poor 'uns usually take the blame. Why, gibbets be too good for they bodysnatchers and . . .'

The constable ignored what was obviously a favourite theme of the steward. 'And who are these young men that make free of that house?'

'They were young medical gennelmen; you know, them that be learning the apothecary art at the hospital.'

Master Drew's eyes narrowed. 'Medical students?' he asked sharply.

'So I did hear. There was something else that I did see.'

'Which was?' Master Drew prompted.

'Unusual cuts on the body, sir,' the man replied.

'What drew your attention to that?'

'I saw one myself and that it was a recent cut.'

'You noticed it just because it was recent?'

Will Cherry looked earnest. 'It reminded me of the work of the sawbone, who shipped with us at sea, when he started cutting the wounded to fish out splinters of ship's wood and musket balls after an engagement. I heard tell some of them gennelmen at the hospital do such things and even that people sometimes sell them

127

corpses to cut around. That be common among those learning about bodies.'

'I know there is a trade in bodies. What makes you think that, in this case?'

Will Cherry did not seem disturbed at the idea.

'I keeps me eyes open. Just trying to be helpful, Constable.'

'You don't seemed shocked that such a thing can happen?'

'I've been too many years in this world to be shocked. We live in a warren of rats. Is not the Bankside known for it? Aye, master. And rats probably live a sight cleaner than we do, for they do not turn upon each other unless it be for survival. No, we are a pretty species to come and give account of ourselves on the Day of Judgement.'

'If you knew of such trade, I am wondering why you did not make profit yourself, having discovered the corpse? You might have taken it on yourself to sell at the hospital.'

The former seaman now expressed his distaste in an exaggerated expression.

'I be a good Christian, master, and making money in dealing with the flesh of others is forbidden.'

'One thing more,' the constable changed tack. 'You were telling me how you picked the name of Robert Armin.'

The steward raised his shoulder in a half shrug. 'I saw the name on a billboard.'

'You attend the playhouses?'

The steward was nervous.

'I pass by them. It is not a matter I would wish the cap'n to know. Nor that I go into taverns. He has certain views on the morality of playhouses and taverns. He would berate me sorely if

he knew I had spent any time in taverns or playhouses. He has
strong views on religious matters. He belongs to one of those new
sects.'

'And you do not?'

'I carry out his orders,' came the fellow's reply.

Seeing there was little else to do, Master Drew thanked the
ex-sailor, who disappeared after his master. Then he turned to
the young boy who had been waiting patiently, remembering the
constable's promise that he would get a coin or two. Master Drew
fumbled in his purse.

'You have done well, lad. Here is another groat for your help.
Do not go far from your usual haunts for, when I track down
those responsible, I may want you to give evidence. You know
where I am to be found.'

The boy seized the coin gratefully.

'Everyone knows you reside at the Pilgrim's Wink,' he grinned.
'That's why it is a place known to be avoided.'

Master Drew chuckled in appreciation as the urchin turned
and trotted away to his more familiar surroundings.

The constable stood at the corner of Angel Court for some
moments and then he retraced his steps back to the old, dark
house. It was easy to snap the lock of one of the lower-floor windows and gain access through it.

The odour that permeated the place was of stale alcohol; a
mixture of beer and cheap wine and spirits mingled with rotting
food and body odours.

He needed a lantern even though it was not yet midday because
the closeness of the surrounding buildings obscured any mean-
ingful light. Drew abandoned the search, exited the house and

made his way back from Angel Court down the road to the Marshalsea Prison where he knew the turnkey well. It took but a moment to negotiate a well-filled lantern and also a stout candle before returning to the dark house and slipping, once again, over the sill into the dark building. Then he lit the lantern. In spite of the outward appearance of the old house, the room in which he found himself seemed well finished, the stale odour of alcohol was, however, noticeable. It was clearly a reception room. If Will Cherry was right, this was where the women were initially entertained.

Master Drew headed through the other rooms. It was in the next room that two things caught his notice. First there was an overturned chair. Then there were scuff marks on the wooden floor. They consisted of two parallel marks as some object had been dragged across the boards. Master Drew examined these closely before beginning to search further, but there was nothing else to make sense of his thoughts.

He had thought that the scuff marks were as if someone had dragged a body across the floor so the heels of their shoes made the scuff marks on the dark wood before the body had been dragged along to a carpeted area. Here and there spots of something caused him to take his knife and scrap one of them off the floor and raise it to look closely. It was dried blood.

Master Drew made a careful inspection of the rest of the house but there was little else he could see that enlightened him further.

He was expecting to find some bloodstained clothes that might have belonged to the woman or even a discarded surgeon's knife. But there was nothing else that presented him with any suspicious sign. Not even the shoes that had created the scuff marks.

After satisfying himself there was little to be learnt, he decided to exit and cross the street to the Tabard Inn. Tim Rowdey, the host of the Tabard Inn, was known to Master Drew, as were most of the landlords of the many taverns and inns through the Bankside. After some pleasantries and a glass of ale, Master Rowdey confirmed that he knew the house of which the constable enquired.

'It belongs to the hospital. They were intending to use it for recoup . . . recuper . . . the like of recovering patients. Although the lordships who ran the hospital never made up their minds how to use it. So young men of a certain mind did so, but not officially.'

'Not officially?'

'Well, several young medical students and doctors use it on weekends. I keep keys for them. It is used by them to have it away with their fancies, if you know what I mean? Why do you ask? Has Captain Borrer been having one of his apoplectic fits complaining of the students?'

Master Drew ignored the question but noted that the captain was known to object to licentious behaviour.

'Tell me more about those who use it?'

'I can only say some young bucks at the hospital more than most. There's about a dozen of them as far as I know.'

'Any do dissection work at the hospital?'

That brought a startled look from Master Rowdey.

'I thought all them medical folk did that.'

Master Drew considered for a moment. 'I presume you know

all the loose women of the area. I mean those who would be taken to that house by these young bucks, as you call them?'

The innkeeper shrugged.

'I keeps a Christian house here and would not condone immoral . . .'

Master Drew ignored him.

'I am going to describe a women to you,' he cut in, sharply. 'Tell me if you recognise the description. Your honesty in this matter will stand you in good stead.'

Master Rowdey gestured his assent.

Master Drew outlined the body's physical points. When it came to the mole on the right cheek, Master Rowdey's expression changed from amazement to concern.

'You recognise the description?' Master Drew asked immediately.

'You are sure you describe a lady of the street?' demanded Master Rowdey.

'I said I describe a woman,' replied the constable, intrigued. 'Who do you think I describe?'

The innkeeper paused then and shrugged.

'It could be a lady that I saw outside here only two or three days since.'

'A lady?'

'I was outside helping with a delivery of some barrels of ale. A coach pulled up nearby. A lady descended and I saw she had a mole on her cheek, just as you describe. She was well dressed and could fit your description. She seemed to be asking directions of the coachman. He pointed across the street and then drove away towards the bridge while she crossed the street in the direction he had indicated.'

'Which was?'

'Angel Court. I was surprised, but then there are a few good houses there. There is the house of Captain Borrer, on the corner.'

'And then?'

'Then? Nothing. I don't have all day to stand staring at my neighbours' comings and goings, nor their visitors'.'

'Did you ask Captain Borrer about the girl, or why the coachman did not wait for her?'

The innkeeper chuckled. 'What makes you think that Captain Borrer would come in here?'

'A retired sea captain living just across the road; I would expect him to make use of a good tavern within a few steps of his front door.'

'Not this one. The captain had strict views on what he called the demon drink. He is one of those Brownists. You must know the type. I remember Master Will Shakespeare saying he had rather be a Brownist than a politician! Me? I'd rather be a rich politician any day than be denounced a heretic.'

The constable remembered that the innkeeper was a frequenter of the local playhouses. He tried to recall from which of Will Shakespeare's plays the quote came. He was proud of his knowledge but it took him some moments before he identified the line from *Twelfth Night* which was actually 'I had lief be a Brownist than a politician.' Ironically, it had been spoken by the actor Richard Armin in the role of the comic character Sir Andrew Aguecheek.

He suddenly became aware that Master Rowdey was waiting for him to speak.

'So, you say the captain is a religious reformer of extreme views? I suppose his servant doesn't come in here either?'

Master Rowdey chuckled cynically.

'He's a different kettle of fish. I have often attended playhouses with him. He comes in here once a week, that being on his day off. He was here the other evening as the captain was away. He likes his brandy and is as garrulous as any I have come across. He only maintains his position as steward because such posts are hard to come by. I will hear more about the lady when next he comes.'

The constable frowned. 'If you say you will hear more, it implies that you have already heard something?'

'I have heard nothing. Master Cherry was imbibing with Sam Pickens and it seemed Will Cherry must have had a windfall for he was doing the spending.'

'Who is this Master Pickens?'

'Works at the hospital, so he claims. Truth to tell, he makes his living selling items given to him by the patients for their fees. You know, items of jewellery, clothes, anything to make enough when they can't afford the physicians fees.'

'But it was Cherry who was in funds?' the constable queried dryly.

'That's not unusual. Sometimes he is in funds, but more often out of funds.'

Another thought occurred to Master Drew.

'Did you notice if the coach had any markings on it that would identify it?'

Master Rowdey screwed up his eyes as if he were trying to conjure a picture of the coach into his mind.

'It was marked with the symbol of The Wayfarer's Rest. That's a small coaching inn north of the river by Blackfriars.'

Master Drew nodded, for he had knowledge of the tavern.

He hesitated a moment before taking his departure and then asked, 'Is the captain aware of his steward's drinking?'

'I doubt that it be so. Will Cherry has done his best to disguise the fact from the captain, for when he has too much brandy taken he will spend the night here. No wenching nor drinking nor any other vice is allowed to be mentioned to the captain.'

'He being a Brownist,' sighed the constable, heavily. Then with a nod to Master Rowdey he made his exit.

The bell of St Anne's was sounding the midday hour when the constable found himself at The Wayfarer's Rest, a small, inexpensive coaching inn, standing near the playhouse run by James and Richard Burbage, who had successfully staged plays there for twenty years. Master Drew lost no time in declaring his business with the elderly innkeeper. The man did not have to consult his ledgers.

'I remember the young lady very well,' he declared immediately. 'She arrived three days since and, after resting the night, immediately hired Jemmy, our coachman, to take her across the river.'

'A lady, you say?' The word confirmed that Master Drew had been right in his assessment. 'Is this coachman about?'

'I'll call him this instant, master,' the innkeeper nodded, suiting the words with action.

'Did the lady have a name?'

'Why, bless you, master, that she did,' affirmed the man. 'She gave her name as Mistress Mary Borrer.'

The constable's eyes widened.

'Borrer, say you?'

'Indeed, master. Come to London from Norfolk to visit her fiancé but she had arrived early so wanted transport across the river.'

A broad-shouldered, tough-looking individual appeared, whose worn leather jerkin and boots, with leather patched trousers and heavy weathered shirt, seemed to proclaim his occupation, even before the innkeeper greeted him.

'Jemmy, the constable here was asking about the lady, Mistress Borrer, whom you took across the river the other day.'

The coachman turned watery blue eyes on him.

'Be there a complaint, master?' he demanded at once. 'I took her where she wanted and pointed out the house she was asking for.'

Master Drew looked at the coachman carefully.

'Which was where?' he demanded, knowing well.

'It were a place up the Canterbury Road, almost opposite the Tabard Inn. She was looking for a seaman who was her uncle. She said it was a house on the corner of Angel Court.'

'And having reached there, what did you do?'

The man frowned, puzzled.

'What should I do? That was where she wanted to go.'

Master Drew showed his impatience with a quick intake of breath.

'What happened when you drew up?' He punctuated his words with a pause between each one.

A look of comprehension grew on the coachman's features.

'Well, I came to the Tabard and used its yard as a turning

136

point for the coach. The lady got out and when I pointed across the road to identify the house she said that she wouldn't need my service further and so I set off back towards the bridge and that was the last I saw of her.'

Master Drew glanced back at the innkeeper after the coachman had finished.

'Did Mistress Borrer leave luggage or personal items here?'

'She did, master. We were expecting her return.'

Master Drew was thoughtful.

'You gleaned no more from Mistress Borrer of her intentions other than she was looking for her uncle who was a sea captain?'

'And if her name be Borrer, then a Captain Borrer do live south side of the river,' affirmed the innkeeper. 'The young lady said she was due to stay at her relative's house and meet her fiancé there. He was an officer serving with the Channel Squadron. She added she was a day or two early in her arrival so she was not sure that he would be at home. Other than that she did not vouchsafe any information about herself other than what I have already told you.'

Master Drew was halfway across the bridge on his way home, when he stopped so suddenly that a pedestrian behind him nearly toppled over him. With a hurried apology, the constable hastened on, ignoring the man's erroneous denunciation on the state of his parentage. At another time, he would have given the man a chance to reconsider his outburst. Now was not the time and, with grim determination, he hurried forward across the bridge to the Canterbury Road. Everything now fell into place.

From the innkeeper at the Tabard Inn, Master Rowdey, Master Drew learnt that Sam Pickens was expected to be at the tavern that night, but Will Cherry had arrived not long after the constable and had already squandered a lot of his coin on brandy. Master Rowdey indicated a darkened corner. Will Cherry, former steward on the *Nonpareil,* was still in a drunken slumber when the Constable of the Bankside Watch, supported by one of Master Rowdey's tap-room assistants, carried the man to the safe-keeping of the warden of nearby Marshalsea Prison. He was satisfied that he would also pick up Sam Pickens later.

At the house on the corner of Angel Court it was Captain Borrer who opened the door with a scowl as he saw the cause of the jangling bell.

'I regret to inform you that the body found by your steward was that of your niece,' the constable said, finding a curious satisfaction in carefully enunciating each word. 'So if you would like to see your niece you will need to go to Master Redweard's mortuary in Bear Alley. For she is dead.'

The captain stared at him in incomprehension, his mouth opening and closing.

'But my steward said that the body was that of some harlot abandoned on the street,' the man finally protested.

'And, as such, you did not care anymore, other than to have her removed from the street lest she distress your dinner guests,' replied the constable. 'Now it is a different matter. You were away when your niece called to see you. Her intention was perhaps to surprise you and join her fiancé. She arrived earlier than expected, driven here by the coachman of The Wayfarer's Rest in Blackfriars.'

'But my steward said no one had called that day.'

'Would he have recognised your niece?'

'What has that to do with it?'

'An answer to my question would be helpful,' the constable said sharply.

'He would not have known my niece,' the captain answered.

'So she was a no one in his eyes and the report he gave you made her a no one in your eyes. Where were you the day before her body was found?'

'I spent the day visiting an old shipmate whose frigate rides at anchor in the Pool of London. Not expecting my visitors until the next day, I did not return much before midnight.'

'Did you tell your steward you were expecting guests?'

'I told him.'

'But you did not tell him who they were?'

Captain Borrer frowned. 'I told him I was expecting guests. It was of no concern of his who they were.'

'So he knew you were out all day. Your steward was alone. The house was empty. But your niece arrived early. I can only say that, aware of your strict moral code, the steward kept secrets from you. Whether from drink or lust, he assaulted your niece and killed her. Perhaps he did not intend to do so. He killed her, stripped her body and placed her outside the house, near to where he knew medical students took their pleasures. He was worried in case you saw the body so he chanced that if he told you he'd found a prostitute on the street you would disdain to view the body. He was right.

'He had another trick up his sleeve. After he stripped the body, he cut it to make it look as if some surgeon had done so. He even attempted to draw my attention to this and mentioned the local hospital in case I missed the point. He left the body outside. As I said, he had to gamble on your attitudes being such that you would choose not to examine the corpse. He had won that gamble and found the two boys to dispose of the body to the mortician. You even gave him money so that the corpse would not spoil your planned evening. It seems he knew your nature and the value you place on your fellows only too well.'

The captain seemed to dwindle in stature, his eyes wide, his mouth open.

'What do you mean to do?'

'I shall make a report to Master William Mayhew, who may view you with some sympathy with regard to your beliefs as he is a vestryman and churchwarden at St Saviour's as well as intending to stand for Parliament. But he is also conscious of his role as a burgess.'

'What of my servant, Will Cherry?'

'Your steward is under arrest in Marshalsea where he will hang, like as not. And that is where his comrade in crime, Sam Pickens, will soon be for receiving the property stolen from your niece.'

Dead for a Ducat, Dead!

How now, a rat? Dead for a ducat, dead!

Hamlet, Act III, Scene iv
William Shakespeare

Master Hardy Drew, Constable of the Bankside Watch, had just turned into Pepper Street and stood within sight of the rooms that he rented above the Pilgrim's Wink tavern, when a harsh voice halted him.

'Master Constable, bide you awhile!' A muscular young man came towards him at a trot. For those who knew the area, they would have recognised the man by his clothing as one of the watermen working the three thousand boats that crowded the River Thames, pulling passengers and light freight to and fro across the river. He wore a coarse linen shirt under his short leather jerkin and leather-patched trousers, the lower parts wrapped in canvas leggings with canvas shoes.

Master Drew recognised the young man immediately, for it was young Tom Redweard, the son of the mortician and apothecary who conducted his business at the corner of Bear Alley and Bankside.

'What is it, Master Redweard?' the constable queried, a little impatient to proceed to the tavern for his midday tankard of ale and beef pie.

'My father requests you come to the mortuary as he is in need of your immediate advice.'

Master Drew gave an exaggerated sigh. 'I suppose he has yet another body to show me that has been fished out of the river?'

The Bankside occupied the south bank of the Thames stretching from the east where the great London Bridge reached to the western end along to the bank of the Paris Gardens. The bridge was a town all to itself, balancing many houses and shops on it, spanning the great river from the City to the pilgrims' road leading to Canterbury. It was the only dry crossing point from the City into Southwark, whose name derived from the 'southern work'. The south end of the bridge had grown into a full borough comprising of an area of low taverns, replete with brothels, gambling dens, bull- and bear-baiting pits and, surprisingly perhaps, with four reputable playhouses which attracted visitors in droves across the river. In this curious mixture were the homes of the wealthy merchants and traders who took advantage of the expanding seaport that the area had become. Intermixed between its taverns and brothels were the mansions of the nobles, of the Bishop of Winchester with his palace, the cathedral and four parish churches. Along the Bankside were some of the most sordid areas and, indeed, the centre of the conceivable criminal activities, over which Master Drew, as Constable of the Bankside Watch, had legal jurisdiction.

Master Drew had often stated that if he were paid a silver groat for every corpse fished from the river he would be a wealthy man. The river was seen as a gigantic open sewer in which bodies were disposed, not merely victims of footpads, but the bodies of the poor whose relatives were unable to pay fees for proper burials. Others saw it as a convenient means to get rid of victims of the bubonic pestilence that often struck the city and its southern neighbour. Indeed, it was claimed that thirty thousand inhabitants had died during the last visitation of the plague, causing the playhouses to close for two or more years.

These thoughts were running through his mind as he regarded the youthful son of the mortician.

'I suppose your father has spotted something unusual about this body, which is why he summons me?'

'I believe so, Master Constable. And, if it please you, having delivered my father's message, I will be on my way.'

The constable sniffed in sarcastic disapproval. 'If I judge the time aright, the Bear Gardens will be opening and we must not deprive Master Henslowe of his penny entrance.'

The constable was not a fan of bear or bull baiting, if the truth be known. He had seen too many deaths in his life. In his youth he had enlisted in the service of Sir Roger Williams, a fiery Welshman, who was much admired by the late Queen for his military capabilities. He had served with the troops Elizabeth had sent to aid Henri IV of France against the Catholic League of the Duc de Mayerne. Three or four years of campaign in Normandy, the Victory at Arques and the Siege of Rouen, were enough for Master Drew to give up the ideas for surviving in the occupation of a soldier. It had left him as a first-class exponent of the clavier long gun with its standard bore and matchlock mechanism. He had been given command by Sir Roger of a small company of *arquebusiers*, as they were called, which would later become musketeers. The constable had become a reader of Sir Roger's military philosophies and planning. He was amused when Master Shakespeare had portrayed Sir Roger as 'Fluellen' in his play *Henry V.* But such accomplishments had not been needed in many walks of civilian life.

These thoughts evoked memories as Master Drew strode along the Bankside to the intersection with Bear Alley where Master Redweard, the mortician, had his place of business. As was his custom, the constable hesitated and brought forth a rose-water impregnated piece of cambric to hold to his nose as he entered. There was only one cadaver on display on a central table at whose side Master Redweard was standing in puzzled thought. His face seemed to brighten as the constable came in.

'Another mysterious corpse out of the river?' Master Drew greeted him. 'Surely not one to warrant such a perplexing creasing of your brow?'

'By the Holy Rood! I think this is one corpse we need take much care of.'

'How so?'

'Examine it for yourself.' The mortician stood back and pointed.

The constable saw at once that the corpse was unusual compared to most. It was a fully dressed youth although with only one leather boot on. But the clothing was of rich cloth and carefully worked by a seamstress. The short, waist-length cape around the shoulders was richly embroidered. Withal, this was the clothing of a wealthy noble. Closer examination showed the body to be a well-proportioned young man, scarcely out of his teens. He had an abundance of fair, corn-coloured hair, well-chiselled features and a wispy fragment of beard and moustache not fully developed. It was clear that he would not have long been in the Thames for the dark, contaminated waters, had not encroached their mark on the rich satins and cottons of the clothing.

Master Redweard had positioned the body with the hands folded before him and the constable could see they were well kempt, the nails had frequently been attended to, pared and shaped and clean. The hands, too, confirmed this was not someone used to any form of manual work. A gold ban of a signet ring was worn on the little finger of the left hand. There was a shield engraved into the gold but Master Drew could not make out the device depicted on it.

'A gentleman,' observed the constable, although the point was obvious.

'A noble,' corrected Master Redweard.

'Why say you so?' Master Drew frowned.

The mortician bent forward and pulled back the short cape. On the left side of the doublet he wore underneath was an embroidery. It was of a shield of red with a design on it of a white lion rampant. Above the lion was a small golden crown.

Master Drew inhaled his breath sharply. 'I presume this device is the same as on the ring?'

'I took the liberty of stamping the ring in hot wax the better to see it with a magnifying lens that I have. Indeed, a noble and . . .' he hesitated, 'a Papist.'

Master Redweard pulled back the water-soaked ruffle around the throat. Round the neck was a small but ornate silver crucifix. 'That's what makes me say it. As to the lion rampant design, I do hear that the Scots use a similar shield and lion rampant. Think you, it be a relative of the Scottish King?'

It was a year since James VI of Scotland had assumed the throne of England as James I but he was still referred to as the Scottish King.

'I am no expert on heraldic devices,' the constable admitted. 'But had there been a connection, there would surely have been a hue and cry resounding throughout the city. Whence comes this body?'

'It was brought here by some watermen only this morning from the Bull's Stairs. They found it floating among the moored vessels. Well, they be honest men who, realising this was someone of wealth and influence, have not disturbed the jewellery, the silver Papist cross, the signet ring nor the embroidery of shield and lion badge from which they might make some living. Also, in the purse on the belt there are a few foreign ducats.'

The constable sniffed. 'So we should maintain the same honesty. Anyway, it could be argued that if this body was found at the Bull's Stairs it is out of my jurisdiction, laying as it does in Christ Church parish.'

'Fie, fie to that. I know of no other mortician on this stretch of the river that would dispute my right to a reward if we can find to whom this corpse belongs.'

'Perhaps you should consult Master Francis Langley, for he has the manor there and 'twas he that built the Swan playhouse,' suggested the constable.

The door suddenly opened and Master Drew immediately recognised the newcomer as the local justice, William Mayhew. He was not only the justice but one of the two local members of

Parliament and, withal, a very influential man, having the ear of several of the King's advisors in Westminster Palace.

'Master Redweard,' the justice began immediately, 'I come looking for your son to hire his wherry . . .' He suddenly halted and saw the constable. 'Give thee a good day, Master Drew. Forgive my intrusion but I need a wherry to keep an appointment across the river. There has been some altercation on the bridge which impedes the progress of my carriage so I needs must use the river crossing.'

'Please, sir, my son is not here but he has a comrade at the Bear Steps who could take you.'

'By your leave, Master Mayhew,' Master Drew interrupted, 'I know you to be informed as to heraldic devices through your acquaintances in the Parliament. Would you honour me with your knowledge by looking at this emblem sewn to this young corpse's doublet? The body is but lately fished from the river at the Bull's Stairs and appears to be a gentleman.'

Frowning in irritation, Justice Mayhew stepped to the corpse and peered down at the badge. To Master Drew's surprise his change of expression was sudden. His face paled, his jaw dropped and it seemed that his eyes popped out of his sockets.

'Lord, have mercy! What can you tell me of the youth's death?'

'We know nothing. In fact, as the body was fished from the river at the Bull's Stairs, we were discussing whether it should be in our jurisdiction.'

'Damn the jurisdiction!' Justice Mayhew snapped to their surprise. 'How was he killed?'

The mortician almost trembled before the threatening tone of the justice.

'I was about to tell the constable, your honour. Foul play is obvious. I can only point out several wounds to the back. He was stabbed. The roughness and jagged edge mean it was not the dagger of a gentleman or of a rapier. It was a dagger used by a street fighter. The wounds were caused by an attack from behind. He fell or was dumped into the river whence some honest watermen retrieved the body and brought it hither.'

'Honest, say you?' Justice Mayhew cried cynically.

'If not honest then they would have taken the jewellery and clothing from the corpse, for such fine cloth and riches would fetch a pretty price,' the mortician countered.

Justice Mayhew glanced curiously at Master Drew. 'You know not the meaning of that design on the shield?'

'I know little of such things, your honour, which is why I sought your advice.'

Justice Mayhew turned to the mortician without saying a further word. 'I pray thee, Master Redweard, cover this corpse and keep it as best you can, keep it safe, until I or the constable return with instructions. I promise you will be well rewarded for your effort.' Then he turned to Master Drew. 'You shall accompany me to the Palace of Westminster immediately. I absolve you of all your immediate duties. You are under my authority now.'

'I am at your service, your honour, but what is afoot?'

'God a'mercy, Constable! If I am right, we might be at war before the week is out. I will say no more until we reach Westminster.'

The journey across the river was passed in silence much to the puzzlement of the two muscular wherrymen, who Justice Mayhew had engaged in answer to the inevitable question when hiring a boat – 'sculls or oars?' The price was higher for oars, the wherry being rowed by two men as opposed to one, and the choice of oars was an indication that Justice Mayhew was concerned for a speedy crossing of the choppy tidal waters amidst the coasters and grain ships, brigs and barges of the wealthy and nobles that crowded the river. The oarsmen redoubled their effort as they came round the bend of the river against the tide and headed towards the Kentish ragstone-fronted walls of Westminster Palace where, apart from the royal apartments that surrounded St Stephen's chapel and its river-fronted gardens, the *curia regis*, the advisors to the King, met, and where, scarce sixty years ago, Edward VI had allowed the representatives of the Commons to sit to make their deliberations in the disused part of St Stephen's chapel.

The oarsmen were pulling towards the steep stone steps that led upwards through an entrance into the gardens, moving between several anchored vessels. The tide was running fast and the constable knew that it rose and fell all the way up to the Royal Palace at Hampton Court, sometimes as much as twenty-three feet. Master Drew felt sorrow for the sweating wherrymen as they negotiated their way through the anchored vessels. He was about to say something when his eyes caught sight of a banner fluttering at the stern mast of one of these vessels.

A red flag with a crowned lion rampant on it in white. Underneath on the wooden name board, depicted in curious lettering, was the name *Der Silberne Löwe*.

The constable turned to Justice Mayhew with his mouth opening but the justice shook his head, immediately signalling him to silence. Master Drew glanced curiously at the vessel as they passed. It was distinctive and, from his knowledge of the river and ships, he could recognise that it was a fairly modern vessel. The sails were gaff-rigged, with a single mast and stays that gave it great speed. It was obvious that the mast could be dissembled to negotiate the low arches of London Bridge to bring it upriver thus far. He wondered what its nationality was and what it meant in connection to the body of the young man.

Then they were bumping against the Westminster Steps and the constable scrambled after Justice Mayhew who hurried across the gardens that spread between St Stephen's chapel and the river front. This led them to a series of buildings at which guards were placed. Justice Mayhew seemed well known and went unchallenged by the guards. The constable followed him into a large hall where several people sat or stood waiting. He was told to wait while the justice went to a side door. There was a quick exchange with the official outside before he vanished beyond the door.

The constable stood nervously with no wish to engage in conversation with any of the wealthy or noble-looking members who were occupying parts of the room. Each of them seemed to be wrapped in their own thoughts; with various expressions of boredom, trepidation or irritation. He saw several glances cast in his direction as his clothes alone excluded him from their company. Some were clearly foreign individuals, judging by their apparel, decorations and manner.

Suddenly the justice re-emerged from the side door and crossed the room to him.

'I am to leave you. You are to go in to see His Grace, the Earl of Salisbury. He will instruct you in this matter.'

The constable was astonished. He was about to summon up

questions when the official, carrying a cane of office, who had conducted the justice beyond the door, intervened.

'You will follow me, Master Drew,' he instructed in a voice used to being obeyed.

The justice glanced meaningfully at the constable, before turning and hurrying away.

Master Drew hesitated and then, hearing the exasperated cough of his would-be guide, he turned and allowed the man to lead him through the door. Beyond was a dark corridor, although a lantern here and there illuminated it. At the end of the corridor, the man stopped before a sturdy oak door and, using his cane of office, rapped three times upon it before opening it and motioning the constable to enter.

Master Drew did so and found himself in a large room, one wall of which consisted of a lattice window of frosted and coloured glass that illuminated the room in a gloomy haze. A great fire blazing in the hearth at one end, along with several lamps, immersed the room in a curious, flickering half-light.

What made Master Drew focus his attention was a large desk behind which a man sat. He was a thin man, in his fifties, sharp-featured with a fashionable thin moustache and short, spade beard. His dark, brooding eyes examined the constable as if troubled by what he saw. Then he allowed his thin lips to form a smile of what seemed to be a welcome.

'So, you are Constable Drew of the Bankside Watch?'

'I am, your grace.' The constable realised that he was addressing the Earl of Salisbury, Secretary of State, Lord High Treasurer, the foremost minister to His Majesty.

The man rose abruptly and revealed himself short of stature, almost a head shorter than the constable. He came round the desk in a strange, shambling motion and stood before Master Drew, examining him intently with his body seemingly bent to the left. The constable remembered that he heard the earl suffered from a curvature of the spine that made him lean to one side. He had heard several things about this Robert Cecil, who King James had only recently ennobled as Earl of Salisbury, but none of them were inspiring. Gossip had it that Cecil had been in possession of Catesby's plot to blow up Parliament for a long time but had continued to allow the plotters to go so far as to plant the gunpowder kegs, almost allowing Captain Fawkes to ignite them, before swooping on the conspirators. It was said he had done so to make an example of the plot and conspirators and ensure the country would never tolerate Catholicism again. Drew realised he was dealing with a man with little mercy to those he saw as enemies of the state.

'Come, Master Constable, we will sit before the fire and take a pipe.'

'I do not use tobacco, your grace,' murmured the constable as he was directed to a chair.

'Good,' agreed the earl, 'for I have no liking of the weed myself, but a glass of Sack will surely not go amiss?'

After he had taken a few sips of the sweet sherry, Lord Salisbury began: 'I hear you are well regarded by Justice Mayhew and have some reputation for resolving distasteful conundrums. That being so, I have a task that I wish you to complete. I am assured by Justice Mayhew that you are to be trusted. In this matter the trust must be well placed, for you shall be acting in the name of His Majesty.'

The unexpected was happening at such a pace that Master Drew found difficulty following what Lord Salisbury was saying. Then his natural faculty came to his aide.

'In what capacity and for what purpose?' the constable replied hesitantly.

Lord Salisbury's smile was approving.

'You are a cautious man, Constable. I applaud you on that. Indeed, I need a cautious man. You will act in the capacity you now hold. No more. No less.'

'And what am I to do?'

'No more than that which you may have been preparing to do when you visited the mortician a while ago. Yes, Justice Mayhew has given me the full story. But I must give you some preliminaries to your investigation. His Majesty has a daughter.'

'The Princess Elizabeth?'

'Just so. Already many foreign princes have seen the advantage of a marriage with the daughter of the King of England and Scotland.'

'But the girl . . . er, the princess, would surely not be of marriageable age for another few years.'

The earl's brows raised a fraction. 'You are well informed about such things, Master Drew.'

'I try to keep abreast of all things, your grace.'

'As I have told you, many foreign princes plan their advantages well in advance. She may only be eleven years old now, but already several princely houses on the continent are soliciting attention to make alliances. We have to be guardians to ensure any prospective alliance is one that we may profit by.'

'I am perplexed. I am no marriage broker.'

153

The earl snorted with sardonic humour. 'That will not be your endeavour. In the hall, awaiting your attention, is the captain of a brig which you have seen at anchor in the river. I am told you have a quick eye and will have noticed the emblem and name of the vessel, *Der Silberne Löwe*. The name means "The Silver Lion". The captain is a foreign noble. The Rheingraf von Amberg. He was escorting Prince Gustav of Braunschweig on a courtesy call to the palace. The young prince is some years older than Princess Elizabeth. He is a cousin to the Elector Palatine of the Rhine and Holy Roman Emperor, therefore he has been met with all due courtesy.'

The earl suddenly looked troubled. 'In all honesty, the King's advisers have decided that he would not be suitable for a future liaison. There is a matter of religious persuasion. Prince Gustav and his immediate family are of the Papist persuasion. However, there is the problem of alliances and the princes of the Rhineland are a sure and certain bulwark against the Spanish intrigues.'

The constable said nothing but waited.

'As I said, he is received with the courtesy due to foreign princes. To our dismay His Majesty and the princess herself received the prince with more than a little enthusiasm. His Majesty would not hear our caveats of how his subjects would perceive such an alliance following the years of our conflicted history.'

He paused again. 'To cut to the chase, Master Drew, we must have a clear report of how the prince, for I think we can be sure that the body is his, came by his death. The boy was a guest of His Majesty. This morning, Rheingraf von Amberg required an urgent meeting with my steward who, in turn, reported to me.

Prince Gustav did not return aboard last night and, indeed, has not been seen since dusk.'

The constable knew what was coming.

'Justice Mayhew reported to me that a body was taken from the river into your jurisdiction on the Bankside whose description meets that of Prince Gustav.'

'You wish me to discover how the prince has got himself killed and wound up in the river?'

'By and by. In the hall, at this moment, is the Rheingraf von Amberg. In the first place you will escort him to where the body of the unfortunate youth lays. If the identification is positive, and I have no doubts it will be so, the body must be taken on board the ship which, with your report, will be allowed to sail as soon as possible. Hopefully, your report will illuminate any culpability.'

'So this . . . this Rheingraf? He is in charge?'

The earl was impatient. 'It is a German title, but he insists on using it in place of what we would term as "count". It is a particular type of count. He is not only captain of the ship but steward of this young prince. He will identify the body. This, I suspect, will be that of Prince Gustav. You will then release the body to the Rheingraf so that they can return in all haste to obsequies in their own land. It is not politic that any ceremonial should happen here. It involves matters of statecraft that you need not bother about. This must remain a confidential matter. The country has settled after the Papist plots to kill the King and his family, and the matter of a Papist prince having been entertained with the prospect of an alliance by marriage would not be politic to reveal to the people.'

'Surely there are protocols . . ?' the constable protested.

'In my position, I make the protocols,' the earl said grimly. 'Anyway, you are to write a report of the circumstances in which the boy drowned or was attacked by riverside footpads. Then I will affix my seal and this country will be released of any obligation to the family of this Papist prince.'

'I foresee problems, your grace,' the constable remarked slowly. 'We know the boy was not drowned. The mortician, Justice Mayhew and I were witness to the dagger wounds that ended his life . . . as were the boatmen who found the body. Neither was he robbed. Doubtless I should then enquire to find the culprit or culprits?'

The earl's features dissolved in anger for no more than a second and then he relaxed and smiled.

''Sbodikins! I run ahead of myself, Constable,' the earl admitted. 'Of course, your finding should not be pre-empted. But the quicker matters can be concluded, the better. However, I would presume that the young prince, if indeed the body is his, was abroad on his own. Then there would be plenty of footpads about, attracted by fine clothes, a fat purse and a foreign language which marks one out as fair game for the cut-throats that scour the docks and landing places of this city.'

Master Drew was troubled. Questions came to him, but he decided to suppress them. Meanwhile, the earl rang a small hand bell and a man entered. It was not the foreign count but a man in the flamboyant uniform of a palace guard. He was a man of sallow features, narrowed, almost sinister, hazel eyes, with a thin-set, immobile mouth. He stood in an attitude of attention, saying nothing.

The earl barely acknowledged him.

'I have no wish to teach you your job, Master Drew, but it would be wrong of me not to provide you with assistance in the fulfilment of your task. This is Captain Rolfe. He will organise transport for you as you wish. And now, all else, you may learn from Rheingraf von Amberg. My steward has advised him of the news that you and Justice Mayhew have brought here. He will be persuaded to give you all the intelligence you require. Meantime,' the earl rose swiftly and went to his desk and took up a paper, 'here is my commission to act in this affair on which I have already placed my seal. You should conclude this matter as quickly as you can and see no word leaks out, for, as I have said, we want no more conspiracies of the type that this may give rise to. Now . . .'

He reached forward, picked up his handbell and rang it again. In answer, his steward entered with the Rheingraf. He was a tall, man, whose features seemed sunken with worry. His eyes drooped as if he had not slept in a while.

Master Drew noticed that he had been formally elevated in rank for he was introduced to the noble as 'Ritter zu Bankside'. He knew this meant some sort of knighthood, presumably to allow him to exercise authority to deal with the count, who was intent on following convention and etiquette.

It seemed a short time elapsed before Master Drew was seated alongside the taciturn count in the stern of a skiff rowed by two taciturn oarsmen dressed in palace livery. Captain Rolfe sat in the bow. Master Drew found conversation with the count stilted and difficult and he soon lapsed into silence. He had tried to pose a few questions but the count was curt in pointing out that such questions and his answers would be superfluous until the body was identified.

They landed at the steps by Bear Alley. Captain Rolfe ordered the boatmen to remain before accompanying the count and Master Drew to the mortician.

The constable felt that he should make some attempt to assert himself as a guide to the aloof noble. 'Forgive me, sir, but as this is a mortuary, there will be foulness of odours, so I suggest you cover your nose to protect yourself.'

Rheingraf von Amberg shook his head impatiently. 'I have experienced the stench of battle,' he said. 'It does not trouble me. Let us go in and view this body.'

So saying, he pushed into Master Redweard's mortuary. The constable followed and greeted the surprised mortician, who, recognising the rank of the foreign dignitary, bowed obsequiously before him and drew back the canvas covering from the body.

The count stared at the body for a second before exclaiming: '*Grosser Gott! Dies kömmtem Kieg bedeuten!*'

His shoulders sagged with the shock of recognition. The constable waited a moment for the count to say something in English. When he did not, he ventured to ask: 'I presume you formally state that this is Prince Gustav?'

The count stared at him for a moment. Then he sighed; '*Ja; das ist der Körpe von Prinz Gustav* . . . it is the prince's body.'

'Very well.' Master Drew had not expected anything other than a positive identification. 'We must have the body transported immediately across the river to your ship.' He turned to Master Redweard. 'I am told that the protocol is for the body to be preserved so that it can be transported back to the prince's country for interment. How quickly can that be done?'

'If the body is immersed in alcohol in a barrel . . .' began the mortician.

The Rheingraf interrupted sharply. He had abruptly pulled himself together after his initial shock.

'My ship's surgeon will deal with this matter once the body of the prince is securely placed on board.'

Captain Rolfe stepped forward. 'I will take charge of the body, Master Constable, and see it safely taken to the ship.'

'Very well,' Master Drew said, before turning to the Rheingraf. 'I shall need to ask some questions for my report to His Grace, the Earl of Salisbury, who will then approve my report. Similarly, you will need the earl's seal to take to the prince's family.' Then he turned back to Captain Rolfe. 'I suggest the boatmen take us directly back to the ship and then you can return here to fetch the body. That will give the Rheingraf time to order his crew to make the necessary preparations.'

While the captain gave orders to receive the body and fulfil his tasks, Master Drew sat uncomfortably with the Rheingraf in the captain's cabin of *Der Silberne Löwe*.

'I would presume that the prince would have a manservant and he would be intimate with him regarding his assignations?'

To his surprise, the Rheingraf shook his head. 'We are a small brig and carry no such personal attendants. However, I have made diligent enquiries in the ship. I have found one witness to Prinz Gustav's leaving the ship last night. He is only a sailor but one who speaks some of your language.'

'Then let us have him in,' the constable replied.

The Rheingraf called loudly without stirring himself from his seat: '*Sag Günter, er soll soforts in meine Kabine kommen!*'

Almost immediately the cabin door opened and a short, weather-beaten man entered. His occupation was obvious from the tough, tanned body and characteristic canvas breeches, loose shirt and woollen cap. He lifted his knuckled fist to his forehead in a typical salutation.

'*Günter, das is ein englischer Beamter. Sie warden seine Fragen beantworten.*'

'*Jawohl!*'

Master Drew guessed the man was being ordered to answer his questions.

'I am told you were a witness to the prince leaving this ship last night. Tell me how you saw this?'

The small man hesitated, trying to find the right words. His English was good although not perfect.

'I was on watch, sir. It was early evening, what they call the dog watch. It's when Sirius, the dog star, is first seen and so the watch is named from that.'

Master Drew knew full well the fairly recent adoption by English ships of naming the dog watches from the German or Dutch method and using Sirius.

'So, it was early evening but dark and you were on watch?' he prompted.

They were interrupted by a sudden rap on the cabin door and Captain Rolfe entered.

'Your pardon, sirs. Come aboard with the remains. The ship's surgeon has taken charge. Can I transport you anywhere, Master Constable?'

'For the moment, no. I need to ask this man some questions.'

Captain Rolfe eased himself into the cabin, to the constable's surprise. As the Rheingraf did not raise an objection, he decided to carry on.

'You were saying, Günter? You were on watch?'

'Just so, *mein herr*. The prinz came to the rail and peered up and down. Then he saw me standing there. He turned and said he was going ashore but only into the palace grounds. I asked if I should call a guard to accompany him. He refused and said he was waiting for a companion who he had met in the palace.'

'He had met this person in the Palace of Westminster?'

'He indicated the place with his hand.'

'So you called no guard?'

'No, *mein herr*. A short time later, a rowing boat came alongside and a voice called.'

'Saying what?'

'*Ich bin hier*. Then the prinz turned to me and assured me I would get a good whipping if I uttered a word. He was going to enjoy himself at a local place of entertainment with his friend.'

'Why did you not report this immediately to . . . to your captain?'

'I did not want a whipping, Herr Ritter.'

It was a fair enough answer. 'You saw him join this friend?'

'I saw him descend into a boat which came below the gangway.'

'But the figure was, of course, in darkness,' Captain Rolfe suddenly interrupted.

'Not entirely,' the seaman said. 'The sidelight on the ship by the port entrance was lit. A storm lantern. The rower was a slight figure. He wore a dark cloak but his red hair glinted in the flickering light. Ah, yes, and I saw a dark line across the forehead, down across the left eye.'

'A dark line?' queried the constable.

'It might have been a scar rather than a shadow,' corrected the sailor.

He heard a sharp intake of breath from Captain Rolfe.

'You recognise something?' he asked.

Captain Rolfe hesitated. The constable caught a slight look of embarrassment. 'The description sounds familiar. I think such a vagrant whelp has been observed by my men around the palace and the river entrances.'

'Then we must search these places.'

'That should be a task for my men and myself, begging your pardon. You may know the southern bank, but matters are different and strange on this northern bank.'

Master Drew considered for a moment. Captain Rolfe was right. Furthermore, after they had thanked the sailor and the Rheingraf and returned to shore, Master Drew realised he was in need of a good meal and a flagon of ale.

As they stepped ashore from the skiff at the palace dock, Master Drew and the Rheingraf were hailed by none other than Justice Mayhew.

'How goes your work, Master Constable,' he greeted. 'My work here is over and I was just going in search of sustenance. What of you? Would either of you gentlemen care to be my companion in a local tavern for a cut of beef and a bottle of good wine?'

Captain Rolfe immediately excused himself, saying he had eaten earlier but would seize the time to set a search in progress for the youth he felt matched the description that Günter had given. If the truth were admitted, Master Drew felt a little uneasy, but he had already been diverted from his meal that morning and he did not wish to forgo being entertained by the justice.

Justice Mayhew led the way to a small tavern outside the palace walls where, apparently, he had access to a private chamber. The meal was leisurely and the justice was full of good humour, informing Master Drew that he was his guest and not to spare himself in his choices. In fact, time passed pleasantly and, before he knew it, he had to suggest to the justice that the skies were darkening. Captain Rolfe always seemed to make a surprise entrance and it was no more surprising when, at that very moment, he burst into the private dining chamber, much to the protestation of the tavern landlord.

'You would not believe such success that has been my lot, masters!' declaimed the burly captain of the guard.

'What means you by this?' Justice Mayhew replied in irritation.

'Why, the young footpad has fallen into my lap. The brigand was haunting the docks for further victims when I spied him.'

Master Drew began to rise.

'Stay a moment,' Justice Mayhew advised. 'Let's hear this news completely.'

''Tis as I say. I gave my men a description, as given by the German sailor, but as I was walking down by the Old Star tavern, I saw the whelp. Clear as I see you now. I came upon him and cried on him to yield to me. Why, so hot-headed was the urchin that he drew forth a dagger and would have impaled me but

I stepped back, defended myself with my cutlass and before you could draw a breath it was he that lay impaled.'

'Is he dead?'

'Aye, dead, say I.'

'You have surely not let him lay there?' queried the justice.

'Not I, sir. I called up two of my men to stand over him and, knowing that the constable would be here, I came with utmost speed to impart the news.'

The constable frowned. 'But we needs must have more proof that this is the assassin; proof that he was the culprit.'

'I will swear to it. A callow youth, with a scar across the forehead and left eye, with fair tumbled hair. A dark cloak and known to be a piece of gallows bait haunting the docks of this northside. Moreover, you shall come and see the body for yourself.'

Justice Mayhew was nodding. 'I shall accompany you.'

There was a crowd gathered outside a tavern a short distance along the reinforced bank. Captain Rolfe roughly pushed them aside and pointed to the body. It seemed exactly as the palace guard had described it. To one side lay an old cheap dagger.

'Perhaps you should examine it?' suggested the justice.

The constable went down on one knee and noticed an old cloth purse hanging from a cheap string belt. He took the purse and felt it. There was something inside. He drew back the strings and pulled out the contents: a large foreign silver coin, which he held up.

'A ducat,' explained the justice.

It was the second object which caused Master Drew immediate unease and he tried not to show it.

It was a signet ring with an emblem; the same emblem that

had been embroidered onto the doublet of the dead prince; the same emblem flying on the jackstaff that flew on *Der Silberne Löwe.*

'That ends it,' cried the justice, almost in a note of triumph. 'No more need be said.'

The way the words were expressed was as if Justice Mayhew was telling Master Drew the matter was finished. Drew stood looking down at the body. It could have been any one of the hundreds of homeless young ruffians, cut-throat villains, who haunted the riverbanks on both sides of the Thames.

One of the guards turned to Captain Rolfe and whispered, 'I've seen this youth before. Wasn't he page to . . .'

'Of course you've seen him before,' the captain interrupted irritably. 'That's how I recognised him. A thief lurking about the docks here. Now, away with the body.' He turned to Master Drew and pointed to the coin and signet ring. 'You will need those items for evidence alongside your report to His Grace.'

Master Drew had realised the implied message. When the justice suggested that he accompany him to the palace where he could write his report, he did not demur nor was he surprised. Obediently, he followed Justice Mayhew and spent but a short time in a room that the justice secured. With quills, ink and parchment, he sat down, tightened his jaw and wrote firmly as he knew he was bidden to. Above all, Master Drew was a pragmatist. At the end, the justice took the report and began to read through it.

'I am delighted to see you have the faculty of brevity,' he observed. 'You also write with a fair hand, too. And this was your conclusion, freely arrived at, after your investigation?'

165

'That is the report I wish to submit,' the constable replied evenly.

Justice Mayhew's expression did not alter as he began to précis the content.

'The young prince, apparently an adventurous boy, absconded from his guardian, Rheingraf von Amberg, leaving his ship one evening, as witnessed by a sailor named Günter, the better to see the sights around the Palace of Westminster. He fell in with a young footpad who preyed on foreign visitors to these parts. Once cornered in a darkened alley, the prince was attacked and stabbed. He died immediately of the wounds. Whereupon the prince was robbed of several items, except his crucifix, which may or may not be of significance. The body was tossed into the river from where, the day following, it was found and thence identified.

'On questioning of divers folk by Master Drew, Constable of the Bankside, whose signature is appended, the footpad was identified by one Captain Rolfe, by the description of the said sailor given in the presence of Rheingraf von Amberg and the said constable. Captain Rolfe and his men discovered the culprit by a riverside tavern and attempted apprehension. The thief disputed the attempt to take him prisoner. He attacked the captain and, by his prompt action, the thief was killed. The sum of a golden ducat, among those stolen from the young prince's purse, was found on the footpad's body. Likewise, the prince's signet ring, showing the arms of his house, was also on the body of the thief at that time.

'As the footpad lived as a vagrant on the streets, it has been impossible to discover if other coins and items of jewellery taken from the prince's person, have been disposed of and, if so, to whom. It has been most lamentable that this murder happened within His Majesty's capital and within the shadow of his palace of Westminster. It is hoped that the swift discovery and death of the vagrant involved might ameliorate the sadness of the loss and be of some solace and atonement . . .'

The justice stopped his recitation.

'Indeed, you write a fair hand. Nay, I would say you would be well fitted in diplomatic spheres. If you have nothing further to add, I will place my seals upon your effort and straightway take it to the earl for his approval. Thus we can dispatch *Der Silberne Löwe* the quicker from our territory.'

'With this I have submitted the report as His Grace wished.'

'Then I shall call for wax and we will put our seals on it. Then I shall place it in His Grace's hands and we will call for a wherry to take us across the river and home.'

It was on the evening of the next day when there was a rap at the door of Master Drew's rooms above the Pilgrim's Wink tavern. The constable set down the brief report he had been reading. On calling out an invitation to enter, he found himself staring in surprise at the form of the justice, Master Mayhew.

'I trust I do not disturb you, Master Constable?'

'I was just reading a report from the keeper of the King's Bench about some argument between householders in Newcomen Street,' the constable said, attempting to rise.

'Sit you down, sit you down.' The justice motioned him to be re-seated and took another chair himself. 'Newcomen Street? Ah yes, it's an old argument about ownership of a piece of land at the back. It led to fisticuffs the other night. A few days in jail will calm both parties.'

He paused and then seemed to be trying to make up his mind about something before speaking. Then he reached in his purse and drew forth a small bag that clinked with obvious coinage.

'This is your fee to cover your endeavours yesterday.'

As the constable made no effort to reach for it, Justice Mayhew set it down on the table between them. 'I am led to understand that His Grace was well satisfied with the outcome of yesterday's affair. That little sack contains fifty of the newly minted gold half crowns.'

'Then his satisfaction seems well expressed,' Master Drew observed dryly. 'When a parson can expect twenty pounds for his salary, I should be well content.'

'Yet you seem a little troubled, Master Constable.'

'Only that I trust the Rheingraf von Amberg was so overcome with grief that his powers of observation were not accurate.'

The justice frowned. 'What say you?' he asked sharply.

'Money and the signet ring were still on the prince's corpse when he was dragged from the river. They remained so in the mortuary until Captain Rolfe took charge of the corpse.'

The justice's lips compressed a moment.

'I think Master Redweard's mortuary was not well lit,' he suggested. 'A minor point in which the mind may well have been confused. Do you not agree?'

'Indeed, I would agree.'

'Exactly so. You would approve, however, of the alacrity with which Captain Rolfe acted?'

'The footpad met his end. Dead, dead for a ducat. Ah well, I am pleased that the earl has endorsed the account. That is how I wrote my report.'

'And how it should remain,' Justice Mayhew said in a reflective tone. 'I have paid Master Redweard for his troubles as a mortician and thus come to deliver your fee.' He paused. 'In these days, Master Drew, some unpleasant actions need be taken to protect the state. Conspirators from all manner of religions intrude; those who want to insert themselves in government. Many factions want to see branches of the Tudors, or of the Stuarts all clinging to power. Papists, Protestants, all manner of non-conventional faiths and politics.'

'I am aware of the problems that beset our country,' replied Master Drew gravely.

'And the harsh ways with which these problems must be dealt? Just so. Just so. We are surrounded by enemies, Master Drew. Such matters as this one weigh heavily on the mind of His Grace who, as you know, is subject to frailty of the body. He has several men who try to second guess his commands. You have been working hard recently. I would suggest that you find some purpose for investigation outside of the parish for a while until certain folk think the recent days are a distant memory. I think you have my meaning. I have a cousin who owns a farm in Malling who has been troubled by the theft of his cattle. He would pay you well to find a solution to the problem.'

It was a full month later, after word came from the justice that it might be expedient for Master Drew to return to his old apartment and endeavours, that found the constable strolling down Bear Lane and passing Master Redweard's mortuary when the mortician was exiting his premises.

'Still doing your business from the river corpses?' Master Drew asked cynically.

169

'It goes fairly, thanks be. The river remains replete with cadavers. One recently was of your acquaintance, if I recall.'

'How so?' the constable frowned.

'Well, he accompanied you here over the affair of the noble foreigner.'

Master Drew had a dark thought. 'Of whom do you speak?'

'A palace guard named Rolfe.'

Master Drew looked at the mortician uncomfortably.

'Captain Rolfe, you say?'

'That was he. He was dragged from the river a few weeks ago. It seems he had not been so quick in dealing with the cut-throats as he had been that time with you. He was attacked, robbed and being dead was thrown into the river. They only left him with a florin in his purse.'

Master Drew was silent for a while and then he remarked cynically, 'Was it a foreign ducat or an English groat?'

Not understanding, Master Redweard simply shrugged and shook his head. 'I would not know, Master Constable. At least the thieves were not thorough at their trade to leave a coin behind.'

'Some can be even more thorough by doing so,' the constable smiled without humour and inclined his head before turning to walk along the Bankside, leaving Master Redweard thorough perplexed.

Now Go We in Content

Now go we in content
To liberty, and not to banishment

As You Like It, Act I, Scene iii
William Shakespeare

'If I were paid a silver groat for every corpse that floated along this river, I doubt not to be able to buy myself both title and estate somewhere with a good trout stream running through it.'

With such disdain Master Hardy Drew, Constable of the Bankside Watch, spoke to the young boy who had brought him an appeal to attend Master Redweard's mortuary to view such a cadaver.

The one event that irritated the constable was being disturbed at the end of a long day when he was about to confront a good meal. That evening he had decided to visit the Cock and Pie and had just taken his seat in the smoke-filled snug and ordered a quarter of a freshly baked beef pie and pickled cabbage, for which the hostess, Mistress Gosforth, was renowned. He had barely taken a sip from his tankard of ale, when he became aware of the young boy standing nervously on the other side of the table.

He scowled.

'What seek you, boy?' he snapped.

'Be you the constable, sir?' enquired the ragged urchin.

'That I am,' Master Drew grunted, 'and about to partake of my supper, which I hope to do in peace. Therefore, if you have aught to do but ogle me, I say – be off with you.'

'But I am sent to find you, if it please you, sir.'

'It pleases me not,' the irritated constable replied. 'Come, state your business if you have any.'

'I was sent by Master Redweard.'

'The mortician?' Master Drew was surprised that the Bankside undertaker had sent a street urchin to find him and at such an hour when the day was drawing to a close.

'And having found me, what then?' he prompted.

'I am to entreat you attend him at his apothecary without delay, sir. He wishes you to regard a corpse but lately taken from the river by London Bridge, sir.'

After giving the boy his philosophy on the number of corpses that were daily found in the river by London Bridge, he enquired, 'Master Redweard asks nothing else?'

'Only that, sir.'

The constable had realised that the mortician knew him well enough to have some good reason for the summons. He gave a deep sigh and took up his tankard of ale, downing its content with one thirsty draft. Then, wiping his mouth, he rose from his seat. He noticed the boy still standing there and, in a moment of guilt reached for the purse on his leather belt.

'Please you, sir,' interrupted the boy, guessing his intent, 'Master Redweard did give me a farthing to come and find you.'

In spite of his bad humour, Master Drew smiled and felt into his purse to withdraw a coin. 'Then, for honesty's sake, you shall have another farthing to make the halfpence. You need not delay for I know well where Master Redweard dwells.'

With an apology to Mistress Gosforth and an assurance that he would return to demolish the meat pie and pickled cabbage as soon as he was able, he left the tavern at the corner of Maiden Lane and began to walk with quickening pace towards Bear Alley where, at the Bankside entrance, Master Redweard practised his art.

This was the area of the Clink Liberties, stretching along the south bank of the River Thames from Gravel Lane almost to the great London Bridge which crossed north into the City of London. It was an area that the constable had come to know well; from the taverns and brothels, together with the large round buildings where the bear and bull baiting attracted larger crowds than any of the other entertainments. The animal rings were marked by the names of several squares and alleys such as Bear Garden, Bear Alley, Bull Wharf and Bull Alley.

What the constable particularly liked about the area was that, nestling among the maze of alleys, were four popular playhouses: the Rose, the Swan, the Hope and the Globe. They straddled either side of Maiden Lane, which ran parallel to the Bankside. The playhouses had first appeared in Southwark when the pious aldermen of the City forbade such popular entertainment to be erected north of the river. So the playhouses attracted crowds who crossed the river from the city either by boat or over London Bridge. The constable enjoyed free entrance to all the playhouses, as was his due, and thus was a frequenter of the performances.

Rich and poor mixed freely here and untimely death was a

natural occurrence. It was a place comprising of the dregs of humanity, perhaps emphasised by the fact there were five prisons located within the small borough. It was the largest number of jails for any similar sized area in London. The thieves and cut-throats, who counted other peoples' lives at nought, lived cheek by jowl with honest folk; with intellectuals, artisans and entertainers. It was a place where the spacious mansions of the nobility interspersed those of the clergy and local churches. And none was more spectacular than Winchester Palace, the London home of the Bishop of Winchester, and his church, St Mary Overy, the old word for 'over the water', which since the Reformed Church had been named St Saviour's and designated a cathedral.

Master Drew had become intimately knowledgeable about the area for he was the law enforcer along the Bankside.

At the end of Bear Alley, Master Drew halted for a moment outside the bleak building where Master Redweard carried out his business. He reached in his pocket for a square of rose-scented cambric and held it to his nose before entering. In the room were several tables on which sackcloth covered three or four corpses.

As the door swung shut behind him, with the faint jingle of a bell to announce his presence, a figure emerged from among the tables; tall, pale-faced and looking emaciated, the mortician, in black broadcloth, almost resembled one of the cadavers.

'Give you a good evening, Master Redweard,' the constable greeted.

'And to you, Master Constable,' replied the man in a croaky voice.

'You sent a boy to bring him hither?'

'That I did and for you to see a corpse lately fished from the river.'

'Why so?' The constable frowned. 'Corpses are fished from the Thames every day. Is there something special about this one?'

'You must be witness as to that.'

Master Drew suppressed an impatient sigh. It was certainly not unusual for corpses to be fished daily from the river in all manner of condition.

Master Redweard pointed to a nearby table and, reaching forward, drew back the sackcloth covering.

The constable moved forward. It was the body of a man who seemed strongly built and hardly beyond his youthful prime. There was nothing particularly outstanding about his clothing except that it was not that of a beggar but rather of an artisan; one used to manual work but of a commanding position. The good leather jerkin and boots, the quality, once-white linen shirt and coarse-thread trousers, underscored that view. There seemed, however, something familiar about the head whose river-flattened black hair clung about the face.

'Bring your lamp closer, Master Redweard,' instructed the constable.

The mortician did so, holding the lamp over the face.

The constable breathed out sharply.

'So, you recognise him?' the mortician queried with some satisfaction in his voice.

'It is Master Penheskin, the overseer at the wharf and docks at St Mary Overy.'

The wharf and docks were used by boats and barges landing cargoes for the cathedral and its estates. It had been an Augustinian priory but, following the Reformation, it was now incorporated with the residence of the Bishop of Winchester.

The constable hesitated as he viewed the body. 'Had he been in drink? Was he inebriated that he came into the river?'

'Not a smell of drink upon him. But observe that the head be cut and bloodied. See the broken bone fragment protruding? I'll wager that a heavy cudgel did for the poor man before he was pushed into the river.'

'The work of footpads?'

'Incompetent footpads, Master Constable, for there was money in his purse. He had two groats, five pennies, one half pence and a farthing. A day's wages for some.'

The constable glanced quickly at the mortician because he was surprised at this admission. It was well known that a good proportion of Master Redweard's income came from selling the clothes of the corpses that were fished from the river if they had anything worth salvaging on them. If coins had been left, it was astonishing the mortician would be so forthright in admitting it.

'You are candid as to this total of thirteen and three-quarter pence?' He could not keep the cynical tone from his voice.

Master Redweard managed to look indignant as he took the coins from a drawer and slammed them on the table.

'Master Penheskin was a friend to my own son. But, importantly, suspicion often falls on one who carries this . . .' He held out another coin.

The constable took it and turned it over. 'A *reales* of Philip of Spain.'

'I recognised the style from when we were forced to accept them in the time when he was the husband of Queen Mary.

A Spanish *reales*. When I saw it to be a Papist coin, I judged I should report it and leave all matters of it to you.'

The constable smiled thinly. 'Coins have no religion, my friend, unless it be the religious sin of avarice. Anyway, it is three years since the ambassador of Philip of Spain signed the Treaty of London ending the war between Spain and England. Spaniards are now free to trade across the English Channel.'

Master Redweard sniffed dourly. 'Aye, but it was only last year that the last of the Papist conspirators were executed. When they failed to blow up Parliament on the day the King opened it, it was said that Papist Spain was behind that plot. Now there are rumours that others are willing to take their place.'

'They are all now executed,' the constable pointed out. 'There's no harm to having a Spanish coin now. As for plots, were not all the Papist priests ordered to quit the shores of this kingdom at that time? So we should be rid of Papist plots.'

'There are still many suspects. Why, as well you know, the chief of all Romish priests is still locked in the Clink and, unless he be executed, he'll be there for the rest of his life.'

'Are you suggesting that Master Penheskin, because he had a *reales* on him, was a Papist?' queried the constable.

'Of course not,' the mortician answered immediately. 'He was a friend to my son. God-fearing lads, the two of them. I just wanted no part in dealing with any Papist coins. No part . . . other than my fee.'

Master Drew was somewhat amused by the idea. 'Well, silver is silver, however it is minted. But, tell me, how came the corpse to your mortuary?'

'By the wherry of my son. You know he works as a waterman

and is as dexterous a single-oared steersman as any along the river . . .'

'How came he by the body?' interrupted the constable.

'He was sculling upriver through one of the piers of the Bridge and saw the corpse entangled in a mooring line near the Pepper Alley Stairs.'

'Pepper Alley Stairs?' enquired Master Drew. He had rooms above the Pilgrim's Wink tavern in Pepper Street. His windows almost gave sight of the landing place giving access from the river.

'It was a few hours ago and the day still light. My son saw that the corpse wore a leather coat of worth so he rowed across with the intent to retrieve it. Leather jerkins fetch a goodly price. Only then did he recognise the body of his friend. Thinking not to abandon him, he dragged the body on board and brought him straightway to me. After I examined the corpse and saw the wound and further saw that he was not a victim to robbery, I decided to send for you.'

'There was nothing else unusual?'

'Nothing except . . .' The mortician hesitated. 'Well, the coins were almost buried in black mud, which I found unusual.'

Master Drew raised a quizzical eyebrow. 'Black mud?'

'More like black grit, as if he had grabbed a handful of it and thrust it into his purse among the coins. It was the consistency of dye. I had to wash it out to clean the coins.'

'Where is your son now?'

'He went to take the sad news to Mistress Penheskin. She and her husband dwell in a tenement at the back of the George tavern. They were all good friends.'

'Very altruistic of you not to collect your fee immediately in these hard times,' the constable remarked cynically. The mortician did not seem insulted.

'Master Penheskin worked on the estates of the Bishop of Winchester. I would seek my legal fees from the comptroller of the estates, rather than be suspected of some petty theft or even being involved in some plot having found the *reales*. The comptroller is a man who is so fanatic in his Protestant faith that he is suspicious of anything smelling of Popery, even to the use of coins.'

The constable shrugged disdainfully. 'Very well. Place the coins and clothes somewhere safe until we have made a conclusion of this business. I am sure Mistress Penheskin will want what is rightfully her own. But she will agree your fees most honestly. Tomorrow at first light I shall attend the wharf at St Mary Overy to see what is to be discovered. As for now, I am returning to finish my interrupted supper and another tankard of ale at Mistress Gosforth's tavern.'

It was a chilly and bright late autumn morning when the constable exited his lodging at the Pilgrim's Wink and turned along the narrow alleys in the direction of Clink Street. At the intersection before the entrance to the south side of St Saviour's he was arrested by a combination of delicious odours overpowering the usual rank smell of the streets. At the corner a small wagon was halted while the driver was adjusting a strap on the sturdy little mule that was its locomotion. The cart was specially constructed so that it was filled with trays of pies and tarts that had been freshly baked and still had not lost their aromas.

'Abroad early delivering your master's wares, Jebediah?' the constable greeted, recognising the elderly driver. 'Wither away this fair morning?'

The old man raised himself from his task of adjusting the bearing rein and terret on the mule. He respectfully raised a knuckled hand to touch his forehead.

'I be off to Winchester Palace to deliver these pastries to His Grace's kitchens for my master.'

'The bishop has a fine taste to send out for Master Bostwick's best pastries. But why order so many and such variety?' Master Drew glanced over the contents of the trays.

'Aye, but His Grace has several guests who have fine tastes, for I delivered such pastries and pies yesterday and was told they be all but vanished.'

Master Drew sniffed appreciatively as he cast his eyes over the trays. 'Warden Pies, if I mistake them not. Hard-baked with pears and impregnated with spices, why ... what's this? Posset, damn my eyes, such sweet stuff of sugar, eggs! I do swear I smell lemon combined in such a potage. And even marchpane tarts? His Grace must be playing host to royalty and not sparing expense, for I know Master Bostwick is renowned as the master of his craft and his prices reflect it. Such delicacies. Even I could not afford to purchase a pie from his bakery.'

The constable knew that Master Bostwick's bakery, along St Olave's Street, had a reputation that was the envy of many.

The old man shrugged. 'Indeed, Master Drew. His Grace's guests are all men of wealth and influence. I heard from His Grace's cook that they be all churchmen, and at least one bishop among them. I am told they be all learned scholars of the Church.'

'But not unusual guests for His Grace to play host to,' mused the constable.

'Not unusual except in their number, rank and entertainment. Apparently, a dozen of them began to arrive a few days ago. Some came by river and some by coach.'

Master Drew was intrigued. As constable he liked to keep abreast of the tittle-tattle of the area. What happened around the Bishop of Winchester's palace was a good source of judging the news of the country.

'What do you mean about their unusual entertainment?' he asked, realising what the old man had said.

Master Jebediah leaned forward confidentially. 'I was told by the cook that they shut themselves in the palace dining room and have been heard arguing fiercely with one another. Apparently, betimes they sent for a bottle of Sack or Malmsey, and were heard discoursing in what sounded gibberish.'

'You mean in a foreign tongue?'

'Not just so, sir. It seemed English but with a number of strange words as discussing the meaning of some ancient tongue.'

'Strange ancient words? Were His Grace's guests a group of scholars then?'

'If you say so, sir. I would not know. Cook said that one of his men reported that His Grace had ordered that "The Westminster Committee" required two more bottles of Sack and half a dozen candles.'

'He used the term – The Westminster Committee?' Master Drew shook his head, not recognising the term.

'The very words, Constable.'

Master Drew realised that old Jebediah was anxious to be off to make his delivery, so he bade him farewell and turned towards Clink Street.

There was a faint wind blowing from the north-east and, as the constable neared the riverside, he could smell the foul odours from the river and from the crowded tenements and buildings that straddled London Bridge. He reminded himself once more to purchase another sweet-smelling posy or rose water as distraction from the putrid smells. He turned into the narrow cobbles of Clink Street, pausing to have a word with Master Skelton, the turnkey who happened to be outside the ancient prison entrance.

Having imparted the news of Master Penheskin's demise, for the wharf overseer was well known, he found Master Skelton was not one to be saddened by the news. Death was a constant companion among the warrens and narrow alleys of the buildings which spread around beyond the ecclesiastical grounds and gated mansions. Indeed, one of Master Skelton's more recent tasks was to escort some of the heretics to their deaths on the bonfires in Smithfield across the river.

'I saw the man only the evening before yesterday,' the rotund turnkey admitted. 'He told me that he had to remain at the docks that evening for he was expecting a barge arriving late.'

'Was that the last time you saw him?'

'Indeed it was. But I did see Mistress Penheskin coming along about noon that same day. I passed the time with her for she is a comely wench. She told me she came to demand that her husband give her money to pay their landlord. I would fain guess money was the only reason for her concern. I have heard stories . . .'

Master Drew quickly interrupted. 'You did not see Penheskin

again or know whether he oversaw the arrival of this barge? Was it not unusual for a barge to arrive so late?'

'I have lived here since my boyhood; it is not unusual for the occupants of Winchester Palace, whoever the incumbent may be, to entertain frequently and well. So barges of watermen or small boats of wherrymen coming at all times would not be unusual. You should know the area well enough for that.'

Master Drew raised his hand in thanks and continued to the end of Clink Street and turned to the open river and the wharf that was named after St Mary Overy. At the end of this was a small inlet of the river, with banks reinforced with stone, in which a few boats were moored. The barges tended to moor on the eastern side of this little inlet where it was easier to unload their heavy goods to be carried through the entrance of the church buildings and into the Bishop's residential estate.

The area was fairly deserted as there were no vessels tied up alongside the riverside as the constable made his way across the stone flags to the bollards where vessels were usually tied. A solitary man sat atop a bollard staring moodily along the river and sucking on a long-stemmed clay pipe. At the sound of the constable's footsteps on the flagstones, the man turned and slowly rose with a crooked smile.

Jack Grimes was known to the constable as assistant overseer of the wharf. Master Drew immediately told the man of his errand. Grimes took the news stoically, perhaps accepting that this meant his elevation to overseer. He had not been a great friend of his former master. In fact, he gave a sly wink at the constable.

'I reckon there might be two who will not be lamenting wholeheartedly at the obsequies for Master Penheskin.'

The constable scowled. 'Explain yourself.'

Grimes pursed his lips before responding. 'It was well known that Mistress Penheskin was more of a friend to young Master Redweard than ever her husband was, if you catch my meaning? But I'll not be one for hearsay.'

Master Drew cast him a scathing glance and asked: 'When did you last see Master Penheskin?'

Grimes shrugged. 'On the evening before last. We were unloading a barge come up from Chertsey Meads.'

'What cargo?'

'Some old religious items for His Grace, the Bishop. A gift from Doctor Hammond who recently acquired the old abbey.'

The constable was aware that Dr Hammond was physician to the royal household and had recently bought the abbey from Sir William Fitzwilliam. In turn, he had taken ownership when the Benedictine monks were evicted during the Reformation.

'Master Penheskin oversaw the unloading of the barge? That was the last time you saw him? Was any other vessel expected that night.'

'Yes, one more,' responded Grimes. 'But Master Penheskin said he would not need my help with it for the barge was fully manned and carried only kegs of ale for the Bishop's cellars. So I left him. When I returned yesterday I found no sign of him so I made enquiries at the local tavern where he often drank, but none had seen him.'

'You did not think to enquire at his home?'

'Not yesterday for there were a couple of landings to be dealt with. I was going to see the comptroller of the Bishop's estate this morning, for he is the ultimate authority over landings on these particular wharves.'

'And who might that be?' The constable was always confused by the plethora of offices within the Bishop's household. He knew only the captain of the household guard, Sir Edward Pollard, for he had previous business acquaintanceship with him.

'Do you not know Dean Speakwell.'

'I know him not.'

'He is not one that you would really get to know. An austere, unfriendly pastor who would not stand out in a group of Puritans. Truly, I think he disapproves even of the Bishop and the revelries that His Grace holds here from time to time.'

'So if Dean Speakwell was the ultimate authority of the wharf, being of the Bishop's household, he might have been here to receive the kegs of ale. He could have seen Master Penheskin that evening?'

Grimes shrugged. 'I would imagine it so. The barge would have been late in unloading, so done by torchlight. I am sure Dean Speakwell would have been anxious at the lateness. I would say . . .' Grimes halted, staring over Master Drew's shoulder. 'Well – speak of the devil . . . forgive any blasphemy, Master Constable, but here is Dean Speakwell approaching.'

The constable turned and hailed the cleric, who seemed to scowl as he came towards them.

'Somethings ails you, Master Constable?' The constable may not have known the dean, but the man seemed to know him. The high-pitched, accusatory voice carried a querulous tone of authority. Jack Grimes's description seemed apt, for the dean was a tall, thin, white-faced man whose countenance exuded none of the joys of life. He was downright ugly with thin bloodless lips and ice-cold eyes. His features seemed set in a permanent expression of gloom. The dour expression was firm set and withal totally disapproving.

'Your overseer, Master Penheskin, has been brought lifeless out of the river. I have enquiries to make.'

Dean Speakwell sniffed disdainfully.

'I know nothing of it, except I know he has been absent from his work for a full day and I must now find a replacement for him.'

'I would enquire when you last saw him?'

'He was one of the workers here. I encountered him whenever I came to these docks.'

'By your leave, that is not what I asked.' The constable was not a man to be intimidated by rank or office. 'Did you not receive a cargo on this wharf the night before last? I am told it was a barge carrying goods for His Grace's household.'

The dean made a strange dismissive motion with his hand.

'And so?'

'So Master Penheskin, as overseer, must have been here also.'

'He was not. So I had to receive the cargo myself. There were some kegs which the watermen unloaded and I had to show them along the alley to His Grace's house. Penheskin did not appear and now business has withheld me from coming here before today to dismiss him from working for me.'

The constable realised that there was little further information he could extract from the curt-mannered comptroller of His Grace's household. So he thanked the dean and turned to make his way through the grounds of St Saviour's. There were a few workers from the church estate and the various clerical buildings who recognised the constable as he strode by and they politely bade him a good day or saluted him as was their wont.

Master Drew left the ecclesiastical grounds and joined the main street of the borough at the start of the great road that led from London Bridge and across the hills of Kent to Canterbury; along the route that pilgrims once took and still did. He passed St Thomas's with its renovated work on the former Augustinian infirmary. It had been closed during the Reformation, but recently allowed to re-open by royal charter as a Church of England hospital.

So, by easy walking, he approached the George inn. At the inn, he found a potman, lazily sunning himself before the entrance to the courtyard, sucking on a foul-smelling pipe. The new whim of tobacco was a habit Master Drew disapproved of, not only because he found the odours distasteful, but because he was cognisant of personal hygiene, having come to the area when yet another pestilence was devastating London.

'Business must be good, for I hear that weed fetches more than two pennies a pound,' he greeted the potman.

'I doubt the Scots King will be hurrying to declare it illegal with all the revenues he personally extracts from its importation and sale,' returned the potman without stirring from his seat. It was not many years since James of Scotland had arrived in London to be crowned King of England. But many disgruntled folk still called him the Scots King. Indeed, antagonism was so widespread that when the King's ministers proposed that the parliaments of England and Scotland should be joined together, which was the new King's dearest wish, the English Parliament had totally rejected the idea. They had no wish to see England and Scotland united in one state.

'I will not debate with you,' the constable replied in an easy fashion. 'But I will ask some information. Can you tell me where I might find Mistress Penheskin?'

The man pointed to a dark alley nearby leading into a warren of misshapen, decaying tenement buildings.

'She be up along,' he grunted. 'First stair you come to, just follow the stench of stale ale and beer.' He paused before adding an afterthought in deference to the quality of the clothing that the constable was wearing. 'Take good care on the stair lest they be rotten and do you a mischief.'

Master Drew was tempted to add that the entire confusion of old tenements were so rotten and they had best be disassembled and burnt. But he said nothing. With a gruff word of thanks, he turned and had walked a few paces when he heard the sound of a coach rattling with iron-shod wheels over the stones of the main street. He halted and turned towards the sound as the noise of wheels and the ringing metal of the horses hooves caused all other sounds to fade.

The constable watched as a coach and four careened into sight around a slight bend in the road. He took in the driver and postilion and four outriders, who were clearly some kind of élite guard. On the west side of the street were small lanes which led into the northern entrance of Winchester Palace. It was clear that the driver of the vehicle was slowing his team to make the turn in that direction, for already the leading guards had made the turn. The coach swung dangerously and for a moment or two the constable thought it would surely overturn, balancing for those moments on two wheels. However, the driver quickly righted it and it swerved past the constable and down the lane.

As it did so, the constable noticed two things. The first was that the blinds were drawn securely in the interior of the coach, masking the passengers. The second was a glimpse of the arms painted in bright yellow and blue on the door of the carriage. The constable had sometimes made the trip north of the river to the Abbey of Westminster and he was surprised when he recognised the escutcheon. These were the arms of Richard Bancroft, Archbishop of Canterbury.

For a few moments Master Drew stood gazing thoughtfully after the disappearing coach. He wondered whether, should the coach truly contain the Archbishop, it had anything to do with the arrival of the mysterious party of clerical scholars that His Grace was entertaining. Then he shrugged and went in search of Mistress Penheskin.

He found her oblivious to the world in a snoring, drunk stupor, still clutching an empty black bottle in one hand. Master Drew sniffed at it and noted with disapproval that it had been a bottle of Sack, the sweet wine from Spain. He knew it would cost twelve times more than a good English brewed ale. He was even more disapproving as he gazed at the person who lay in a similar stupefied coma beside her. He had often seen Master Redweard's son, the wherryman. It was no use expecting any coherent information from either the woman or her lover for many hours, even if they had any to give. He decided to allow them more time to sleep off the drink before rousing them.

On retreating to the main street he almost collided with a tall man in his mid-twenties, with an abundance of ginger hair, who

189

was looking, head down, intently at some papers in his hand. The constable deftly moved aside and caught hold of the young man by the arm.

'Well met, Master Fletcher. What brings you slumming south of the river?'

The young man gathered his wits, recognised the constable and gave a cheery grin.

'Well met, indeed, my literate constable.' It was well known that Master Drew was an eager attender at the playhouses, and had even been known to frequent the Blackfriars Playhouse on the northern side of the bridge. 'Buy me a noggin of ale in yonder George and you shall have the tale of my coming hither.'

The constable smiled thinly. 'I probably have it already but, for friendship sake, and the gift of a seat in whatever playhouse you are going to perform the play whose script I see gripped in your hand, you shall have your mead.'

Master Fletcher roared with laughter. 'Swop me bob! But you have a sharp eye, Master Drew. Indeed, this is why I have come to your nest of warblers who strut the stages here and claim to be actors. I have a new play which I wrote in collaboration with Master Beaumont, we have entitled it *Cupid's Revenge* and I am in search of a new theatre in which to launch it. Our play *The Woman Hater* has had short success, but its text will soon be printed by Master Hodgets in St Paul's Yard. So I am hither bound to consult with Master Falconer, who has some influence among the playhouses here. But, come, a libation first.'

Master Falconer was a printer and bookseller whose premises lay but a few steps away on St Margaret's Hill.

They repaired into the George and found a snug while the

same potman who had greeted the constable earlier hurried forward, this time with due deference, to attend them.

'So the names of John Fletcher and Francis Beaumont are gaining reputation?' Master Drew observed as they sipped their ale.

'One day it will be just plain John Fletcher who will be delighting the crowds. I have sworn it, just to spite the shade of my father.'

Wisely, Master Drew made no comment, for he knew Fletcher's father had been Bishop of London and, although it was now a decade since his death, Bishop Fletcher had a reputation for the severity of his disapproval of actors and entertainers. As Dean of Peterborough's cathedral, he had been on the scaffold at the execution of the Queen of Scots and presided over her funeral. It was while thinking of Master Fletcher's father, the Bishop, that another thought came to the constable.

'It is a coincidence that I have just seen the coach of the prelate who succeeded your father as Bishop of London.'

The young playwright smiled wanly. 'You mean Bancroft, who is now elevated to Archbishop of Canterbury?'

'The Archbishop's coach was driving into Winchester Palace as if an army of heretics were after him,' the constable agreed. 'I wonder if something is afoot? Just earlier this morning I had intelligence that nearly a dozen venerable scholastics of the church were also in residence with the Bishop of Winchester as host. Now the Archbishop himself arrives.'

To the constable's surprise, Master Fletcher simply shrugged without interest.

'It will probably be a meeting of the First Westminster Committee,' he replied in an offhand tone.

'What say you?' Master Drew demanded in surprise. 'Why, Westminster Committee was the very name I heard tell.'

'Come, come, Master Constable,' chided his playwright friend. 'It is but three years since the Hampton Court Conference when the Scottish King went back on all the things that he promised, affecting the affairs of the Reformed Church.'

The constable gave a quick, nervous glance around to ensure no one had overheard the remark.

'I pray you modulate your tone, Master Fletcher. As you said, we continue to live in difficult times. Tell me, and softly, what it is you mean?'

'Oh, 'tis history now. Did not the Scots King promise the Earl of Northumberland that, once he was King of England, he would not pursue the persecutions of Papists, Puritans nor Presbyterians? But, by accepting the position of King of England, he accepted that he and none other was Supreme Head of the Church, which he would govern through his bishops as temporal princes as well as spiritual? Certainly, he went back on his word at Hampton Court, for all Papist priests were expelled from the country, then all Puritans were dismissed from any living within the Anglican Church. God knows what he has in store for the Presbyterians. At this time, all are treated the same unless they swear the Oath of Allegiance to him as Supreme Head of the Church of England. That is no more than the truth.'

'Oft-times, it is diplomatic not to mention the truth,' pointed out the constable softly. 'So what of this Westminster Committee and how do you know of it?'

'I confess that, as son of my late father, the Bishop, I grew up with the offspring of ecclesiastics; break bread and exchange gossip with them. I still hear many things.'

'And so?'

'And so, my literate constable, you should know one of the King's decrees that the Hampton Court Conference undertook was to order the production of a new translation of the New and Old Testaments. The King so ordered it done to replace the previous English translations, for he claims they are all mightily flawed.'

Master Drew closed his eyes and uttered a deep sigh as he remembered.

'It was ordered that the best scholars of the church be formed into committees.'

Master Fletcher smiled. 'Indeed, forty-nine scholars all told. There be two committees in Westminster, two in Cambridge and two in Oxford. Bishop Lancelot Andrews, the Bishop of Winchester, was made overseer of the first Westminster Committee. There are about ten scholars in all who every now and then meet at council to discuss their work. They are supposed to be excellent scholars, claiming intimacy not just with Greek and Latin but with Arabic and Hebrew.'

'And the Archbishop of Canterbury?'

'His Grace was named Chief Overseer of the entire project. He presides over all six committees.'

'Then, this Westminster Committee must be meeting here now,' murmured the constable thoughtfully.

'It is logical. Let us hope that among these scholastic prelates there be some with a good turn of English phrase in their translations, for I do fear that some of their discourses, or those that I have read, are badly wanting in drama, let alone in metre and rhyme. Why, I even heard they are but poor lexicographers in English and would be better employing the likes of Master Shakespeare or Jonson or some other popular wordsmiths. Ah, this reminds me of my immediate endeavours. I must away to St Margaret's Hill to Master Falconer.'

'I'll walk a way with you as his shop is on my path back to Bankside,' the constable decided.

Some interest caused Master Drew to accompany his friend within the shop of the bookseller and printer. Perhaps it was the sight of some Bibles arranged for sale therein. Master Falconer was younger than the constable had expected. A youth scarcely come from university but with sound knowledge and a talent for the art of setting matter in type or making woodcuts, however, he employed others in this field and took it upon himself to represent such matters as sales. He welcomed them both and Master Fletcher acceded to the constable to make his enquiry first.

'When this new translation of the Bible is ready, I suppose your trade will be eager to put forward submissions to acquire the task of setting it up in print for the sale of such a work?' the constable had opened his question.

Master Falconer shook his head with a rueful smile. 'Not so, as Robert Barker in St Paul's Yard has already made supplication to His Majesty to be allowed that concession. As for me, I shall carry on with selling the Bishop's Bible. It is still popular.'

'Isn't there danger in that? It is the Bible admired by ardent Protestants and Puritans alike and therefore disliked by King James.'

'There is no pleasing the minds of people in these tempestuous times,' interposed Master Fletcher. 'However, it is the very Bible that the King ordered his translators to be guided by.'

'But it will surely conflict with the new version when it appears?'

'Something of truth in that,' agreed the bookseller. 'Now no one is allowed to see or possess the English translation done at Rheims-Douai, it being ascribed as Papist. Aye, and some early attempts such as Coverdale's New Testament are claimed as being heretical. I tell you, good gentlemen, being a bookseller and printer is to have one faction or another screaming for your blood and preparing a stake for your public burning. Personally, I do not want to make an acquaintance of any scaffold because I sold the wrong book. We will see what comes of the new translation, if it is allowed to emerge, and I shall be guided by the law and not religion.'

'Do you say there are factions who would be determined enough to see this new translation destroyed before it appears?' the constable asked in a thoughtful tone.

'That same determination caused the Papist Robert Catesby to attempt to blow up King and Parliament, when King James went back on his word not to persecute them further.'

Master Fletcher smiled thinly. 'And Puritans and Protestants are now thrown from their livings and restricted in their rights. Maybe it might put them at common cause with Papists against this new Church of England as blessed by King James as Supreme Head?'

Master Falconer grimaced in agreement. 'I would not go so far as to say Papists would agree a common cause with the Puritans and Protestants, or any other who claim to be dissenters from the

Church of England. I only say that Puritans and Protestants would fain keep to the Bishop's Bible. As to the Papists, they would keep to their Douai Bible. Both would wish ill luck to the King's translators as they pursue their tasks.'

A few moments later Master Drew was striding rapidly down the hill in the direction of Winchester Palace, his mind suddenly filled with the horror of an idea that had begun to coalesce in his mind based on the information he had heard. The word 'kegs' kept filling his mind and the reference to Catesby's plot. Had not Catesby been heir to a knighthood, lineal descendant of Richard III's most influential chancellor and Speaker of the Commons? If he had chosen to rebel then . . . Things were forming a frightening picture in Master Drew's mind.

At the palace gates he demanded to see his acquaintance, Sir Edward Pollard, steward of the Bishop's household, as well as commander of the Troop of Gentlemen, who were the guards responsible for the security of His Grace, the Bishop. Master Drew, being no stranger to Sir Edward, found little difficulty in being shown to his chamber and cutting short the pleasantries of greeting.

'I am much concerned, Sir Edward. I believe there are great dangers here. If it please you, allow me to put some questions directly before I explain.'

Sir Edward stared in surprise without speaking, but then motioned the constable to proceed.

'It is my understanding that a gathering of theological scholars are meeting here; scholars known as the Westminster Committee.'

'Little secret in that,' Sir Edward replied. 'His Grace, Bishop Lancelot Andrews, is the leader of this group.'

'The group being part of those now undertaking the commission of His Majesty, to devise a new translation of the Holy Bible?'

'That is so.'

'His Grace, the Archbishop of Canterbury, Bishop Bancroft, has but recently arrived here. What role does he play in this?'

'As might be expected, he is the Chief Overseer of the project. How did you know that the Archbishop was here?'

'I chanced to see his coach arriving. This committee, the Archbishop and His Grace of Winchester, are all met together here deliberating on the task of this commission?'

'They are. But they are only one of the committees who have undertaken this onerous task of a new translation. There are committees at Oxford and at Cambridge as well as here. In fact, the Archbishop proceeds tomorrow to Oxford after his business is finished here. Now what ails you that you appear so perturbed, Master Constable?'

'There are many factions within the country who would not like to see this Bible that King James has commissioned coming to fruition?'

'Disagreements about translation have existed as long as Eusebius of Stridon was commissioned by Pope Damasus to select, translate into Latin, having construed from Greek and Hebrew, the first texts we call the Great Book, over twelve centuries ago.' Sir Edward, who liked to think himself a scholar, smiled.

'But the matter is taken seriously?'

Sir Edward shrugged. 'There is no debating that point, Master Drew. The Papists have their own New Testament, produced in English at the so-called English College of Douai in Rheims in France. They boast that soon they will have the Old Testament printed and available to act as a Papist rival to this proposed version.'

'I also hear that the Puritans and other extreme Protestants and Dissenters are not supportive of the King's commission to present a new Bible in English?' pressed the constable.

Sir Edward sighed and nodded. 'Again, you are well informed. The last English translation of the Holy Bible is much favoured by those factions and they feel that His Majesty will compromise it, with an express order to leave, in this new work, many things to appease the Papists. The King is still suspect, bearing in mind his mother, Mary, the Scottish Queen, was an ardent Papist. These Dissenters say the new Bible will support the divine right of kings, and will condone the state politic by which His Majesty remains Supreme Head of the Church to rule it through his bishops as temporal princes as well as lords spiritual. So they are as much against the rejection of what is called the Bishop's Bible as the Papists are against the rejection of their Douai Bible.'

'So an attack might come from anywhere,' the constable muttered. 'We have been assured that after the recent public executions, the Papists are quiet. Do we still need fear them?'

Sir Edward looked surprised.

'After Catesby's failure to blow up His Majesty and Parliament two years ago, and the fierce resolve with which that plot was dealt with, I believe the Papists have been tranquil. Even the Pope condemned the plot and ordered all Papists in the country to remain subdued in obedience to the laws of the kingdom. On the other hand, I hear many Puritans are organising passage on ships to the New World for fear they will be next to feel the King's anger at their non-conformity.'

'And the Puritans have no such central authority like the Papists,' Master Drew observed thoughtfully. 'Their philosophy is to meet in isolated groups with no ordained ministers to instruct them . . .' The constable hesitated. 'Did you say the Archbishop was here just for this one committee meeting?'

'He journeys on to Oxford tomorrow morning.'

'Tomorrow?' The constable was suddenly concerned. 'Then he is only here today with this Westminster Committee?'

'That is so. In fact, the meeting is about to convene momentarily so it may finish early to allow the Archbishop to partake of a meal and entertainment before he continues on his journey.'

Master Drew was suddenly cold. 'The meeting is about to take place now? Where is the meeting taking place?'

'They are using the banqueting room on the lower floor.'

'What stands under that room?'

Sir Edward stared at him.

'Come on, good sir,' snapped the constable. 'Perhaps the hour-glass has already run its course.'

'Underneath are only the cellars for the purpose of storing wines and beers.'

'Is it accessible from the docks?'

'All the cellars are accessible by divers passages. But what are you saying?'

'Show me the quickest way to those cellars. Gather some of your guards to accompany us.' The constable's voice had risen sharply and he was already starting for the door.

Moments later, Master Drew and Sir Edward had descended into the cellars and were proceeding along a series of tunnels at the head of four armed members of the guards, each carrying the latest flintlock pistols. They came through an arch into a large cellar and the first thing Master Drew saw was the stack of kegs almost forming a pyramid in the centre. The next was the figures of a burly man on his knees together with the tall figure of Dean Speakwell trying to adjust one of the open kegs. A lantern stood nearby.

It happened quickly. Seeing the emergence of the guards, Dean Speakwell threw himself towards the lantern with the obvious intent to smash it against the kegs. There was a roar, a flash and an acrid smell of smoke from one of the flintlock pistols held by a guard that caused the burly man to fly backwards, blood streaming from his head. A second, almost simultaneous, blast caused Dean Speakwell to spin round, the lantern flying from his hand. Thankfully it flew and shattered on the stone slabs of the cellar some way from the kegs and was quickly extinguished.

Dean Speakwell, in spite of his shattered, bloody shoulder, had drawn a dagger with his other hand, but it was quickly knocked from his grasp by another of the guards who then secured him.

'Have good cheer, Dean Speakwell.' Sir Edward was smiling grimly as he moved forward. 'We have no intention of allowing you to harm yourself, or to leap from the scaffold to encompass your own death as Master Fawkes did. You shall have the full measure of your sentence and be hanged, drawn and quartered as other Papist conspirators.'

Dean Speakwell glowered at him.

'The Devil and all his crew take you. You think I am a Papist? Why, you and that damned Scots King who dares sit on the throne of a Protestant country . . . You are all in Rome's thrall. What is he who sits on the throne but the son of a Papist whore!'

Sir Edward was bewildered but the constable intervened grimly.

'The dean here is one of those puritanical Protestants who believes that the Church of England is rejecting all the Protestant reforms which were introduced by our monarchs Henry, Edward and Elizabeth. Is it not so?'

'The proof is with those knaves now sitting above here,' snarled the dean. 'Lickspittles who will rewrite our good Protestant Bible, changing the truth of the scripture. It will be lost once this Scottish King's work becomes our authority.'

'Ah,' Sir Edward sighed, 'you are of those Dissenters who use the motto *sola scriptura, sola fide.*'

'Scripture alone is the justification for the Faith. The scriptures are the infallible source of authority for the Faith, and to change them is heretical. Those that intend to do so must be destroyed before they contaminate the people. Was not the Bishop's Bible authorised to be used in all parishes and cathedrals but our good Church of England? Was it not authorised forty years ago to be the only scripture to be read in all the churches of England?'

'You will have your chance to argue that before a justice,' Sir Edward replied dryly. 'But it is not a theological discussion which is the ultimate purpose of the criminal charge you face.' He turned to Master Drew. 'I expect you have some explanation of how you came to thwart this plot?'

Master Drew sought to explain in a few words.

'Master Penheskin was by himself on the dock that night when the barge arrived carrying the kegs of gunpowder. He was told they were but kegs of ale for His Grace's cellars. As comptroller of the palace, Dean Speakwell was there to observe the unloading. Penheskin apparently became suspicious. Maybe one of the kegs was knocked and spilt out some of its content. He scooped up a handful of gunpowder, perhaps recognising the black powder for what it was. He put the powder in his purse as evidence. I believe he then hurried to you, Dean Speakwell, with his suspicion, little realising that you were the leader of this plot. You or your confederates knocked him over the head and killed him. He was thrown in the river. The gunpowder was still in his purse, though turned to black liquid by the river. A mistake that you or your men did not search him before throwing his body into the river. You left the gunpowder and some coins in his purse, showing that his death was not the work of footpads.'

On Sir Edward's instructions, the guards dragged the wounded dean from the cellars to temporary accommodation in the Clink. Sir Edward gave instructions to others to start dismantling the kegs and reload them on a barge at the docks.

The constable stayed with him to observe this procedure, watching as the last of the kegs of black powder were placed safely aboard. Sir Edward had put one of his lieutenants in charge with instruction to bring the kegs to the captain of the arsenal at the Tower on the north side of the Thames. They watched the barge pull away and turn between the piers of London Bridge before becoming lost to sight.

The constable finally turned to his companion with a shake of his head in an expression of incomprehension.

'Why are people so afraid of words that they would blow up their fellows or eradicate them in other violent ways?'

Sir Edward regarded the constable indulgently. 'You surprise me, Master Drew, for I am told you are an enthusiastic follower at the various playhouses. You must know the value of words which can bestir all manner of emotions. Words are the most dangerous of weapons.'

'Then, as Master Shakespeare says in his play about Henry Fifth – men of few words are the best of men,' he replied cynically.

'A good observation but, then, it is impossible for all to achieve becoming the best of men. Now, my friend. Will you join me in a glass of Sack, which is well deserved and perhaps necessary since we must report this matter to His Grace?'

'I would not protest that invitation,' the constable replied gravely.

Sir Edward took his arm in friendly fashion, turning back to Winchester Palace and remarking with a slightly mocking tone: 'And now go we in content.'

Here's Ado to Lock Up Honesty

Here's ado
To lock up honesty . . .

A Winter's Tale, Act II, Scene ii
William Shakespeare

Master Hardy Drew, Constable of the Bankside Watch, descended the stairs from the rooms he rented on the upper floor of the Pilgrim's Wink tavern, and entered the tap room where he usually took his breakfast. There were few other people there, some nodded to him in greeting, but most were intent on individual, animated conversations. They spoke low and hurriedly, stumbling over words so that few sentences were clear to him. He was only able to discern some event had occurred in the night. He was about to intervene with a question when Mistress Cuttle, the hostess, came bustling in bearing his small tankard of cider, with fresh baked bread, cold sausage and cheese.

'Lor' a-mussy! Master Constable, here's ado,' she declared, setting down the breakfast tray before him. She was obviously as excited as her customers.

He regarded her with curiosity. 'It would seem some unusual event has occurred to inspire this excitement?'

'Why, did you not bestir yourself during this night amidst such rowdy goings-on?'

Master Drew smiled with a dry sense of humour. 'That I did not, for I was late abed after two days scarce shutting my eyes. I would not have been disturbed had the armies of the King of Spain marched across London Bridge in battle order.'

It was true that during the last two days he had been instructed to go into London and take charge of a prisoner in Newgate Jail but having arrived there he had found that his prisoner, by means of a bribe, had transferred himself to the Fleet Prison on the eastern bank of the Fleet River. Its governor, Thomas Babington, ran a liberal regime for any who could pay. It was said that the Fleet charged the highest fees of any prison so that even turnkeys were paid well by the prisoners for just unlocking the cell doors. The Fleet had once been a cruel place and during its five-hundred-year history it was where the Star Chamber sent its condemned to await their fate. The confusion of prisons had forced the constable to spend a sleepless night in the city before identifying his prisoner and transporting him back across London Bridge to Southwark and the mercies of the Clink by the Bankside before Master Drew finally returned, exhausted but thankful, to his own lodgings at the Pilgrim's Wink in Pepper Steet.

'Then you have not heard that the house of Sir Hugh Rowse has been left a smoking ruin and himself found a corpse within it?'

The constable's eyes widened a little.

'The house of the custodian of Marshalsea Prison?' He did not need to ask the question as Sir Hugh was well known.

'Aye, Master Constable. Sir Hugh's house in Flying Pan Alley went up in flames and is but a charred cinder this morning.'

'I know it,' Master Drew replied thoughtfully. There was nothing unusual in the frequency of fires among the dark alleys and courtyards of Southwark with their wooden houses. But he had thought Sir Hugh's house was of more quality with much stonework and its own well. 'Did the watermen not rally to help douse the flames?'

The only means of fighting fires were with gangs of watermen, those who made their living from the coasts on the river, who would volunteer for payments. Usually, the only method of dousing the flames was carrying buckets of water from the river or a nearby stream. But Sir Hugh had a well. He was one of the richer inhabitants, such as the Bishop of Winchester, who had actually bought some hand-held pumps such as those that had been used in Swabia and Bavaria since the previous century. But they were not as effective as a bucket of water accurately thrown.

Thinking on the matter, the constable uttered a silent prayer of gratitude that Marshalsea Prison was not in his jurisdiction. Technically it was part of the Courts of Justice of the royal household and its governance came under a Knight Marshal. In reality the prison was leased to governors who ran the prison for profit, for any comfort could be bought for a price. These governors, in turn, granted the tenure to what they termed as custodians or keepers. Master Hardy could remember that Sir Thomas Way had been a keeper for forty years, and when he died ten years ago it passed to Sir Edmund Verney's family, who hired Sir Hugh Rowse to run it.

'Will you not be going there, Master Constable?' asked Mistress Cuttle.

'I shall take a walk to view the damage but I am only

Constable of the Bankside and what happens at Marshalsea is looked after by the justice appointed by His Majesty's household,' he explained.

Having finished his breakfast, Master Drew made his way southerly along the Bridge Road. This was the main road leading off London Bridge, up the high street of Southwark, and past St Mary Overy and the grim edifice of the Marshalsea Prison itself. He joined the groups of curious onlookers heading down the narrow streets that led to Frying Pan Alley, where the crowds had gathered to stare at the still smoking blackened ruins of what had once been Sir Hugh's house.

He had no sooner halted on the edge of the crowd than a voice hailed him.

'Master Drew! 'Ods bud! Methought 'twas you.'

The constable turned to see a small coach with a single pony in its shafts, drawn up behind him. It was of the new fashion from France called a *fiacre*, which was becoming popular in the city. The carriages were already being made by a workshop in Hackney, north of the city. An elderly man, richly attired, was leaning from it and beckoning Master Drew to come forward.

Master Drew recognised William Mayhew who had been elected to Parliament for the borough some years before. He was a wealthy man, owning two breweries in the area and stables for dray horses. The constable knew well that he was a justice and recalled that Master Mayhew, with his fellow member of Parliament for the borough, Sir William Smith, had governance over Marshalsea.

'Give you good day, your honour,' Master Drew greeted respectfully.

Master Mayhew appeared relieved to see him.

'Can you spare me some of your time, Master Constable?'

Master Drew was surprised for a moment. 'I can,' he replied, hesitantly.

'Then if it please you, I would be obliged if you would follow me to my house in Three Crown Court.'

The place was but a short distance away. The constable knew it contained several fine houses of which Master Mayhew kept one as his house in the area.

'Lead on and I shall follow,' replied Master Drew, realising the small carriage was barely large enough to take the burly figure of the justice and his driver. The carriage could barely move at a walking pace through the narrow, crowded streets, so he had no difficulty in keeping pace with it. He found himself smiling to himself as he recalled that Mayhew was one of the members of Parliament who had supported the bill to restrain the excessive construction and use of coaches in the city, claiming that the use of such vehicles to cross the Bridge between the City and South-wark was taking the bread out of the mouths of the Thames watermen who earned their livelihoods ferrying passengers to and fro across the river.

Once at his house, Mayhew led the way into his study, indicated the constable should seat himself, and ordered one of his servants to bring glasses of Malmsey as refreshment.

'I will come straight to the point, Master Constable. You have seen the condition of Sir Hugh's house and doubtless heard that he was found dead within the ruins?'

'I heard gossip on the street. A terrible way to meet one's death.'

'The gossip is only partially correct. You know that he was custodian of Marshalsea Prison?'

'I know it, your honour.' The constable frowned at the comment which preceded the question.

'I am, as you may know, appointed by the King and Parliament to be part of a commission to consider the reforms of Marshalsea together with my good friend and fellow member Sir William Smith.'

Master Drew inclined his head but waited quietly for Master Mayhew to continue.

'To cut to the chase, I have a problem,' sighed the justice. 'You will know that Master Tucker is the constable of this area. Master Tucker is suffering from an ague; a feverish condition which renders him unfit for the activities of his office. I lack someone to take charge of the matter of this fire.'

Master Drew was puzzled.

'But houses burn down frequently among the small alleys of this place. The only matter of disquiet is that Sir Hugh was caught in the blaze and perished. I would have thought the deputy custodian of Marshalsea has enough knowledge to submit a report on the matter.'

Master Mayhew gave a low expulsion of breath as if the troubles of the world were suddenly upon him.

'Unfortunately, it is not so simple. When the remains of Sir Hugh were taken from the burnt building, the mortician alleged that Sir Hugh was already dead when the fire started. Furthermore, it has been charged that he was murdered.'

Master Drew tried not to show his surprise. 'How came the mortician by such a conclusion?'

The justice peered among the papers on his desk and drew one forth.

'I have his deposition here.' He wrinkled his nose in distaste. 'Sir Hugh's body was not entirely consumed in the conflagration. A section was untouched, that being the area above the heart and the front of the neck. From the wounds there, Master Sportle – that's the mortician – took oath that Sir Hugh was thrice stabbed to the heart and then his throat cut.'

Master Drew pursed his lips thoughtfully. 'So many wounds? It sounds like an attack conjured from personal malevolence. But, it occurs to me, a man of Sir Hugh's standing might have several implacable enemies.'

'True enough. But he was said to be alone in his house except for three servants.'

'Three? A man of such standing?'

'Ah, just so. He had remained a few days at his town house here with, as you remark, only a few servants to attend his wants. His main household had already repaired to his country estate in Luddesdowne where Sir Hugh had been shortly to journey. The few servants who remained here were to look after the town house while he was away. The servants escaped the inferno unscathed. Yet Sir Hugh died. I have had the servants taken as suspects to the King's Bench Prison in the High Street to await questioning.'

The constable shook his head. 'As the custodian of Marshalsea, Sir Hugh would not be lacking in enemies,' he pointed out. 'Are there good grounds for the suspicion to fall on his servants?'

'That is just it. Two of the servants claimed to be at the Swan playhouse when the fire broke out and did not return until it was

over. Sir Hugh was alone in the house with but one servant and
she is now the prime suspect, having left the house unharmed at
the time of the fire. Of course, she denies the deed most vehemently and sought sanctuary at St George's Church.'

Master Drew felt unease about the matter.

'Why cannot Sir Hugh's deputy custodian take charge of this
affair? It would appear a straightforward inquiry.'

'For these reasons: the deputy custodian, Master Lupton, has
a record of not being in accord with Sir Hugh on matters of the
prison regime. It was known he coveted Sir Hugh's position and
once challenged him to a duel.'

Master Drew suppressed a snort.

'The nobility, and those who would try to imitate them out of
self-conceit, are a set of ill-informed buffoons. Even the King has
ordered that those taking part in duels should be tried by the
Court of the Star Chamber, and I know not how many cases have
been heard by the Solicitor General since the order was made.
The trouble is, there are folk who take duelling lightly, not thinking to fight to kill but merely to prick their opponent with a
sword point to restore their honour.'

Master Mayhew, who had no title nor seemed to want reward
for his public service, did not seem affronted by the constable's
views.

'Having consulted with Sir William Smith,' he went on, 'we
have both decided it needed someone learned in such matters as
ferreting the truth from unwilling lips to conduct this investigation. When I saw you, having realised Constable Tucker had
betaken himself to his bed with fever, I believed my prayer
answered. So I entreat you, Master Drew, will you undertake this

211

inquiry to ensure all is done legally? What say you to two crowns as a fee for what may be half a day's work?'

The constable did not need time to think because a refusal to the justice would be going against one of the most powerful men in the borough, titled or untitled. Master Mayhew gave a short sigh of relief at Master Drew's acceptance of the case.

'You tell me that the servants of Sir Hugh's household are now in the King's Bench Prison?' said the constable.

'I gave orders for the steward and cook to be held at the Court of the King's Bench to await your examination,' he said. 'The rector of St George's came this morning about the third servant who had sought refuge with him. I ordered him to take her there so that she was also detained to await your pleasure.'

He looked at his desk and produced another piece of paper. 'This is a list of their names to guide you.'

'Then the only thing it needs,' the constable said, 'this being not my jurisdiction, is a warrant signed and sealed by your honour, giving me authorisation to carry out this examination.'

The provision of the warrant was forthcoming in a matter of minutes, and the constable found himself striding from Three Crown Court, out through the narrow streets onto the wider stretch of the High Street before turning down towards the Bridge, where the small prison had its main entrance.

Master Drew approved that the small independent prison of the King's Bench, lying next to Marshalsea, was an appropriate place to hold the suspects. It had been built a decade after the bigger prisoner and held little more than seventy male and female inmates. In previous years, it had held its share of those whose bad fortune it was to be following the wrong religion of the day, and who would be incarcerated there before being taken across the river to be burnt at the stake in Smithfield. But now its inhabitants were only debtors.

The turnkey, a gap-toothed, stubble-haired man of indiscernible age, but badly in need of a wash and better clothing, knuckled his fist to his forehead as Master Drew demanded entrance. The man recognised the constable while Master Drew searched his memory for the turnkey's name. Caleb Dobbs had been senior turnkey at the prison for some years. The constable thought it prudent to hold out his warrant for inspection. Dobbs peered forward to examine the red wax seal on the warrant, for he could barely read and the flowery signature of Master Mayhew would have been beyond his comprehension.

'How can I be of service, Master Constable? Give me your instruction,' the turnkey intoned, handing back the warrant.

'I am here to question the household servants of Sir Hugh Rowse. They are to be separated, and I need a small room in which to examine them individually.'

The turnkey scratched his ear as if trying to encourage some thought.

''Tis difficult, master, as we are overcrowded and wanting in room. I was forced to put them all into one room already and, I do confess, though they be only two women and one old man, to hear them shout, each intent in denouncing the other, you would think a riot were taking place. In fact, I was just about to concede to Master Lupton's suggestion.'

'What suggestion did the deputy custodian of Marshalsea make?'

'That he take one of the prisoners to hold at Marshalsea. Needless to say, he chose the young girl.' The turnkey gave a lewd grin. Master Drew did not bother to comment.

'I could use a room in the nearby Angel Tavern to carry out my investigations,' he mused. 'We will discuss where they will be held after my interrogation. No one is to be moved until I have done so. Of course, this would involve transporting them under guard individually there and back as I need.'

The Angel Tavern was but a few steps away in Foul Street. The turnkey frowned.

'That might be difficult, Master Drew.'

The constable thought for a few moments. 'I will require the services of one or two men to escort the prisoners. It should not be arduous. I shall pay each man a groat for their service.'

The turnkey's face brightened suddenly; a speculative expression crossed his coarse features. 'For two silver groats, master, I will do the service myself.'

'What of your duties here?' enquired the constable.

'For two groats I can take care of it,' the turnkey grinned. 'I shall bring the prisoners one by one as you want while my assistant takes charge here.'

After the arrangement was made, Master Drew exited the King's Bench with the turnkey, and turned immediately into Foul Lane where the old tavern stood. Having secured the use of a room for the interrogations, the turnkey was despatched to bring the first of the servants that had been held for questioning.

Master Drew had chosen to question the male prisoner first. He was named as Jacob Falstone on the list the justice had handed him. He was a small, elderly man with a shock of white hair and pale blue eyes. He seemed nervous and kept massaging the side of his nose as if it troubled him. Having delivered the man to the constable, Caleb Dodds sat in the tap room with a small beer to await further instructions.

'How long have you been in the service of Sir Hugh?' the constable opened up sharply.

'I entered his service in the year there was all that talk about the late queen marrying the Duke of Anjou, your honour,' the old man said in a tremulous tone, having paused to bring the memory back.

The constable tried to stretch his own memory. 'So you have served him at least five and twenty years?'

'That be so.'

'What do you do as steward for the household?'

'I see the servants have their orders, I await instruction from Sir Hugh, answer the door to his guests and attend the running of the house. I can read, write and add figures, so I keep accounts of his affairs.'

'Tell me of the conditions leading to the fire.' The constable suddenly switched the subject of his questions. It was a trick of his to catch the unwary.

'Conditions, your honour?' The old man was puzzled.

'Tell me what happened yesterday evening, the evening of the conflagration.'

'Sir Hugh was due to go to his country estate on this very day and had already sent most of the household there yesterday morning to await his arrival. We had all made ready. I, with Mistress Diddlebury, who is the cook, and young Mistress Tanner, the chambermaid, were to remain here to take care of the house.'

'Was that normal whenever Sir Hugh went to his country estate?'

'Normal? Ah, Sir Hugh trusted me and Mistress Diddlebury to look after the house when he was not there. We had done so many times before. We have been in his service for many years.'

'And Mistress Tanner?'

A look of disapproval hovered on the man's face. 'She was but new come to his service, your honour. New come to any degree of work, if you ask me. Scarce out of swaddling clothes, in my opinion.'

'Yet you call her Mistress Tanner?'

'I do not doubt that a year ago she would still have been addressed as miss. But, the fashion is, that when a miss comes to adulthood, she must be addressed as mistress. Sir Hugh was particular that proper forms of address be used.'

'She was not liked within the household?' Master Drew quickly caught on to the man's tone of disapproval.

'The household? Well, it is not for me to say. She had disagreements with Mistress Diddlebury.'

'Concerning what?'

'She was young and seems an affliction of the young,' observed the old steward.

'Nothing else in particular?' pressed Master Drew.

'I think the girl's attitude was that she did not respect Mistress Diddlebury's age and service.'

'I hear that she is suspected of setting the fire because she was the only one left alone in the house with Sir Hugh when the fire started. Mistress Diddlebury and you went to a playhouse that night. Is that the basis of your suspicion against the girl?'

216

The old man shook his head. 'I did not make that accusation,' he said after some hesitation. 'However, it is not beyond logic.'

'Then the accusation is made by Mistress Diddlebury?'

'You should get the accusation from her, Master Constable. All I say is that from long association, I have known and respected Mistress Diddlebury's opinions.'

'But opinions are not facts.'

'That is why I ask that you hear from her rather than ask me to repeat her words. There is logic to her argument.'

'A reasonable request. But is it not also a logical suspicion to ask how came, on the very evening before Sir Hugh was about to leave for the country, leaving you and Mistress Diddlebury to look after it, you quit the house to go to a playhouse? Was it not an odd time to leave your master alone in the house to go seeking entertainment?'

'It was Sir Hugh's own wish that we do so.'

'Indeed. So where were you when the fire started?'

'Mistress Diddlebury and I were at the Swan theatre.'

Master Drew frowned. 'The Swan? All right, what was being presented there?'

'A new comedy by Tom Middleton.'

'And its title?'

'*Wit at Secret Weapons.*' The response came back easily enough and the constable, who was a follower of the Bankside playhouses, knew it was one of the presentations at the Swan.

'Do you often go spending a penny on such frivolity? And this is approved of by Sir Hugh on the night he was supposed to leave?'

'Why, bless you, master, it was because he was leaving for his estate at Luddesdowne that it was Sir Hugh himself who gave us the two pennies and a further two pennies to spend on fruit or ale to have while we enjoyed the performance.'

'He seemed a generous master,' the constable remarked in surprise.

'He was that, your honour, to those who served him well.'

'I gather Mistress Tanner did not go to the theatre with you?'

'She did not.'

The constable was not sure if he heard some implication in the old man's tone.

'So, as far as you knew, she remained in the house.'

'As far as we knew, yes; she stayed in the house, alone with Sir Hugh.'

Master Drew frowned. The man did not have to add that remark. As Caleb Dodds said, it was logical, but by commenting on it, the old man seemed to be drawing his suspicion to the constable's attention.

'Very well. When did you return to the house?'

'After the play, we met some friends and retired to a tavern and drank and discoursed before making our way back. Before we reached there we realised that there were alarums. The house was well and truly ablaze. There was no saving it. Some watermen were rushing buckets from a nearby stream but it was soon seen that it was hopeless. The only thing saved was Sir Hugh's horse, which had been tethered in the back, ready for his journey that morning. We tried to discover what had happened. Among those staring at the smoking pile we recognised Master Mayhew, the justice. Then we heard a body had been discovered. The deputy custodian,

Master Lupton, was there and we heard Sir Hugh had perished in the conflagration.

'At first we thought Mistress Tanner must have perished also. But when we were told that only Sir Hugh's body had been found, we realised she had come away safe but was not to be found.'

'So when did you see Mistress Tanner and know her to have escaped the flames?'

'Not until she was put in the cell in the King's Bench to await questioning where we had been taken by Master Lupton. She was brought in later by a young man.'

'A young man? Did you know him?'

'I knew him not.'

'Were you told why you were taken to the King's Bench?'

'When it was told that the body found was that of Sir Hugh, the justice said an investigation had to be made and he ordered Master Lupton to escort us to the prison to be held until we could be questioned and all the details assessed. We were then joined by the girl, apparently someone had caught her.'

The constable called to Turnkey Dodds and dismissed the old man into his charge. 'I will see Mistress Diddlebury next,' he instructed.

When Mistress Mercy Diddlebury was announced, Master Drew immediately rebuked himself for his preconceptions. He usually associated cooks with kindly, motherly women, more on the rotund side than otherwise. Mistress Diddlebury was thin, almost skeletal, with sharp features, a beak of a nose, thin lips, and darting dark eyes that never seemed still. Her head thrust forward from a scrawny neck, baleful and in a manner as if ready

to attack. There was no doubting, from her dark choice of clothing, that she was in service.

Master Drew motioned her to be seated. She sat hesitatingly,
hands clasped before her, only glancing slyly at her inquisitor.

'You have been with Sir Hugh a long time,' he opened pleasantly, for he realised sharpness would only breed sharp replies.

'It was the year that the theatre was opened in Shoreditch, for
it is Shoreditch that I came from,' responded the woman.

'Some thirty years ago?'

'I expect so. I came to join Sir Hugh's house as a maid to his
mother. After her death, I became cook for Sir Hugh.'

'So you and Jacob Falstone had been with Sir Hugh a long
time and, withal, you were good friends?'

'We were servants in the household. We knew our station in
life, constable,' replied the woman testily. 'But we were trusted
enough by Sir Hugh to be able to tend to his house whenever he
withdrew to spend time on his country estate.'

'He was due to ride to Luddesdowne this morning, so I am told.'

'He was.'

'It seems odd, then, that he told you both to leave the house
last evening to go to a playhouse? Why would he do that, leaving
him alone, at a time when your services might be needed?'

The woman sniffed, as if it expressed some deep meaning.

'He was a good master and it was not our place to express a
thought about his decisions,' she eventually said. 'He knew that
after he left the house today, we would have to be there to attend
to all matters until his return. I presume that he released us last
evening as his way of expressing appreciation of our service.'

'Did he make that clear?'

'It was implied but he also said that he had special business to attend to that evening which would keep him occupied late.'

'Was that when he gave you the pennies for your trip to the Swan?'

'No, sir,' she replied at once. 'We were in the kitchen preparing to leave when that . . .' she hesitated, 'when Mistress Tanner entered and handed us the coins.'

'She handed you the coins for the theatre?' Master Drew was surprised.

'She told us that Sir Hugh had forgotten to give them to us and he told her to take the coins to us. In fact, the coins were wrapped in a bill advertising the new play at the Swan. She told us that Sir Hugh was not to be disturbed further until breakfast the next morning.'

'So you went away to the theatre?'

'We did, Master Constable.'

'And then? After the play?'

'We fell in with some we knew and were drinking awhile until well beyond midnight. We were coming up Deadman's Place when we saw the tumult; saw the crowds around Frying Pan Alley and smelled the smoke and flames. The house was almost gone and just cinders left.'

'So, as far as you knew, you had left Sir Hugh safe in the house with Mistress Tanner in attendance?'

The old woman was suddenly shaking with rage.

'That harlot and ill-gotten daughter of Satan's mistress! We should have been warned of what she was about.'

'Which was?' Master Drew asked softly without changing his expression.

'She wanted to consummate her sinful intentions. When Sir Hugh, a gentleman of firm morals, declined her overtures, she set a fire in order to punish him and then absconded, leaving him to die in the flames.'

'And you have proof of this?'

'Proof?' exploded the old woman. 'Why, proof is in her sinful, shameless body. Anyone can see the licentious invitation of her form. Why, she hardly ever wore a cap to cover her head when working in the house. The proof of profligate thoughts was before our very eyes.'

'Did she give any indication of such intentions? How long had she worked for Sir Hugh?'

'She was only two full months in the house, employed as maid and Sir Hugh unmarried. He was a widower these last two years.'

'Would you not say that it was curious to employ a young girl in a bachelor household and employ her as a chambermaid,' asked the constable, puzzled by the thought.

'There were other women of the household,' Mistress Diddle-bury pointed out sharply, as if the constable had overlooked her sex. 'Sir Hugh doubtless wanted to train her up for when he remarried. I do believe, and wish to spread no gossip, but I did hear that he was in hope of marrying again. He would then need the services of a trained maid for whoever his choice of wife fell on.'

'One thing,' the constable said. 'When Sir Hugh gave you the evening off and said he had matters to attend to, did he imply what these matters were?'

'At the time, I presumed it was to do with his work as custodian of Marshalsea. I can't recall now, but earlier I knew he had to give instruction to Master Lupton, his deputy. So I expect he was alone in the house when that slovenly harlot tried her dissolute ways with him and was rejected and sought vengeance.'

The constable sat for a moment or two drumming his fingertips on the wooden board of the table. He realised he would only get more prejudice from the old woman and so returned her to the turnkey, instructing him to bring forth Mistress Tanner.

When Mistress Anne Tanner entered, the constable could see why Mistress Diddlebury disliked her. She was everything in looks that Mistress Diddlebury was not. Even in the frightened and almost pathetic mode in which she had been escorted from the prison, she walked with a more upright and elevated manner than the shuffling cook. Her heart-shaped, fresh-faced features were finely chiselled, with attractive dimples in her cheeks and red lips to which a smile came more naturally than not. It was hard to see if her eyes were green or blue. Fine corn-coloured hair escaped from under the hood of her cloak. She stood chin thrust forward with defiance in spite of the attempt to suppress her fears.

The girl stared at him boldly and even before he spoke she had opened the questioning herself.

'I know you will not believe me since that harridan, Mistress Diddlebury, will doubtless swear my life away out of spite. Also, you will wish to protect Sir Hugh's reputation. Therefore, there is little point in me wasting time in telling you the truth.'

Master Drew did not react. He sat silently regarding the girl for a moment or two before he said softly: 'I am here to protect only one thing and that is the truth, however unpleasant it may be for some. I intend to discover the truth. This is your opportunity to tell me your truth.'

The girl sniffed in disbelief. 'Ever since I came to Southwark seeking work, two months ago, I feel that the worst thing I have done was seek Sir Hugh's service. Truth is not valued there.'

'Sit down and tell me how you came to work for Sir Hugh,' invited Master Drew.

The girl hesitated and then lowered herself into the chair he indicated.

'I am from Lewknor. A little village by Oxford. The curate there, knowing my father was recently dead and that I was desirous of work, suggested I came here in search of his friend, the rector of St George's – a Master Johas Cartwright. It was he who recommended me to Sir Hugh's employ. Alas, he knew he was a prison custodian and said to be a moral man and patron of his church.'

'And for two months you were happy in that employ?'

'No, sir. There were many innuendoes that I endured and inappropriate touching. I reproved the culprit and I tried to show that I did not enjoy nor seek such attention.'

'Are you speaking of Sir Hugh as the culprit?'

'I am, sir. I hoped Sir Hugh would desist when he realised my reproaches.'

'Let us come to last night.'

'While all the servants were in the house, Sir Hugh lacked opportunity . . . Last night the majority of his servants had gone off to his country estate. Perhaps he had arranged it, I don't know. Even when he sent the old steward and cook to the playhouse, I did not think he would ignore my previous admonishment. But he saw this as an opportunity.'

'An opportunity for what?' The constable knew well enough but did not want to leave things as a matter of insinuation.

'An opportunity to press his attentions on me.'

'You say that you did not encourage him in this.'

'I made it plain, I would rather lay with a pig!' snapped the girl. 'But immediately the other servants had left the house, Sir Hugh summoned me and without any more ado told me that I was old enough to know how best to serve him. He started making his lewd intentions known. A fear gripped me. I did not know what to do.'

'The charges are that you stabbed him several times and then set a fire to destroy the house and the result of your deed,' pointed out the constable.

The girl gave a sharp cry of protest.

'Not true, sir. I swear it by the Faith.'

'Then tell me what you did?'

'I would protect myself but knew the man's pursuit of me would end one way for me. Therefore I begged Sir Hugh's pardon and said before he began his endeavour I must take me to the privy for nature had called me to such.

'He grumbled but let me go from the room to attend the privy. I had but one plan. I grabbed some necessary belongings from my room which was on the lower floor opening into the back yard.

I was trying to open the window when I heard Sir Hugh at my door. Thankfully, I had turned the key, but I knew it would take but a moment for him to burst open the door while I was struggling with the window latches.'

The girl paused. Master Drew waited. 'And so?' he prompted after he felt long enough had passed.

'When I had given up hope, there came the sound of the bell chain being pulled at the front door. I heard Sir Hugh hesitate and then I heard him swear before his steps receded.'

'He went to answer the door?'

'I presume so for I turned to open the latch and luck was with me for I opened the lattice window and pulled myself through with my bundle. I dropped the short distance into the back yard but the only way to clear the house was along the path at the side of the house to the main street.'

'The street was the same as where the front door was situated?'

'It was. I halted at the corner, hoping the person at the main door had gone. They had not.'

'I don't suppose you discovered the identity of this caller?'

'I did not, sir, I remained hidden by the corner of the house. I heard some conversation though. Sir Hugh was speaking sharply.'

'What did he say?'

'He declared that he would not endorse something. The other voice said that there would be ledgers to sign off before Sir Hugh left for his estate. There was silence as if Sir Hugh hesitated. Then he said that if the ledgers must be signed, then they must. He was still very angry, presumably because I had eluded him. I heard the main door bang shut and thus I took to my heels.'

Master Drew rubbed his chin thoughtfully.

'I think I know what happened next, but confirm it to me. Where did you go?'

'I went to Master Cartwright, rector of St George's. I told him what had taken place and pleaded for sanctuary. He was shocked but promised to help me.'

The constable stared at her thoughtfully for a moment.

'I don't suppose you knew what time you fled to Master Cartwright?'

The girl suddenly looked confident. 'I was already some time with him when nine hours were indicated.'

The constable stared at her in surprise. He did not have to articulate the question because the girl replied, 'Master Cartwright pointed to a strange mechanism that stood nearby that uttered a bell-like sound. Its single pointer, he called it a hand, indicated the letters on its curious face. He told me that it was an horology . . . I had not heard the word before . . . an horology piece. A miniature of the mechanism that stood in the Hampton Court Palace which King Henry had erected there. Master Cartwright told me that people could even tell by it when there was high water under London Bridge and thus warn the watermen.'

Master Drew was intrigued as he was much interested in horology, especially as he had once seen the tiny clock which was called a wrist clock that the Earl of Leicester had presented to Queen Elizabeth. Such a better method of keeping time would, in his eyes, be a great asset in his task of tracking down the culprits of crime. He felt that he should have words about the new developments in time-keeping with the rector if he was such an enthusiast. There was exciting news from Italy of a clock working by pendulum that would give increased accuracy to . . .

He paused, realising he had fallen silent in his distraction. He rebuked himself with a shake of his head and returned to the matter in hand.

'So, you made no stir after you reached Master Cartwright's house? Where did you stay?'

'I shared a room with his housekeeper, in the rectory behind the church. I was given food and a good bed and Master Cartwright promised to discuss my case with the justice the next morning.'

'The housekeeper would, of course, vouch for this?'

'It is the truth, sir. There would be no reason not to.'

'Then if the rector promised to help, how came it about that Master Cartwright escorted you to the King's Bench prison this morning to await interrogation?'

The question did not seem to perturb the girl.

'When I was awakened this morning and breakfasted, Master Cartwright came to me. He had been abroad early and told me the news of the burning of Sir Hugh's house and the finding of his body. I was truly shocked and sickened, sir. The rector told me that he had gone to the justice, Master Mayhew, and relayed my story. Master Mayhew said the matter, due to Sir Hugh's death, was too serious to ignore. He had already been to the ruins of the house and met with Sir Hugh's deputy custodian and he had taken Mistress Diddlebury and Master Falstone to a prison to await interrogation. Therefore, I must go too. Master Cartwright told me to be of good cheer for the investigation must be made. The justice had instructed him to take me to this prison. Once over, he would endeavour to help me.'

'You were not concerned that you would be a suspect?'

'I knew the truth and told it. There was nothing to be concerned about except the prejudice of others.'

Master Drew gave a deep sigh. 'That is more than enough to be concerned about,' he observed quietly. 'There was no one but you in the house with Sir Hugh, and you could easily have set the fire.'

'That is not so. I have told you that when I left, he had a visitor at the door. So I was not the last to have seen him alive last night.'

The constable smiled thinly.

'Indeed, so you say. But you did not recognise this visitor.'

'The visitor had gone inside with Sir Hugh when I fled down the street. So I did not see him, nor did he see me.'

Master Drew thought for a moment. Then he asked, 'In your short time at Sir Hugh's, did you ever encounter a Master Lupton?'

'The deputy custodian to Sir Hugh? His name was known to me. Only Master Falstone was allowed to answer the summons at the door. But I think, once or twice, I might have passed him on the stair when he came to visit Sir Hugh bearing ledgers and other things connected with the business of their office.'

'But you never saw him?'

'I did pass a visitor being shown into Sir Hugh's study once, maybe twice, by Master Falstone. Being in service, one is told to keep one's eyes to the floor when you pass visitors.'

The constable screwed his lips in a thoughtful grimace. 'He seemed to know you, because he recognised you at the King's Bench,' he added thoughtfully.

'Well, I did not know him.'

Master Drew stretched back in his chair, letting his fingers perform another tattoo on the table. Then he smiled softly to himself. He rose, went to the door and looked out.

Caleb Dodds, the turnkey, was sitting outside, nursing another tankard of beer.

'You may go now,' he instructed.

The man rose reluctantly to his feet.

'If please you, Master Constable, have you forgotten that I am to escort the wench to Marshalsea now you have done? Remember, conditions being crowded at the King's Bench, I was told to remove her to Marshalsea to make space.'

'I have taken charge,' the constable replied. 'There is no need for her to go to Marshalsea now.'

The turnkey knuckled his forehead without a dubious look. Master Drew, remembering the agreement, took some coins from his purse and handed them over.

'You are now released from this duty.'

As soon as the man disappeared, he turned to the girl. 'Come with me, and do so quickly.'

The girl looked defiant. 'I have my few belongings at the King's Bench,' she began.

'They will be sent for shortly. But you will come with me now.'

They turned out of the inn onto the High Street and he hurried, almost propelling the girl quickly before him. A few people stared curiously at him, recognising him and his office, and thereby examined the young girl, undoubtedly wondering what crime she had committed. They came to St George's and he impelled through the grounds towards the rectory beyond. As it happened, a young man was coming from the house who was clearly Master Cartwright.

'Master Constable, I . . .' he began.

'I am on my way to report to the justice,' the constable interrupted. 'I want you to take charge of this young girl and keep her well and safe until you hear further from me. You are to release her to no one else except me. Is that understood?'

'I shall do so,' the young man frowned. 'But . . .'

'Keep her well, for I fear she might be in some danger. Remember that I act in the name of the justice. He is a member and honoured representative of His Majesty's Parliament and will not take kindly if this instruction is not obeyed.'

A short while later the constable was being shown into Master Mayhew's study in his mansion in Three Crown Court.

'You have examined Sir Hugh's servants?' the justice asked, rising to offer the constable a glass of Malmsey. 'You have made a decision in this matter?'

'I have a question for you before I give that assessment.'

'A question for me?' The justice raised his eyebrows in surprise.

'You told me that you had ordered Master Cartwright, the rector, to take Mistress Tanner to the King's Bench. I presume Master Cartwright had reported to you what she had told him about why she had fled the house?'

The justice did not seem to be perturbed.

'He did. Johas Cartwright, being a friend of mine, as I am a warden of the church, was frank. He had found the girl weeping in the church and took her to the rectory. She carried her belongings wrapped in a shawl and sought sanctuary or help to get on the road back to Lewknor, a place near Oxford from whence she came.'

'And the rector informed you what she said in explanation?'

'That Sir Hugh had behaved as no gentleman of breeding should. She thought he had contrived to send the cook and steward away so that he could be alone to carry out his intent. She rejected him and fled the house.'

'Was it a story to which you could give credence?' asked the constable.

'We are all of flesh and blood and I doubt Sir Hugh is any worse or better than many men in his authority. But, I wondered whether she had fled the house for that reason and whether she set it afire to bring retribution on him. There were three suspects and when I appointed you, I left it to you to discover which of the three the culprit was.'

'Or who was the fourth culprit,' corrected Master Drew.

'Meaning?' frowned the justice.

'I refer to the unexpected visitor who unwittingly saved the girl from the further attentions of Sir Hugh. She heard him announcing at the door that he had important ledgers and business to be seen to before Sir Hugh left for his country estate the next morning. Matters that could not wait.'

A grim expression formed at the corners of the justice's mouth.

'Was this person identified by the girl?'

'Not exactly. But I believe identification could be achieved by what he said.'

'That being?'

'What sort of man had urgent business with the custodian of Marshalsea that needed to be dealt with, ledgers looked at, before he repaired to his country estate? Urgent business that meant Sir Hugh had to invite the man in. What man, when, learning there were no servants there, with motive to attack Sir

Hugh, killed him and sought to cover his crime by setting the entire house afire?'

'The girl did not identify him, as you say.'

'But he identified himself.'

'How so?'

'Well, this man knew the girl was last in the house; maybe Sir Hugh told him. Maybe Sir Hugh . . . anyway, the two old servants of Sir Hugh were taken into custody by the deputy custodian after the fire by your command. If Sir Hugh hadn't told him of the girl's escape certainly the busybody Mistress Diddlebury told him that the girl had been left alone in the house with Sir Hugh and she lost no time with providing her gossip as evidence.'

'You are saying the deputy custodian . . .'

'Master Lupton went to check on his prisoners after Master Cartwright had taken the girl there to await my interrogation. He had no difficult in recognising her. He went to pains to get her transferred to Marshalsea. But the turnkey had been ordered to await my orders. So he instructed that after she had been questioned the girl would immediately be taken to Marshalsea. She would have probably disappeared in there.'

Master Mayhew rubbed the back of his neck thoughtfully.

'So we release the girl and the old servants and Master Lupton is summoned before us? It is a curious web that you have unwoven. But however did you start unpicking this web?'

The constable smiled thinly. 'I am not the person who mentioned the thread to start picking at.'

'Who then?'

'Why, it was yourself who first mentioned it.'

The justice was astonished.

'I?'

'Yours is the credit. You told me at the start that Master Lupton was desirous of Sir Hugh's office. You told me how much enmity he held against Sir Hugh. Even to the point where a duel had been threatened and that was why you had not handed over the matter of investigating his death to the man. Last night he was handed the ideal situation to get rid of the object of his twisted jealousy.'

'Jealousy. Envy. The oldest motive of all,' sighed the justice. 'Was it not Livy that said that those possessed by envy overlook all reason that should alleviate and eliminate the condition? *Caeca invidia est.*'

'Alas,' the constable replied, 'I am not as learned as you, your honour. I can understand Lupton's jealousy, his wanting to replace this superior and become a gentleman with power. I can even comprehend the jealousy of old Mistress Diddlebury, with her envy of a young girl of attractive qualities that inspired a man like Sir Hugh to abandon moral considerations. Such stories, such distortions of envious minds! Why, such ado, taking place in blistering imagination, is enough to lock up honesty.'

The Game's Afoot!

The game's afoot!

Henry V, Act III, Scene i
William Shakespeare

When the shrill voice of a boy, accompanied by an incessant thudding against his door, awoke Master Hardy Drew that morning, the Constable of the Bankside Watch was not in the best of moods.

He had retired to his room, which he rented above the Pilgrim's Wink tavern in Pepper Street, in the early hours that morning. Most of the night he had been engaged in dispersing the rioters outside the Cathedral of Southwark. It had been a well-organised protest at the publication of the Great Bible, which had been authorised by King James. This Great Bible had been the production of fifty scholars from the leading universities, resulting in a work that the King had ordained to be the standard Bible used throughout his realms.

While it had been obvious to Master Drew that the Catholics would seize the opportunity to express their outrage at its publication, he had not expected the riots organised by the Puritan Party.

Not only were there rumours and reports of popish plots and

235

conspiracies this year, but the activities from the extreme Protestant sects were far more violent. King James's moderate Episcopalian governance angered the Puritans also. Only last month the Scottish Presbyterian reformer, Andrew Melville, had been released from the Tower of London in an attempt to appease the growing anger. The King had admitted that his attempt to break the power of the Presbyterian General Assembly in Scotland had not met with success. Rather than placate the Presbyterians, Melville's release had increased the riots, and he had fled into exile in France where, rumour had it, he was plotting his revenge. James had fared little better with imposing his will on the English Puritans.

The kingdoms of England and Scotland echoed and re-echoed with treasonable conspiracies. Indeed, a few months previously, another attempt to install James's cousin Arabella Stuart on the throne had resulted in the unfortunate lady being confined to the Tower. Times were dangerous; Master Hardy Drew had been reflecting on this while quelling the outburst of anger of Puritan divines. Even his position of constable was fraught with political danger. There were many who might falsely inform on him for his religious affiliations or, indeed, for his lack of them, in order to secure the position of constable for themselves, together with the small patronage that went with it.

The knocking increased in volume, and Master Drew rolled out of his bed with a groan. 'Ods bodikins!' he swore. 'Must you torture a poor soul so? Enter and have a good reason for this clamour!'

The door opened a fraction, and a dirty young face peered round.

Master Drew glared menacingly at the child. 'You had better have a good reason for disturbing my sleep, little britches,' he growled.

'God save you, good master,' cried the young boy, not entering the room. 'I've been sent to tell you that a gen'leman be lying near done to death.'

Master Drew blinked and shook his head in a vain attempt to clear it. 'A gentleman is – ? Who sent you, child?' he groaned.

'The master what owns the inn in Clink Street. The Red Boar, Master . . . Master Pen . . . Pen . . . some foreign name. I can't remember.'

'And precisely what did this Master Pen ask you to tell me?' Master Drew enquired patiently.

'To come quick, as the gen'leman be stabbed and near death.'

Master Drew sighed and waved the child away. 'Tell him that I'll be there shortly,' he said.

Had the news been of anyone other than a *gentleman* who had been stabbed in an inn, he would have immediately returned to his interrupted slumber. London was full of people being stabbed in taverns, alleys, or along its grubby waterfront. They were usually members of the lower orders of society, whom few people of quality would miss, much less shed a tear over. But a gentleman . . . now that was a matter serious enough to bring a Constable of the Watch from his warm bed.

Master Drew splashed his face with cold water from a china basin and hurriedly drew on his clothes. Below, in the tavern, he spent a half-pence on a pot of beer to cut the slack from his dry throat and, outside, chose an apple from a passing seller to munch for the balance of his breakfast.

Clink Street was not far away, a small road down by the banks of the Thames, along the very Bankside that was Master Drew's main area of responsibility. He knew of the Red Boar Inn but had little occasion to frequent it. Perhaps *inn* was too grand a title, for it was hardly more than a riverside tavern full of the usual riffraff of the Thames waterfront.

There was a small crowd loitering outside when he reached there. A small boy was holding forth to the group, waving his arms and pointing up to a window. Doubtless, this was the same urchin who had brought the message to him. The boy pointed to the constable as he approached and cried, 'This is 'im naw!' The small crowd moved back respectfully as Master Drew halted before the dark door of the inn and pushed it open.

Although the morning was bright outside, inside candles were alight, but even so, the taproom was still gloomy, filled with a mixture of candle and pipe smoke, mingling with odours of stale alcohol and body sweat.

A thin, middle-aged man came hurrying forward, wiping his hands on a leather apron. He had raven-black hair but his features were pale, which caused his shaven cheeks to have a bluish hue to them.

'We do be closed, good sir,' he began, but Master Drew stopped him with a cutting motion of his hand.

'I am Constable of the Bankside Watch. Are you the host of this tavern?'

The man nodded rapidly. 'That I do be, master.'

'And your name?'

'Pentecost Penhallow.'

Master Drew sniffed in disapproval. 'A Cornishman, by your name and accent?'

'A Cornishman I do be, if please you, good sir.'

Master Drew groaned inwardly. This day was not starting well. He did not like the Cornish. His grandfather had been killed in the last Cornish uprising against England. Not that he was even born then, but there were many Cornish who had come to London during the reign of the Tudors and stayed. He regarded them as a people not to be trusted.

The last uprising had been caused by the introduction of the English language into church services in Cornwall. The Cornish rebels had marched into Devon, even captured the suburbs of Exeter after a siege, before defeating the Earl of Bedford's army at nearby Honiton. That was where Master Drew's grandfather had been killed. The eventual defeat of the Cornish rebels by Lord Grey, and the systematic suppression of the people by fire and sword, the execution of their leaders, had not brought peace to Cornwall. If anything, the people had become more restless.

Master Drew knew that the English court feared a Catholic-inspired insurrection in Cornwall, as well as other of the subject nations on the isles. Cornwall was continuing to send her priests to Spain to be trained at St Alban's College of Valladolid.

Master Drew took an interest in such things and had read John Norden's recent work surveying Cornwall, in which it was reported that, in the western part of the country, the Cornish tongue was most in use among its inhabitants. Master Drew felt it best to keep himself informed about potential enemies of the kingdom, for these days they all seemed to congregate in the human cesspool that London had become.

He realised that the innkeeper was waiting impatiently.

'Well, Master Pentecost Penhallow,' he asked gruffly, 'why am I summoned hither?'

'If you would be so good as to go above the stair, good master, you may find the cause. One of my guests who do rent the room above do be mortally afflicted.'

Master Drew raised an inquisitive eyebrow. 'Mortally afflicted? The boy said he was stabbed? What was the cause? A fight?'

'No, no, good Master Constable. He be a gentleman and quite respectable. A temperate, indeed he be. This morning, as is my usual practice, I took him a noggin of mead. He do never be bestirring of a morn without his noggin. That 'twas when I discovered he be still abed with blood all over the sheets. Stabbed he be.'

'He was still alive?' demanded Master Drew, surprised.

'And still be but barely, sir. Oh, barely!'

'Godamercy!' exclaimed Master Drew in annoyance. 'Still alive and yet you sent for me and not a physician?'

Pentecost Penhallow shook his head rapidly. 'Oh, sir, sir, a physician was sent for, truly so. He do be above the stair now. It be he who do be sending for thee, Master Constable.'

The constable exhaled angrily. 'What name does your gentleman guest go by, and which is his room?'

The innkeeper pointed to the head of the stairs. 'Master Keeling, do be his name. Master Will Keeling. The second door on the right above the stair.'

Master Drew went hurrying up the stairs. On the landing he

almost collided with a young girl carrying a pile of linen. He caught himself, but the collision knocked some sheets from her hand onto the floor. The constable swiftly bent down and retrieved them. The young girl was an exceptionally pretty dark-haired lass of perhaps no more than seventeen years. She bobbed a curtsy.

'*Murasta, mester,*' she muttered, and then added in a gently accented English, 'Thank'ee, master.'

The constable gave a quick nod of acknowledgment and entered the door that the tavern owner had indicated.

A thin-faced man with a shock of white hair, clad in a suit of black broadcloth, making him appear like some Puritan divine, was sitting on the edge of a bed. On it a pale-faced young man lay against the pillows. Blood stained the sheets and pillows. Some bloodstained clothes were pressed against the man's chest.

The thin-faced man glanced up. 'Ah, at last. You have not come a moment too soon to this place, Master Constable. He has barely a moment more of life.'

'God send you a good morrow, Doctor Tate,' replied Constable Drew in black humour. He knew the elderly physician and acknowledged the man before he moved to the bedside.

The young man was, indeed, barely conscious and obviously feverish. There was a bluish pallor that lay over his skin, which showed the swift approach of death.

'Master Keeling,' he said loudly, bending to the dying man's face. 'Who did this thing? Who stabbed you?'

The young man's eyes were open, but they were wandering about the room. He seemed to be muttering something. The constable leaned closer. He could just hear the words, and their diction indicated a person of some education.

'What's that you say, good fellow? Speak clearly if you can.'

The lips trembled. 'Oh, for . . . for a Muse of fire . . . that would ascend the . . . the brightest heaven of invention . . .'

Master Drew frowned. 'Come, good fellow, try to understand me. Answer you my simple question . . . What manner of knave has done this to you?'

The young man's eyes brightened, and Master Drew suddenly found a hand gripping his coat with a power that one would have not thought possible in a dying man. The lips moved; the voice was stronger. 'Once more unto . . . unto . . .' He began to cough blood. Then suddenly he cried loudly, 'Let the game begin!'

The words choked in the man's throat. The pale blue eyes wavered, trying to focus on the constable's face, and then the pupils dilated as, for a split second, the young man realised the horror of the imminent fact of death.

The constable gave a sigh and removed the still-clutching hand from his jacket and laid it by the side of the body. He whispered softly: 'Now entertain conjecture of a time, when creeping murmur and the pouring dark fills the wide vessel of the universe . . .'

'What's that?' demanded the physician grumpily.

'No matter,' Master Drew replied as he moved aside and gestured to the body. 'I think he has run his course.'

It did not need the physician's quick examination to pronounce that the man was dead.

'What was the cause of death?' asked Master Drew.

'A thin-blade knife, Master Constable. You will see it on the table where I placed it. It was left in the wound. One swift incision was made in the chest, which I deduced caused a slow internal bleeding, thus allowing him to linger between life and death for the last several hours.'

'Presumably not self-inflicted?'

'Most certainly not. And you will notice that the window is opened and a nimble soul might encounter little difficulty in climbing up with the intention of larceny.'

'You have an observant eye, Master Physician.' The constable smiled thinly. 'Can it be that you are interested in taking on the burdens of constable?'

'Not I!' laughed the physician. 'I need the prospect of a good livelihood.'

Master Drew was turning the knife over in his hands. It told him nothing. 'Cheap,' he remarked. 'The sort that any young coxcomb along the waterfront might carry at his waist. It tells me little.'

Dr Tate was covering the body with the bloodstained sheet. 'Poor fellow. I didn't understand what he was saying at the end. Ranting in his fever, no doubt?'

'Perhaps,' replied the constable. 'But articulate ranting nonetheless.'

Dr Tate frowned. 'I don't understand.'

'Perhaps you don't frequent the Globe?' The constable smiled. 'He was reciting some lines out of Master Shakespeare's play *The Life of King Henry the Fifth*.'

'I didn't take you for one who frequents the playhouses.'

'A privilege of my position,' Master Drew affirmed solemnly. 'I am allowed free access as constable. I find it a stimulation to the mind.'

'There is too much reality to contend with without living life in make-believe,' dismissed Dr Tate.

'Tell me, good doctor, did the young man say aught else before I came?'

'He said nothing, but raved about battles and the like. Something about St Crispin's Day, but that is not until next October, so I do not know what he meant by it.'

The physician had turned from the body and was packing his small black bag.

'I can do no more here. The matter rests with you. But I would extract my fee before I depart.'

'Take your fee and welcome,' sighed the constable, glancing round the room. It was untidy. It appeared as if someone had been searching it, and he asked the physician if the room had been disturbed since he had arrived.

The physician was indignant. 'Think you that I would search for a fee first before I treated a gentleman?' he demanded.

'Well, someone has been searching for something.'

'And not carefully. Look! Some jewels have been left on the table there. I'll take one of those pearls in lieu of a coin of this realm.'

Master Drew pulled a cynical face. 'A good profit in that, Doctor Tate. However, I'll not gainsay your right.'

The physician scooped up the pearl and held it up to the light. The smile on his face suddenly deepened into a frown, and he placed the pearl between his teeth and bit sharply. There was a crack, and the physician let out a howl of rage. 'Paste, by my troth!'

Master Drew walked over and examined the other pieces of jewellery scattered nearby. There were some crushed paste jewels on the floor. A small leather purse also lay there with a few coins in it. He took out the coins.

'Well, paste jewels or no, he was not entirely destitute. There is over a shilling here, which will pay for a funeral if we cannot find his relatives. And here, good physician, three new pennies for your fee.' He grinned sourly. 'I wager that the three pennies are closer to the value of your service than ever that pearl, had it been real, would have been.'

'Ah, how is a poor physician to make a decent living among the impoverished derelicts along this riverbank, Master Constable? Answer me that, damme! Answer me that!' The physician, clutching his coins, left the room.

Master Drew gazed down at the shrouded body of the young man and shook his head sadly.

An educated young man who could recite lines from popular theatrical entertainment but who used cheap paste jewellery. Surely this was a curious matter? He turned and began to search the room methodically. The clothes were many and varied, and while giving an appearance of rich apparel, on closer inspection were actually quite cheap in quality and often hastily sewn.

He noticed that there were some papers strewn around the room, and bending to pick them up, he saw a larger pile on the floor under the bed. He drew these out and examined them. It was a text of the play *The Life of Henry V* by Will Shakespeare. The lines of Henry V had been underlined here and there.

'Well, well, Master Keeling,' the constable murmured thoughtfully. 'This sheds a little light in the darkness, does it not?'

He gathered up the script and turned out of the room, closing the door. There was nothing more he could do there.

The innkeeper was awaiting him at the bottom of the stair. He appeared anxious. 'The physician says the gentleman do be dead now, Master Constable. Did he identify his assailant?'

'Indeed he is dead, Master Penhallow. Some words with you about your gentleman guest.' Master Drew frowned suddenly, and an idle thought occurred to him. 'Pentecost, is that your first name, you say?'

'That it be,' agreed the man, somewhat defensively.

'Your parents being, no doubt, pious souls?'

'Not more so than anyone else.' He was defiant, but then he realised what was in the constable's mind. 'Pentecost be a good Cornish name; the name of my mother's family. *Pen ty cos* means "dwellers in the chief house in the wood".'

Master Drew found the explanation amusing. 'Well now, Master Pentecost Penhallow, how long has Master Keeling been residing here?'

'One . . . nay, two months.'

'Do you know what profession he followed?'

'Profession? He be a gentleman. What else should he do? You've seen his clothes and jewels?'

'Is that what he told you? That he was a gentleman?'

The innkeeper's eyes narrowed suspiciously.

Suddenly a dark-haired woman appeared from a shadowy corner of the tavern. Twenty years ago, she must have looked much like the young girl whom he had encountered on the landing, thought Master Drew. She began to speak rapidly to him in a language that Master Drew did not understand. It sounded a little like Welsh, but he guessed that it was Cornish.

'Wait a moment, good woman,' protested Master Drew. 'What is it you say?'

'*Meea navidna cowza Sawsneck,*' replied the woman in resignation.

'*Taw sy!*' snapped her husband, turning with an apologetic smile to the constable. 'Forgive my wife, sir. She be from Kerrier, and while she has some understanding of English, she does not be speaking it.'

'So, what does Mistress Penhallow say?'

'She complains about the late hours Master Keeling did keep, that's all.'

'Was he late abroad last night?'

'He was.'

'When did you last see him alive?'

'At midday, but my wife saw him when he came in last night.'

He turned and shot a rapid series of questions at his wife in Cornish.

'She says that he came in with his friend, another gentleman, about midnight. They were a little the worst for drink.'

The woman interrupted and repeated a word that sounded like *tervans*.

'What is she saying?' demanded Master Drew.

'That they were arguing, strongly.'

'Who was this man, this friend?'

There was another exchange in Cornish, and then Master Penhallow said, 'My wife says that he was a young man that often used to drink with Master Keeling. Another gentleman by name of Cavendish.'

A satisfied smile spread over Master Drew's face. 'Master Hal Cavendish? Was that his name?'

'That do be the name, Master Constable. A fine gentleman, I am sure. Have you heard tell of him?'

'That I have. You say that the two came here last night, drunk

247

and arguing? Is it known when Master Cavendish left Master Keeling's room?'

'It was not by the time that my wife and I retired.'

'Where were you when Master Keeling came in that you did not see him?'

'I was out . . . on business.'

'On business?'

The man hesitated, with a swift glance at his wife, as if to ensure that she didn't understand; then he drew the constable to one side. 'You know how it be, good master.' He lowered his voice ingratiatingly. 'A few shillings can be made from cock fights –'

'*Kessynsy!*' sneered his wife.

'You were gambling, is that it?' Master Drew guessed the meaning of her accusation.

'I was, master. I confess I was.'

'So you did not return until late? Was all quiet then? . . . I mean, you heard nothing of this argument overheard by your goodwife?'

'All was quiet. The place was in darkness.'

'And when was this?'

'About the middle watch. I heard the night crier up on the bridge.'

London Bridge stood but a few yards away. Master Drew computed that was between three and four o'clock. He rubbed his chin thoughtfully. 'And did your daughter notice anything before she went to bed?'

Master Penhallow's brows drew together. 'My daughter?'

'The girl that I met on the landing; I presume that she is your daughter? After all, she addressed me in your Cornish jargon.'

A look of irritation crossed the man's face. 'I do be apologising for that, master. I know 'tis thought offensive to address one such as yourself in our poor gibberish. I will speak harshly to Tamsyn.'

Master Drew stared disapprovingly at Pentecost Penhallow, for he heard no genuine regret in his voice.

What was it Norden had written? *And as they are among themselves litigious so seem they yet to retain a kind of concealed envy against the English who they affect with a desire of revenge for their fathers' sakes by whom their fathers received their repulse.* He would have to beware of Penhallow's feigned obsequiousness. The man resented him for all his deferential speech, and Master Drew put it down to this national antipathy.

'Is that her name? Tamsyn?' he asked.

'Tamsyn Penhallow, if it please you, good master.'

'Did she notice anything unusual last night.'

'Nay, that she did not.'

'How do you know?'

'Why, wouldn't she be telling me so?'

'Perhaps we should ask her?'

'Truly, good Master Constable, we cannot oblige you in this, for she has only just left to go to the market by the cathedral.'

Master Drew sighed. 'I will be back soon. In the meantime, no one must enter into the room of Master Keeling. Understand?'

Pentecost Penhallow nodded glumly. 'But when may we clear the room, master? It is not pleasing to have a corpse lying abed there, for when the vapours do be emanating –'

'I will be back before midday,' the constable cut him short, and left the Red Boar Inn, still clutching the script he had gathered from the floor of Keeling's room.

249

Although it was still early in the day, he made his way directly to the circular Globe playhouse, which was only a ten-minute walk away. He was greeted by the elderly gatekeeper, Master Jasper.

'A good day, Master Constable. You are abroad early.' The old man touched his cap in respectful greeting.

'Indeed I am, and surprised to see you here at this hour.'

'Ah, they are rehearsing inside this morning.' The old man jerked his thumb over his shoulder.

'I had hoped as much. I'll lay a wager with you, good Jasper.' The constable smiled in good humour. 'I'll wager you what new play is in rehearsal.'

The old doorkeeper laughed. 'I know well enough not to lay wagers with the Constable of the Watch. But for curiosity's sake, do make your guess.'

'*The Life of King Henry the Fifth.*'

'The very same,' chuckled Master Jasper in appreciation.

'Is Master Hal Cavendish playing in it?'

'You have a good memory for the names of our players,' observed the old man. 'But young Hal Cavendish be an unhappy man because Hal cannot play Hal in this production.'

'Explain?' asked Master Drew, allowing the old gatekeeper a few moments to chuckle at his own obscure joke.

'Young Hal Cavendish fancied himself as playing the leading part of King Hal, but now must make do with the part of the Dauphin. He is bitter. He is understudying the part of King Hal, but if he could arrange an accident to he who plays the noble Harry Fifth, young Cavendish would lief as not be more than content.'

Master Drew stroked the side of his nose with a lean forefinger. 'Is that the truth of it?'

'Aye, truth and more. Hal Cavendish is a vain young man when it comes to an assessment of his talents, and that is no lie. Mind you, good Constable, all those who tread the boards beyond are of a muchness in that vanity.'

'Do you also have a player called Will Keeling in the band of King's Players?'

To Master Drew's surprise, Master Jasper shook his head.

'Then tell me, out of interest, who plays the part of Henry the Fifth, whose role Hal Cavendish so desires?'

'Ah, a young Hibernian. Whelton Keehan. He has newly joined the company.'

Master Drew raised a cynical eyebrow. 'Whelton Keehan, eh. What manner of young man is he? Can you describe him?'

Master Jasper was good at descriptions, and at the end of his speech, the constable pursed his lips thoughtfully. 'I would have a word with Master Cavendish, good Jasper,' he said.

The old man saw the grim look in his eyes. 'Is something amiss, Constable?'

'Something is amiss.'

Master Jasper conducted the constable through the door and led the way into the circular auditorium of the theatre.

An elderly lean-faced man was standing on stage with a sheaf of papers in his hand. There were a few other people about, but the central figure was a young man who stood striking a pose. One hand held a realistic-looking sword, while the other hand was on his waist and he was staring up into one of the galleries.

'Crispian Crispian shall never . . .' he intoned, and was

interrupted by an angry stamp of the foot of the lean man, who shook his wad of paper at him.

'God's wounds! But you try my patience, Master Cavendish! *Crispin* Crispian shall ne'er go by – ! Do you aspire to rewrite the words of Master Shakespeare or can it be that you have grown indolent as the result of your previous success as Macduff? Let me tell you, good Master Cavendish, an actor is only as good as his last performance. Our production of *Macbeth* ended last night. You are now engaged to play the Dauphin in this play of *Henry the Fifth*, so why I am wasting time in coaching you to understudy the part of King Hal is beyond me.'

The young fair-haired man waited until the torrent had ended, and then he began again.

> *'And Crispin Crispian shall ne'er go by*
> *From this day to the ending of the world*
> *But we in it shall be remembered.*
> *We few, we happy few, we band . . .'*

His voice trailed off as he suddenly noticed Master Hardy Drew standing nearby with folded arms.

The lean-faced man swung round. 'And who might you be, who puts my players out of rhythm with their parts? Can you not see that we are in rehearsal?'

Master Drew smiled easily. 'I would have a word with Master Cavendish.'

'Zoots!' bellowed the man, and seemed about to launch into a tirade when Master Jasper drew him to one side and whispered something.

'Very well, then,' sighed the man in irritation. 'Ten minutes is all we can spare. Have your word, master, and then depart in peace! We have a play to put on this night.'

The young man was frowning in annoyance as Master Drew approached him. 'Do I know you, fellow?' he demanded haughtily.

'You will, fellow,' the constable replied in a jaunty tone. 'I am Constable of the Bankside Watch.'

The announcement registered little change of expression on the player's features. 'What do you want of me?'

'I gather that you are a friend of Master Whelton Keehan.'

Hal Cavendish's features formed a grimace of displeasure. 'A friend? Not I! An unwilling colleague on these boards, this will I admit to. But he is no more than an acquaintance. If he is in trouble and needs money to bail him, then pray go to Master Cuthbert Burbage, who manages our company. Perhaps he will feel charitable. You will not extract a penny from me to help him.'

'I am afraid that he is beyond financial assistance.' Master Drew smiled grimly. Then without explaining further, he continued: 'I understand that you accompanied him back to his lodgings last night?'

Hal Cavendish sniffed dismissively. 'If you know that, then why ask?'

'Let me make it plain why I ask.' Master Drew's voice rose in sudden anger at the young man's conceit. 'You stand in danger unless you answer me truthfully. Why was he known at his lodgings as Will Keeling?'

'It's no crime,' Cavendish replied indifferently. 'He was but a few months arrived in this city from Dublin and thought to better his prospects by passing himself off as an English gentleman at his lodgings. Poor fool – he had not two farthings to jingle in his pocket. I'll grant you, he is a good actor, though. He borrows props from here, costumes and paste jewellery to maintain his image at his lodgings and thus extend his credit with that sly old innkeeper. Ah . . . tell me, has his ruse been discovered? Are you carting him off to debtors' prison?' Hal Cavendish began to laugh in good humour.

Master Drew waited patiently for him to pause in his mirth. 'Why should that give you cause for merriment, Master Cavendish?'

'Because I now can play the part of King Hal in this production. Keehan was never right for the part. In truth, he was not. A Hibernian playing King Hal! Heaven forfend! That is why we argued last night.'

'Tell me, Master Cavendish, how did you leave Master Keehan? What was his condition?'

'Truth to tell, I left him this morning,' the young man admitted. 'He was not in the best of tempers. We had been drinking after the last performance of *Macbeth* and visited one or two houses of . . . well, let us say, of ill repute. Then we fell to discussing tonight's play.'

'You were arguing with him.'

'I do not deny it.'

'About this play?'

'About his inability to play his role. He had the wrong approach to the part, which rightfully should be mine. He had the audacity to criticise my part as the Dauphin, and thus we fell to argument. A pox on the man! May he linger a long time in the debtors' jail. He deserves it for leading the innkeeper's daughter on a merry dance with his assumed airs and graces. She, being a simple, country girl, was beguiled by him. There is no fun in debauching the innocent.'

Master Drew raised an eyebrow. 'Debauching? In what way did he lead Master Penhallow's daughter on?'

'Why, in his pretence to be an English gentleman with money and fortune. He gave the poor Penhallow girl some of his worthless jewels and spoke of marriage to her. The man is but a jack-in-the-pulpit, a pretender.'

The constable considered this thoughtfully. 'You say that Keehan promised to marry the Penhallow girl?'

'Aye, and make her a rich and great lady,' agreed Cavendish.

'He gave her paste jewels?'

'Poor girl, she would not know the like from real. I think she had set her heart on being the mistress of some great estate which only existed in Keehan's imagination. He gambles the pittance that Master Burbage pays us and visits so many whorehouses that I doubt if he has not picked up the pox, which will cook his goose the sooner. I have never known a man who had such an excess of love for his own self. I rebuked him for it. By the rood! He had the audacity to recourse to a line from this very play of ours, *Henry the Fifth* . . .'

The young man struck a pose.

' "Self love, my liege, is not so vile a sin as self-neglecting." One thing may be said of Master Keehan, he never neglects himself.'

'This Master Whelton Keehan does not sound the most attractive of company,' agreed the constable.

'I doubt not that this view is shared by the father of the Penhallow girl. I never saw a man so lost for words when he espied

Master Keehan treading the boards last night and realised that Keehan was none other than his gentleman lodger.'

'What?' Master Drew could not stay his surprise. 'Do you mean to tell me that Master Pentecost Penhallow knew that his lodger was a player and residing at the Red Boar under a false name?'

'He knew that from last night. He was there in the ring having paid his penny entrance to stand in the crowd before the stage. Keehan did not see him, but I did. In fact, as I was coming off-stage, Master Penhallow accosted me to confirm whether his eyes had played him false or not. I had to confess that they had been true. He went away in high dudgeon. He was in no better spirits when I saw him later at the Red Boar.'

'You saw Master Penhallow at the Red Boar? At what time was this?'

Master Cavendish considered for a moment. 'I confess to having indulged in an excess of cheap wine. I scarcely recall. It was late, or rather, it was early this morning. He was coming in as I was going out.'

The elderly white-haired man came forward, clicking his tongue in agitation. 'Sirrah! Can you desist with your questioning? We have a play to rehearse and –'

Master Drew held up his hand to silence him. 'Cease your concern, good master. I shall leave you to your best efforts. One thing I have to tell you. You must find a new player for the part of King Hal this evening. Master Keehan is permanently indisposed.'

'Confound him!' cried the elderly man. 'What stupidity has he indulged in now?'

Master Drew smiled grimly. 'The final stupidity. He has gotten himself murdered, sir.'

Arriving back at the Red Boar Inn, he found Master Pentecost Penhallow moodily cleaning pewter pots. He started as he saw the dour look on the constable's face.

'You lied to me, Master Penhallow,' Master Drew began without preamble. 'You knew well that Will Keeling was no gentleman, nor had private means. You knew that he was a penniless player named Keehan.'

Pentecost Penhallow froze for a moment, and then his shoulders slumped in resignation. 'I knew,' he admitted. 'But I only knew from last night.'

'Are you a frequent playgoer then, Master Penhallow?'

The innkeeper shook his head. 'I never go to playhouses.'

'Yet you paid a penny and went to the Globe last night. Pray, what took you there?'

'To see if I could identify this man Keeling . . . or whatever his name was.'

'Who told you that he was a player there?'

'Two days ago, one of my customers espied him entering the inn and said, "That's one of the King's Players at the Globe." When I said, nay, he be a gentleman, the man laid a wager of two pence with me. So I went, and there I saw Master Keeling in cavorting pretence upon the stage. God rot his soul!'

'So you realised that he was in debt to you and had little wherewithal to honour that debt?'

'Indeed I did.'

257

'So when you returned home in the early hours of this morning, you went to his room and had it out with him?'

When Penhallow hesitated, Master Drew went remorsefully on.

'You took a knife and stabbed him in rage at how he had led you and your family on. I gather he gave fake jewels to your daughter and promised marriage. Your rage did wipe all sense from your mind. It was you who killed the man you knew as Will Keeling.'

'I did . . .' began Master Penhallow.

'*Na! Na, tasyk!*' cried a female voice. It was the young woman the constable had seen on the landing that morning. Penhallow's daughter, Tamsyn.

'*Cosel, cosel, caradow,*' Penhallow murmured. He turned to Master Drew with a sigh. 'This Keeling was an evil man, Constable. You must appreciate that. He used people as if they meant nothing to him. Yet every cock is proud on his own dung heap. He crowed at his vice when I challenged him. He boasted of it. His debt to me is but nothing to the debt that he owed my daughter, seducing her with his glib tongue and winning ways. All was but his fantasy, and he ruined her. No man's death was so richly deserved.'

The young girl came forward and took her father's arm. '*Gafeugh dhym, tasyk,*' she whispered.

Penhallow patted her hand as if pacifying her. '*Taw dhym, taw dhym, caradow,*' he murmured.

Master Drew shook his head sadly as he gazed from father to daughter and back to father. Then he said, 'You are a good man, Master Penhallow. I doubted it for a while, being imbued with my prejudice against your race.'

Penhallow eyed him nervously. 'Good Master Constable, I understand not –'

'Alas, the hand that plunged the dagger into Master Keehan was not your own. Speak English a little to me, Tamsyn, and tell me when you learnt the truth about your false lover?'

The dark-haired girl raised her eyes defiantly to him.

'*Gorteugh un pols!*' cried Penhallow to his daughter, but she shook her head.

She spoke slowly and with her soft accent. 'I overheard what was said to my father the other night; that Will . . . that Will was but a penniless player. I took the jewels which he had given to me and went to the Dutchman by the Blackfriars House.'

Master Drew knew of the Dutchman. He was a jeweller who often bought and sold stolen goods but had, so far, avoided conviction for his offences.

'He laughed when I asked their worth,' went on the girl, 'and said they were even bad as fake jewels and not worth a brass farthing.'

'You waited until Will Keehan came in this morning. But he came in with Hal Cavendish.'

'He was in an excess of alcohol. He was arguing with his friend. Then Master Cavendish departed, and I went into his room and told him what I knew.' Her voice was quiet, unemotional. But her face was pale, and it was clear to Master Drew that she had difficulty controlling her emotions. 'He laughed – laughed! Called me a Cornish peasant who had been fortunate to be debauched by him. There were no jewels, no estate, and no prospect of marriage. He was laughing at me when –'

'Constable, good Constable, she does not know what she is saying,' interrupted Pentecost Penhallow despairingly.

'That was when you came in,' interrupted Master Drew. 'One

thing confused me. Why was it left until morning to raise an alarm? I supposed it was in the hope that Keehan would die before dawn. When he did not, good conscience caused you to send for a physician, but hoping that he would depart without naming his assailant. That was why you asked me if he had done so. That was your main concern.'

'I have admitted responsibility, Master Constable,' Penhallow said. 'I will admit it in whatever form of tale would best please you.'

'You are not a good teller of tales, Master Penhallow. You should bear in mind the line from this new play in which Keehan was to act, which says, as I recall it to mind, "men of few words are the best men." Too many words allow one to find an avenue through them. Instead of saying nothing, your pretence allowed me to discover your untruths.'

'I admit responsibility, good Constable. She is only seventeen and a life ahead of her, please . . . I did this –'

'Enough words, man! Unless you wish to incriminate yourself and your family,' snapped the constable, 'I have had done with this investigation.' He put his hand in his pocket and drew out a purse. 'I found this in Master Keehan's room. The physician took his fee out of it. There is enough to give Master Keehan a funeral. Perhaps there might be a few pence over, though there is not enough to clear his debt. But I think that debt has now been expunged in a final way.'

Pentecost Penhallow and his daughter were staring at him in bewilderment.

Master Drew hesitated. Words were often snares for folk, but he felt an explanation was needed. 'Law and justice sometimes disagree. You have probably never heard of Aristotle but he once wrote, "Whereas the law is passionless, passion must ever sway the heart of man." Rigorous adherence to the letter of the law is often rigorous injustice.'

'But what of –?'

'What happened here is that a penniless player met his death by the hand of a person or persons unknown. They might have climbed the wall and entered by the open window to rob him. It often happens in this cruel city. Hundreds die by violence, and hundreds more by disease among its teeming populace. The courts give protection to the rich, to the well connected, to gentlemen. But it seems that Master Keehan was not one of these; otherwise, I might have had recourse to pursue this investigation with more rigour.'

He turned for the door, paused, and turned back for a moment.

'Master Penhallow, I know not what conditions now prevail in your country of Cornwall. Do you take advice, and if it be possible, return your family to its protective embrace and leave this warren of iniquity and pestilence that we have created by the banks of this foul-smelling stretch of river. I doubt if health and prosperity will ever be your fortune here.'

The young girl, eyes shining with tears, moved forward and grasped his arm. '*Dursona dhys!*' she cried, leaning forward and kissing the constable on the cheek. '*Durdala-dywy!* . . . Bless you, Master Constable. Thank you.'

Smiling to himself, Master Drew paused outside the Red Boar Inn before wandering the short distance to the banks of the Thames. The smells were overpowering. Gutted fish and offal. The stench of sewerage. Those odious smells, to which he thought that a near lifetime of living in London had inured him, suddenly seemed an affront to his nostrils. Yet thousands of people were arriving in London year after year, and the city was extending rapidly in all directions. A harsh, unkind city that attracted the weak and the wicked, the hopeful and the cynics, the trusting and the swindler, the credulous and the cheat. Never was there such an assemblage of evil. The Puritan divines did not have to look far if they wished to frighten people with an image of what hell was akin to.

He sighed deeply as he glanced up and down the riverbanks.

A boy came along the embankment path bearing a placard and ringing a handbell. Master Drew peered at the placard.

It was an announcement that the King's Players would be performing Master Will Shakespeare's *The Life of King Henry V* at the Globe Theatre that evening.

Master Whelton Keehan would not be playing the role of King Hal.

Master Hardy Drew suddenly found some lines from another of Will Shakespeare's plays coming into his mind. Where did they come from? *The Tragedy of Macbeth*! The last performance Whelton Keehan had given.

> *Tomorrow, and tomorrow, and tomorrow,*
> *Creeps in this petty pace from day to day,*
> *To the last syllable of recorded time;*
> *And all our yesterdays have lighted fools*
> *The way to dusty death. Out, out brief candle!*
> *Life's but a walking shadow, a poor player*
> *That struts and frets his hour upon the stage*
> *And then is heard no more.*

Some Cupid Kills

Some cupid kills with arrows, some with traps

Much Ado About Nothing, Act III, Scene i
William Shakespeare

Master Hardy Drew, Constable of the Bankside Watch, halted at the western end of the Bankside and the corner of Gravel Lane with a perceptible sigh of satisfaction. It was a bright, sunny morning, and, although it was Saturday, the crowds had not yet begun to gather to head towards the two circular buildings which were the separate centres for bull and bear baiting. These were the most popular entertainments of the borough of Southwark, sprawling along the south side of the River Thames.

Although Master Drew had been a constable for several years, he was not a follower of such spectacles. If the truth were told, he despised them. It was true that the old Queen's father, Henry, had closed such entertainments, but they had been revived by Elizabeth herself, who was known to be fond of bear and bull baiting and even partial to cockfighting. She and her courtiers came south of the river to revel in such questionable delights.

Master Drew often argued with himself that the only reason why he remained committed to his occupation was his interest in keeping some sort of law and order in the warren of blood sports, crime, brothels and disreputable taverns. It was a peculiarity that among these warrens there had grown the centre of the most popular playhouses serving the capital. Among the wretched streets had arisen the Globe, The Rose, The Swan and a new theatre being built, to be called The Hope, and Master Drew was an assiduous playgoer.

It was too early before noon to see the crowds streaming south across the Thames into this hub of entertainment; too early before the one solitary bridge crossing from the City into Southwark would be blocked by carriages and horses of the fortunate with wealth; too early for the many to start hiring among the three thousand wherrymen who plied their trade on the waterway, to bring them safe to the several landing points along the south bank. Yet, withal, it was even too early for the constable to make his way back to his lodgings in Pepper Street and sample the delights of Mistress Cuttle's luncheon pies. The hostess of the Pilgrim's Wink, in whose tavern Master Drew rented rooms, was renowned for her pies.

Master Drew stood undecided for a moment. The end of Bankside was also the end of the Liberties of the Clink and of the estates of the Bishop of Winchester, of which he was constable. It was here that the jurisdiction changed to the Liberties of the Paris Gardens. Here he could end his first circuit of the morning. Yet it was too early for a midday repast. However, he smiled. It was not too early for a tankard of good ale in the Falcon Inn, which stood down by the river at the Falcon Steps, the landing stage for many of those crossing the Thames into this area. The

Falcon Inn stood on the very borders between the Liberties of the Clink and those of the Paris Gardens.

For a moment he found his mind idling over the Paris Gardens. Many visitors were intrigued by the fact the gardens seemed to share a name after the capital of the French. Master Drew smiled for he had discovered the old name was Parry's Gardens, and that Parry was but the Welsh name of some retainer of Henry Tudor; Henry who had defeated Richard of York, the last English King to be killed in battle defending his throne. Thereafter, London had swarmed with Tudor retainers from Wales. Some even were bold enough to say that Parry was the illegitimate son of the new King because the name came from the Welsh 'ap-Harry', son of Harry. This had soon changed in the English pronunciation to Parry and hence Parry's Gardens and now the Paris Gardens. Constable Drew liked to muse on such obscure conundrums.

With a shake of his head, he bestirred himself and was about to cross the street towards the Falcon Inn, only to be arrested by someone crying his name in a cracked and feeble tone. He turned and saw an elderly man limping hurriedly towards him. He frowned for the little gusts of wind off the river blew the old man's loose clothing this way and that, and caused the man to hold tight to his hat, keeping his face in shadow. It took a few moments for Master Drew to recognise who it was.

'Master Jasper! I haven't seen you for a month or so. I was told you had left the Globe.'

The constable knew that for years Master Jasper had been employed by Richard Burbage and his brother, Cuthbert, to take charge of tending to the fabric of their theatre.

The old man halted before him, breathing with some difficulty as if he had run a distance.

'I succumbed to an ague for a while . . . I thank God for my recovery . . . I fell in with Master Henslowe who rented the Swan. He offered me a similar job to that I had at the Globe. When I saw you, I thanked God.'

Master Drew frowned. The Swan lay south-west, in the Liberties of the Paris Gardens, just across the meeting of the roads where they now stood. The theatre had been the concept of Master Langley in 1589, but ill-fortune seemed to possess the playhouse. It had started with Ben Jonson's play *The Isle of Dogs*, which had opened there in 1597. Albeit Jonson had written it with Thomas Nash, it was said that the old Queen flew into a fury and nearly had him executed. Elizabeth declared the play was a personal affront to her and brought her into ridicule. Jonson declared that he had only meant to satirise the courtiers around her, but the Queen was not best pleased and had the playwright thrown into jail and then ordered he be exiled for the rest of his life from London. It was not the first time that Ben Jonson had acquaintanceship with prisons, and he had narrowly escaped execution.

Thanks to its association with Ben Jonson, the Swan achieved little popularity nor made any money after that. Yet it was certainly the most impressive of the theatres on the south bank of the Thames.

'Come now, Master Jasper, why do you come to me praising God for seeing me?'

'Master Drew, you know me for an honest fellow.'

'I know you to be so. Therefore, why so?'

'I was opening the theatre but a while ago. I was at my duties when I came to the area where the actors change . . . Master Constable, I found a body. The body of a young woman, well dressed withal and clearly a lady of some worth. I knew not what to do. That is why, on exiting the theatre just now, when I spied you across the millpond I thanked God.'

Master Drew was certainly interested but he was a man of some obedience to rules affecting his occupation which he felt should be rigidly applied.

'We have known each other these past years when you served at the Globe, but now your theatre stands in the Liberties of the Paris Gardens, which is outside my jurisdiction.'

'Ah, I am old but my brain is not shrunken with age. I went first to the house of young Master Jabez Topcliff, who is constable there. He resides in the Old Paris Gardens Lane . . . Master Drew, he is ailing with some fever that turns his skin like ochre, what some call the yellow death, and he cannot stir from his bed. Certainly, I would not enter his house. Thereafter, I returned to the theatre not knowing what to do. That was when I saw you.'

'I am sorry for this intelligence for I served as deputy to his father, Master Edwin Topcliff, when he was constable here.'

'What could I do, Master Drew? The girl lies dead. Who else should I go to?'

'Well, so long as the constable is indisposed it is still in the purview of Justice Mayhew, to whom all constables to the watch make an account. I can take a look and report to him. You say this was a lady? You did not recognise her?'

The old man's concerned features relaxed at the constable's assurance. Then he shook his head.

'She was stretched on her side with her back towards me. I could not bring myself to turn the body to see her face. I saw only that the clothing looked of good quality, but that there were bloody marks on it as if the poor girl had been stabbed several times in the back. Methinks it was strange simply by the clothing.'

'So it was not someone who had any transaction or interest with the theatre? Very well. Let us go to see what we can construe from this matter.'

The old man, with just a beckoning gesture, turned back across the street towards the tall theatre building. Master Drew, with one longing glance towards the Falcon Inn, turned and followed.

The theatre was deserted. Master Drew followed the old man as he made his way to the back of the ornate stage and pushed through heavy curtains. There was a jumbled heap of clothing in one corner; a mass of various items, some identifiable as ancient costumes and hats. There were even some pieces of painted armour although here and there cracked and, on closer inspection, seen to be pieces of painted pasteboard. To one side of this assorted pile was clothing that did not fit the carelessly dumped items. As Master Drew advanced on it he saw that it was a woman's dress of some finery, although the aspect he saw was very bloody. It took only a moment to realise a body was still in the clothing with its back towards him.

As he stared down, he noticed there was something strange about the angle of the coiffured hair. It seemed as if knocked a little sideways. It was obviously a blond wig. There was nothing odd in that, for many ladies of fortune styled themselves with wigs these days. Even the old Queen had affected a red wig in her later years, refusing to submit to the will of chronos and the inevitable turn of the Zodiac Wheel to show the passing of time. But there was something about this body that caused him concern. It looked initially like a young woman, but somehow the neck and shoulders were of a more muscular alignment.

The constable made a decision and glanced at old Master Jasper.

'A hand, please you,' he instructed and, reaching forward, took the shoulders and turned the body over with the old caretaker helping with the legs. The wig fell away, revealing fairly short blond hair, handsome male features, a small nose but a pronounced jaw and blue sightless eyes wide open. The entire face was covered in white lead and adorned in red paint to the lips and black to the eyes. The make-up was that which exaggerated the facial features.

Behind him, Master Jasper gave a startled cry.

'So not a woman at all?' mused the constable dryly, glancing at the old man.

'No, Master Constable. It is one of the players.'

'A young lad.' It was more of an observation than a question.

'He is one of the lads who take the female parts in the play.'

Master Drew knew there had been one or two experiments at women playing female parts in the theatre, but these were quickly abandoned due to the extremity of the law. It was known there were street performers and performances at notorious venues, but the Puritans exerted power so that it would be a few decades before the Crown and Church confronted each other and a Royal Charter gave permission for women to play their own sex on stage. At this time, even by using young boys to play these parts seemed an affront to religious morality. The Puritan divine John Rainolds had recently declared in his booklet that it was a filthy spectacle of lust and vice that young men should put on women's attire because it kindled unclean affections.

'Does he have a name?' The constable indicated the body.

'Aye. He be Cudworth Culborne,' the old man replied. 'I never did see the boy in this costume afore. I did not recognise him at first.'

Master Drew ignored the old man's justification.

'Culborne? The name is unknown to me. Is he among the regular players? Is this the only playhouse he appears in?'

'Well, master, he be no Christopher Beeston,' the old man mentioned a leading boy actor, famed for his women's roles at the Globe. 'I think he had only been here a few weeks, since they began to rehearse this play.'

'Which company?'

'They have a patent as Lady Elizabeth's Men, contracted to Master Philip Henslowe. They are rehearsing something called *The Mad Pranks of Merry Moll of the Bankside*.'

Master Drew stared at the caretaker in disbelief.

'I thought I saw a script of that name by John Day?'

'Truly, sir. I heard Thomas Middleton was the writer, or writing his play from some text on this Moll Cutpurse and he being assisted on it by Thomas Dekker.'

Master Drew knew the names of all three playwrights and knew they were acquainted with one another. He was also aware the underworld of the city had knowledge of Moll Cutpurse. Of all the remarkable characters that emerged in the curious world of thieves, cutpurses, highwaymen, smugglers and prostitutes, none were known better than Mary Frith. The daughter of a Barbican shoemaker, she was never seen without a pipe in her mouth and a sword in her hand, despising Puritans by dressing in men's clothing and even riding astride like a man wagers. It was in August of the previous year that Master Drew had been shown a text of John Day's script purporting to show her life. Now Middleton and Dekker seemed to be re-creating this work.

'So, this Culborne was playing the part of Moll?'

'That he were, sir.'

'Did he have relatives here, in the borough?'

'He lodged at Nell Barry's house on Gravel Lane. I never did hear of relatives.'

'Is it Master Henslowe who is in charge of this play? Or is it Tom Middleton himself.'

'Master Henslowe pays the bills. But Master Dekker directs the players and plays the part of an old apothecary, Hippocrates Gallipot or some such name.'

Master Drew glanced round the deserted theatre.

'Why is it I see no players rehearsing?'

'It was decided to make a late start on the rehearsal after noon this day.'

'Do you know aught of this boy? His friends? Who he mixed with? When did you last see him?'

'Last night, Master Constable. He was the last to leave – him and Tom Chard. I locked up after them. I had the impression Master Culborne was going directly to his lodging.'

'And who is Tom Chard?'

'He plays another female in the play, a Mistress Prudent.'

'So they both went back to Mistress Barry's?'

The old caretaker shook his head. 'Not they, master. For one thing, young Tom lodges with another player in a cottage along by Henry Maxer's house. But for another thing they were parting not on the best of terms.'

'How so?'

'They had been having an argument before they left the theatre and so I am sure they turned in different directions.'

'So they were at enmity?'

'Why, bless you, master, you know well these players are always arguing with each other.'

'I don't suppose you know what the argument was about?'

'Jealousy, as it is with most arguments in playhouses. Tom Chard thought the role of Molly should be his. She is what the play was all about. Mistress Prudent was the wife of the old apothecary. Tom Chard maintained he was better known among the players than Master Culborne, who – as you yourself pointed out – was not well known.'

'Where will I find this Tom Chard? At his lodgings?'

At that moment a distant bell caused the old man to lift his head with a smile.

'That be the noon bell, Master Constable. Within the hour or so the players should all be coming in for the afternoon rehearsals.'

Master Drew thought for a moment before deciding his next course.

'I must leave you for a while. I would go and speak with this Mistress Barry, who you say this Culborne lodges with, so that I might have more intelligence of him. I will send for Master Red-weard, the mortician, for we will need his services for legal

272

purposes. I have to leave it to you to set a guard over the body until Master Redweard or I return. Let none of the players near the body, nor allow them to leave the playhouse once they arrive. Will you do this service?'

Master Jasper nodded. 'I will, sir, and will do so in the authority of your name, for I am but the keeper of this playhouse and my word is not regarded.'

'Then make sure you stress it is my authority and I shall be the one they account to.'

The constable then left the Swan playhouse. Outside he halted a young lad of likely disposition and engaged him for a bright penny to run to Master Redweard's mortuary at the corner of Bankside and Bull Lane and bring him to the Swan, where a body awaited him. He would be in touch later. Having sent the boy about this mission he turned up the broad thoroughfare of Gravel Lane and sought the lodging house of Mistress Nell Barry.

To his surprise, Mistress Barry was not a middle-aged woman as he presumed most hostesses of lodging houses would be. She was in her early twenties, but fleshy and with ill-chosen make-up, and withal a sullen expression on her pouting, over-rouged lips. A few years ago she would have been an attractive, uncorrupted spirit, but now her circumstances, and passing innocence, had set her on the path to joining the brawny harridans that were more likely to be seen among the taverns and brothels of the area.

'What seek you?' she demanded as he stopped before the door.

'I am told that you keep a lodging house?' he opened.

She folded her arms belligerently across her apron.

'And so?' Her voice was as hostile as her stance as she examined him. 'You have not the appearance of one looking for rooms.'

'I am Constable of the Bankside Watch.'

The woman opened her mouth to reply, then suddenly sniffed and glanced back into the room behind. The constable could see it was her kitchen.

'I must see to my saffron cake less it be over-baked,' she said, turning away reluctantly. 'You'd best come in for a moment.'

Master Drew watched approvingly as she removed the backing tray from the small brick bread oven in the corner. He was partial to saffron cake and its aroma.

'Do you sell those, Mistress Barry?' Master Drew asked, thinking of the future.

'I do not. I bake saffron cake only once a week. I nearly had to miss today because I had to go this morning to old Mistress Pencothan to buy saffron. I was sure I had left enough on the shelf here, so when I could not find it, I had to run round to get some more, not wishing to disappoint my young lodger who relishes it.'

'Your young lodger?' interrupted the constable as he was brought back to the business in hand. 'You let rooms to some of the players in the theatres?'

'And if I do?' There was a slight change in her manner. The arms folded again and the shoulders seemed to hunch a little.

'You have a tenant named Cudworth Culborne?'

'What do you seek with him? He is a young lad, albeit a player at the Swan.'

Master Drew decided to be blunt. 'I do not seek him, for he lies dead in the theatre. I now seek information about him.'

The woman gave a scream and her body became loose as she

stepped back as if she were about to fall. Master Drew held out a steadying hand and lowered her to a stool.

'Need you water?'

She breathed deeply once or twice and seemed to recover.

'How, what . . .?' she began.

'The how and what is that which I shall determine. Will you answer my questions?'

Mistress Barry gave a mute nod, rose and went to the sideboard. She took a jug that was clearly cider and poured some into a mug and drained it, swallowing without drawing breath. Then she slumped back onto her wooden stool.

'Dead, you say?' she asked hollowly.

'He was stabbed,' Master Drew replied without further preamble. 'How long has he lodged here? What do you know of him?'

'I know little enough. He came here last Martinmas from somewhere up York way, so he told me. He was in search of work in the playhouses. He has made himself a likeable and responsible tenant; an asset to this house.'

'You liked him?' the constable asked. 'I thought that lodgers, especially players, were often regarded as a nuisance and possessors of an untrustworthy income?'

'He met his dues, unlike some who have a reputation for expecting to put their hosts on their list of creditors.'

'So he was not one such?'

'I have seen worse.'

'You seem young, Mistress Barry, to have experience of tenants and to become acquainted with such cares as a lodging house, especially in this district?'

'I inherited the house from my husband,' she replied defiantly.

'Inherited?'

'My husband went for a soldier in the Dutch wars and was killed three years since. Thanks be, his father had the good sense to leave him this house, and so it was left to me as his only kin. I was not wanting except for a husband.'

'So, you took in this youth as a lodger, and that, you say, was nearly six months ago? Was he a good tenant?'

'There were a few periods when he did not have work and had long since run out of items to exchange. But he was careful to repay when he could. I did allow him to remain in return for jobs to be done about the house.'

'And he was then engaged at the Swan?'

'They have been in rehearsal there for a week or more.'

'Do you have any other players from the Swan in your house?'

'Not from the Swan.'

'But other players?'

'Only Master Blithford,' she replied at once.

'Prosper Blithford?' The name was recognisable to Master Drew as someone often treading the boards of the Rose and the Globe in various performances.

'Is he performing at the Swan?'

'He is not, sir. He rehearses a new play at the Globe, or I am told. In truth, sir, I have no interest as I like not the man. He is under notice to quit my house.'

'Why so?' the constable asked, slightly surprised at her vehemence.

'It is not for me to say.'

'If it is for you to expel him from your house, if he displeases you, then it is for you to explain that displeasure,' admonished the constable.

The woman pouted. It made her features cast into an ugly form.

'He is a creature of lewd habits. A vain and licentious creature without a soul.'

'Lewd, mistress? In what manner?'

'He consorts with younger men to contrive their corruption. I did hear Pastor Portal preach on the subject only last week and he said all such are condemned to Hell fire. I realised I must protect my . . . my household.'

'Apart from young Culborne, you have other young men in your household?'

The woman blushed. 'Cudworth was my only other tenant.'

'Pastor Portal is one of those Puritan divines who follows William Bradshaw of Cambridge, is he not? The only reason why he has survived the displeasures of the Church is that, while refusing any ecclesiastical jurisdiction, he ensures he preaches that the King is the general overseer of all the churches in the kingdom. Are you of that sect?'

'I know aught faction or divisions. But Pastor Portal does preach right from wrong.'

'How long has Master Blithford lodged with you?'

'Nearly two years. Just after I heard my husband had died in the Dutch wars.'

'So he has been your lodger for quite a time; indeed, longer than Master Culborne. In fairness wouldn't the last comer be the first to go if there were a problem in your mind?'

'Why, no, indeed,' the woman was adamant. 'Cudworth needed . . . needed protection. Not Master Blithford.'

'I have heard Pastor Portal preaching against the playhouses and, in particular, the employment of young men to play women in the performances. The Pastor would better spend his time preaching against the law which forbids women to act upon the stage playing their own sex. Otherwise the playwrights should remove the characters of women in their works entirely.'

On this Master Drew held sincere beliefs and had once heard Master Shakespeare speak vehemently upon the matter, pointing out that a fifth of his major characters were women. He was silent for a moment before coming back to the present. It was clear that Mistress Barry was part of one of the Puritan sects.

'So, you felt you must protect young Master Culborne?'

'My duty, as the mistress of this lodging, was clear, sir. Cudworth . . . Master Culborne . . . was in need of my protection. I felt I could draw Cudworth back to a holy path. I could have offered him work to upkeep this lodging house.'

'Master Blithford lost his lodging. There is confusion here. If you believe Pastor Portal then surely you should have expelled both him and Master Blithford?'

'It is done. Master Blithford left his room early this morning before anyone was up. I presume that he has gone to find another lodging. He left a note to say he will return to take up his belongings this evening.'

'Did he leave for the theatre at the same time as Master Culborne?'

'He was gone before I came down to prepare breakfast for Cudworth . . . Master Culborne. Master Culborne had his breakfast and left not long afterwards.'

'So Master Blithford did not breakfast here?'

'Indeed, Master Blithford would not sit at my table after I had told him my mind. He probably went out to some tavern.'

'My understanding would be that the rehearsal at the Swan was not due until this afternoon. Why would Master Culborne go out so early?'

'He told me that he had to try on the costume he had to appear in. It was new; an elaborate dress which is difficult to assume if you have never tried one before. This one had especially difficult laces at the back.'

'Tell me, apart from Master Culborne, did you know any others at the Swan?'

'I would not waste my time in playhouses. But one young man, Tom was his name, I believe, called for him a few times.'

'Tom Chard?'

'I heard only the name of Tom. He sought a room here and I refused him.'

'Yet you take in players?'

'I have a living to earn and a house to maintain. But I try to maintain standards. I did not like his manner.'

'Mistress, I swear I feel there is some inconsistency here. So you would not know if Master Culborne was in enmity with anyone?'

'I think Cudworth would have confided in me if he had made some enemy.'

'Regarding Master Blithford, do you not think the seeds of enmity would have been sewn by yourself?'

The young girl frowned angrily.

'What do you imply, sir?'

'That you decided to throw out your lodger of some long-standing because you did not wish him to associate with your younger guest. That had he known this was the reason he lost his room, that fact would have fermented his ire and perhaps led him to seek vengeance?'

The girl's eyes narrowed as she thought on the matter. It was as if an angry smile momentarily passed over her lips and was gone before Master Drew was sure it was there.

'Much to be thought over in what you say,' she finally said.

'I might have need to call on you again, Mistress Barry,' the constable replied. 'Once the matter is cleared, the obsequies and funeral will probably fall under the guidance of Master Red-weard. Doubtless you know of the mortician?'

Something led Master Drew's footsteps next to the Globe playhouse and, on enquiry there, he was directed to the nearby Groat and Smile tavern where some of the players had repaired to reinforce themselves before the rest of the day's rehearsals. Master Drew glanced around the smoky atmosphere of the alehouse and it took him a few moments before he saw the person he was looking for.

Prosper Blithford was well featured with flaxen hair that put the constable in mind of a young Viking warrior. Recalling that the player was from York, a fact once boasted during some entertainment he had witnessed, he doubted not that Blithford had such ancestry. It was clear that he liked to be of attention for he sat with several others recounting some anecdote, head thrown back and with a loud, punctilious pronunciation to his discourse. The constable halted before him.

'Spare me a moment of your time, Master Blithford.'

The player looked up in annoyance at being so interrupted, but one of his companions, who recognised the constable, greeted him in a loud voice so that Master Blithford would realise who he was.

'Why do you seek me, constable?' The player amended what was going to be his previous formation of words in greeting.

'If it please you, a moment of your time.' He nodded to a recently emptied snug. 'You may bring your pipe, if you will.'

'I do not use a pipe,' the young man said in surprise.

'Ah, methought you were a tobacco user by the stains on your fingers,' the constable responded, for he had noticed the yellowing marks on the man's hands which were so often those of frequent familiarity with users of the weed.

'It is bad for the voice projection,' explained Prosper Blithford as he seated himself. 'What can I do for you, Master Constable?'

'This morning I called on Mistress Barry.'

At once the player's face turned into a sneer.

'Has that wench sworn a complaint against me? She is one to bear ill-will, for all her youth and wiles, Master Constable. I know of few who offend the name of womanhood as she has done.'

Master Drew noticed the man's vehemence. 'You intrigued me, sir. All she has told me is that she asked you to find new lodgings.'

Master Blithford uttered a short bark of laughter.

'And did she tell you why? She says that she felt I would corrupt young Cudworth Culborne, and him corrupt enough already to cause the Devil's ass to blush with shame.'

'What say you, sir?' demanded the constable.

'Little to say. Some of us try to bring respectability to our profession, others use it to hide the reality of themselves and their desires. It is a bit like the Papist priests, sir, those who use their priestly caste so that one questions them if they do not behave as ordinary men and women. So, too, is it claimed that, because there are young boys playing women, they must be subverted souls to know not what sex to lie with.'

Master Drew frowned but acceded that what the actor said was true. 'I'll grant you that it is a criticism of the playhouses in the Bankside. But you condemn it?'

'Of course I condemn it. But not from any Puritan view. It is the likes of the Puritan sects and others of rigid faith that are the loudest in their commendations. They would have no plays at all to entertain and education the people.'

'Mistress Barry is of such a sect?'

'A recent convert when she discovered the predilections of young Culborne.'

'Recent?'

'I tell you this, after I went to lodge at her house, when the news of her husband's fate in the Flanders war had but recently made her a widow, she was of free temperament.'

'But she converted?'

'Only after Master Culborne came to lodge and after, it seems, she felt they were good friends. Even then it was more recently that she joined with the naysayers like those followers of the Puritan Divine Bradshaw.'

'Those who locally follow Pastor Portal?'

The actor smiled without humour.

'Indeed. Pastor Portal, the great friend of culture who would burn all books, destroy all theatres and probably lead the ignition of the flames to execute any who dared raise a song to lullaby young children to sleep. For such, singing is an affront to God.'

'You speak in bitterness?'

'I speak as I see it.'

'I presume that you were the object of Mistress Barry's attentions before the arrival of Master Culborne?' Master Drew asked sharply.

For a moment, Master Blithford hesitated and blinked.

'It amused me for a while,' admitted the actor, assuming a smile. 'But I am a man of easy passions, and while there was a convenience to the affair, I saw it as no more than what it was.'

'But you are telling me that it was Mistress Barry who ended it?'

'She did when she became enamoured of Culborne. She could not do enough for him. Always preparing his favourite food, in spite of the expense. Those saffron cakes she always made on a certain day, for example . . .' He paused and sniffed in disgust.

'You accepted this?'

'Why would I not do so? I knew that Culborne cared not one way or t'other. And since he started rehearsals at the Swan, I think he met one of the players with whom he formed an attachment.'

'Do you claim that he in no way encouraged Mistress Barry?'

'Of course he did. Or rather, let us speak plainly, he did not discourage her. She was, in the end, giving him free lodgings, a free bed and meals. Why, only this mid-morning I saw her taking a basket of food to the Swan because Culborne had missed breakfast.'

Master Drew stared at the player. 'But you had left before breakfast. How did you know that he had missed breakfast and that Miss Barry took his breakfast to the theatre later? You must have seen her doing so.'

'You are perceptive.' Master Blithford was not put out. 'I was at the Sign of the Gates opposite the Swan when I saw her going into the theatre.'

'What were you doing there?'

'When one is rehearsing, all the actors must play their part and do all manner of chores for the production. I was asked to pick up some costumes for the Queen of Sicily that had been left there.'

An astounded look crossed the constable's face, causing the actor to burst into laughter.

'Zounds, good Constable! Do you forget that we are players? We are rehearsing Master Shakespeare's new play *The Winter's Tale* and Hermione is the Queen of Sicily – a leading character in it.'

'And what part do you play?'

'I am Camillio, a noble of Sicily. So I was picking up some costumes for our production.'

'You mention that Mistress Barry's attentions were not reciprocated by Culborne?'

'Especially not after he was engaged by Henslowe at the Swan. No, he had some amour among the players. In fact, I believe that Mistress Barry has been immortalised through the young man's acquaintance with Tom Middleton. He suggested some line to Middleton about unfortunate discontented women who lose their husbands and, with their wants unfulfilled, become Molls, after the character in his play. He was so proud of offering that line to the playwright.'

'Are you suggesting that he had an intimate acquaintance with Middleton?'

''Zblood! No, no. 'Twas with a young member of the troupe, but he never spoke a name to me.'

'You did not feel resentment against Culborne when you were told to leave the lodgings? After all, in some way he was responsible for Mistress Barry throwing you out.'

Blithford chuckled. 'In a way, I must be grateful to the young cove. Perchance he saved me from a fate worse than death.' The player was rising from his seat. 'Now, if please you, I must return with my companions. Master Shakespeare is a hard taskmaster over ensuring his actors know their parts.'

'What play did you say it was?' asked the constable.

'A new play – *A Winter's Tale*. I am sure someone of your position would be welcome to observe its course.'

'I wish I could do so. However, I still have a task to perform.'

Master Blithford suddenly stood still and uttered a groan.

''Zlife!' he exclaimed. 'I had forgotten the reason that had brought you in search of me. Has Mistress Barry sworn some charge against me?'

'You need not be a-feared of that, but Master Culborne is dead.'

Blithford stared at him. 'So she could not stand his rejection?' He stood quietly for a few moments and Master Drew watched him carefully. Then the actor sighed. 'Then I durst not return to her lodgings to pick up my bags.'

'I would restrain yourself from that. It will be my endeavour to come to the Globe this evening and I shall bring you back your belongings.'

A short time later, Master Drew was reflecting on matters as he turned down Bear Alley and paused before Master Redweard's mortuary at the corner of the alley and the Bankside. As was his custom, Master Drew took out a crumpled piece of rose-scented cambric from his pocket before entering. The thin, dark-clad figure of Master Redweard looked up from where he was covering a cadaver on a table in a corner. On recognising the constable he smiled with thin, bloodless lips.

'I have been expecting you, Master Constable.'

'So you have picked up the body from the Swan?' It was an unnecessary question.

'I did so and brought it here for examination and your coming to advise as to how to dispense with it. Master Jasper, at the Swan, said it was all in your hands. The only thing was Master Dekker, who directs the play, demanded that the costume the corpse was wearing be returned to him as it was the property of the company. I complied.'

'So long as you can confirm how he died. I am also sure Mistress Barry, in Gravel Lane, where he had lodged, will fund enough to ensure his burial.'

Master Redweard sighed. 'You can never be sure in these hard times, especially with players. Anyhow, my brief examination showed he was stabbed several times in the back.'

'Nothing else?'

'Only that the stabs were made in fury and not with any degree of science.'

'What makes you say so?'

'The random pattern of the blows as if done in anger. Some glanced off the bone, but two drove upwards, missing the bone and entering the heart. Those caused blood to squirt out in such a manner that the boy was dead within seconds.'

Master Drew sniffed cynically. 'And with all that blood, you were asked to remove the costume because the players were in need of it?'

'Well, 'twas not as if it were the boy's own clothes. Just a play actor's costume. They said it had just been delivered that morning for the boy to try on for the rehearsal.'

'I suppose these things cost?'

'As do funerals, Constable,' the mortician observed. 'I would think the cost is enhanced by the fact that the knife tore some of the dress, meaning there was some serration on the blade. Did you find the knife by the body?'

The constable was thoughtful. 'I did not. Some serration, say you? That would make it an unusual weapon?'

'Well, it was certainly no gentleman's dagger, nor a weapon with a clean pointed blade. That's probably why the victim was stabbed so many times. For example, the new-fashioned stiletto from foreign parts, now favoured, would have produced a quick kill with one thrust. This was a dirty weapon. When I was removing the clothing I saw little scraps of dried pastry and meat. Such tiny morsels that I would not have noticed had I not been intent to undo the bodice of the clothing.'

'You are saying that these were left on the blade before it was thrust in and out of the body? That the knife had not been cleaned after a meal, and the remains were caught on the clothing?'

'Exactly what I am saying, Master Constable, and that is why I asked you if you had found the weapon.'

'Master Redweard, you have been of great help. For that, much thanks.'

As he completed the short walk to the Swan he found the well-known figure of Master Thomas Dekker waiting impatiently for him on the steps of the main entrance. There were very few people among the population of the borough like Dekker, whose multitude of plays over the last few years had caused him to become as well known as Master Shakespeare, Jonson and Middleton. Dekker was a tall, sallow-skinned man in his early forties but, alas, it was rumoured that his best days were behind him and these days he was but trying to produce other people's plays for whatever theatre would hire him. So badly had his previous plays prospered that his last one he had ironically entitled *If This Be Not a Good Play, Then The Devil Is In It*. It had been a failure. Now he was trying to direct Middleton's play.

He greeted Master Drew nervously.

'You must clear up this dreadful business, Constable,' were his first words.

'That is truly my intention, Master Dekker,' replied the constable. 'I have come from Master Redweard who has charge of the cadaver. Do you still have the dress that the young man was murdered in?'

'I was about to send it across to old Chickabiddy Gross who does the washing down by the Millpoint.'

'It is not sent yet? May I see the dress?'

Master Dekker led the way into the theatre. Several people stood or sat about in states of nervous tension. They were obviously waiting for the constable or for some direction. A woman stood near a bundle of clothing. Master Drew told her what he wanted and she extracted the piece of clothing with a look of distaste. The constable took the clothing and turned it over so that he could examine the back where it laced up. The blood was still damp. He turned it to the light and examined the holes where the laces went through. Master Redweard's discerning eye had been right. There were areas where it seemed the clothing had been ripped. It was clear the jagged edges were caused by a knife being inserted and had passed back and forth with considerable energy.

Master Drew's eyes narrowed as he inspected the tears and the holes where the laces had been tied. Then he put his hand in a purse on his belt and drew out a magnifying lens. He liked using this tool which, it was said, Sir Roger Bacon had developed at Oxford. He now applied the rounded piece of convex glass to the area of the dress. Master Redweard's sharp eyes were correct. Mixed with the blood here and there were tiny traces of meat and pastry. He sighed and put the glass away.

'You may take the clothes to the laundress,' he instructed.

'Who do you need to question?' demanded Master Dekker.

'Are all your players assembled? I should say, only those who had business in the theatre this morning.'

Master Dekker spread his hands. 'So far as I know, today there was only Master Jasper to open the theatre, but that you know well for he raised the alarm. Only the victim was needed to try on the costume. The rest of the players came at noon or after.'

'These half-dozen?'

The players had begun to emerge from the corners of the stage where they had been waiting as the two men were speaking. The constable turned to face them.

'Did any of you have business in the playhouse this morning, earlier than this afternoon's rehearsal?' he asked.

Old Jasper stepped forward as expected.

'As you know, sir, I was supposed to be first here, a little before noon, to open up and prepare for the rehearsals.'

'Indeed, and I neglected to ask you, did you find the doors open?'

'The main doors were shut, Constable.'

Master Drew exhaled in a deep sigh. 'There's the rub. Our victim left his lodging this morning after breakfast, but came to the theatre early to try on his costume, the very costume in which he was found murdered. So how did he enter the theatre and how did the murderer do so?'

The players began to mutter and stare suspiciously at one another.

It was Master Dekker who unexpectedly cleared his throat.

'I provided the key of the side door, knowing that the seamstress would be delivering that costume early this morning.'

'So you gave it to the seamstress?'

'No, I gave it to one of the players to oversee the delivery.'

'And that was . . .?'

'Thomas Chard.'

'And where is he?'

One of the players pointed to a dark corner of the stage. 'He was over there, sir, a few moments ago.'

'Wait here,' instructed the constable, and strode in the indicated direction. In a dark corner a young man was seated on the floor, his knees drawn up and arms wrapped around them. He was clearly in distress, his shoulders heaving. The gasping sobs were palpable and intense. The constable needed no lantern to judge the young man's obvious tear-stained face.

'Are you Tom Chard?' he demanded, unnecessarily. 'What ails thee?'

The young man sniffed.

'I have lost a friend.'

'More than a friend, I fancy,' Master Drew responded. 'Yet I hear you quarrelled over the parts you play in this performance.'

'That was just a player's vanity,' replied the boy in a broken voice. 'In truth, I had not envy on that score.'

'But you had enmity with each other, nevertheless. You had a love for Master Culborne?'

'I am not afeard to say so. But he would neither say "yea" nor "nay" and he made sport of my feelings and boasted of other lovers.'

'Indeed? So you killed him?'

'Not I, not I, sir!' sobbed the boy.

'But you knew he came here this morning to try on a costume? And you were given the key to let in the seamstress who came to deliver it. Culborne was killed in the costume, so this was done after the costume was delivered by the seamstress and Culborne had put it on. That means you had already opened the playhouse for the seamstress and Culborne.'

'Aye, sir. The seamstress came, I let her in and Cudworth Culborne. The seamstress left as he was trying on the costume. Then we fell to our argument again and this time I was provoked to anger. I demanded that he make a choice. He laughed. He saw it as a joke. That was his way with everything, sir. Life was a joke and everyone was to be used to his advantage.'

'Did he tell you of his choices?'

'He boasted of the hostess at his lodgings and mentioned an older player. But he said they meant no more to him than I did.'

'So you were inspired by jealousy?' the constable pointed out.

'I was jealous, true. We quarrelled, true; but that was all. How could I kill what I loved? We ended our quarrel and, in a rage, I turned and departed, leaving Cudworth here alone but well.'

'So, you left. What did you do with the key?'

The young man caught himself with a frown. 'I am not sure. It was a heavy key. I think I left it in the door.'

The constable swung round. 'Master Jasper, have you examined the outside door, the small side door that the seamstress would have been admitted to?'

The old man was gone for some moments before he returned with the key.

''Twere in the lock as plain as day. Any one could have used it.'

'Anyone, including our killer,' mused Master Drew. 'I begin to see through Cupid's traps.' He turned to Master Dekker. 'I will let you know shortly if you and your players are needed again in this investigation.'

A short while later Master Drew was striding back up Gravel Lane to Mistress Barry's lodging house. The young woman met him at the door with a scowl on her fading, pretty features. She did not greet him pleasantly.

'Why do you pester me now?' she demanded.

'To pursue my legal enquiries.' He stepped forward so that the young woman was forced to move backward and allow him inside. 'Do you mind if I look at his room?'

'What do I care? Top of the stairs and first left.'

His room was surprising empty but there was one bag on the end of the bed. A canvas bag such as seamen were wont to use.

Master Blithford had already packed his belongings. The constable turned out all the contents on the bed and started to methodically go through them. He was not expecting to find that which he sought, nor was he disappointed when he came to a negative end. He replaced the contents back in the bag. He had only conducted the exercise as a means of reinforcing what was in his mind. Afterwards he went downstairs, carrying the bag, to find Mistress Barry boiling potatoes. She looked up with a sniff as she saw him.

'You are confiscating his bag?' she demanded. 'I shall need a receipt in case he claims I have stolen it.'

'I said I would return the bag to him,' smiled the constable. He eyed her culinary measures. 'Tell me, did you make a meat and potato pie these last few days?'

She looked astonished at the question. 'Did I . . .?'

'It is a simple question.'

'I don't deny it. I managed to get a shin of beef which I mixed with a half-pint of ale and some onion and potato with a shell of pastry. Do you want to know more?'

Master Drew smiled grimly. 'I trust you were not sparing the seasoning – salt and peppers with a touch of thyme might have enhanced the taste.'

The woman swore softly.

'You accuse me of not knowing how to cook . . .'

'I am sure you are the finest. Tell me where you keep your knives to prepare such a pie?'

Mistress Barry frowned for a moment and then indicated a drawer.

The constable opened it and sorted the items with a trained eye before he picked one with a fairly long blade, but which was old and well used to the point where the blade had not been regularly sharpened. There were a couple of nicks in it.

'What are you about?' the young woman said nervously.

'Tell me, mistress. Have you been here all day?'

'Why, of course.' She paused and corrected herself. 'No. I had to go to Mistress Pencothan to get some more saffron. I had in mind to make a saffron cake and she gets a good store of it, being from Cornwall and . . . But you came here when I was baking it.'

'And you were out for how long?'

'Not long. But long enough to need to replace the logs on the fire before I could boil my potatoes.'

Master Drew nodded and stood looking in satisfaction at the knife he held, almost lovingly, in his hands.

'Well, no doubt this is the weapon that murdered young Cudworth Culborne.'

Mistress Barry gave a scream and began to protest.

'I did not say that you had killed him.' He held up a hand to silence her. 'However, I may need you to bear witness after I present my case to Justice Mayhew.'

At Master Mayhew's house a short time afterwards, the justice was shaking his head.

'So you intend to arrest this play actor after the performance this evening? You have no doubts?'

'It is a simple motive, as all such motives are when Cupid's arrow goes awry,' replied the constable. 'A handsome youth wanting to make his way in the playhouses usually gets consigned to play the women's roles, and while women in playhouses are condemned by our ecclesiastics, boys have to take on their roles, as is legal, and are even more vehemently condemned.'

'Yes, there is much debate about that,' nodded Master Mayhew, who was one of two members of Parliament for the borough. 'But, explain.'

'Well, the boy found himself in a love situation. Three people had emotional snares for the boy. One woman, the mistress of his lodgings, and two fellow players. All came under my suspicion. But only one of them acted from a violent anger with malice enough to do the deed and plot to place the blame on another: the actor, Prosper Blithford. The malice was engendered by Mistress Barry, who threw him out of his lodgings when she recognised him as a rival to her own affections, although she disguised them, claiming to be a convert to the Puritans and just wished to protect the boy.'

'So how did you reach the conclusion that it was Blithford?'

'By the very fact that Blithford sought to create a drama by which he thought I would fall for the tale. I should also explain that the victim cared for none of his would-be lovers. He acted the innocent to Mistress Barry because he wanted to make use of her lodging house. But he boasted this to the others, to Blithford and to Chard, playing one off the other.

'Having left his lodgings, after being told he was not welcome, Blithford had already created his design. True, the man relied on luck, for like any plan it could have gone wrong. He knew that morning the victim had to go to the Swan to try on a costume. Indeed, the victim told Blithford that fact and that Master Dekker had given a key to one of the other players, his would-be lover Chard. To implicate Mistress Barry, he left early, having

taken her kitchen knife. He was prepared to commit two murders if necessary – Culborne and Chard. He would do so with
Mistress Barry's knife. To make the story real, he needed to
replace it in her kitchen. He had a plan for that even before he left
that morning. I will come to that.

'Blithford claimed that he had seen Mistress Barry carrying a
meal to the Swan for Culborne. Someone was lying because
Mistress Barry said Culborne had eaten breakfast heartily with
her before he went to the theatre. Blithford said he was collect-
ing costumes for his own play opposite the Swan, which gave
him an excuse to observe the entrance to the Swan. He was
there, and fate was with him because he saw Tom Chard run
from the theatre after his argument. It was then that Blithford
entered and stabbed his victim many times using Mistress Barry's own meat knife.'

'What then? You said you found it in her kitchen. So how had
he been able to replace it and thus, as you say, incriminate her?'

'He prepared for that. He knew she was due to bake a saffron
cake for Culborne that day. He knew roughly when she would
stoke up the oven to be hot enough to bake it. So, before he left,
he took her saffron from the shelf. He was back hiding at a dis-
creet distance when she realised she could not find her saffron,
and emerged to go to Mistress Pencothan. He took the opportunity to slip in, place the knife back in the drawer and then
vanish to the Globe.'

'What set you on this convoluted path?' the justice asked in
surprise.

'Saffron. When you touch it, it can leave a yellow stain on your fingers. It did so with Blithford. When he denied using tobacco, I realised what it was.'

Master Mayhew shook his head sadly.

'I tell you, Master Constable, Cupid is not a loving creature. His arrows are sharp and draw much blood, they can sever the heart strings, leaving the heart as dead as if a real arrow had penetrated it.'

Satan in the Star Chamber

I will make a Star-chamber matter of it

The Merry Wives of Windsor, Act I, Scene i
William Shakespeare

The noise reminded Master Hardy Drew of the distant report of cannon except that it grew curiously louder and louder. Then he realised that he was awakening from a deep sleep and the noise had resolved itself into a furious knocking at the street door below. It was still black night. He lay for a moment in his warm bed, cursing the fact that his manservant was not at home that night. Exhaling with a sound like a groan, he swung out of bed and padded across the cold wooden floorboards to the lattice window and opened it a fraction.

'Who's there?' he demanded in his best stentorian tone. 'Who disturbs the slumber of honest citizens at this hour?'

Peering down, he could see two men, one with a lantern held high, in the cobbled street below. By its flickering light he could see that they were clad in livery, although he could not discern the crests they bore, which would denote in whose service they were employed. Both men were girthed with swords.

'Be you Master Hardy Drew, the Constable of the Bankside

Watch?' cried the man with the lantern, lifting it towards the upper window as if to catch sight of him.

'I am,' replied Master Drew.

'Then you must accompany us at once, Master Drew. It is a matter of urgency.'

Master Drew's brows lowered in annoyance.

'Must accompany you?' he replied coldly. 'Whither? And by whose request?'

'To the Palace of Whitehall, good Constable. By the request of my Lord Ellesmore.'

Only a fraction of a second passed before Master Drew bid them wait but a moment to allow him to dress, assuring them that he would be down directly. It would not do to allow the Lord Chancellor of England and Keeper of the Seal to be kept waiting. It was but a short time before he was hurrying behind the two royal guards down the narrow alley that led onto the Bankside, by the dark Thames' waters, where he found two boatmen, also in royal livery, awaiting with a skiff. No word was exchanged as he clambered into the stern of the boat while the others took up positions facing him, their faces stoic and uncommunicative. The boatmen grasped the oars and sent the little vessel speeding across the dank waters of the great river.

From Bankside, on the south bank of the Thames, across to the Palace of Whitehall, on the northern bank, it was a short distance, but with the darkness and dangerous tides it took fifteen minutes to traverse the stretch of black water.

No challenge was given as they came to the jetty at the water entrance of the Palace, though clearly they were within sight of many royal sentinels. The two guards were out first, the one still holding the lantern to aid Master Drew to clamber from the boat onto the stone jetty. Then, still without a word, his guides turned and hurried forward through the gates. Guards with halberds stood watch here and there but no one issued any challenge as they hurried through arches into a series of small courtyards before coming to a door which was immediately opened to them. Here the two guards stopped and the man who had opened the door, an elderly man but also in royal livery, beckoned Master Drew to follow. He proceeded to lead him down a maze of darkened corridors before halting before a door on which he tapped respectfully.

He paused a moment and then opened it and coughed hollowly before announcing: 'Master Hardy Drew, the Constable of the Bankside Watch, my lord.'

Master Drew found himself ushered inside.

There was only one man in the room. He was an elderly man, with a shock of snow-white hair, still handsome and with a sharp pointed beard of which style, Master Drew observed, was favoured by the King himself. The old man was slightly stooped at the shoulders, but with bright blue eyes sparking with humour. He was bending in his chair, pulling on a pair of fashionable shoes. The constable had no difficulty recognising the seventy-one-year-old Thomas Egerton, Lord Ellesmore, the Lord Chancellor and Keeper of the Seal.

'Sit you down, Constable,' the Lord Chancellor said, pointing to a chair as he adjusted his footwear. 'Excuse me for I am having a little difficulty with these new shoes. I'd fain sign an execution warrant for my cobbler after this. Do you know who I am?'

Master Drew inclined his head and sank nervously onto the edge of the chair.

'I do, my lord.'

'How so? I might be anyone. Do you rely on the word of those who brought you hither?'

'No, my lord,' replied Master Drew, raising his chin defensively. 'Two days ago, at the installation of our new Lord Mayor of London, Sir John Swinnerton, you were in attendance. I was nearby and heard Sir John and divers others greet you tenderly by name. I would not think that they be all mistaken in their greeting.'

For a moment it seemed that Lord Ellesmore was about to break into a smile but instead he nodded slowly.

'I have good reports of your sagacity, Constable. Both from my predecessor in this office, my Lord Burghley, and also Sir Thomas Bennett.'

Master Drew said nothing and so Lord Ellesmore continued.

'They spoke most highly of your capabilities, Master Drew. They told me that you have an uncanny talent in the solving of riddles. Moreover, they spoke of your discretion. May I trust your discretion, Master Drew?'

The constable frowned thoughtfully.

'My lord, prudence is important in many of the tasks that I have undertaken and unless they be matters that are inimical to the safety of His Majesty and the Kingdom, or impinge on the liberty of my conscience, then my discretion is something that may be trusted from the lowliest subject to the King himself.'

Lord Ellesmore raised an eyebrow and then he smiled wanly.

'You have answered well, Master Drew. You are an honest man and speak forthrightly without fear or favour. Your wisdom and discretion are both needed this night. I am soon to show you something that, if 'twere known outside of these walls, might cause civil war to devastate these now united kingdoms. Do you swear what you see will go no further?'

'My caveat is as I have said, my lord,' replied Master Drew, resolutely. 'I cannot foreswear to secrecy until I know what this threat may be and whether my secrecy may serve the well-being of His Majesty and the kingdom.'

'That word is good enough for me, Master Drew,' replied Lord Ellesmore after a moment's hesitation. 'Be so good as to follow me and prepare yourself for something I never dreamt I would see the like of.'

The Lord Chancellor moved to a side door and led the way down a narrow corridor. Once more, it seemed to Master Drew that he was being led through a maze of passageways until they paused before a pair of dark oak doors. Lord Ellesmore drew a large iron key from the leather purse that hung at his waist. He inserted it in the lock and turned it. They entered into a large chamber with a high vaulted ceiling. It was the ceiling that immediately caught Master Drew's attention. It was blue and gold and painted with a star pattern. The panelling was of dark oak and there were chairs arranged in a semi circle around what looked like a raised wooden platform, only one foot higher than the floor but with a single chair placed on it. At one end of the room was another even higher platform, on which were seven ornate chairs, one of which had all the regalia of a royal seat. Above these hung banners and shield crests.

'Do you know where you are?' asked Lord Ellesmore as he closed the door behind them and locked it.

Master Drew shook his head. He had never been in the Palace of Whitehall before.

'This is the Court of the Star Chamber.'

The constable suppressed a shiver that involuntarily began to catch his spine at the name. Back in medieval times the king's royal council used the chamber, but in the days of Henry VII it had become a judicial body. During the reigns of the Tudor dynasty, it had even over ruled all the lower courts. The Star Chamber Court would order torture and imprisonment and now, under King James, its power had grown considerably, being used to suppress opposition to the royal policies, arraigning nobles who were thought too powerful. Its acts were done in secret session with no right of appeal. Here, in this terrible place, punishment was swift and severe to any falling out of favour with the Crown.

'Why am I here?' asked the constable nervously.

Lord Ellesmore simply pointed to the far end of the room, opposite the royal seats.

It was only then that Master Drew realised this area was in a great state of turmoil. Some chairs were overturned and there seemed a table on which various items had been upset or knocked over, items like candles made of black wax, scrolls of some ancient quality, a golden hilted dagger and curious icons the like of which he had never seen before. One of these was a candleholder with many arms, of the type that he knew came from the faith of the Jews, and there was a strange pentacle star.

Master Hardy Drew took all these things in at a glance before alighting on the dominant object that lay stretched on the door.

It was the body of a young man. His throat had been cut and he had bled profusely. Blood stained everything. His eye caught sight of bloody footprints leading from the body and moving across the chamber but ending abruptly in mid-floor. For

303

a moment or two, they held the constable's frowning attention. Then he pursed his lips and glanced at the Lord Chancellor.

'It seems that there is great evil afoot here, my lord. These seem to be the devil's accoutrements.' He gestured towards the objects on the table.

The tall man sighed.

'Know you what day this is, Master Drew?'

The constable started as he realised it.

'It is now All Hallows' Day.'

'And this last night was All Hallows' E'en.'

'God save us,' whispered the constable. 'The night when witches and warlocks are abroad to hold their wicked revels.'

He glanced again at the partially obscured face of the body of the young man.

'Has he been identified, my lord?'

'You know him not?' queried the Lord Chancellor with meaning in his voice.

Master Drew hesitated. Then a cold feeling began to come over him. He bent down on one knee for a better examination.

'His features are passing familiar. He . . .'

He exhaled sharply, the breath hissing through his partially closed mouth.

He knew the features of Henry Fredrick Stuart, Duke of Rothesay, Lord of the Isles, Duke of Cornwall, Prince of Wales and heir to the thrones of England and Scotland and Ireland.

He came slowly to his feet. There was an oppressive silence. Lord Ellesmore was gazing keenly at him. His expression was serious.

''Twere better if names were not uttered,' he counselled.

'Who did this thing?' replied the constable, aghast.

Lord Ellesmore allowed himself a sardonic chuckle.

'This mystery is for you to make a resolution of, Master Constable. Not only who did it but why it was done. Not even His Majesty has been woken to be told as yet, but when we do awake him at daylight, as is the custom, it would be better for all of us if we had some answers to give to the questions that he will shower upon us.'

Master Drew's lips compressed.

'It lacks only four hours until daylight,' he muttered. Then he turned back to the scene. He bent down and picked up a strangely curved dagger with foreign symbols that was lying near the body. It was covered in drying blood. He peered closely at the alien engraving. 'It does not need great wisdom to see that some devil's ritual was being made here.'

'You have seen the like before?' demanded the Lord Chancellor curiously.

'Not I. But I have a passing familiarity with the work *Daemonologie* that the King himself wrote nearly a score of years past. In my duties as Constable, I have had to make myself familiar of this subject as many lay charges of witchcraft against others. I see many things here that are described within His Majesty's book. These strange hieroglyphs on this dagger, for example.'

Lord Ellesmore glanced at him in grudging approval.

'It is true that His Majesty did write that treatise which denounced witchcraft and which many scholars hold in high esteem. Alas, good Constable, His Royal Highness . . .' He paused a moment and corrected himself. 'The young man trod paths of impropriety consistent with his station in life. He was corrupted by some of those around him. Many at court, I included, feared for the future. Yet, withal, I find it hard to believe he dabbled in the black arts.'

'And yet 'twas witchcraft that seems to be in evidence here,' replied the constable quietly. 'Who first discovered His Royal . . . the body?' He corrected himself with a gesture that encompassed the scene.

'The Serjeant at Arms, one Ned Strong. He is a trustworthy man, long in royal service. A man of silent tongue, to be sure. He has served me well and is loyal to me. Knowing that I was residing in the palace this night, pursuing some weighty matters of state, he straightway came to inform me of his discovery, having secured this chamber from idle curiosity.'

'And where shall I find this Ned Strong?'

'He is waiting in the guards' chamber in readiness to answer your interrogation. The Serjeant at Arms, as commander of the guard here, is allowed a special chamber for his use.'

'Then let us to him this instant and examine his story.'

Ned Strong had been in royal service for thirty years and had been privy to many sights that ordinary men could only dream of. He was stalwart, calm of spirit, yet with bright brown eyes that seemed piercing and missed nothing. His auburn hair was greying but he was of a muscular, thickset build and, doubtless, he could give a good account of himself with his sword and dirk in spite of the advancing years. He was dressed in the livery of the royal guards, a leather jerkin covering his red and white undershirt with its white ruffs, red breeches tucked into heavy leather riding boots, with wide bucket tops above which the boothose showed. He wore a sword and a dirk at his waist. A short cape hung from his shoulders on which was the royal crest.

He stood respectfully as Lord Ellesmore and Master Drew entered his small chamber in which he had been sitting, awaiting them.

With formalities of introduction over, the constable asked:

'How came you to make your grim discovery, Master Serjeant?'

'It is my duty to proceed through the corridors of this part of the palace at the tolling of each bell, signifying the passing of the night watch.'

'Is it your habit to inspect the . . . the Star Chamber?'

The man shook his head quickly.

'The chamber is usually locked and no one is admitted except when the Court of the Star Chamber is in session.'

'Yet you have a key?'

'As Serjeant of Arms, I am given keys of all the chambers that are locked. This is done in case of emergency. I have served in this palace for thirty years. I served our good Queen Elizabeth, God grant her peaceful rest. Now I serve King James.'

Master Drew frowned slightly. Had he detected a slight change in the man's tone at the mention of the King?

'So you must have served the late Queen for over twenty years?'

The Serjeant at Arms drew himself up proudly.

'I had that honour, good master.'

'And on her death, you continued in service?'

'I did.'

Again was there a slight change in tone. It was a sharper note of disapproval. Master Drew decided to pass over it.

'So what made you open the door on this occasion instead of passing on and continuing your watch?'

'I was approaching down the corridor when I heard a sound as of an object falling. A soft, muffled thud of a sound. I paused and heard the noise of rapid footsteps. Then, no more.'

'And so?'

'I took the key and opened the door. The scene that greeted me in the light of the lantern I held was as I have showed his lordship earlier. A body lay on the ground and there were scenes that something diabolical had been enacted there. Once I perceived the body to be that of His Highness the . . .'

Lord Ellesmore coughed warningly.

'Once you perceived the body, you came straightway in search of me,' he cut in meaningfully.

The Serjeant at Arms blinked and then nodded quickly.

'That I did and right quickly, sir.'

'Locking the door behind you?' queried the constable.

'Aye, sir.'

'You touched nothing? Moved nothing?'

'By the rood, I lay not a hand on anything, good Constable.' His voice was indignant.

'It is well to confirm these things, Master Strong,' pointed out the constable in a conciliatory tone. 'But there arise some questions. You say that you were alerted by the noise of a soft thud as if something heavy had fallen. Might that be consistent with the fall of a body to the floor?'

The man looked mollified.

'It would, good Constable.'

'And you then say that you heard sounds of footsteps?'

'That I did.'

'After the thud?'

'Aye, afterwards.'

'That presupposes that there was another in this very chamber at the time the body fell.'

'That was confirmed, for I also perceived footprints, bloody footprints, which led from the body.'

Master Drew nodded slowly.

'These footsteps that you heard, how long did they proceed before you did not hear them again?'

Master Ned Strong shrugged.

'I do not know what you mean.'

'A few seconds, some time? How long a passage of time?'

The Serjeant at Arms was diffident. 'I do not know.'

'I say this because I saw these prints and they led only five paces from the body, bloody prints, and then disappeared abruptly. Judging from their shape, I would say they were left by a male wearing solid wedge-shape shoes with low heels, unlike the high-heeled new fashion that is common today with both men and women.'

Master Strong was frowning in bewilderment.

'I do not understand, Master Constable. I only know what I heard.'

'Very well. Someone was in the chamber with the . . . the victim. You agree to this observation?'

'It seems logical to deduce as much,' replied the man.

'And you were standing at the main chamber door during this time. So what other entrances or exits to this chamber are there?'

'Apart from the main doors, I know of only one such entrance or exit and that is at the back of the chamber where prisoners are brought before it or taken below for punishment. The prints, as I recall, led in that direction. A tapestry disguises the door.'

'Then you must straightway show me.'

They returned to the Star Chamber with the Lord Chancellor, carefully locking the door behind them. The Serjeant at Arms marched clumsily across in his riding boots, passing the body and, carefully avoiding the footprints, went to a tapestry, pulling it aside. A small door of solid oak, with reinforced metal studs and hinges, stood behind it. It was locked.

'You notice that the bloody footprints have come to a halt long before reaching this door?' Master Drew pointed out.

The Lord Chancellor frowned.

'Is that important?'

'Notice how thick the blood is on the prints right until they cease. Why would they cease? There would have been enough blood still on them to make marks, even smudges, not to cease so abruptly. It is as if the person walked to the middle of the chamber and then . . . then disappeared into thin air.'

Lord Ellesmore looked worried.

'You imply that there is some devilry here? Some evil phantom at work?'

Master Drew smiled wanly.

'That devilry was at work here is obvious. But, no; I do not ascribe the explanation of this mystery to the supernatural, if that is what you mean.'

He turned abruptly.

'Have you the key to this door?'

The Serjeant at Arms nodded and produced a key from his ring.

'This only leads to the dungeons and guardhouse, Master Constable.'

'Let us proceed,' Master Drew said.

Led by the Serjeant at Arms they went down a small corridor and came to a second door that he unlocked. Beyond it was a room in which two surprised guards had been sitting at a table with a flagon of beer between them and dice on the table. They scrambled to their feet, astounded at the sight of the Lord Chancellor and the Serjeant.

'How long have you men been here?' demanded Master Drew.

One of the men raised his knuckles to his forehead.

'If please you, sir, we came on watch at midnight.'

'On watch?'

'We guard these cells,' explained the other, pointing to several doors that led off the room.

'You have been here all this time?'

'We have.'

'What prisoners are in the cells?'

'Just three. An Irish noble, Lord O'Donnell, and the lords . . .'

Master Drew waved his hand impatiently.

'Has anyone come this way since you have been here, from midnight, you say?' He jerked a thumb over his shoulder at the corridor behind.

Both men shook their heads.

Master Drew indicated that the Lord Chancellor and Serjeant should return with him to the Star Chamber.

'If the person who made these footprints did not exit by that route,' offered Lord Ellesmore once they were back by the body, 'then there is only one other entrance.'

Master Drew frowned.

'But the Serjeant was at that door.'

The Lord Chancellor shook his head.

311

'I mean there is a special door that leads directly to the royal apartments.'

'You did not tell me of this.' Master Drew swung round in annoyance to the Serjeant.

The man gestured with raised shoulders and outspread arms.

'Even I do not have a key to that door leading to the royal bedchambers,' he protested.

'Show me where this door is,' instructed Master Drew, irritably.

It was Lord Ellesmore who led the way across the chamber, behind the dais on which the seats reserved for the King and his leading courtiers were placed. He swung back another tapestry behind them and then let out a gasp.

The door stood open and there was a key still in the lock.

Master Drew looked thoughtful. His keen eyes caught a dark stain on the handle and he bent forward, touching it with his fingertip. The blood was not quite dried.

'Was this door checked by you, Master Serjeant?'

The man shook his head quickly.

'I have said, once I observed the body and recognised who it was, I went straightway to Lord Ellesmore. I made no investigation.'

'Yet you heard footsteps in the room? Did it not occur to you that the culprit had escaped, and if it wasn't through the guard-room and cells then it must have been through this door?'

'To the royal apartments?' demanded the Serjeant in astonishment.

Master Drew did not answer but turned to Lord Ellesmore.

'And when you returned here with the Serjeant, my lord, you did not demand any inspection of this door?'

The Lord Chancellor shook his head uncomfortably.

'I resolved that the matter must be placed in competent hands immediately. That is why I sent for you.'

Master Drew let out a sigh.

'Then I suggest we proceed through this door, for the stains of blood show us the way.'

Master Drew went first with the Serjeant bearing his lantern close behind. Beyond the door was a narrow passage ending in a long flight of stairs that went straight up between stone walls. Now and then the constable would halt to examine a dark stain which merely confirmed that someone with blood on his or her hands or clothes had passed this way. There was a small landing at the top of the first flight, but no doors leading off, and then another flight of stairs led up to the dark oak door. Another key was needed and again Master Drew saw that it was still in the lock of the door.

He swung it open slowly.

Beyond was a tapestry that disguised the door from unknowing passers-by in the passageway beyond. This red yew-panelled passage was hung with portraits and lit by occasional lanterns. It was opulent in its decorations and furnishings.

Behind him, Lord Ellesmore leaned close to Master Drew.

'These are the royal apartments,' he whispered.

The red wood made it difficult to discern bloodstains and the constable was momentarily at a loss as to how to proceed.

It was at that moment a woman came from one of the chambers along the corridor, carrying a china bowl of water and a towel. She was tall, with golden hair, and strikingly handsome. She saw them and halted in confusion.

'What are you doing here, my lord?' she demanded of the Lord

Chancellor, recovering from her surprise. She obviously recognised him at once.

Lord Ellesmore contrived to give a courtly bow in the confined space of the corridor.

'A grim task brings us hither, my lady. We . . .'

Master Drew stepped forward.

'We wish to know how you obtained the bloodstain on your sleeve, lady, and . . .' He peered closely into the bowl. 'Why you carry water so intermixed with blood in that receptacle?'

The woman flushed with indignation.

'How now, sir! I know you not.' Her chin came up defiantly. 'Who are you to dare question me?'

Lord Ellesmore coughed in embarrassment.

'Master Drew, the constable, is acting under my instruction, lady. Master Drew, this is the Lady Ivowen, lady-in-waiting to the Queen's Majesty.'

There was a silence and then Master Drew said: 'We await an answer, lady.'

'You are impertinent, sir,' snapped the woman.

'As you have heard, I act for my Lord Ellesmore.'

Beside him the Lord Chancellor nodded unhappily.

'We would not trouble you, lady, were it not of great import.'

Lady Ivowen sniffed.

'If you have to know . . . I cut myself on the arm and was tending to the wound.'

'I see.' Master Drew smiled. 'I am acquainted with such wounds. Perhaps you'll be good enough to show me that I may advise you . . .'

'Really, sir. You are impudent!'

314

Behind her, a door opened and a tall young man stood there in his shirt, the white sleeves of which were stained with blood. He was tall and had the same features and burnished hair as the woman but without the determined chin. His eyes were red and cheeks tearstained. His lower lip trembled. Master Drew had the impression of an oversized petulant child whose treasured possessions had just been confiscated for misbehaviour.

'It is no good, sister,' the young man said in a resigned but tremulous voice. 'They have tracked me down and I must face their questions.'

The woman turned to him in agitation.

'No, no, Cedric. You are in no condition to . . .'

The Lord Chancellor moved forward, frowning, his voice suddenly angry and accusing.

'Lord Deenish! We have come from the Star Chamber. Do you admit responsibility . . .?'

'Of course he does not!' snapped Lady Ivowen. 'He is innocent of any wrongdoing. How dare you . . .?'

'Madam, I dare because I am Chancellor. Your brother's liaison . . .' he chose the word carefully, 'with Prince Henry is the scandal of London.'

Master Hardy Drew raised a hand for silence. He was thinking rapidly. Certainly, Lord Ellesmore was right. Lord Deenish was the talk of certain quarters of the city as being the favourite companion to the Prince of Wales. And the talk was, as Lord Ellesmore pointed out in unsubtle fashion, that they were more than just companions. Deenish was about twenty-one, three years older than Prince Henry, and rumour had it that he had enticed the young prince into the paths of vice and evil.

'It would be better to repair to Lord Deenish's chamber than discuss this matter in the discomfort of this passage,' the constable said firmly. 'Serjeant, do you stand guard here by the door while we retire within.'

Everyone seemed mesmerised by his quiet command of the situation and Lord Deenish backed before them into the room, which was an anteroom to his bedchamber. A fire blazed in the hearth and there were chairs and a table nearby. Master Drew stood back and motioned Deenish's sister, Lady Ivowen, to enter, still bearing her bowl of water and towel. These she then replaced on the table. Lord Ellesmore followed and closed the door behind him.

'Now, my lord, my lady, what means this?' the Lord Chancellor demanded, pointing to Deenish's bloodstained clothing. 'You cannot deny that you were in the chamber below with His Royal Highness.'

As Lady Ivowen began to reply, still with a belligerent expression on her features, Master Drew held up his hand again.

'With your indulgence, my lord,' he said to Ellesmore, 'I would like to conduct this in my own way. First, Lady Ivowen, you are not wounded and were not washing the blood from any such cut or abrasion on your person. I would like you to tell us the truth. Tell us what you were about before we turn to the matter of what your brother was doing.'

There was a silence. Her mouth remained in a thin slit, her jaw pugnacious.

'You know whose body lies in the Star Chamber?' Master Drew pressed on firmly. 'This is not merely a matter of murder, but it might be construed as an act of High Treason.'

Brother and sister exchanged a startled glance.

'We are innocent of any act,' Lady Ivowen replied, her voice less combatant than before. 'I was awoken by my brother coming into my chamber in a state of great agitation and with blood upon his hands and clothes . . .'

'Your chamber is where?'

'Next to this.'

'Continue. I presume you were asleep?'

'I was. His coming awoke me. It took much persuasion on my part and Malmsey wine to calm his agitation. He said that he had gone looking for Prince Henry and found his body below . . .'

'In the Star Chamber?'

She nodded quickly. Master Drew noticed that she suppressed a shudder.

'What else did he tell you?'

'He was incoherent for much of the time. My brother is . . . was . . . very close to Henry. They were bosom companions. I brought him here to his own chamber and, believing the blood was from some wound, I took water and towel and washed the blood away. My brother then confessed that the blood was from Prince Henry's death wound. By that time, my brother was calm and told me what exactly he had discovered. He . . .'

Master Drew made a slight cutting motion with his hand.

'As your brother is here with us there is no need for you to tell us this. Your brother may give his account first hand. Now, did you at any time go down into the Star Chamber to verify this story?'

She shook her head.

'Have you attempted to raise the alarm?'

'I have only just calmed my brother and not discussed what we should do,' she responded. 'I was about to get rid of the bowl of water when you appeared.'

Lord Ellesmore grimaced in contempt.

'This looks bad, young Deenish,' he said in a brittle tone. 'You have affronted God by your conduct here and now you have gone too far, for I have no doubt that it was you who persuaded the young prince to dabble in the black arts. The case against you is obvious.'

The young man blinked rapidly.

'I did not do this. You must believe me.'

Master Drew contained his annoyance at the Lord Chancellor's intervention.

'We have yet to hear your story, my lord. Let us start with what you might know of the diabolical materials that are laid out in the chamber below.'

The young man was pale.

'It was Hal's humour,' he muttered.

'Prince Henry's humour?' snapped Master Drew. 'You must explain more explicitly.'

'You know that His Majesty wrote a work on *Daemonologie*, a work that is highly regarded among the clerics?'

Master Drew gave a sign that he was acquainted with the book.

'Hal – His Highness, that is – was lately out of favour with his father, the King's Majesty, and in filial rebellion against him. I mean,' the young man added hastily, 'the rebellion that a young man has against his father.'

The constable smiled with humour.

'The challenge of the young bull to the old bull. It happens to all, kings or commoners.'

'Hal – that is, His Highness – knowing rightly that his father deemed himself a great expert on witchcraft and that his book has been produced in authority at the various trials of witches and warlocks throughout the realm, thought he would amuse himself by holding a Black Mass in his father's very court – in the Star Chamber. He enlisted my support . . .'

The young man hesitated and licked his lips.

'And did you give it?' demanded Lord Ellesmore harshly.

'I never stirred to help him. I swear so by the holy rood. As much as I loved the prince, I am yet a Christian, and not even to form an amusement or play act would I participate in such a theatre. His Highness was petulant and called me many names, saying that with or without me he was determined to perform the acts referred to in his father's books at midnight on the eve of All Hallows' Day in the very spot where his father, the King's Majesty, sat in judgment on all his kingdom.'

Master Drew nodded slowly.

'And this came to pass?'

'It is as you have seen. Right until the final moment I refused to accompany His Highness.'

'Until the final moment? Did you then change your mind?'

'Not I. Prince Henry left me before midnight and went down by the stairs his father and other members of the royal family use to enter the Star Chamber. He cajoled and pleaded for me to go with him right until the end, using persuasive tones one moment and harsh and jeering taunts another. After he had gone I sat for a long while here in my room. I heard, eventually, the cry of the night watch proclaiming the midnight hour. I waited a while, waited for what seemed eternity, for His Highness to return.

When he had not, I summoned my courage and went down the stairs.'

He paused and gave a sob and it was some moments before he could control himself.

'You entered the chamber?' pressed Master Drew.

'That I did,' affirmed Lord Deenish. 'I saw His Highness's body immediately. I went over and tried to lift him . . .'

'Hence the bloodstains on your clothes?' queried Lord Ellesmore.

'He was dead, cold and dead.'

'There was no sign of anyone in the chamber?'

'I saw none. As soon as I saw that Hal's throat was cut, a cold fear seized me. I heard someone at the doors and I ran back here to wake my sister.'

Master Drew stood quietly for a while.

'That is exactly as my brother told me earlier,' Lady Ivowen said, feeling a need to break the silence. 'My brother is incapable of any violence, least of all to his . . . his best friend.'

'It looks bad, nevertheless,' replied Lord Ellesmore. 'What say you, Constable?'

Master Drew smiled softly.

'Are those the shoes you have been wearing all evening, my lord?' he asked abruptly, glancing down.

Lord Deenish started in surprise and glanced down at his shoes.

'I suppose so, why?'

But Master Drew had turned to Lady Ivowen.

'And you, my lady?'

Lord Deenish's sister was gazing at him as if he had lost his senses.

'I wore these shoes before I retired for the night and put them on after my brother disturbed me.'

Master Drew glanced at Lord Ellesmore.

'A word alone with you, my Lord Chancellor. Is there an adjacent chamber to which we may retire?'

'We will use Lord Deenish's bedchamber, with his permission. Remember, the Serjeant is without,' he added to Deenish and his sister.

The young man gestured helplessly.

Lord Ellesmore picked up a candle from the table and led the way into the darkened room. Master Drew closed the door behind him.

'I am now sure of the identity of the culprit, my lord,' he whispered, placing a finger to his lips to indicate that Ellesmore should respond in a low voice.

'Deenish?' demanded Lord Ellesmore, in satisfaction. 'I agree. God help me, but Henry was a weak and indolent young man and his actions were an affront to God and our good Protestant religion. I am afraid it may be said that his death will be of much benefit to the future of our kingdom. Young Prince Charles will be next in line now and being yet a boy we can, perhaps, raise him with a sense of responsibility and protect him from evil influences such as Deenish.'

Master Drew did not reply at once. Then he said: 'I know that there were many in the kingdom who were unhappy when Her Majesty died and her councillors made the decision to invite James the Sixth of Scotland to ascend the throne of England also.'

The Lord Chancellor looked momentarily surprised.

'Eight – no, nine – years have passed since then. We have had to make our peace with His Majesty.'

'Nevertheless, there were those who were unhappy.'

Lord Ellesmore shrugged.

'Some pointed out that Her Majesty never made a will and that when she died the nation was ill advised to invite a Scot to govern them. It is no secret that I was initially among that number. Many greeted His Majesty as a foreigner, one who speaks in a strange accent and who brought forth all his favourites out of the court of Scotland and placed them over those of England. His Majesty inevitably made enemies; Catesby's plot some years ago nearly deprived him of his life; Melville has been in the Tower these six years, and plots and rebellions occur throughout the kingdom.'

Master Drew pursed his lips thoughtfully.

'The Golden Age of England is thought to have passed with Her Majesty,' he observed. 'Is not her speech to the House of Commons, barely eighteen months before her passing, now called her "Golden Speech"? The one in which she spoke of her love of her people and her people's love of her.'

Ellesmore grimaced.

'I know it well. I was there when she made it.'

'There are many, such as you, my lord, who loyally served and loved Elizabeth well. Many supported a continuance of the Tudor dynasty by inviting a distant cousin to take to the throne.'

Ellesmore's face hardened.

'I know not what you are suggesting, Master Constable. His Majesty of Scotland now has as much Tudor blood in his veins as anyone. Is he not descended from the Princess Margaret, daughter of Henry, the Seventh of his name to sit upon the throne of England?'

'All I am saying is this, plots and rebellions have been many since His Majesty of Scotland came to London. The fact that the heir to the throne of England is . . . *was* an indolent young boy who preferred the company of young men to women was scandalising many. I believe that this latest indulgence – the performance of a blasphemy in the very chamber where Her Late Majesty, Elizabeth, held court – was, when it was discovered, seen as a final sacrilege and insult to England. The person could not restrain their outrage and slaughtered him.'

Lord Ellesmore was staring at the constable aghast.

'How now, Master Drew, be you serious in this matter?'

'Never more,' the constable assured him.

'And thus are you saying that Lord Deenish must be innocent of it?'

'I am.'

'Then do you accuse his sister, Lady Ivowen?'

Master Drew turned to the door.

'Give me a moment more of indulgence,' he said.

They re-entered the chamber where Lord Deenish rose uncertainly from the chair where he had been sitting. He had removed his bloodstained shirt and pulled on a woollen doublet. His sister continued to sit moodily staring into the fire.

The constable went to the door and called in the Serjeant at Arms.

'A favour, good Serjeant,' he said, when Master Strong entered. 'Be so good as to go and fetch me the shoes that you were wearing when you were doing your guard rounds tonight.'

The Serjeant at Arms stared at him in bewilderment for a moment.

The Lord Chancellor was frowning.

'Shoes? You seem to have a preoccupation with shoes, Master Constable.'

Master Drew nodded, his eyes not leaving those of the burly Serjeant at Arms.

'I am not so unobservant that I did not realise a night watch in the corridors and halls of a palace does not stalk these echoing chambers in heavy, clumsy riding boots. You have changed your footwear, Master Strong. Shall I tell you how?'

There was a tense silence in the room. The Serjeant was now white-faced.

'This night you went on your rounds as usual, clad in your normal footwear. You came to the doors of the Star Chamber and something caught your attention. Perhaps some noise. You quietly unlocked the chamber door and entered and saw . . . well, God alone knows what you thought. Here was the ultimate sac-rilege. The young Prince of Wales, heir to the throne, performing some unspeakable satanic rite, in the very chamber where your own beloved Queen Elizabeth once held court among her loyal subjects. You had served her well and loyally, and your religious scruples reinforced your anger. You grabbed the ritual dagger from the young man's hand and killed him.'

Master Drew paused. There was no denial, no response, no movement from Master Ned Strong.

'You began to move away from the bloody body, half a dozen paces, before you realised the reality of what you had done. You suddenly grasped the fact that you had blood on the underside of

324

your shoes. They left an accusing trail. So you stepped out of your shoes, there and then, and picked them up. Thus the trail ended. Bearing them in your hands you walked in stocking feet back to the doors, re-locked them, and removed yourself to your guard-room where you put on the only other available footwear – your riding boots.

'Then I think you decided to resume your watch and came back to the door of the Star Chamber when you heard movement within. You opened it but Lord Deenish, who had just discovered the body, had fled back to wake his sister. She was the only person he could confide in. Knowing someone must have made the discovery, you pretended to have discovered the Prince's body for the first time and went off to alert Lord Ellesmore. Am I right?'

Ned Strong glanced to Lord Ellesmore. Some look, a slight nod of acknowledgement, passed, and then he cried, 'God bless Queen Bess. God bless England!'

The cry startled them all with its abrupt passion.

Then Master Ned Strong was sinking rapidly to the floor. He was dead before he reached it. The dirk was no longer in the sheath at his waist but buried deep under his ribs, through the heart, and his blood was pumping over his clothing.

Master Hardy Drew stood looking down at him in sadness. He had not been prepared for such an act. At his shoulder, Lord Ellesmore was more cynical.

'How shall we describe him, good Constable? A patriot? A religious fanatic? A regicide?'

The constable shook his head.

'That is not my concern, my lord. But think long and hard about this affair. Should the truth of this be voiced abroad it

might do irreparable damage to a realm that is already in turmoil. I am no counsellor, my lord, but things have happened here
that the common good dictates should not be revealed to anyone
outside these walls.'

Lord Ellesmore glanced sharply at him.

'Then I shall return to the question that I asked you earlier –
can I count on your discretion?'

Master Hardy Drew returned his gaze earnestly.

'My lord, I have not been here tonight.'

It was five days later, on 6 November, that London awoke to
the announcement from St James's Palace that His Royal Highness Henry Frederick, Prince of Wales, Duke of Rothesay, Lord
of the Isles and Duke of Cornwall, heir to the thrones of England, Scotland and Ireland, had died of typhoid fever. He had
been removed to his darkened bedchamber early in the morning
of 1 November, where not even his family were allowed entrance,
nor even his chaplain, Reverend Dr Daniel Price, could see him
because of the contagion. The announcement provoked a widespread outpouring of public and private grief, English and
Scottish poets wrote moving elegies reflecting on human vulner-
ability, ballads were sung, sermons preached and even madrigals
called 'songs of mourning' were performed. The realms of England and Scotland joined together in the grief-stricken release of
hopes and expectation for their future king who was now no
more. All eyes were turned on the eleven-year-old Duke of
Albany, Marquess of Ormonde, Earl of Ross, Baron of Ardmannoch and Duke of York – Charles – the new heir apparent.

Only Master Hardy Drew gave passing thought to the gossip
surrounding the swift departure of Lord Deenish and his sister,

Lady Ivowen, who had sailed from Gravesend to make a new life for themselves at Jamestown in Captain John Smith's new colony of Virginia, even before the funeral obsequies of Prince Henry.

It was four years later that Master Drew was attending the funeral of Lord Ellesmore himself.

He was seated next to an elderly and loquacious man.

'A great man, Lord Ellesmore,' the man offered. 'He was one of Her Late Majesty's most trusted servants and ardent supporters of her dynasty. Did you know him, Master Constable?'

'I knew him briefly some years ago,' admitted Master Drew. 'And you?'

'I served him as a guard when he was Chancellor. Serjeant Strong was my senior then.'

'Serjeant Ned Strong?' Master Drew stirred uncomfortably.

'Aye, did you know him?'

'I have heard the name.'

'A fine soldier was Ned Strong. Fiercely loyal to Lord Ellesmore.'

Master Drew stirred uneasily.

'Is that so?'

'Indeed it is. You would have recognised him easily had you known him. A strong, muscular man who was proud of the livery he wore. We used to jest with him, for when he was on duty, he liked to dress in full uniform, even down to riding boots. Whoever heard of wearing riding boots within doors! But that was his only eccentricity.'

The constable felt suddenly cold.

'It was his custom to wear riding boots indoors?'

The elderly man chuckled.

'He said a uniform was not properly worn without them. But he was a man who would lay down his life for what he believed right. Poor Ned Strong. He disappeared some years ago. The story was that he was probably set upon by footpads one night outside the palace and his body dumped into the Thames. A sad end.'

Master Drew nodded slowly. He was suddenly remembering the first time he had seen Lord Ellesmore, seated in his chair and pulling on a new pair of shoes. All that he had accused Strong of doing could equally apply to . . .

It was then the funeral cortège of Lord Ellesmore entered the church.

'A sad end,' he echoed. 'Ah!' he added, with a little savagery in his tone. 'I think I am getting too old to be constable. I miss the obvious.'

An Ensuing Evil

Yet I can give you inkling
Of an ensuing evil . . .

Henry VIII, Act II, Scene i
William Shakespeare

'It's a body, Master Constable.'

Master Hardy Drew, Constable of the Bankside Watch, stared in distaste at the wherryman. 'I have eyes to see with,' he replied sourly. 'Just tell me how you came by it.'

The stocky boatman put a hand to the back of his head and scratched as if this action were necessary to the process of summoning up his memories. 'It were just as we turned mid-river to the quay here,' the wherryman began. 'We'd brought coal up from Greenwich. I was guiding the barge in when we spotted the body in the river, and so we fished it out.'

Master Drew glanced down to the body sprawled in a sodden mess on the dirty deck of the coal barge.

The finding of bodies floating in the Thames was not an unusual occurrence. London was a cesspool of suffering humanity, especially along these banks between London Bridge and Bankside. Master Drew had not been Constable of the Watch

329

for more than ten years without becoming accustomed to bodies being trawled out of this stretch of water whose southern bank came under his policing jurisdiction. Cut-throats, footpads and all manner of the criminal scum of the city found the river a convenient place to rid themselves of their victims. And it was not just those who had died violent deaths who were disposed of in the river, but also corpses of the poor, sick and diseased, whose relatives couldn't afford a church burial. The pollution of the water had become so bad that this very year a water reservoir, claimed to be the first of its kind in all Europe, had been opened at Clerkenwell to supply fresh water for the city.

However, what marked this body out for the attention of the constable, among the half-dozen or so that had been fished from the river this particular Saturday morning, was the fact that it was the body of a well-dressed young man. Despite the effects of his immersion, he bore the stamp of a gentleman. In addition, he had not died of drowning, for his throat had been expertly cut – and no more than twelve hours previously, by the condition of the body.

The constable bent down and examined the features dispassionately. In life, the young man had been handsome, was well kempt. He had ginger hair, a splattering of freckles across the nose, and a scar, which might have been the result of a knife or sword, across the forehead over the right eye. His age was no more than twenty-one or twenty-two years. Master Drew considered that he might be the son of a squire or someone in the professions – a parson's son, perhaps. The constable's expert scrutiny had ruled out his being of higher quality, for the clothes, while fashionable, were only of moderately good tailoring. Therefore, the young man had not been someone of flamboyant wealth.

The wherryman was peering over the constable's shoulder and sniffed. 'Victim of a footpad, most like?'

Master Drew did not answer, but keeping his leather gloves on, he took the hand of the young man and examined a large and ostentatious ring that was on it. 'Since when did a footpad leave jewellery on his victim?' he asked. He removed the ring carefully and held it up. 'Ah!' he commented.

'What, Master Constable?' demanded the wherryman.

Drew had noticed that the ring, ostentatious though it was, was not really as valuable as first glance might suggest. It boasted no precious metals or stones, thus fitting the constable's image of someone who wanted to convey a sense of style without the wealth to back it. He put it into his pocket.

There was a small leather purse on the man's belt. Its mouth was not well tied. He opened it without expecting to find anything, so was surprised when a few coins and a key fell out. They were as dry as the interior of the purse.

'A sixpenny piece and three strange copper coins,' observed Master Drew. He held up one of the copper coins. 'Marry! The new copper farthings. I have not seen any before this day.'

'What's that?' replied the wherryman.

'These coins have just been issued to replace the silver farthings. Well, whatever the reason for his killing, robbery it was not.'

Master Drew was about to stand up when he noticed a piece of paper tucked into the man's doublet. He drew it forth and tried to unfold it, sodden as it was.

'A theatre bill. For the Blackfriars Theatre. A performance of *The Maid's Tragedy*,' he remarked.

He rose and waved to two men of the watch, who were waiting

on the quay with a cart. They came down onto the barge and, in answer to Master Drew's gesture, manhandled the corpse up the stone steps to their cart.

'What now then, Constable?' demanded the old wherryman.

'Back to your work, man,' replied Master Drew. 'And I to mine. I have to discover who this young coxcomb is . . . *was*, and the reason for his being in the river with his throat slit.'

'Will there be a reward for finding him?' the wherryman asked slyly. 'I have lost time in landing my cargo of coal.'

Master Drew regarded the man without humour. 'When you examined the purse of the corpse, Master Wherryman, you neglected to retie it properly. If he had gone into the river with the purse open as it was, then the interior would not have been dry, and neither would the coins.'

The wherryman winced at the constable's cold tone.

'I do not begrudge you a reward, which you have taken already, but out of interest, how much was left in the purse when you found it?'

'By the faith, Master Constable . . .' the wherryman protested.

'The truth now!' snapped Master Drew, his grey eyes glinting like wet slate.

'I took only a silver shilling, that is all. On my mother's honour.'

'I will take charge of that money,' replied the constable, holding out his hand. 'And I will forget what I have heard, for theft is theft and the reward for a thief is a hemp rope. Remember that, and I'll leave you to your honest toil.'

One of the watchmen was waiting eagerly for the constable as he climbed up onto the quay. 'Master Drew, I do reckon I've seen this 'ere cove somewhere afore,' he said, raising his knuckles to his forehead in salute.

Master Drew regarded the man dourly. 'Well, then? Where do you think you have seen him before?'

'I do be trying 'ard to think on't.' His companion was staring at the face of the corpse with a frown. ''E be right. I do say 'e be one o' them actor fellows. Can't think where I see'd 'im.'

Master Drew glanced sharply at him. 'An actor?'

He stared down at the theatre bill he still held in his gloved hand and pursed his lips thoughtfully. 'Take him up to the mortuary. I have business at the Blackfriars Theatre.'

The constable turned along the quay and found a solitary boatman soliciting for custom. The man looked awkward as the constable approached.

'I need your services,' Master Drew said shortly, putting the man a little at ease, for it was rare that the appearance of the constable on the waterfront meant anything other than trouble. 'Blackfriars Steps.'

'Sculls then, Master Constable?' queried the man.

'Sculls it is,' Master Drew agreed, climbing into the small dinghy. The boatman sat at his oars and sent the dinghy dancing across the river to the north bank, across the choppy waters, which were raised by an easterly wind.

As they crossed, Drew was not interested in the spectacle up to London Bridge, with its narrow arches where the tide ran fast because of the constriction of the crossing. Beyond it, he knew, was the great port, where ships from all parts of the world tied up, unloading cargoes under the shadow of the grim, grey Tower.

The north bank, where the city proper was sited, was not Constable Drew's jurisdiction. He was constable on the south bank of the river but he was not perturbed about crossing out of his territory. He knew the City Watch well enough.

The boat rasped against the bottom of Blackfriars Steps. He flipped the man a halfpenny and walked with a measured tread up the street towards the tower of St Paul's rising above the city, which was shrouded with the acrid stench of coal fires from a hundred thousand chimneys. It was not far to the Blackfriars Theatre.

He walked in and was at once hailed by a tall man who fluttered his hands nervously. 'I say, fellow! Away! Begone! The theatre is not open for another three hours yet.'

Master Drew regarded the man humourlessly. 'I come not to see the play but to seek information.' He reached behind his jerkin and drew forth his seal of office.

'A constable?' The man assumed a comical woebegone expression. 'What do you seek here, good Constable? We have our papers in order, the licence from the Lord Chamberlain. What is there that is wrong?'

'To whom do I speak?' demanded Master Drew.

'Why, to Master Page Williams, the assistant manager of our company – Children of the Revel.' The man stuck out his chin proudly.

'And are any of your revelling children astray this afternoon?'

'Astray, good master? What do you mean?'

'I speak plainly. Are all your company of players accounted for today?'

'Indeed, they be. We are rehearsing our next performance, which requires all our actors.'

'Is there no one missing?'

'All are present. Why do you ask?'

Master Drew described the body of the young man that had been fished from the river. Master Page Williams looked unhappy.

'It seems that I know him. An impetuous youth, he was, who came to this theatre last night and claimed to be a playwright whose work had been stolen.'

'Did he have a name?'

'Alas, I have forgotten it, if I were even told it. This youth, if it be one and the same, strutted in before the evening performance of our play and demanded to speak with the manager. I spoke with him.'

'And what did he want?' pressed Master Drew.

'This youth accused our company of pirating a play that he claimed to be author of.'

Constable Drew raised an eyebrow. 'Tell me, was there reason behind this encounter?'

'Good Master Constable, we are rehearsing a play whose author is one Bardolph Zenobia. He has written a great tragedy titled *The Vow Breaker Delivered*. It is a magnificent drama . . .' He paused at the constable's frown and then hastened on. 'This youth, whom you describe, came to the theatre and claimed that this play was stolen from him and that he was the true author. As if a mere youth could have penned such a work. He claimed that he had assistance in the writing of it from the hand of some companion of his –'

'And you set no store by his claim, that this play was stolen from him?'

'None whatsoever. Master Zenobia is a true gentleman of the

335

theatre. A serious gentleman. He has the air of quality about him . . .'

'So you know him well?'

'Not well,' confessed Master Williams. 'He has been to the theatre on divers occasions following our acceptance of his work. I believe that he has rooms at the Groaning Cardinal tavern in Clink Street –'

'Clink Street?'

It was across the river, in his own Bankside jurisdiction.

'What age would you place this Master Zenobia at?'

'Fully forty years, with greying hair about the temples and a serene expression that would grace an archbishop.'

Master Drew sniffed dourly. Theatre people were always given to flowery descriptions. 'So did the youth depart from the theatre?'

'Depart he did, but not until I threatened to call the watch. When I refused to countenance his demands, he shouted and threatened me. He said that if he did not recover the stolen play or get compensation, his life would be in danger.'

'His life?' mused Master Drew. 'Marry! But that is an odd thing to say. Are you sure he said it was *his* life in danger, not the life of Master Zenobia? He did not mean this in the manner of a threat?'

'I have an ear for dialogue, good master,' rebuked the man. 'The youth soon betook himself off. It happened that Master Zenobia was on stage, approving the costumes for his drama, and so I warned him to beware of the young man and his outrageous claims.'

'What did he say?'

'He just replied that he would have a care and soon after departed.'

'Is he here today?'

'No. He told me he would be unable to see the first performance of the play this afternoon but would come straightway to the theatre after the matinee.'

'A curious attitude for an aspiring playwright,' observed Master Drew. 'Most of them would want to be witnesses to the first performance of their work.'

'Indeed they would. It seems odd that Master Zenobia only calls at our poor theatre outside the hours of our performances.'

Constable Drew thanked the man and turned out of the theatre to walk back to the river. Instead of spending another halfpenny to cross, he decided to walk the short distance to the spanning wooden piles of London Bridge and walk across the busy thoroughfare with its sprawling lopsided constructions balanced precariously upon it. Master Drew knew the watch on the bridge and spent a pleasant half an hour with the man, for it was midday, and a pint of ale and pork pie at one of the grog shops crowded on the bridge was a needed diversion from the toil of the day. He bade farewell to the watch and came off the bridge at the south bank, turning west towards Clink Street.

The Groaning Cardinal tavern was not an auspicious-looking inn. Its sign depicted a popish cardinal being burnt at the stake. It reminded Constable Drew, with a shudder, that only the previous year some heretics had been burnt at the stake in England. Fears of Catholic plots still abounded. Henry, the late Prince of Wales, had refused to marry a Catholic princess only weeks before his death, and it was rumoured abroad by papists that this had been God's punishment on him. Protestants spoke of witchcraft.

Master Drew entered the tavern.

The innkeeper was a giant of a man – tall, broad-shouldered, well muscled, and with no shirt, just a short, leather, sleeveless jerkin over his hairy torso. He was sweating, and it became evident that he was stacking ale barrels.

'Bardolph Zenobia, Master Constable?' He threw back his head and laughed. 'Someone be telling you lies. Ain't no Master Zenobia here. He do sound like a foreigner.'

Constable Drew had come to the realisation that the name was probably a theatrical one, for he knew that many in the theatre adopted such preposterous designations.

He repeated the description that Master Page Williams had given him and saw a glint of anxiety creep into the innkeeper's eyes.

'What be he done, Master Constable? 'E ain't wanted for debt?'

Master Drew shook his head. 'The man may yet settle his score with you. But I need information from this man, whoever he is.'

The innkeeper sighed deeply. 'First floor, front right.'

'And what name does this thespian reside under?'

'Master Tom Hawkins.'

'That sounds more reasonable than Master Zenobia,' observed the constable.

'Them players are all the same, with high-sounding titles and names,' agreed the innkeeper. 'Few of them can match their name to a farthing. But Master Hawkins is different. He has been a steady guest here these last five years.'

'He has his own recognisances?'

The man stared at him bewildered.

'I mean, does he have financial means other than the theatre?'

'He do pay his bills, that's all I do say, master,' the innkeeper replied.

'But he is a player?'

'One of the King's Men.'

Master Drew was surprised. 'At the Globe Theatre?'

'He is one of Master Burbage's players,' confirmed the innkeeper.

Constable Drew mounted the stairs and knocked at the first floor, front right door. There was no answer. He did not hesitate but entered. The room was deserted. It was also untidy. Clothes and papers were strewn here and there. Master Drew peered through them. There were some play parts and a page or two on which the name *Bardolph Zenobia* was scrawled.

He took himself downstairs and saw the big innkeeper again.

'Maybe he has gone to the theatre?' suggested the man when he told him the room was deserted.

'It is still a while before the time of the matinee performance.'

'They sometimes hold rehearsals before the performance,' the innkeeper pointed out.

Master Drew was about to turn away when he realised it would not come amiss to ask if the innkeeper knew aught of the youth whose body had been discovered. He gave the man a description without informing him of his death. But his enquiry was received with a vehement shake of the head.

'I have not seen such a young man here, nor do I know him.'

Constable Drew walked to where the Globe Theatre dominated its surroundings in Bankside. Master Hardy Drew had been a boy when the Burbage brothers, Cuthbert and Richard, had built the theatre there fourteen years before. Since then the Globe had become an institution south of the river. It had first become the home of the Lord Chamberlain's Men, who, on the succession of James VI of Scotland to the English throne ten years ago, had been given gracious permission to call themselves the King's Men. Master Drew knew Cuthbert Burbage slightly, for their paths had crossed several times. Cuthbert Burbage ran the business side of the theatre while his brother, Richard Burbage, was the principal actor and director of the plays that were performed there.

Master Drew entered the doors of the Globe Theatre. An elderly doorman came forward, recognised the constable and halted nervously.

'Give you a good day, Master Jasper,' Master Drew greeted him.

'Is aught amiss, good master?' grumbled the old man.

'Should there be?' The constable smiled thinly.

'That I would not know, for I keep myself to myself and do my job without offending God nor the King, nor, I do pray, my fellow man.'

Master Drew looked at him sourly before glancing around. 'Are the players gathered?'

'Not yet.'

'Who is abroad in the theatre?'

Master Jasper looked suspicious. 'Master Richard Burbage is on stage.'

The constable walked through into the circular auditorium, leaving the old man staring anxiously after him, and climbed the wooden steps onto the stage.

A middle-aged man was kneeling on the stage, appearing to be measuring something.

Master Drew coughed to announce his presence.

Richard Burbage was still a handsome man in spite of the obvious ravages of the pox. He glanced up with a frown. 'And who might you be, you rogue?' he grunted, still bending to his task.

Drew pursed his lips sourly and then suddenly smiled. 'No rogue, that's for sure. I might be the shade of Constable Dogberry come to demand amends for defamation of his character.'

Burbage paused and turned to examine him closely. 'Are you a player, good master?'

'Not I,' replied Drew, 'and God be thanked for it.'

'How make you freely with the name of Dogberry, then?'

'I have witnessed your plays, sir. I took offence to the pompous and comical portrayal of the constable in Master Shakespeare's jotting. *Much Ado about Nothing* was its title and, indeed, Master Burbage, *Much Ado about Nothing* was a title never more truly given to such a work. 'Twas certainly *Much Ado about Nothing*.'

Richard Burbage stood up and brushed himself down, frowning as he did so. 'Are you, then, a critic of the theatre, sir?'

'Not I. But I am a critic of the portrayal of a hardworking constable and the watch of this fair town of ours.'

'How so, good master?'

'I judge because I am a constable myself. Constable of Bankside, in which this theatre is placed.'

'Art come to imprison me for defaming the watch then, sir?' asked Burbage stiffly.

Master Drew chuckled with good humour. 'Marry, sir, there be not enough prisons in the entire kingdom wherein to imprison everyone who makes jest of the constable and his watch.'

341

'Then what – ?'

'I am seeking one Tom Hawkins.'

Burbage groaned aloud. 'What has he done? He is due on stage in an hour or so, and I fear we have no competent understudy. Do not tell me that you mean to arrest him? On what grounds?'

'I come not to arrest anyone . . . yet. Where is Master Hawkins?'

'Not here as yet.'

Master Drew looked round. There were a few people in corners of the theatre, apparently rehearsing lines. 'What play are you rehearsing?' he asked with interest.

'Will Shakespeare's *Famous History of the Life of King Henry VIII.*'

'Ah, that is a play that I have not seen.'

'Then you would be most welcome to stay . . .'

'Does Master Hawkins take part in this play?'

'He does, for he is Cardinal Campeius,' came Burbage's immediate response. 'It is a part of medium tolerance, a few lines here and yonder.'

'The elderly harassed-looking doorman approached Burbage. 'I declare, Master Richard, that the fools have not sent us gunpowder. What shall I do?'

Burbage took an oath by God and his angels that all except himself were incompetent fools and idlers. 'Go directly to Master Glyn's gunsmithy across the street and take a bucket. Return it filled with gunpowder, and tell Master Glyn that I will pay him after this evening's performance.'

The old man went scurrying off.

'Gunpowder?' Master Drew frowned. 'What part has gunpowder to do in your play?'

Burbage pointed to the back of the theatre. 'We have mounted a small cannon in one of the boxes on the second floor. The box will not be hired out during any performance.'

'And what will this cannon do, except blow the players to kingdom come?' demanded the constable wryly.

'Not so, not so. In act two, scene four, we have a grand scene with everyone on stage, and the king and his entourage enter, with princes, dukes and cardinals. It is a grand entrance, and Will Shakespeare calls for a sennet with divers trumpets and cornets. I thought to add to the spectacle by having a royal salute fired from a cannon. It will just be the ignition of the gunpowder, of course, but the combustion shall be explosive and startle our dreaming audience into concentration upon the action!'

Master Drew sniffed. 'I doubt it will do more than cause them to have deafness and perhaps start a riot out of panic for fear that the papists have attacked the theatre.' He was about to settle down to wait for Tom Hawkins when he had a further thought. 'In truth, turning to concentration reminds me that I would have you set your mind upon a youth whose description I shall presently give.' He quickly sketched the description of the youth whose body they had fished out of the river.

Richard Burbage's reaction was immediate. 'God damn my eyes, Master Constable, I have been searching for that miscreant since this morning. He failed to turn up at the rehearsal, and I have had to give his part to his friend. Where is the execrable young rogue?'

'Dead these past twelve hours, I fear.'

343

Richard Burbage was shocked. He clapped his hand to his head. But the main reason for his perturbation was soon apparent. 'A player short! If ever the gods were frowning on me this day . . .'

'I would know more about this boy . . .' insisted the constable. Richard Burbage had turned to wave to a man who had just entered the theatre.

Master Drew recognised Richard Burbage's brother, Cuthbert, immediately.

'A good day to you, Master Constable. What is your business here this fine Saturday?' Cuthbert Burbage greeted him as he came forward.

His brother raised his hands in a helpless gesture. 'Fine Saturday, indeed, brother! Tell him, Master Constable, while I am about my business. It lacks only an hour before the play begins.' He turned and scurried away.

Quickly, Master Drew told Cuthbert Burbage of what had passed.

'So, young Oliver is drowned, eh?'

'Oliver?'

'That was the lad's name, Oliver Rowe. Did he fall drunk into the river to drown?'

Master Drew shook his head. 'I said we hauled him from the river, not that he drowned. Young Oliver Rowe had his throat slit before he went into his watery grave. It was not for robbery either, for he still had money in his purse and' – he pulled out the ring from his pocket – 'this ring on his finger.'

Cuthbert let out an angry hiss. 'That, sir, is theatre property. No more than a simple actor's paste. A cheap imitation. I had wondered where it had gone. Damn Oliver –'

'He is damned already, Master Cuthbert,' interrupted Master Drew.

Cuthbert hung his head contritely. 'Forgive me, I quite forgot. I was thinking of his making off with theatre property.'

'Had this Oliver Rowe been long with you?'

'A year, no more.'

'A good actor?'

'Hardly that, sir. He lacked experience and dedication. Though, I grant, he made up for his lack with a rare enthusiasm.'

'Would anyone wish him ill?'

'You seek a reason for his murder?'

'I do.'

'Then I have none to give you. He had no enemies but many friends, particularly of the fairer sex.'

'And male friends?'

'Several within the company.'

'Was Master Hawkins a particular friend of his?'

'Hardly. Tom Hawkins is twice his age and an actor of experience, though with too many airs and graces of late. He is a competent performer, yet now he demands roles which are beyond his measure. We have told him several times to measure his cloth on his own body.'

'Where did this Oliver Rowe reside?'

'But a step or two from here, Master Constable. He had rooms at Mistress Robat's house in the Skin Market.'

A youth came hurriedly up, flush-faced, his words tumbling over themselves.

Cuthbert Burbage held up a hand to silence him. 'Now, young Toby, tell me slowly what ails you?'

'Master Burbage, I have just discovered that there is no gunpowder for the cannon that I am supposed to fire. What is to be done?'

Master Drew pulled a face. 'If I may intervene, Master Burbage? Your brother has sent old Jasper across to the gunsmithy to purchase this same gunpowder.'

The youth gave Drew a suspicious glance and then left with equal hastiness. 'I will ascertain if this be so,' he called across his shoulder.

Cuthbert Burbage sighed. 'Ah, Master Constable, the play's the thing! The player is dead – long live the play. Life goes on in the theatre. Let us know what the result of your investigation is, good master. We poor players tend to band together in adversity. I know young Rowe was impecunious and a stranger to London, so it will be down to us thespians to ensure him a decent burial.'

'I will remember, Master Cuthbert,' the constable agreed before he exited the theatre.

It took hardly any time to get to the Skin Market, with its busy and noisome trade in animal furs and skins. A stallholder pointed to Mistress Robat's house in a corner of the market square.

Mistress Robat was a large, rotund woman with fair skin and dark hair. She opened the door and smiled at him. '*Shw mae. Mae hi'n braf, wir!*'

Constable Drew glowered at her ingenuous features. 'I speak not your Welsh tongue, woman, and you have surely been long enough in London to speak in good, honest English?'

The woman continued to smile blandly at him, not understanding. '*Yr wyf yn deal ychydig, ond ni allaf ei siarad.*'

A thin-faced man tugged the woman from the door and jerked his head in greeting to the constable. 'I am sorry, sir, my wife, Megan, has no English.'

Master Drew showed him his seal of office. 'I am the Constable of the Watch. I want to see the room of Master Oliver Rowe.'

Master Robat raised his furtive eyebrows in surprise. 'Is anything amiss?'

'He is dead.'

The man spoke rapidly to his wife in Welsh. She turned pale. Then he motioned Master Drew into the house, adding to his wife: *'Arhoswch yma!'*

The constable followed the man up the stairs for five flights to a small attic room.

'Was there an accident, sir?' prompted the man nervously.

'Master Rowe was murdered.'

'Diw! Diw!'

'I have no understanding of your Welshry,' muttered the constable.

'Ah, the loss is yours, sir. Didn't Master Shakespeare give these words to Mortimer in his tale of *Henry the Fourth*? . . .' The man struck a ridiculous pose. 'I will never be a truant, love, till I have learn'd thy language; for thy tongue makes Welsh as sweet as ditties highly penn'd –'

Master Drew decided to put an end to the man's theatrical eloquence. 'I come not to discuss the merits of a scribbling word-seller, nor his thoughts on your skimble-skamble tongue,' snapped the constable, turning to survey the room.

There were three beds in the room. Two of them untidy, and

there were many clothes heaped upon the third. There were similarities to the mess he had observed in Hawkins' room. A similar pile of untidy papers. He picked them up. Play scripts again. He began to go through the cupboards and found another sheaf of papers there. One of them, he observed, was a draft of a play – *Falsehood Liberated*. The name on the title page was *Teazle Rowe*.

'What was Master Rowe's first name?' he asked the Welshman. He had thought the Burbages had called Rowe by the first name of Oliver.

'Why, sir,' confirmed the man, 'it was Oliver.'

'Did he have another name?'

'No, sir.'

'Can you read, man?'

The Welshman drew himself up. 'I can read in both Welsh and English.'

'Then who is *Teazle* Rowe?'

'Oh, you mean Master Teazle, sir. He is the other young gentleman who shares this room with Master Rowe.'

Constable Drew groaned inwardly.

He had suddenly remembered what Page Williams, at the Blackfriars Theatre, had said. What was it? Rowe had complained that Bardolph Zenobia had stolen a play written by Rowe with the help of his friend.

'And where is this Master Teazle now?'

'He is out, sir. I don't suppose he will return until late tonight.'

'You have no idea where I will find him?'

'Why, of course. He is doubtless at the theatre, sir.'

'The theatre? Which one, in the name of – !'

'The Globe, sir. He is one of Master Burbage's company. Both Master Rowe and Master Teazle are King's Men.'

Master Drew let out an exasperated sigh.

So both Rowe and his friend Teazle were members of the same company as Hawkins, alias Bardolph Zenobia?

Rowe had accused Hawkins of stealing a play that both he and Teazle had written, and of selling it to the Blackfriars Theatre. A pattern was finally emerging.

'When did you last see Master Rowe?'

'Last night, sir,' the reply came back without hesitation.

'Last night? At what hour?'

'Indeed, after the bell had sounded the midnight hour. I was forced to come up here and tell the young gentlemen to be quiet, as they were disturbing the rest of our guests.'

'Disturbing them? In what way?'

'They were having a most terrible argument, sir. The young gentlemen were quite savage with each other. *Thief* and *traitor* were the more repeatable titles that passed between them.'

'And after you told them to be quiet?'

'They took themselves to quietness and all was well, thanks be to God. Sometimes Master Teazle has a rare temper, and I swear I would not like to go against him.'

'But, after this, you saw Master Rowe no more?'

The man's eyes went wide. 'I did not. And you do tell me that Master Rowe is dead? Are you saying that – ?'

'I am saying nothing, Master Robat. But you shall hear from me again.'

The play had already started by the time the constable reached the Globe again.

He marched in past the sullen old doorman and examined the auditorium. The theatre was not crowded. It being a bright summer Saturday afternoon, many Londoners were about other tasks than spending time in a playhouse. But there was a fair number of people filling several of the boxes and a small crowd clustering around the area directly in front of the stage. He noticed, in disapproval, the harlots plying their wares from box to box, mixing with fruit sellers and other traders, from bakers' boys and those selling all kinds of beverages.

Master Drew saw a worried-looking Cuthbert Burbage coming towards him.

'Where is Master Hawkins?' he demanded.

'Preparing for the second act,' replied the man in apprehension. 'Master Constable, swear to me that you will not interrupt the play by arresting him, if he be in trouble?'

'I am no prophet, Master Burbage,' returned the constable, moving towards the area where the actors were preparing themselves to take their part upon the stage. He looked at them. What was the part that Hawkins was said to be playing – a cardinal? He picked out a man dressed in scarlet robes.

'Are you Master Hawkins?'

The actor raised a solemn face and grimaced with contempt. 'I am not, sir. I play Cardinal Wolsey. You will find Cardinal Campeius at the far end.'

This time there was no mistake. 'Master Thomas Hawkins?'

The distinguished-looking cleric bowed his head. 'I am yours to command, good sir.'

'And are you also Master Bardolph Zenobia?'

The actor's face coloured slightly. He shifted uneasily. 'I admit to being the same man, sir.'

Master Drew introduced himself. 'Did you know that Master Oliver Rowe has been discovered murdered?'

There was just a slight flicker in the eyes. 'It is already whispered around the theatre from your earlier visit, Master Constable.'

'When did you first learn of it?'

'Less than half an hour ago, when I came to the theatre.'

'When did you last see Master Rowe?'

'Last evening.'

'Here, at this theatre?'

'I was not in last night's performance. I went to stay with . . . with a lady in Eastcheap. I have only just returned from that assignation.'

'And, of course,' sneered the constable, 'you would have no difficulty in supplying me the lady's name?'

'None, good master. The lady and I mean to be married.'

'And she will be able to tell me that you were with her all night?'

'If that is what you require. But not just the lady, but her father and mother, for she lives with them. They own the Boar's Head in Eastcheap and are well respected.'

Master Drew swallowed hard. The alibi of a lady on her own was one thing, but the alibi of an entire respectable family could hardly be faulted.

'When last did you see Master Rowe?'

'It was after yesterday afternoon's performance. Rowe asked me to go with him to a waterside tavern after the matinee performance.

I had an appointment across the river before I went on to Eastcheap and could not long delay. But Rowe was insistent. We wound up by having an argument, and I left him.'

'What was the argument about?'

Hawkins' colour deepened. 'A private matter.'

'A matter concerning Master Bardolph Zenobia's literary endeavours?'

Hawkins shrugged. 'I will tell you the truth. Rowe and a friend of his had written a pretty story. Rowe wanted help in finding a theatre to stage it.'

'Why did he not take it to Burbage?'

'Sir, we are the King's Men here. We have a program of plays of surpassing quality for the next several years from many renowned masters of their art, Master Shakespeare, Jonson, Beaumont, Fletcher and the like. Master Burbage would not look at anything by a nameless newcomer. Rowe knew I had contacts with other theatres and gave me the script to read. The basic tale was commendable, but so much work needed to be done to revise it into something presentable. I spent much time on it. In the end, the work was mine, not Rowe's nor that of his friend.'

'I suppose by "his friend", you mean Teazle?'

'Yes, Teazle.'

'So you felt that the play was your own to do with as you liked?'

'It *was* mine. I wrote it. I will show you the original and my alterations. At first, I asked only to be made a full partner in the endeavour. When Rowe refused, saying the work was his and his friend's alone, I put the name of Zenobia on it and took it to Blackfriars. I told Rowe after I had sold it and offered to give him a guinea for the plot. I did not wish to be ungenerous. He refused. Rowe found out which theatre I had sold it to and even went to the theatre after I had left him last night, claiming that I had stolen the work.

'But from what was said yesterday afternoon, I had the impression that Rowe might have accepted the money if Teazle had not refused his share of the guinea. Rowe told me that Teazle thought him to be in some plot with me to cheat him and share more money after the play was produced. I told Rowe that it was up to him to make his peace with Teazle. I think a guinea was a fair sum to pay for the idea which I had to turn into literature.'

'I doubt whether a magistrate would agree with your liberal interpretation of the law,' Master Drew replied dryly. 'Has Master Teazle spoken to you of this business? Where is he now?'

Hawkins gestured disdainfully. 'Somewhere about the theatre. I avoid him. He has a childish temper and believes himself to be some great artist against whom the whole world is plotting. Anyway, I can prove that I am not concerned in the death of young Rowe. I have robbed no one.'

'That remains to be seen.'

Master Drew left him and went to the side of the stage. The third scene of the second act was closing. The characters of Anne Bullen and an old lady were on stage. Anne was saying,

> '– *Would I had no being,*
> *If this salute my blood a jot; it faints me,*
> *to think what follows.*
> *The queen is comfortless, and we forgetful*

*In our long absence: pray, do not deliver
What here you've heard to her.'*

The old lady replied indignantly: 'What do you think me?'
And both made their exit.

All was now being prepared for the next scene.

Master Drew glanced around, wondering which of the players
was Teazle.

Something drew his eye across the auditorium to the box on
the second storey in front of the stage. Someone was standing,
bending over the small cannon that had been pointed out to the
constable earlier. Master Richard Burbage had explained that the
cannon would herald the scene with a royal salute, followed by
trumpets and cornets, and then the King and his cardinals would
lead a procession onto the stage.

The muzzle of the cannon appeared to be pointing rather low.

The constable turned to find Master Cuthbert Burbage at his
shoulder.

'That is going to stir things a little.' The business manager
of the theatre, who had observed Master Drew's examination,
grinned.

'Your brother has already explained it to me,' the constable
replied. 'The cannon will be fired to herald the entrance of the
procession in the next act, but isn't the muzzle pointing directly
at the stage?'

'No harm. It is only a charge of gunpowder which creates the
explosion. There is no ball to do damage. Take no alarm; young
Toby Teazle has done this oftimes before.'

Master Drew started uneasily. 'That is Master Teazle up there with the cannon?'

A cold feeling of apprehension began to grip him as he stared at the muzzle of the cannon. Then he began to move hurriedly towards the stairs on the far side of the auditorium, pushing protesting spectators out of his way in his haste. He was aware of Cuthbert Burbage shouting something to him.

By the time he reached the second floor, he was aware of the actors moving onto the stage in the grand procession. He heard a voice he recognised as the actor playing Wolsey. 'Whilst our commission from Rome is read, let silence be commanded.' Then Richard Burbage's voice cried: 'What's the need? It hath already publicly been read, and on all sides the authority allow'd; you may then spare that time.' Wolsey replied: 'Be't so. Proceed.'

The cacophony of the trumpet and cornets sounded.

Drew burst into the small box and saw the young man bending with the lighted taper to the touch hole. On stage he was aware that the figures of Burbage's King, and the actors playing Cardinal Wolsey and Cardinal Campeius, the urbane figure of Hawkins, had come to the front of the stage and were staring up at the cannoneer, waiting. The constable did not pause to think but leapt across the floor, lacking at the muzzle of the small cannon. It jerked upward just as it exploded. The recoil showed that it had been loaded with ball; its muzzle had been pointed directly at the figure of Cardinal Campeius. The hot metal crashed across the interior of the theatre and fell into the thatch above the stage area.

There were cries of shocked surprise and some applause, but

then the noise of the crackle of flames where the hot metal landed on the dry thatch became apparent. Cries of 'Fire!' rose on all sides.

Master Drew swung round only to find the fist of the young man, Toby Teazle, impacting on his nose. He went staggering backwards and almost fell over the wooden balustrade into the crowds below as they streamed for the exits of the theatre.

By the time the constable had recovered, the young man was away, leaping down the stairs and was soon lost in the scuffling fray.

Master Drew, recovering his poise, hastened down the steps as best he could. The actors, with Cuthbert Burbage, were pushing people to the exits. The dry thatch and straw of the Globe were like tinder before the angry flames. The theatre was becoming a blazing inferno.

Master Drew groaned in anguish as he realised that the young man was lost among the crowds now and there was never a hope of catching him.

It was more than nine months later, in the spring of the following year, 1614, that the new Globe Theatre eventually rose from the ashes. This time it was erected as an octagonal building with a tiled roof replacing the thatch. Fortunately no one had been injured in the fire, and all the costumes and properties had been saved thanks to the quick wit of the actors, and all the manuscripts of the plays had been stored elsewhere, so the loss was negligible.

Apart from Master Oliver Rowe, two other players were not present to see the magnificent new Globe Theatre. Master Tom

Hawkins was languishing in Newgate Gaol. However, he was not imprisoned for the fraudulent misuse of another playwright's work. In fact, *The Vow Breaker Delivered* had been taken off on the third night and had made a loss for the Blackfriars Theatre. No, Master Hawkins was imprisoned for breach of promise to the young lady who lived at the Boar's Head tavern in Eastcheap. As Constable Hardy Drew remarked, *The Vow Breaker Delivered* had been an inspired prophetic title, as apt a title as could have been chosen by Master Bardolph Zenobia.

The other missing player was Master Toby Teazle.

It was the very day after the new Globe Theatre had opened that Constable Drew was able to conclude the case of the murder of Master Oliver Rowe, sometime one of the King's Men. Master Cuthbert Burbage asked Constable Drew to accompany him to the Hospital of St Mary of Bethlehem.

Drew was mildly surprised at the request. 'That is the hospital for the insane,' he pointed out. Most Londoners knew of Bedlam, for as such the name had been contracted.

'Indeed it is, but I think you will want to see this. I have been asked to identify someone.'

An attendant took them into the grey-walled building, which was more of a prison than a hospital. The stench of human excrement and the noise arising from the afflicted sufferers was unbelievable. The attendant took them to a small cell door and opened it.

A young man crouched inside in the darkness, bent industriously over a rough wooden table. There was nothing on it, yet he appeared to be in the act of writing in the blackness. His right hand held an invisible pen, moving it across unseen sheets of paper.

The attendant grinned. 'There he is, good sirs. He says he's a famous actor and playwright. Says he is a King's player from the Globe Theatre. That's why you were asked here, good Master Burbage, just in case there might be truth in it.'

The young man heard the voice and raised his matted head, eyes blazing, mouth grinning vacuously. He paused in his act of writing.

It was Toby Teazle.

'Ah, sirs,' he said quietly, calmly regarding them. 'You come not a moment too soon. I have penn'd a wondrous entertainment, a magnificent play. I call it *The Friend's Betrayal*. I will allow you to perform it, but only if my name should go upon the handbill. My name and no other.' He stared at them, each in turn, and then began to recite.

> *''Tis ten to one this play can never please*
> *All that are here; some come to take their ease*
> *And sleep an act or two; but those, we fear,*
> *We have frightened with our cannon; so, 'tis clear,*
> *They'll say, 'tis naught . . . naught . . .'*

He hesitated and frowned. 'Is this all it is? Naught?' He stared suddenly at the empty table before him and started to chuckle hysterically.

As Constable Drew and Master Cuthbert Burbage were walking back towards Bankside, Drew asked: 'Were those his own lines which he was quoting with such emotion?'